Red-Hot Desert Docs

CAROL MARINELLI
AMALIE BERLIN
MEREDITH WEBBER

MILLS & BOON

First Published in Great Britain 2019
by Mills & Boon, an imprint of HarperCollins*Publishers*
1 London Bridge Street, London, SE1 9GF

RED-HOT DESERT DOCS © 2019 Harlequin Books S. A.

Seduced by the Sheikh Surgeon © 2016 Carol Marinelli
Challenging the Doctor Sheikh © 2016 Amalie Berlin
The Sheikh Doctor's Bride © 2015 Meredith Webber

ISBN: 978-0-263-27486-8

0419

MIX
Paper from
responsible sources
FSC® C007454

This book is produced from independently certified FSC™ paper to ensure responsible forest management.

For more information visit: www.harpercollins.co.uk/green

Printed and bound in Spain
by CPI, Barcelona

SEDUCED
BY THE SHEIKH
SURGEON

CAROL MARINELLI

CHAPTER ONE

IT WASN'T BECAUSE of lack of opportunity for there had been plenty of them.

In fact, here was one now!

A late spring storm had come from nowhere and lit up the London sky.

Adele stood at the bus stop across the road from the Accident and Emergency department, where she had just finished working a late shift. The rain battered the shelter and she would probably be better off standing behind it. Her white dress, which was not designed to get wet, clung to her and had shrunk to mid-thigh and her shoulder-length blond hair was plastered to her head.

She wore no mascara so she was safe there—Adele wouldn't be greeting Zahir with panda eyes.

It was ten at night and she could see the blinkers on his silver sports car as he drove out of the hospital, turned right and drove towards her.

Surely now? Adele thought, as she stepped out from the supposed shelter just to make sure that she could be seen.

Surely any decent human being who saw a colleague standing shivering and wet at a bus stop, caught in a sudden storm, would slow down and offer them a lift home.

And when he did Adele would smile and say, 'Thank

you,' and get into the car. Zahir would see her clinging dress and wonder how the hell he had not noticed the junior nurse in *that* way before.

And she would forgive him for a year of rudely ignoring her. Finally alone, they would make conversation and as they pulled up at her flat...

Adele hadn't quite worked out that part. She loathed her flat and flatmates and couldn't really see Zahir in there.

Maybe he would suggest a drink back at his place, Adele thought as finally, *finally*, her moment came and the silver car slowed down.

She actually started to walk towards it, so certain was she that their moment had come.

But then he picked up speed and drove on.

No, his car didn't splash her with water, but she felt the drenching of his repeated rejection, just as if it had.

He must have just slowed down to turn on his radio or something, Adele soon realised, for Zahir drove straight past her.

How could she fancy someone as unfeeling as him? she wondered.

It was a conundrum she regularly wrangled with.

She couldn't console herself that he didn't like women.

Zahir dated.

A lot.

On too many occasions Adele had sat at the nurses' station or in the staffroom as he'd taken a call from whoever his latest perturbed girlfriend had been.

Perturbed because it was Saturday night and they were supposed to be out and Zahir was at work. Perturbed because it was Sunday afternoon and he had said several hours ago that he was only popping in to work.

Work was his priority. That much was clear.

During Adele's last set of night shifts he had been called in when he hadn't been rostered on. Wherever he had come from had required him to wear a tux. He had looked divine. For once he had been utterly clean shaven and his thick black hair had been slicked back. Adele had tried to stammer out the problem with the patient that she and Janet, the nurse unit manager, had been concerned about.

It had proved to be a hard ask.

'He was seen here this afternoon and discharged with antibiotics,' Adele said. 'His mother's still concerned and has brought him back tonight. The paediatrician has seen him again and explained it's too soon for the antibiotics to take effect.'

'What is your concern?' Zahir asked.

His cologne was heavy yet it could not douse the testosterone and sexual energy that was almost a visible aura to Adele. His deep, gravelly voice asked pertinent questions about the patient. She loved his rich accent and each stroke of a vowel he delivered went straight to her thighs.

'Adele,' he asked again, 'what is the main reason for your concern?'

'The mother's very worried,' Adele said, and closed her eyes because mothers were always very worried. 'And so am I.'

Zahir had gone in to examine the patient when a stunning woman had walked into the department. Her long brown hair and make-up were perfect despite the late hour. Dressed in silver, she had marched up to Janet and asked in a very bossy voice exactly how long Zahir would be.

'Bella, I said to wait in the car.' Zahir's curt response

had made the beauty jump. Clearly she only spoke like this out of his earshot.

Janet smothered a smile as Bella stalked off. 'Gone by morning,' she said to Adele.

Zahir had asked that Janet send in Helene to assist him.

More experience was required.

Adele had none.

Well, not with men but it seriously irked her that even after a year of working in Accident and Emergency he seemed to treat her as if she had just started.

And she had been right to be worried about the child.

Zahir performed a lumbar puncture and viral meningitis was later confirmed. The little boy was admitted and ended up staying in hospital for five days.

Not that Zahir told her.

There was never any follow-up for Adele.

And yet, for all his faults in the communication department, Zahir was the highlight of her working day.

Of all her days.

Well, no more, she decided as his car glided past.

He was arrogant and dismissive and it had been outright mean of him not to stop and offer her a lift—she refused to fancy him any longer.

Adele's world was small, too small, she knew that and was determined to do something about it.

The bus finally arrived.

Actually, two of them did. The one that was late and the one that was due.

Spoiled for choice, Adele thought as she climbed onto the emptier one and said hello to the driver.

There were some of the regulars on board and there were a few others.

Adele was a regular and knew she could zone out

for the next half-hour. She rested her head against the window as the bus hissed and jolted its way through the rain, and as it did so she went to her favourite place in the world.

Zahir.

Her conundrum.

She had no choice in her attraction toward him, she had long since decided. She had fought it, tried to deny it, tried to do something about it and she had also tried to ignore it.

Yet it persisted.

It simply existed and she had to somehow learn to live alongside it.

Maybe it was because he was completely unobtainable, she considered as someone started to sing at the back of the bus.

Yes, she needed to get out more and she was starting to do so. On Friday night she had a first date with Paul—a paramedic who had made his interest in her clear.

Just say yes, everyone at work had told her.

Finally she had.

Except it wasn't Paul that she wanted to go out with.

It was, and felt as if it always would be, Zahir.

His name badge read, 'Zahir, Emergency Consultant.'

The patients did not need to know he was Crown Prince Sheikh Zahir Al Rahal, of Mamlakat Almas.

Her heart hadn't needed to know that either. She had felt its rate quicken the moment she had seen him, before she had even known his name.

At first sight, even before their first introduction, this odd feeling had taken residence in Adele.

His hair was black and glossy, and his skin was the

colour of caramel and just as enticing. The paper gown
he'd worn had strained over wide shoulders. There had
been an air of control in the resuscitation room even
though it had been clear that the patient's situation had
been dire.

He had glanced up from the patient he'd been treating
and for a second his silver-grey eyes had met Adele's
and she had felt her cheeks grow warm under his brief
gaze.

'I'm just showing Adele around the department.'
Janet, the nurse unit manager conducting the interview, had explained.

He had given just the briefest of nods and then he
had got back to treating the critical patient.

'As you can see, the resuscitation area has been updated since you were last here,' Janet had said. 'We've
now got five beds and two cots.'

Yes, it had been updated but the basics had been
the same.

Adele had stood for a moment, remembering a time,
several years previously, when she had been wheeled
in here and, given that Janet had been with her on that
awful day, she had perhaps understood why Adele had
been quiet.

Janet had made no reference to it, though; in fact,
as they'd both walked back towards Janet's office she'd
spoken of other things.

'That was Zahir, one of our emergency consultants,'
Janet said. 'You'll have come across him when you did
your placement.'

'No.' Adele shook her head. 'He wasn't here then. I
believe he was on leave.'

'He's been working here for a couple of years now
but, yes, he is away quite a lot. Zahir has a lot of com-

mitments back home so he works on temporary contracts,' Janet explained. 'We always cross our fingers that he'll renew. He's a huge asset to the department.

'I've worked with his brother, Dakan,' Adele said.

They both shared a smile.

Dakan had just completed his residency and was a bit wild and cheeky, and she knew from the hospital grapevine that Zahir was the more austere of the two.

Of course she had heard about his brooding dark looks and yet she had never expected him to be quite so attractive.

Adele hadn't really found anyone that attractive before.

Not that it mattered.

There had been no room in her life for that sort of thing, not that Zahir would even give her a second glance.

'So,' Janet said as they headed back to her office, 'are you still keen to work here?'

'Very.' Adele nodded. 'I never thought I'd want to work in Emergency but during my placement I found that I loved it...'

'And you're very good at it. You shall have to work in Resus, though.'

'I understand that.'

As a student nurse Adele had struggled through her Accident and Emergency placement. She had dreaded going into the room where, even though her mother hadn't died, Adele had found out that she was lost to her.

Janet, knowing all that had gone on, had been very patient and had given Adele the minimum time in Resus and had looked out for her when she was there. Now, though, if Adele wanted to make Accident and

Emergency her specialty, there could be no kid-glove treatment.

'Are you sure it won't be too much for you?' Janet checked.

'I'm sure.' Adele nodded. She had given it a lot of thought and she explained what she had come to realise during her training.

'Really, my mother was in Theatre, in Radiology and ICU. For some reason the Resus room hit me the hardest but I've come to understand that there are memories of that time all over the place.'

'How is Lorna doing now?' Janet asked carefully.

'She's still the same.' Adele gave a strained smile. 'She's in a really lovely nursing home, the staff are just wonderful and I go in and see her at least once a day.'

'That's a lot of pressure.'

'Not really.' Adele shook her head. 'I'm not sure if she knows I'm there but I'd hate her to think I'd forgotten her.'

Janet wanted to say something.

Years of visiting her mother at *least* once a day would take its toll, she knew.

But then Janet understood why it would be so hard for Adele to move on. After all, she knew the details of the accident.

Janet had been working that day.

They had been alerted that there had been a motor-vehicle accident and that there had been five people injured and in the process of being freed from the wreckage of the cars.

Lorna Jenson, a front-seat passenger, had been in critical condition with severe head and chest injuries.

The driver of the other car had abdominal and head injuries and had been brought into Resus too. His wife and daughter had escaped with minor injuries but they had been hysterical and their screams and tears had filled the department.

And finally, as Lorna had been about to be taken to Theatre for surgery to hopefully relieve the pressure on her brain, Janet had gone in to speak with her eighteen-year-old daughter who'd lain staring at the ceiling.

Adele's blonde hair had been splattered with blood and her face had been as white as the pillow. Her chinablue eyes had not blinked, they'd just stared up at the ceiling and her lips too had been white.

'Adele?' Janet checked, and Adele attempted to give a small nod but she was wearing a hard cervical collar. 'Can you tell me your full name?' Janet asked as she checked the wristband. She had been busy dealing with the critically injured patient and had to be very sure to whom she was speaking.

'Adele Jenson.'

'Good.' Having confirmed to whom she was speaking, Janet pressed on. 'I believe that Phillip, the consultant, has been in and spoken with you about your mother.'

'He has,' Adele said.

Phillip had been in and had gently told her just how unwell her mother was and that there was a real possibility that she might not make it through the operation.

His glasses had fogged up as he'd looked down at Adele and told her the grim news.

Adele didn't understand how the doctor had tears in his eyes and yet hers were dry.

Now Janet was looking down at her.

'She's going to be going to Theatre very soon.'

'How's the man…?' Adele asked.

'I'm sorry, Adele, I can't give you that information.'

'I can hear his family crying.'

'I know you can.'

'How badly are they hurt?'

'I'm sorry, Adele. Again, I can't give you that information, it's to do with patient confidentiality.'

'I know it is,' Adele said. 'I'm a nursing student. But I just need to know how he is, if he's alive.'

'It's very hard for you.' Janet gave her hand a little squeeze but gave her no information. 'I wondered if you'd like me to take you in to see your mother before she goes up to Theatre.'

Adele tried to sit up.

'Just lie there,' Janet soothed. 'We'll wheel you over on the gurney. I can take that collar off you now, Phillip just checked your X-rays and says your neck is fine. It just had to be put on as a precaution.'

Gently she removed it.

'How do you feel?' Janet asked.

'I'm fine,' Adele said, though, in fact, she felt sick and had the most terrible headache, possibly from sitting in the car as the firefighters had used the Jaws of Life to peel back the roof. The noise had been deafening. The silence from her mother beside her had been far worse, though.

Janet could hear the sound of police radios outside the curtain and one of them asking if they could speak with Adele Jenson.

'Just one moment,' Janet said to Adele. She took the police to the far end of the corridor, well out of Adele's earshot.

'I'm just about to take her in to see her mother. Can this wait for a little while?'

'Of course,' the officer agreed. 'But we really do need to speak with the other driver.'

'*Learner* driver,' Janet said, and with that one word she asked that they tread very carefully.

The officer nodded.

Janet left them then and wheeled Adele in to see her mother.

At the time Janet was quite sure Lorna wouldn't make it through surgery.

But she did.

Now Lorna clung to life in a chronic vegetative state.

And her daughter, Janet rightly guessed, was still paying the price for that terrible day.

CHAPTER TWO

'THAT WAS SOME storm last night,' Janet said.

'You're telling me!' Helene responded. 'Hayden was driving and I had to get him to pull over.'

Adele was on another late shift and they were sitting at the nurses' station. They had been discussing annual leave before the conversation had been sidetracked.

Adele really wasn't in the mood to hear about Helene's son's driving lessons.

Again!

Helene had, a few months ago, come back to nursing after a long break away to raise her perfect family, and she spoke about them all the time.

'Did you get home okay, Adele?' Janet checked.

'I did,' Adele said, glancing over at Zahir, who had his back to her and was checking lab results on the computer. He was wearing navy scrubs and his long legs were stretched out. He was still taking up far too much space in her mind. 'A lovely man stopped and gave me a lift.'

She watched as Zahir briefly stopped scrolling through results but then he resumed.

'Who, Paul?' Janet asked, because they all knew that Adele had a date with him tomorrow night.

'No.' Adele shook her head. 'It was just some random

man. As it turned out, he'd escaped from police guard in the psychiatric unit, but I didn't feel threatened—he didn't have his chainsaw with him.'

Janet laughed. She understood Adele's slightly off-the-wall humour. 'You got the bus, then.'

'Yes, I got the bus.'

Chatter break over, they got back to business.

'Adele, you really need to take some annual leave.'

Janet placed the annual leave roster in front of her and Adele frowned as Janet explained. 'Admin don't like us to hold too much over and further you haven't taken any in the time you've been here.'

'Nice problem to have!' Helene said.

'What about September?' Adele suggested, because there were several slots there and Janet nodded and pencilled a fortnight in then. 'You need to take two weeks before that, though.'

The trouble with that was it was now May. The upcoming summer months were all taken. In fact, a couple of months ago Adele had cancelled her leave when Helene had won a competition to take her perfect family on an overseas holiday.

'How about the first two weeks of June?' Janet suggested. 'There's a spot there.'

'But that's only three weeks away.'

'That will give you time to book something last minute and cheap,' Janet said. 'I've been telling you to take some leave for ages, Adele.'

She had been.

'What might you do?' Helene asked once Janet had gone.

'I have no idea,' Adele admitted.

The truth was, even if she could afford to jet off to

somewhere nice, she could not bear the thought of leaving behind her mum.

And a fortnight without the routine of work wasn't something that Adele wanted either.

She didn't like the flat where she lived, and, feeling guilty about acknowledging it to herself, neither did she want to spend even more time at the nursing home.

Perhaps she could do some agency work and try to get enough money together to start looking for her own place.

'How is Mr Richards now, Adele?' Zahir asked about the patient whose notes she had been catching up on when the subject of annual leave had arisen.

'He's comfortable.'

'And how are his obs?'

'Stable,' Adele said.

Mr Richards was on half-hourly obs and they were due, oh, one and half minutes from now.

Basically, Zahir was prompting her to do them.

Well, she didn't need him to remind her, as he so often did, but she said nothing and hopped down from her stool.

Mr Richards had unstable angina and as she did the observations Adele smiled down at the old man, who was all curled up under his blanket and grumbling as the blood-pressure cuff inflated.

'I want to sleep.'

'I know that you do,' Adele said, 'but we need to keep a close eye on you for now.'

His blood pressure had gone up and his heart rate was elevated. 'Do you have any pain at the moment?' Adele asked.

'None, or I wouldn't have, if you'd just let me sleep.'

Adele went to tell Zahir about the changes but was

halted by a very elegant woman. She had a ripple of long black hair that trailed down her back and she was wearing a stunning, deep navy, floor-length robe that was intricately embroidered with flowers of gold. Around her throat was a gold choker and set in it was a huge ruby.

She was simply the most stunning woman Adele had ever seen.

'I am to meet with Zahir…' she said to Adele. 'Can you tell him that I am here?'

Adele would usually ask who it was that wanted to speak with him but there was something so regal about her that she felt it would be rude to do so. As well as that, she had heard Zahir asking Phillip to cover him for a couple of hours as he and Dakan were taking their mother out for afternoon tea.

This was surely his mother—the Queen.

'I'll just let him know.'

There was only Zahir in the nurses' station now. He was still on the computer but just signing off. 'Zahir,' Adele said.

'Yes?' He didn't turn around.

'There's a lady here to see you. I think that it might be your mother.'

'Thank you,' he stood. 'I shall take her around to my office. When Dakan comes, would you tell him where we are?'

'Actually…' Adele halted him. 'I was just coming in to tell you that Mr Richards's blood pressure and heart rate are raised.'

'Does he have pain?'

'He says not, he just wants to sleep.'

'Okay.' Zahir glanced at the chart she held out to him. 'Could you take my mother to my office and have her wait there?'

'Of course,' Adele said. 'What do I call her?'

'I answer to Leila!'

Adele turned and saw that Zahir's mother had followed her into the nurses' station. 'I apologise.' Adele smiled. 'Let me take you through…'

They walked through the department. Leila said how lovely it felt to be in London and to be able to go out with her sons for tea. 'Things are far less formal here than they are back home,' she explained. 'I prefer not to use my title when I am here as people tend to stare.'

They would stare anyway, Adele thought. Leila was seriously beautiful and it was as if she glided rather than walked alongside her.

'I thought you'd have bodyguards,' Adele said, and Leila gave a little laugh.

'My driver is trained as one but he is waiting outside. I don't need bodyguards when I have my sons close by.'

'Zahir's office is a little tucked away…' Adele explained as they walked through the observation ward, but then she frowned as she realised that the Queen was no longer walking beside her.

She turned around and saw that she was standing and had her fingers pressed into her forehead.

'Are you okay?' Adele checked.

'I'm just a bit…' Leila didn't finish. Instead she drew in a deep breath and Adele could see that she was terribly pale. 'Could you show me where the restroom is?'

'It's there,' Adele said, and pointed her to the staff restroom. 'I'll just wait here for you, shall I?'

Leila nodded and walked off and Adele waited for her to come out.

And waited.

Perhaps she was topping up her make-up, Adele decided, but then she thought about how pale Leila had suddenly gone and Adele was certain that she had been feeling dizzy.

She was loath to interrupt her. After all, Leila was Zahir's mother and she was also a queen.

But, at the end of the day, she was a woman and Adele a nurse and she was starting to become concerned.

Nursing instinct won.

She pushed open the door and stepped in but there was no Leila at the sink washing her hands or doing her make-up. 'Leila?' Adele called into the silence.

'Please help me…' Leila's voice came from behind the cubicle door.

'It's okay, I'm here.' Adele took out the coin that she kept in her pocket for such times. She turned it in the slot and pushed open the door, relieved that it gave and that Leila wasn't leaning against it, as had happened to Adele in the past.

'Don't let my sons see me bleed,' Leila begged.

'I shan't.'

She was bleeding and on the edge of passing out.

'Put your head down,' Adele told her. 'Has this happened before?'

'A couple of times. I am seeing a doctor on Harley Street.'

Adele didn't want to leave her sitting up in case she passed out, but neither did she want to lie her on the floor. She opened the main door to the rest room, at the same time as keeping an eye on her. She saw Janet bringing a patient into the obs ward.

'Janet!' Adele called out in a voice that made the other woman turn around immediately. As she did so Adele ducked straight back into the cubicle, knowing that Janet would follow her in.

'Just take some nice big breaths,' Adele said to Leila.
As Janet entered, Adele brought her up to speed.

'This is Leila, Zahir's mother. She's bleeding PV.'

'I'll go and get a gurney.'

'Janet,' Adele added, before she dashed off, 'she doesn't want Zahir to see.'

It was all swiftly dealt with. Leila was put onto a gurney and oxygen given. Adele put some blankets over her to make sure that she was covered before they wheeled her through.

Of course Zahir had finished with Mr Richards and was making his way to his office as they passed by.

'What happened?' he asked and then he gave a look at Adele as if to say, *I left her with you for five minutes!*

'Your mother fainted,' Adele told him as they walked quickly into the department.

'Maria,' Janet called out to the female registrar who was on duty today.

'I will take care of my mother,' Zahir said as they arrived at the cubicle.

He started to walk in but Adele blocked his path.

Well, she hardly blocked it, because she was very slight and he could easily have moved her aside or stepped around her, but there was something in her stance that was a challenge. 'Zahir!' Adele said, and she looked up at him and, for only the second time in twelve months of their history, their eyes met properly.

'Adele, let me past.'

'No,' she said, and stood her ground. 'Zahir, there are some things a mother would prefer her son didn't see.'

As realisation hit he gave a small nod. 'Very well.'

'We've got this,' Adele reassured him.

He was like a cat put out in the rain but reluctantly he stepped back. 'Could you keep me informed?'

She nodded.

Poor Leila, Adele thought as she got her into a gown and did some obs. Leila point blank refused to allow Adele to remove her jewellery.

Janet inserted an IV and Maria ordered some IV fluids. In a short space of time Zahir's mother was starting to look better.

'I've been unwell for a while,' she explained. 'I came over last month to have some time with my sons but I also had some tests done. I'm supposed to be having a hysterectomy tomorrow. I don't want my husband to know.' She took a breath. 'As awkward as it might be, I was going to tell my sons today at afternoon tea.'

Maria went through her medical history but at first Leila was very vague in her responses.

'How many pregnancies have you had?' Maria asked.

'I have two children.'

'How many pregnancies?' Maria asked again.

'Three,' Leila said, and Adele saw a tear slip from her eyes and into her hair. 'I don't like to speak of that time.'

Maria looked at Adele, whose hand Leila was holding, in the hope Adele could get more out of her. 'The doctor needs to know your history, Leila. She needs to know about your pregnancies and labours and any problems you have had.'

'My womb causes me many problems. I got pregnant very quickly with Zahir but he was born prematurely. It was a very difficult labour.'

They waited for her to elaborate but she didn't.

'And the next pregnancy?' Adele prompted.

'It took five more years to get pregnant and then I had Dakan. Again it was very difficult, he had very large shoulders. Two years later, I was lucky and I fell pregnant but my body did not do well… I had the best healer and a specialist *attar* but there was little they could do for me.'

'*Attar*?' Adele checked.

'He makes up the herbs the healer advises. I took the potion every day yet I still felt very unwell, and I started to vomit.'

'At what stage of the pregnancy?' Maria asked.

'He said I had four months left to go,' Leila answered. 'I was getting worse and I insisted that I be flown to a medical facility overseas. My husband and the healer were very opposed to the idea but I demanded it. In Dubai they said that I had to deliver the baby and that my blood pressure was very high. I called my husband and he said the healer had told him it was too soon and that the baby would die and that I needed to come home. Fatiq flew to Dubai to come and bring me back home…'

Leila started to cry in earnest then. 'But by then I had delivered and the healer was right. A few hours after my husband arrived our son died.'

'I'm so sorry,' Adele said.

'I have a picture of him.'

Adele got Leila's bag and watched as she took out her purse and showed them the tiniest most beautiful baby. 'We named him Aafaq, it means the place where the earth and sky meet.'

'It's a beautiful name,' Adele said, and she looked at a younger Leila and a man who looked very much like Zahir and was probably around the age his son was now.

They were both holding their tiny baby and he was off machines.

'What a beautiful baby,' Adele said.

They were a beautiful family, Adele thought, despite the pain. The King's arm was around his wife and he was gazing down at his son and you could see the love and sorrow in his expression.

'We cannot even speak of Aafaq,' Leila sighed. 'There is too much hurt there to even discuss that time. I think that my husband blames me for turning my back on the healer and yet he loves me also. I want for us to be able to speak about the son we lost but we can't. Aafaq would have been twenty-five years old next month and time still hasn't healed it. I miss him every day.'

It was so sad, Adele thought, and she continued to hold the older woman's hand as Maria examined her. A while later an ultrasound confirmed fibroids and Maria went through the options.

'We have a private wing here and I can speak with the consultant gynaecologist, Mr Oman. Or you can be transferred to the hospital you're already booked into, though I doubt they'd operate tomorrow. You might need a few days to rest and recover from this bleeding.'

'I think I would rather stay here but I shall discuss it with my son. Will you speak with him, please?' Leila asked Maria. 'He will be so worried and I am so embarrassed.'

'Stop thinking like that,' Adele told her. 'Zahir is a doctor, he deals with this sort of thing all the time.'

'Adele's right,' Maria said. 'Can I tell Zahir that you were already planning to have surgery?'

'Yes.' Leila nodded. 'But please don't mention what I said about Aafaq.'

'I shan't. Do you want him to come in when I've finished speaking with him?'

'Please.'

'Check first, though,' Adele called, as Maria left. 'I'm just going to help Leila freshen up.'

Adele left to make preparations so that she could give Leila a wash and change of sheets. When she came back into the cubicle Leila was staring at the photo but then she placed it back in her bag.

It must be so hard for her, Adele thought, not to be able to speak of her son. She wondered if Zahir even knew about the baby his mother had lost.

'Were you going to tell your husband after the operation?' Adele asked as she washed her.

'Yes,' Leila said. 'I might even have told him before or got one of my sons to. I know it is hard to understand our ways,' Leila said. 'Most of the time I am very grateful for the care I receive. There are times, though, that more is needed.'

Aafaq had been one of those times, Adele guessed.

Soon she was washed and changed.

'Thank you for caring for me,' Leila said.

'It's my pleasure. I'm just going to take your blood pressure again.'

She was doing just that when Maria checked that Leila was ready to receive visitors and a concerned-looking Zahir and Dakan came in.

They came over and Zahir gave his mother a warm embrace and spoke kindly to her in Arabic.

'It's okay,' he said. 'You could have told me that you have not been well.'

'I have been trying to deal with it myself.'

'Well, you don't have to. You have two sons who are doctors.'

'The healer seems to think…'

What was being said, Adele did not know but she watched as Zahir's jaw gritted.

'Zahir, don't just dismiss it out of hand. The potion

helped at first but in the end was not working. It was the same when...' She didn't finish.

Zahir looked down at his mother's swollen eyes and he knew that she would have been asked about previous pregnancies.

And he knew that subject must not be raised by him.

'When things were getting no better, the healer suggested that when I was in London perhaps I could see someone.'

Zahir frowned. 'He suggested it?'

'Yes,' Leila said, 'but please don't tell your father that. I don't want the healer to get in trouble.'

It was a long afternoon that stretched into the evening, Dakan got paged to go to the ward and Zahir saw patients while keeping an eye on his mother.

Mr Oman came and saw Leila. It was decided that she would be admitted to the private wing and that surgery would take place on Monday.

'For now we'll have you moved somewhere more comfortable and you can get some rest.'

He spoke with Zahir on his way out. 'You know that I shall take the very best care of her.'

'I do. Thank you.'

'Try not to worry. It will be a laparoscopic procedure and there will be minimal downtime.' Mr Oman said.

Zahir knew that.

It was a straightforward operation that his mother had had to travel for ten hours to get access to.

Dakan came in to visit again and they persuaded their mother that Fatiq, the King, needed to be informed as to all that had happened today, and finally she agreed.

'Go easy on him, Zahir,' Leila said, for she knew how they clashed, especially on topics such as this. 'He will be so worried and scared for me.'

Zahir nodded.

And at the beginning of the call, knowing how deeply his parents loved each other and the shock this would be, he was gentle. He sat in his office, explaining as best he could what had happened and that his mother would have surgery on Monday.

'No,' his father said and Zahir could hear the fear in his voice. 'I want her here. Last time she went into hospital…' He didn't finish.

They never did.

That topic was closed for ever.

'Zahir, if anything should happen to her—'

'She needs surgery,' Zahir interrupted, but they went around in circles for a while, with Fatiq insisting that surgery was unnecessary and that the healer could sort this.

Zahir bit back the temptation to tell his father that the healer had been the one who had suggested it.

That had surprised Zahir, yet it pleased him also.

Perhaps some progress could finally be made.

'She is seeing one of the top surgeons in London,' Zahir said. 'I will ensure that she gets the very best of care and shall keep you informed.'

The call ended and Zahir replaced the receiver. He squeezed the bridge of his nose between finger and thumb and took a deep breath to steady himself. He was so angry with his father about the health care back home and it was a battle they had fought for way more than a decade.

It was the reason he was here.

CHAPTER THREE

'ARE YOU OKAY?'

Her voice was soothing.

Pleasant.

He opened his eyes and there, standing at the office door, was Adele.

Zahir thought he had closed it and was uncomfortable that she'd caught him in an unguarded moment.

'I'm not about to have my second Al Rahal faint on me today?' Adele checked, and Zahir gave a reluctant smile.

'No.'

'We're just about to move your mother to the private wing.'

'Good,' Zahir said, and then glanced at the time. 'You must be finishing up. Thank you for all your help with her today.'

'You're welcome.'

'Who's taking her up to the ward?'

'I am,' Adele said.

His mother had insisted on keeping Adele around and, because queens were something of a rarity, the rules had been relaxed.

'She wants to know if you've spoken with her husband.'

'Tell my mother that he knows. I'll come and speak

with her on the ward. I just have a couple more patients to see.'

It took ages to settle Leila into the private wing. She was lovely but extremely demanding and by the time Adele had everything to the Queen's liking and had handed over it was way past the end of her shift and she was exhausted.

'I shall see you in the morning,' Leila checked as Adele wished her goodnight.

Zahir had come in to check that his mother was settled too.

'No.' Adele shook her head.

'But you said you started tomorrow at seven.'

'Yes, but I work in Emergency.'

There was an exchange in Arabic between mother and son. A rather long one and finally Zahir translated what was being said.

'She wants to know if you can nurse her. I've just explained that that is not how things work.'

Leila spoke now in English. 'I want Adele to be my nurse.'

'She's very used to getting her own way.' Zahir gave a wry smile and then went back to speaking in Arabic.

His mother was adamant and, seeing that she was getting upset, Adele intervened.

'Leila, I would love to care for you but it isn't my specialty and I'm already rostered on to work in Accident and Emergency tomorrow. They're very short of staff. I can come and visit you, though.'

'You'll visit me?'

'I'd love to.' Adele nodded. She often caught up with patients once they were moved to other wards and few were more interesting than Leila. 'I can come in during my lunch break tomorrow. For now, though, you need to get some rest. It's been an exhausting day for you.'

Adele headed down and changed out of her scrubs and into jeans and a T-shirt. It was well after ten and she had missed her bus and would have to wait for ages for the next one.

It wasn't the first time it had happened and it certainly wouldn't be the last.

It was, however, the first time that the silver sports car that usually glided past pulled in at the bus stop.

The window slid down and Zahir called out to her.

'The least I can do is give you a lift home.'

Even though Adele was still sulking about last night, she knew it would be petty to refuse.

Finally she sat in the passenger seat.

'You don't drive?' Zahir asked.

'No.' Adele shook her head. 'There's no real need to in London.'

She gave her regular excuse, but the truth was that since that awful day even the thought of getting behind the wheel made her feel ill.

'Surely it's better than getting a bus late at night?'

'Maybe.' Adele gave a shrug.

Perhaps she couldn't afford a car, Zahir thought. He had heard that she was saving up to move out of her flat.

He would buy her a car, Zahir decided.

It was as if cultures had just clashed in his brain.

That was what his family would say—buy her a car, repay the debt, return the favour tenfold—and yet he knew that she would find such a move offensive.

Today was not a debt that needed to be repaid to Adele.

It was her job. Nursing was what she did.

And she did it very well.

It wasn't her fault that he was terse with her at times. It was necessary for him to function.

She entranced him.

She was funny and open and yet private and deep.

Adele was the woman he kept a distance from because she was the one person he would really like to get to know.

And no good could come from that.

'I really am grateful for all your help today,' he said.

'I was just doing my job.'

'I know, but you helped my mother a lot. I know that she would have been scared, given that she is so far from home, and that she would have needed someone to talk to.' Zahir hesitated. He thought of his mother's eyelids, swollen from crying. He hoped she had given her full history to the doctors. 'Did she mention that she lost a baby?'

Adele frowned as Zahir glanced at her. From the way Leila had asked that it not be mentioned, Adele had assumed Zahir didn't know about his brother. She thought about it some more and realised he would have been about seven when it had happened.

When she didn't answer the question, Zahir elaborated.

'I don't really know the details,' he admitted. 'It's a forbidden subject in the palace. I just know she was having a baby and that she flew to Dubai. Then my father left and they all returned. Aafaq is buried in the desert but to this day...' He glanced at her again, hoping he might glean something.

Anything.

'You need to discuss that with your mother,' Adele

said, though there was regret in her voice. She knew how it felt to be kept in the dark. She could still clearly remember trying to get information out of Janet. It was awful knowing someone held facts that were vital to you but could not be shared. 'I'm sorry.'

'I know,' Zahir admitted. 'And I'm sorry to have put you in that situation. I just hope she has been frank with Mr Oman.'

Adele didn't answer.

Zahir respected her for that.

'Just here,' Adele said, and they pulled up at a large building with heavy gates.

'Again—thank you again for your help with my mother today.'

'No problem. Thank you for the lift.'

'Any time.' Zahir gave an automatic response.

She let out a short, incredulous laugh. For a year he had driven past her; last night she had been drenched and he'd utterly ignored her. And, yes, it might seem petty but she would not leave it unsaid. 'Any time you feel *obliged* to, you mean.'

Zahir stared ahead but he was gripping the steering-wheel rather tightly.

He knew that Adele was referring to last night.

Of course he had seen her.

It had taken all he had not to stop.

'Goodnight, Zahir.'

She got out and opened the gates.

Zahir knew he hadn't dropped her at her flat. This was a nursing home. He knew that Adele's mother was very ill and that she visited her often.

He had never delved.

Zahir had wanted to, though.

He wanted to explore his feelings for Adele. He wanted her more than he had ever wanted anyone.

But he had been born to be king, which meant at all times he kept his head. His emotions he owned and his heart had to remain closed until marriage.

And he would marry soon hopefully.

It was the last bargaining tool he had with his father.

King Fatiq wanted a selection ceremony to take place and for Zahir to choose his future bride.

There were several possibilities and the union must be the one to best benefit the country, yet Zahir had refused to commit himself so far.

Only when he had free rein to rebuild the health system in his own country would Zahir choose a bride. His father had resisted but Zahir was now thirty-two and the King wanted his son married and home.

And so Zahir chose to remain aloof in relationships, knowing, hoping, that at any given time his father might relent and summon him home and the work on the health system in his country could truly begin.

There was nothing aloof about his feelings for Adele, though.

It could only prove perilous to get involved with her.

The last time he had been home he had sat in the desert and asked for a solution.

Always he asked for help regarding Aafaq and the clash with his father, and always he asked how best to serve his people. Lately, he had asked about Adele.

There could be no solution there, Zahir knew.

Yet he had asked for guidance and in the quiet of deep meditation the answer had been the same.

Have patience.

In time the answers will unfold.

Do what is essential.

Zahir's patience was running out.

He watched as Adele pressed the buzzer and then she turned around and frowned.

She was surprised that the man who left her standing in the dark night after night seemed to want to see her safely inside.

Within a matter of moments she was walking into the nursing home and towards her mother's room.

'Hi, Adele.' Annie, one of the nurses, had just finished turning her mother and smiled at Adele as she came in.

'I know that it's late but I couldn't get here this morning and...'

Adele stopped herself. They always told her that she didn't need to give a reason if she couldn't come in. Tomorrow she wouldn't be able to—she was on an early shift and, even though the nursing home was close by, she was going out on that date with Paul.

The trouble was she wasn't particularly looking forward to it.

'Hi, Mum,' Adele said, and took a seat and held one of her mother's hands.

Lorna's nails were painted a lovely shade of coral. Adele did her mother's finger- and toenails each week. Her once brown hair was now a silver grey. Adele had used to faithfully do her roots but in the end she had stopped that.

Oh, she knew she had to get a life and yet it was so hard not to come in and visit.

And people simply didn't understand.

Lorna had been so vibrant and outgoing. A single mum, she had juggled work and her daughter, along

with an active social life. She'd had a large group of
friends and at first they, along with relatives, had filled
the ICU waiting rooms and then later they had come by
to visit when Lorna had been on the ward.

Over the years those visits had all but petered out.

Now the occasional card or letter came and Adele
would read it out then add it to the string on her mother's wall. Lorna's sister, Adele's aunt, came and visited
maybe once or twice a year. Another friend dropped in
on occasion but apart from that it was just Adele.

And so she brought her mother, who lay with her
eyes closed, up to date on what was happening in her
life.

'I finally my got my lift from him,' Adele told her
mum. 'It was very underwhelming.' It really had been,
she thought. 'Anyway, I'm over Zahir. I really do mean
it this time. I'm going out with Paul tomorrow night.
He's one of the paramedics,' Adele explained to the
silence. 'He's asked me out a few times and I decided
maybe I should give him a chance after all. I guess I'm
not going to like everyone in the same way I do Zahir.'

It really was time to get a life.

But then she told her mother the real reason she had
stopped by after work.

It wasn't just that she might not be in tomorrow, there
were bigger reasons than that for her being here tonight.

If her mother would just squeeze her hand or blink
or do one thing to acknowledge that she knew Adele
was here, it would help.

This was agony, it truly was, sitting here day in, day
out, and yet she was all her mother had.

But Adele made herself say it out loud.

'Mum, I've got some annual leave that I need to take
and I'm thinking of going on holiday.'

It was a huge thing for her to say.

Yet she knew she couldn't live this life for ever.

To pay for the nursing home and the legal fees when the other family involved in the accident had sued, the family home had been sold and Adele now shared a small flat with Helga and James.

Adele had deferred her studies for two years, but they had been spent dealing with the aftermath of the accident. She hadn't had a holiday in years. Any weekends or leave had always been taken up with other things, such as university, work, visiting her mother, getting the house ready for the market or dealing with lawyers, doctors and real estate agents.

Finally, when her mum had been placed in this home and things had started to settle, Adele had started her role in Accident and Emergency.

Now she felt as if she was coming up for air and she simply wanted to get away and maybe just grieve for her mother.

Of course she would still visit, Adele thought as she walked the small distance home to her flat.

But she had to work out some sort of balance.

Helga was in the kitchen, making an enormous fry-up for herself and James, and she had her music up loud.

Adele was so tired but she lay on her bed, trying not to think of what she had just told her mother and trying to consider where to go on holiday.

Greece perhaps?

She woke to that thought.

Adele took out her laptop and looked at several destinations and then saw a wonderful package deal for the South of France.

Oh!

It was more expensive than she had planned for.

Then again, she hadn't really planned to be going away.

Walking towards the bus stop, she saw that a one-bedroom flat nearby had just come up for rent.

Perhaps the money would be better spent moving out than on two weeks overseas.

Arriving at work, she smiled at Janet, who was waiting for the rest of the early-shift staff to arrive before they had handover, which wouldn't take long, given that the place appeared dead.

Zahir was sitting on hold on the phone and not looking in the sunniest of moods.

'How's the holiday planning going?' Janet asked as Adele came over.

'I've seen something nice for the South of France.'

'*Ooh, la la,*' Helene said as she joined the group. 'Will you go topless?'

'I might.' Adele said. 'And I might find myself a nice French man...'

'What about Paul?' Janet checked.

'Oh, yes.' Adele said, her voice a touch deflated.

'You've got your hot date tonight!' Janet reminded her, and Adele rolled her eyes. 'Where's he taking you?'

'No idea.' Adele shrugged.

Zahir tried to ignore the conversation. Adele was going out on a date, well, of course she was.

She was beautiful, seriously so, and it had nothing to do with him what she did in her free time.

But this wasn't her free time.

'Is it appropriate,' Zahir said tartly as he hung up the phone, 'to be discussing topless bathing and dating in a corridor.'

'Er, Zahir.' Janet, who knew a thing or three, and

had been enjoying winding him up, answered with her own version of tartness. 'There are absolutely no patients around. I can handle my nursing staff, thank you.'

She smiled as Zahir stalked off.

Oh, yes.

She knew full well that he liked Adele.

CHAPTER FOUR

I<small>T WAS A</small> busy morning and lunchtime soon came around. Adele made good on her promise to visit Leila.

'You are looking so much better.' Adele was delighted to see the other woman sitting up and that she had some colour in her cheeks. Her hair was up and, despite wearing a hospital gown, she looked amazing.

'I am feeling it,' Leila agreed. 'Thank you for all your help yesterday. Honestly, I shudder to think what might have happened. We could have been at afternoon tea!'

'Don't think like that.' Adele smiled.

'It's hard not to,' Leila sighed. 'There's not much else to do here. It is so nice to have you come and see me. I am used to being very busy. To just lie in bed is so frustrating. Zahir and Dakan have been in, of course, and the nurses here are very kind, but I am so bored.'

'Will your husband come and visit you now that he knows you're having surgery?'

'No.' Leila shook her head. 'He does not like hospitals.'

It must be lonely for her, Adele thought.

'He was going to send one of my handmaids but I have told him not to. I have asked Dakan to bring my embroidery from the hotel. That will take my mind off things.'

Leila was so easy to talk to. She was the complete opposite of Zahir, who, Adele guessed from the little she had gleaned, took after his father. Leila was more open and outgoing, rather like Dakan.

'So you have days off this weekend?' Leila asked.

'I do.' Adele nodded. 'Then I'm on night duty for a fortnight.'

'They must be tiring,' Leila said, and then looked at Adele and saw the smudges under her eyes and her pale features. 'Though you look tired now, even before you have started your night duty.'

'I am tired,' Adele admitted, and not just to Leila but to herself. It had been an exhausting few years and Janet was right to insist that she take her leave. 'I've got a holiday coming up.'

'That's exciting. Are you going anywhere nice?'

'I haven't decided yet. I'll have a think about it this weekend.'

As they chatted Adele revealed that she was going on a date that evening.

'A first date.' Leila beamed.

'I'm actually not looking forward to it,' Adele admitted. 'I'm thinking of cancelling but I can't come up with a good enough excuse.'

'What do your parents think of him?' Leila asked.

'They...' Adele paused. 'I think your idea of a first date and mine are a little bit different, we're just going out for dinner.'

'Oh, yes.' Leila nodded. 'I sometimes forget. By the time I had my first date with Fatiq he was already my husband.' She laughed.

'Had you met him before you married?'

'Yes, there was a selection ceremony two months before the wedding. I knew though that I would be chosen. Or rather I hoped. From when I was a little girl I always knew who I would marry. I told him that I came with conditions, though,' Leila said, and tapped the ruby at her throat.

Adele guessed Leila meant she had told Fatiq that she must be kept in splendour.

'Well, I can't see myself ever marrying Paul,' Adele admitted. 'I can't even picture getting through dinner.'

'Your parents haven't met him, then?'

'No.' Adele shook her head. 'My parents divorced when I was very young and my father has never had anything to do with me.'

'And your mother?'

'She was in an accident,' Adele said. 'She's very unwell and is in a nursing home. I see her every day.'

'And you're visiting me too!'

'No, I *like* visiting you,' she said, and then closed her eyes on the sudden threat of tears.

Adele never cried but she was suddenly close to it now as she had practically admitted the truth—she didn't like visiting her mum.

Leila's hand went over hers.

It was unexpected and also terribly kind, given what she had just said.

'She can't talk or react,' Adele told Leila. 'She's just a shell of herself. I don't even think she knows that I'm there.'

'You know that you're there for her, though,' Leila said. 'That's the important thing.'

Finally, someone who understood, Adele thought.

Her family, friends and colleagues all encouraged her to step back. Even the nursing staff at the home gently implied that Adele didn't need to visit quite so much.

Adele knew that she had to sort out her life—she

didn't need to be told that but it was so nice to have someone understand.

'I'm worried about going on holiday,' she admitted.

'Can I tell you something?' Leila offered. 'I want to have a holiday. I love my country and my people but because of certain ways...' She hesitated and then explained. 'Always there must be a royal in residence. Fatiq was already a king when we married so I never even had a honeymoon. Now one of my sons steps in if we have to go away for formal occasions. Usually it is Zahir, but both of them have busy lives, so they only return when they must. I know that a holiday would be rejuvenating. I dream of having some time away with my husband to replenish myself, although I can't see it ever happening. Take some time for yourself, Adele, and you will return refreshed and better able to take care of your mother.'

It helped to hear that.

The wise, gentle words made Adele feel better about taking a short break.

'I must get back to work.' It had been nice talking and before she went Adele wished Leila well for her operation on Monday.

'I doubt you'll be up to visitors on Monday night but I'll come in after my shift on Tuesday morning.'

'I shall look forward to it,' Leila said. 'Enjoy dinner tonight.'

Adele did.

Her date went well, in fact. Paul was nice, and perfectly fine, except she didn't fancy him.

Not a bit.

And it neither started nor ended with a kiss.

It just wasn't there.

For Adele at least.

Monday came and in the afternoon Adele lay in bed, trying to get some sleep before her night shift.

Then Helga and James started to row.

Again.

She had gone to look at the one-bedroom flat, along with many others. She had put an application in and all Adele could do now was hope.

Oh, Leila was right, she needed a break.

She had two weeks of night duty to get through and then the world was her oyster.

Not quite.

She sat up and reached for her laptop and checked her bank account.

Still, it didn't stop her from daydreaming. She liked the look of Greece though she was still considering the South of France when an advert for exotic honeymoon destinations caught her eye.

Well, not the honeymoon word. Adele couldn't even get the excitement up for a second date. Paul had called over the weekend, suggesting that they go to the movies, but she had said no.

There was no point.

No, it was the destination that had her pause.

Mamlakat Almas.

That was where Zahir was from.

Adele clicked on it and immediately she was swept away.

She found out that the name translated to Kingdom of Diamonds.

It looked incredible. Adele watched a short film. It was taken from the air and she saw the azure water and the pristine white beaches. From snatches of conversations when she had worked with Dakan and from the odd comment Zahir had made, she had thought it was all ancient buildings and desert. And, yes, there was all of that—the film led her through the desert and she saw a caravan of camels and Bedouin tribes as well as colourful souqs. The city skyline, though, was modern, with golden high-rise buildings that shimmered in the sun.

And there, most beautiful of all, was Qasr Almas.

Diamond Palace.

Zahir's home.

It was spectacular—an imposing white residence with beach and ocean on the one side yet the desert started directly behind and spread into the distance.

The palace was dotted with stones, rubies, emeralds, and sapphires and some diamonds too.

Adele wanted to see it and she wanted to be there in the souqs and especially out in the desert.

She read the comments and most agreed it was an amazing destination. There was a certain magic to it, many said, and it was perfect for a honeymoon or romantic getaway.

Then Adele read the negative comments and they were all pretty much the same.

Don't get taken ill there!
Bring your own medication!

And one was aimed at a tour guide.

He couldn't even answer why the palace is called Diamond Palace and yet it is mainly coloured stones.

Oh, she would love to go there.

Right now, though, she needed to sleep.

It was bad enough trying to sleep when she was working days—her flatmates liked to party hard, it didn't matter what day of the week. Trying to sleep during the day was almost impossible—there were doors slamming, arguments breaking out. After a fitful sleep Adele woke to the sound of the television blaring and loud chatter from the kitchen as supper was being made.

She was tired before her shift even started. It was going to be a very long night.

Zahir also wasn't having the best of days.

While he was grateful that his mother's operation had gone smoothly, he was furious that it had to come to this.

There was only one small hospital in his home town. Zahir had had several architects working on plans for a new one, yet his father had halted him every step of the way and in the end the project had been abandoned.

The whole health system in Mamlakat Almas needed to be addressed and better ways implemented.

The main reason that Zahir and his brother had chosen to study medicine had been so that they could knowledgeably implement the changes that were needed, yet they were thwarted at every turn. Their father refused to move forward and over and over he came up with reasons why the plans for the hospital could not go ahead.

Zahir had now had enough.

Finding out that his mother had had to travel to another country just to get suitable treatment did not sit well with him.

He looked at his mother, drowsy from anaesthetic, and was told by Mr Oman that surgery had gone well.

'I'm surprised she waited so long,' the surgeon commented.

Zahir was sure his mother had been struggling for a long time and it meant his mood was not the most pleasant as he made his way back to the emergency department after visiting her.

And Zahir's already dark mood did not improve when he saw a woman holding a large bouquet of flowers asking one of the nurses if they could be delivered to Adele Jenson.

'She's not on duty till tonight,' the nurse said, taking the flower arrangement. 'But I'll see that she gets them.'

Once the delivery woman had gone a debate took place as to who had sent the flowers.

'She had a date with Paul on Friday,' someone said.

Zahir did not want to think about that but the flowers seemed to follow him everywhere.

They were in the nurses' station as he wrote his notes. And when, having checked on his mother again in the late afternoon, he went to make a drink, someone had moved them through to the staff kitchen.

He went to his office to make a call to his father.

The King.

He sat at the desk for a long moment, thinking hard. There was a lot on his mind. Admin were demanding his signature on a new contract, as they had every right to do.

Zahir knew, though, that he needed to go home and not just for a visit this time.

He was thinking of going head to head with his father so that he could get the hospital under way.

There was another reason, though, that he hadn't signed his new contract—Adele.

The attraction had been instant and troublesome. He

could still vividly remember the first time he'd laid eyes
on her. Working on a patient, usually nothing could have
drawn his attention, yet for a fleeting moment she had.

Her china-blue eyes had met his and Janet had explained that Adele was there for an interview.

He hadn't wanted her to get the job.

That was how much he was attracted to her. Even
before they had spoken, he would have preferred that
they never had. Of course she had been given the role
and two weeks later he had walked into the nurses' station to the sound of her laughter and her fresh fragrance.

'Zahir,' Janet had said. 'This is Adele. She is a graduate nurse…'

'Adele.' He had responded with a brief nod.

'Hi!' She had smiled.

'Adele did her training here,' Janet had explained,
'so she's familiar with the place.'

Zahir had shut her out at every possibility. He'd asked
for more senior staff when possible. He'd ignored her
slightly wacky humour and had not rewarded it with
a smile.

He'd dated sophisticated beauties and he'd told them
upfront that he was in no position to settle down.

Currently he was dating Bella.

That was about to end and he knew Bella sensed it.
He had used the excuse of his mother being sick this
weekend not to see her and now she had come up with
tickets to the theatre next week.

He would end it before then.

Soon he would marry a bride considered suitable.

Of course he would be consulted, but the effect of
her laughter on the edge of his lips would not be taken
into consideration. Neither would the fact that the mere
scent of her made him want to turn around.

There would be a more logical thought process when it came to the selection of the future Queen. Perhaps her country would have a considerable army, for it would be a marriage of countries rather than hearts. Of course Zahir was not considering Adele for such a role. Yet, on sight, his guard had gone up and he'd known he'd have to be wary of the attraction he felt.

It was an attraction so intense that over the last year every time he had driven past her at the bus stop he had wanted to slow down and tell her to get in. Not to take her home but to take her to his bed.

To make slow, tender love to her.

Yes, he had slowed down the car once, but the sight of her in that short wet dress had been too much.

She was a relentless assault to his senses and six feet three of turned-on sheikh had decided it was safer to drive on.

It was hell to drive past her and leave her standing in the dark. It was hell to work alongside her.

It was hell.

And perhaps time away was needed before self-control ran out.

Nothing could come of them, Zahir knew that. It was the reason that he kept his distance.

His feelings for Adele were serious and that was why he held well and truly back. But it was getting harder to do so.

And it was another reason why it might be better to return to his country.

Zahir rang home.

'I have just come from visiting the Queen.' Zahir spoke formally with his father. 'She is doing very well.'

'How long until she can come home?' The King asked.

'Not until she is ready,' Zahir said. 'I have spoken

with Mr Oman and usually it would be several weeks before she could fly but, given she will be on the royal jet, I don't expect it to be that long. And I shall accompany her, of course.' He took a breath and then told his father what he had decided. 'I am not renewing my contract at the hospital. I'm coming home to sort out the building of the new hospital. I'm going to be speaking with architects over the coming weeks. I shall do my best to find someone who can understand the need to respect our traditions, as well as incorporate the new. When I return things will immediately get under way.'

'Nothing is to get under way without my permission.'

'Too many lives have been lost,' Zahir said. 'Your delay in implementing changes has caused your own wife to collapse. What about all our people?'

'I am King.'

'And I am Crown Prince and I refuse to do nothing until your death. I shall be returning with the Queen and change will happen.'

'Don't speak of this now, Zahir. Not when I am concerned for my wife—'

'No,' Zahir interrupted. 'You can no longer ignore that fact that there are better ways. The Queen collapsed while she was visiting me at work. What if she had been at a formal dinner or a royal event? Luckily she was in a hospital at the time.'

Zahir let out a tense breath, embarrassed on behalf of his mother as to how events could have panned out.

He was so grateful that Adele had dealt with things so discreetly.

Adele.

All roads led to her.

Even in the middle of a difficult conversation he

smiled at the memory of her blocking his path as he had tried to get into the cubicle to care for his mother.

Then his smile faded and he returned to the subject.

'We shall discuss this in person,' Zahir said to his father. 'For now, know that she is resting comfortably and that she is receiving *excellent* medical care.'

'If you are returning then there shall be a selection ceremony and a wedding.'

'You know where I stand on that,' Zahir said. 'I will not marry and have children when I cannot ensure adequate health care for them.'

Zahir hung up.

He saw a few more patients and then went through to the staffroom. Those flowers really were following him. They had been placed on the table and the word 'Adele' had been written on a sheet of paper, as well as an arrow, a row of hearts and a lot of question marks.

It was tease from the other nurses, informing her that she would need to explain!

Zahir did not want to hear it.

Adele walked into the staffroom fifteen minutes before the start of her shift to the beautiful sight of Zahir stretched out and asleep on a sofa. His mouth was slightly open, he needed to shave, but she'd prefer that he did not. But then her heart sank when she saw the large floral arrangement and the note with her name on it. Not for a second did she hope that the flowers were from Zahir. With trepidation she opened the card and read the message.

Adele
    Thanks for a great night. Hope to do it again
very soon.
Paul x

Unlike their date, there was a kiss at the end.

Zahir awoke to the sickly scent of flowers and to Adele's blue eyes as she stood in the middle of the staff-room.

She looked over as he stirred and wondered what it would be like to wake up beside him.

'You got flowers.' He stated the obvious.

'I did.'

But not from you, her eyes accused.

Never anything from you.

Not even a smile.

'How is your mother?'

'She's doing well.' Zahir stretched his long body. 'The operation went smoothly.'

'That's good.' she said, wondering how the mere sight of him stretching had her on slow burn. How a night being wined and dined by a friendly and good-looking Paul couldn't garner a kiss, yet she could happily go over and straddle Zahir right here and right now.

Honestly!

She had never slept with anyone but she could almost feel the pull in her groin to walk over to him, to bend her head and to kiss that sulky mouth.

He sat up and she was very glad that he did.

'My mother said that you have been visiting her and are going to see her again.'

'I just thought with her being so far from home—' Adele started to explain, but Zahir cut in.

'I appreciate it,' he said, and then abruptly stood and left.

It didn't feel as if he appreciated it, Adele thought as he stalked off.

Still, she wasn't visiting Leila to earn favours from him.

She liked his mother and enjoyed their conversations.

Adele missed talking with her mum so much and Leila helped with that.

Zahir went home and it was a quiet night in Emergency, which made it a very long one. By morning, all Adele wanted was to go to sleep but she remembered she had promised to visit Leila.

'Don't forget your flowers,' Janet called out as she left.

Blasted things, Adele thought, but then she decided they might brighten the room up a little for her visitor.

'Flowers!' Leila was wearing a gorgeous nightgown, had all her jewels on and was back to looking stunning. She smiled when Adele knocked on her door and quickly dabbed her eyes with a handkerchief. 'You shouldn't have.'

'I didn't,' Adele admitted. She knew Leila had been crying. 'The man I went out with on Friday sent them.' She rolled her eyes.

'Do tell.'

Adele did.

Well, a little bit.

'It didn't go well.'

'Why?'

Because he wasn't your sexy son!

'It just didn't,' Adele said. 'I kept wanting to check my phone. That's not a good sign, is it?'

Leila laughed.

'Then he called over the weekend and asked me out again and I said no. I thought he'd got the message but he sent these. I didn't want to look like an idiot on the bus, and I thought they might cheer you up.'

'Well, they have.'

They were like a snowflake in a snowstorm, though, Adele thought as she looked around.

There were flowers everywhere.

'How do you feel?' she asked Leila.

'I had a lot of pain in the evening but they changed my pain control and now I feel much more comfortable. I've just had my first drink of tea. I asked Mr Oman when I can go back to the hotel. He says not for a few more days.'

'You've got on your jewels.'

Leila nodded. 'I was appalled when they told me I had to have them off for surgery. I insisted they were brought to Recovery and I was to wake up with them on.'

Adele smiled.

'Adele,' Leila said, 'I've been thinking.'

'About what?'

'Well, I need a private nurse and I would very much like it to be you.'

'I'm on night shift for the next couple of weeks,' Adele said.

'No, I'm not talking about back at the hotel. I mean for you to fly back with me. You said that you wanted a holiday.'

Adele's shocked expression was misinterpreted.

'I wouldn't be making too many demands on you,' Leila said quickly. 'I would just feel safer knowing I had a nurse for those first few days at home, and then you could do what you wanted. I would page you if required. You would have your own wing with its own beach and of course you would be well reimbursed.'

'Leila…' Adele didn't know what to say.

She was stunned to be asked and very flattered too.

And the more she thought about it, the more excited she felt.

There, in her chest, was something that had been missing for so long—the hope of adventure.

The thought of Zahir didn't enter her head. Not at that moment. He would be here, working. This had nothing to do with him.

It was the thought of a holiday at such an exotic location. Yes, it would be a working holiday perhaps but that suited Adele even better—it didn't have to be a holiday *or* a new flat, she could have both.

Yet hope was dashed even before it took form.

'Ah, Zahir!'

Adele, who had been perched on the bed, hurriedly stood up as Leila greeted her son. He was dressed in a suit for now. No doubt later he would be wearing scrubs, but for now he was all glossy and freshly showered, and the scent of his cologne as he came over was more heady than a room full of flowers. 'I was just saying to Leila that I need a private nurse and she had told me that she has some annual leave coming up. I thought—'

'I will arrange your nurse,' Zahir interrupted, and his voice was terse.

'I don't need you to arrange anything,' Leila said. 'I would like Adele—'

'Adele is a junior emergency nurse. I shall find a surgical nurse who specialises in women's health to take care of you. In fact, I already have. She will be looking after you when you go back to the hotel.'

'Zahir!' Leila reprimanded her son.

'It's fine.' Adele halted them. Her cheeks were on fire and she was angry and hurt at Zahir's cutting words. Clearly he didn't even think her capable of nursing what would by then be a two week post-op patient. 'It was lovely of you to think of me, Leila... I really do have to go now.'

She said goodbye and gave a very brief nod to Zahir.

'Zahir,' his mother admonished once they were alone. 'You were very rude to speak like that in front of her.'

'I work with Adele.' He shrugged. 'I shall find a more suitable nurse. Anyway, perhaps *you* were the one who was rude. Adele might already have plans.' He tried not to think of her topless on a beach in France and then he thought of Paul. 'Maybe she wants to go away with her boyfriend...'

'Rubbish,' Leila said. 'She doesn't have one. In fact...' She gestured to her locker and those flowers really were following him everywhere because Zahir caught sight of them as Leila continued to speak.

'She had a disastrous date on Friday. She said all she wanted to do was to check her phone. She spends all her spare time taking care of her mother and I want to do something nice for her.'

Zahir held in an exasperated sigh.

There was a debt to be paid and his mother had now come up with a way to pay it.

'I shall think of a more suitable way to thank her,' Zahir said, and then he asked a question. 'Why do you want Adele?'

It was a question he had asked himself many times over the past year.

'I find her easy to talk to and she knows about...' Leila shook her head and lay back on her pillow and closed her eyes. 'It doesn't matter. I'm going to have a little rest now. I've been up since five.'

The subject was closed.

So many subjects were closed.

He could see that she had been crying and Zahir thought about what Adele had said to him in the car: *You need to discuss that with your mother.*

He didn't know how to, though.

He could speak with grief-stricken parents, he could tell someone, with skill and care, that they did not have long to live.

Yet this was a conversation that was almost impossible to start. From seven years old he had been warned not to ask questions. Not to upset his mother or anger his father by bringing the subject of his brother up.

But they weren't at the palace and things had been left unsaid for far too long.

'I miss him too,' Zahir said to his mother, and he watched her face crumple. 'I know I never saw him, but I still think of him and when I go to our desert abode I pray for him each time.'

As Leila started to cry he let her and then after a while she asked him something.

'Could you pass my bag?'

She took out her purse and Zahir saw his brother for the first time as his mother spoke. As he finally found out what had happened Zahir wasn't in doctor mode, or crown prince mode, he was just remembering the sadness and the silence that had returned with his parents to the palace and he looked at the tiny, beautiful reason why.

'Zahir, I had to tell the doctor about Aafaq and Adele was there when I did so. I don't want to go through it all with another nurse. I am very tearful at the moment. I know that. Mr Oman says it is to be expected after such an operation and it may continue for a few weeks. Maybe the nurse you arranged can care for me at the hotel—'

'You don't need to be in a hotel,' Zahir said. 'Please come back to my home.'

'Your home is in Mamlakat Almas,' Leila told him. 'I would prefer to stay in a hotel.'

Despite being more open than Fatiq, she did not approve of his lifestyle here. Leila did not like the fact that Zahir and Dakan dated when there was an array of brides waiting for them to choose from.

Staying in a hotel was her protest.

'Please let me have Adele care for me.'

'I'll think about it,' he said.

Adele was all he could think about of late.

He had been about to head to Admin to tell them he was taking the last fortnight on his contract as leave and that he would not be renewing it.

The ramifications of a relationship with Adele had long troubled him—his father frowned on his lifestyle here and certainly any serious relationship would be even more frowned upon. It would be dire indeed if anything happened in Mamlakat Almas. He could never choose Adele. The rift it would create between him and his father would be irreparable.

The King was a stickler for tradition and those traditions did not allow for a woman without a title who had dated before.

He could well be exiled and unable to fulfil his duty to his country.

No, he did not want to consider his mother's request.

He was trying to get away from Adele.

Not bring her to his home.

CHAPTER FIVE

FOR A MOMENT there Adele had thought that her luck was finally changing.

You make your own luck, Adele told herself.

She just didn't know how.

It was her second week of nights and she couldn't wait for them to be done and for her two-week break to commence.

She was still smarting at Zahir.

It was six p.m. and there was a staff accreditation that Adele needed to have signed off. She wanted to get it done before she went on annual leave.

She wasn't going to the south of France. Despite the offer still being available, it remained too expensive, so she had decided she would take the Eurotunnel to Paris.

In the morning she would book it.

It really was time to move on with her life, while still including her mother.

And she *was* going to have a holiday romance.

Absolutely she was.

She was tired of her lack of a love life and that she was twenty-four years old and still a virgin.

And, as she went over to the nurses' station and Zahir didn't even acknowledge her, she decided was tired of having feelings for someone who thought so little of her.

He looked immaculate. He was wearing his suit and clearly hoped to get away quickly.

'Zahir,' Meg asked, 'is there any chance of you staying back?'

'I can't,' he said. 'I have to finish at six. Bella is waiting for me to pick her up. We are going to the theatre.'

Ouch, Adele thought.

'I just need to write up this drug regime and then I'll have to go,' he said.

With all the drama of his mother being sick and settling her into the hotel, as well as the constant calls back home, he had forgotten to tell Bella they were over. Zahir did not want to put it off for even one more night. He would tell her tonight soon after the curtain came down.

Helene came in then, all ready for staff accreditation too before her night shift.

The staff rotated, and did two weeks of nights every twelve weeks or so.

'You made it!' Janet smiled.

'I nearly didn't.' Helene gave a dramatic sigh. 'I took Hayden out for a driving lesson this afternoon and I've decided I'd rather pay for an instructor. I actually value my life. Honestly, he's—'

'Adele.' Janet halted Helene's latest rant about her son. 'Could you get the annual leave roster from my desk?'

Janet had seen Adele's eyes shutter.

It wasn't Helene's fault. She didn't know.

Few did, but Helene loved to give dramatic blow-by-blow accounts of her day, and with her son just learning to drive, it must be pretty hellish for Adele.

'You know Adele's mother isn't well?' Janet checked with Helene once Adele had gone.

'Yes...'

'She suffered a severe head injury. Adele was at the wheel of the car—she was learning to drive at the time.'

'Oh, no.' Helene cringed. 'I didn't know.'

'Of course you didn't, she doesn't really talk about it. Just know that she's had the most awful time.'

Zahir said nothing.

He finished writing up the chart and headed to his office.

There was Adele coming towards him with the roster.

'Adele...' he said, but she didn't stop walking.

In fact, she brushed past him.

She was on the edge of tears at what Helene had said and she never broke down. Right now, she knew, Janet would be having a discreet word with Helen. And she was fed up too with Zahir. She was tired of smiling only to never have it returned, and being offered the dream job just to have it snatched away by him had been the final straw.

At least she hoped that it was.

She was over him for good.

Oh, no, she would not turn around.

'Enjoy the theatre,' she called over her shoulder, and there was a jealous barb in her tone.

She was cross with him and hurt by him and too weary to not let it show.

Still, she had a fun couple of hours spent with mannequins being signed off on her CPR technique. Having found out she was going to Paris, Janet had remembered a beret she had in her locker and had put it on Ken, the mannequin, when it was Adele's turn.

'Ooh, Ken,' Adele said in a terrible French accent as

she knelt over him, 'Why do you just lie there so still?
Let's get this heart racing...'

Janet was laughing loudly and then looked up at the
open door. 'Oh, Zahir, I thought you'd gone.'

'I'm just leaving now.'

She got more reaction out of Ken, Adele thought as,
blushing, she massaged his chest.

The best bit was supper was provided!

Maria came in and grabbed a couple of sandwiches.
'I'm about to go home,' she said. 'Janet I tried not to
admit anyone, but I've got a patient that needs to be in
the obs ward overnight. Her name is Gladys Williams.
She's eighty and had too much to drink and fell and hit
her head. I can't send her home.'

'Of course not.' Janet said.

They were low on staff numbers and would do their
best to keep the observation ward closed for as long
as possible.

At nine they hit the ground running.

Gladys would have to wait to be admitted. For now
her gurney was parked in the corridor where the staff
could keep an eye on her without her taking up a cubicle or having to open the observation ward.

She lay there, singing, and didn't seem to mind at all.

'It's supposed to be a Tuesday night!' Helene moaned
as the place started to look more like Accident and
Emergency on a Saturday after the pubs had turned
out than a weeknight.

A group of young men, all the worse for wear, were
creating a bit of a ruckus in the waiting room. The security guards were in there, watching them, as Adele
called one of the men through.

It wasn't even ten o'clock and the place was full.

She put on some gloves and peeled back the dressing that the triage nurse had put over his eye.

'Sorry, Oliver,' she said as he winced. 'That must hurt.'

It was a nasty cut and was going to require a lot of stitches.

Phillip came in and introduced himself and then took a careful look at the wound.

He was a nice doctor, calm and laid back, and Adele would always remember how kind he had been to her the day he had broken the awful news.

Phillip never referred to it and Adele was grateful for that.

Now, though, she understood the tears in his eyes that day. Phillip was very much a family man and he had a daughter close in age to Adele.

'I want to take my time to suture this,' Phillip told Oliver. 'Which means you might have to wait for a few hours until I'm able to give it the attention it deserves.'

The patient nodded.

'For now, Adele will put on a saline dressing to keep it moist. Adele,' Phillip asked, 'is the overnight ward open?'

'It's about to be.' Adele nodded.

She was going to take Gladys around after this.

'Well, why don't we admit you there?' Phillip said to his patient. 'You can get some rest and then when the place is quiet I'll come and suture you.' He turned to Adele. 'Hourly obs, please.'

'Sure.'

Adele started to dress the laceration as Phillip wrote up his notes and then he opened up the curtain to head out to see the next patient.

It was then Adele heard an angry shout. 'There he is!'

It all happened very quickly after that.

A group of men—not the ones from the waiting room—had come into the corridor and had found who they were looking for.

They barged Phillip aside, and he was knocked to the floor and trampled over in their haste to get to Oliver.

Unfortunately for Adele, she was now the only thing between them and the man they wanted. As Oliver went to jump down, the gurney moved and the punch aimed at Oliver hit Adele's cheek. She fell to one side, her fall broken by a metal trolley to her middle.

It was over in seconds.

The security guards hauled the men out of the cubicle and Adele found out the police had already been alerted as soon as the group had burst into the department.

She could hear the sirens.

Janet moved her away from the drama and onto the computer chair at the nurses station and Adele just sat there, feeling her eye and trying to work out what had just happened.

'You'll be okay,' Janet said as she checked her eye.

And then Adele remembered Phillip and that he had been knocked to the floor.

'How's Phillip?' she asked.

'He's a bit winded. He's in his office. Helene's with him.'

No work was getting done.

The night manager was on her way down and would arrange cover. Ambulances would be placed on bypass for now as the department dealt with what was, unfortunately, not a particularly rare occurrence.

Helene came around then and brought Janet up to date. 'Phillip's okay,' she said. 'Just a few bruises and his glasses are broken.'

'Is Zahir on his way?' Janet checked.
'He's fifteen minutes away,' Helene replied.
Zahir would make it in ten.

CHAPTER SIX

ZAHIR WAS TAKING Bella home when the phone call came in.

Rather, he was taking Bella back to her apartment.

They had loosely dated for a few weeks and though he had been upfront from the start—that they would go nowhere—Bella seemed to have completely blanked out that particular conversation.

When she had rung to say she had tickets to the the- atre, Zahir had told her that he was considering going home.

'I could come over and visit.'

For Zahir it was by far the worst suggestion she could have made.

But it wasn't the rules of his land that made him end things.

He just couldn't ignore his feelings for Adele any more and he was certain that they were reciprocated. Perhaps it wasn't such a foolish idea for her to see where he lived.

If he was going to fight for them.

Zahir had never run from a challenge, yet he knew this was perhaps an impossible one.

Now he chose to face it.

Zahir hadn't rushed from Emergency to take Bella out.

Instead, he had stopped by to visit his mother.

After that he had dropped in at Emergency to hopefully speak with Adele but she was busy making out with a mannequin and making others laugh.

And at the theatre, instead of watching the performance, he had sat in the dark, thinking about Adele and what she had been through.

Who was he to deny her a holiday?

He loved his homeland very much.

Oh, there were problems. Serious ones at that. Yet there was a certain magic to Mamlakat Almas that Adele deserved to experience.

He knew, even if she would be looking after his mother, that she would be beautifully taken care of at the palace. He thought of the golden desert and the lush oases. He thought of steam rising from hot springs and the majesty of the stars at night. How, no matter how many problems you had, the night sky held you in such awe that it reduced them. So much so that sometimes you simply forgot your troubles completely.

Adele could certainly use that.

And as for the two of them?

He didn't know the answer—just that they could not end without a chance.

He was just about to launch into his *it's not you, it's me* speech with Bella when his phone had rung.

Seeing that it was the hospital, he took the call, hoping that there wasn't a problem with his mother.

It was Helene and she sounded somewhat breathless.

'Zahir, there's been a gang fight in the emergency department and some of the staff were in the middle of it. A couple have been injured, not seriously, though.'

'Who?' Even as he asked the question he was executing a U-turn.

'Phillip. He's got a few bruises and his glasses are broken. Adele has a black eye and is a bit winded, and Tony, the security guard, was kicked.'

As they approached the hospital Zahir could see blue lights from several police cars and vans outside the ambulance bay.

'Wait here,' he said to Bella as he pulled into his reserved spot.

Bella though had no intention of waiting in the car, he soon realised, because as he arrived at the nurses' station he turned and saw that she had followed him in.

'It just came from nowhere,' Janet explained to Zahir as he looked around the chaotic department. 'We were already busy. I don't think they intended to hit out at the nursing staff or the doctor. I'm sorry we had to call you in.'

'You were right to call me in,' he said. Phillip was in no way fit to see patients and, as well as that, the staff deserved to be treated at times like this by the most senior staff.

He could see that Adele was sitting in a chair with her arms folded over her stomach. Her eye and cheek were swollen and she looked angry.

'Where's Phillip?' Zahir asked.

'He's in his office. Tony's already in a cubicle.'

'I want Adele and Phillip both in gowns and in cubicles.'

Zahir would do everything to keep this completely professional. As Janet was taking Adele to get changed, Bella chose her moment to speak.

'How long do you think you'll be?' she asked, and Zahir turned impatiently.

'Why don't you get a taxi home? I might be a while.'

'I'm happy to wait in your office.'

Adele heard the brief exchange as she made her way to the cubicle.

Janet had been wrong, it would seem. Bella hadn't been *gone by morning* and never had Adele felt more drab in her baggy scrubs and showing the beginnings of a lovely black eye.

She could hear the sounds of the police radios and tried not to think back to the last time she had been in a cubicle, waiting for a doctor to arrive.

As he waited for Phillip and Adele to get changed, the receptionist, as was protocol, brought up Adele's old Accident and Emergency notes. He flicked through them and tried to be objective. He read about an eighteen-year-old nursing student with minor injuries who had been the driver in a high-impact motor vehicle accident.

Phillip had wanted to admit her to the observation ward but the patient had refused and said she wanted to go and wait near Theatre.

There was a self-discharge form attached to the notes that Adele had signed.

Everything was there, even her muted reaction when Phillip had broken the news that her mother was critically ill, was noted.

It just didn't seem enough, Zahir thought.

Yes, the notes were detailed but there was a brevity to them, to all patient notes here, that Zahir could not logically explain to his colleagues.

First he checked in on Phillip. He now had spare glasses on but there was a small cut over his eye and a nasty bruise on his back. He checked Phillip's abdomen. 'Any tenderness?' he asked.

'A bit,' Phillip admitted.

'I would like his urine checked for blood,' he said

to Janet, and then spoke with Phillip. 'I would like you to stay in overnight.'

'It might be better,' Phillip agreed. 'Meredith will get a fright if I come home in the middle of the night.'

Tony, the security guard, was next and he wanted to get back to work but, having examined him, Zahir said that he should go home.

'Adele.' He came in to see her with Janet. 'I'm so sorry that this happened.'

She didn't respond.

'How are you feeling?'

'Fantastic!' Adele knew her sarcastic response was perhaps a bit harsh but what hurt more than the bruise was that, after a year of being ignored, now that she was a patient he was finally being nice to her.

He went through everything and asked if she'd been knocked out.

'No.'

He went through all the allergies and her medical history and Adele answered him in a monotone.

'Are you on any medication?'

'No,' Adele said. 'Just the Pill.'

She didn't add it was the pill of perpetual hope, hope that one day she would be doing what seemingly every other twenty-four-year-old had already done.

It really wasn't the best of nights.

He picked up the torch and checked her pupils' responses. He tried not to notice unshed tears, but he could see her pain. Oh, his findings were not evidence based, but he could see that there were years of agony there.

'I need to look at the back of your eye.'

He picked up ophthalmoscope and Adele stared

ahead as he moved in close. She managed not to blink and then thankfully it was over.

She felt as if he had just stared into the murky depths of her soul.

His fingers gently probed the swelling around her eye.

'It's a soft-tissue injury,' Zahir said.

'I know.'

'It needs to be iced but you are going to have a black eye. Is it painful?'

'No.'

It was the truth. It didn't really hurt, as such. What pained her more was the shock of what had happened and the indignity of Zahir now being kind to her.

'I need now to look at your stomach,' Zahir said.

'I was just winded.'

'Adele,' Zahir said, 'this will probably go to court and my notes need to be thorough. Lie down, please.'

She did so and Janet covered her neatly with the blanket before lifting her gown. He examined her abdomen and she answered the question before he asked it.

'There's no tenderness,' she said as he probed her stomach. And then she gave a wry laugh.

She hadn't just been talking about her abdomen—there had never been any tenderness from him.

'Did I miss the joke?' Zahir asked, and he gave her a smile as he covered her with the blanket.

And maybe because she was hurting so badly she was allowed to be a little bit mean too.

'I don't need your small talk and your pleasant bedside manner, Zahir,' she told him. 'We don't get on, let's just keep it that.'

She glanced to Janet, who gave her a small smile as if to say, *You get to say what you want to tonight.*

Janet had seen for herself the way that Zahir was with her, though she knew it had nothing to do with them not getting on!

'I would like you to stay in the observation ward to-night,' Zahir said.

'Well, I'd prefer to go home.'

'Who is there to look out for you?'

Adele thought of Helga and James and closed her eyes as Janet spoke. 'I'm not putting you in a taxi to go home to those flatmates tonight. I'm not going to be argued with on this, Adele.'

'Is Phillip going home?' Adele asked.

'Phillip is staying here tonight too,' Zahir answered the question. 'He doesn't want to upset his wife by turning up in the middle of the night.' His mind was made up. 'You're staying in and then I'll sign you off for the rest of the week.'

Adele would far rather have gone home but instead she had to lie there listening to Phillip snoring and Gladys, who was now in the opposite bed, first singing and later talking in her sleep.

And then she too started to snore!

As well as that there was a lot of chatter coming from the staffroom as people went for their breaks.

Yikes, she would be quieter in the future when she took her break, Adele decided.

A light was shining from the desk and Adele asked if the curtain could be pulled around her.

Then, just as she drifted off, it was time for her hourly observations.

And then, a while later, from the other side of the curtain came the balm of Zahir's voice as he asked the night nurse for an update.

'How's Gladys?'

'Sobering up.'

'How's Phillip?'

'His obs are all fine, he's sleeping soundly. What happened with Tony?'

'He was discharged home.'

And then he asked about her.

'What about Adele?'

'Her obs are stable, she's not sleeping very well, though.'

'Okay.'

Zahir went off to see some more patients.

It was an exceptionally busy night but in between seeing patients he made his *it's not you, it's me* speech to a very put-out Bella.

Normally he would have seen her home, but tonight he could not leave the department and he could not string her along so she had gone home in a taxi.

Now, as the day staff started to trickle in, Zahir made coffee.

And he took one in to Adele.

She was finally asleep, not that anyone took such a thing into consideration in the observation ward!

'Adele.'

He watched as she woke up and opened both eyes, and he was pleased to see that her eye had not closed over.

'How are you feeling?' he enquired.

'A bit sorry for myself,' she admitted. 'And I'm sorry if I was rude to you last night.'

'I get it.'

'I doubt it.' She sat up and saw that he was placing a mug of coffee on her locker.

'Ooh, I really am getting the royal treatment this

morning,' she said, and then smiled at her own joke and Zahir found that he did too.

'I've discharged you,' he said. 'Roger comes on at seven and I shall bring him up to speed with all that happened last night and then I shall drive you home.'

'I don't want you to drive me home, Zahir,' she said.

She didn't.

All she needed was to get away from him, from the torture of being crazy about someone. He had been horrible to her, rude to her, and while she understood that he might not fancy her she loathed the sudden false niceness.

'I'm going to call a friend to come and get me,' Adele said.

'No, you're not,' Zahir refuted. 'We need to talk.'

'About?'

'We shall discuss things in the car.'

He made no secret that he was taking her home. In fact, when Phillip asked Adele how she was getting home, Zahir responded that he would take her himself.

And, really, no one gave it a thought.

Janet had offered her a lift and so had Helene and a couple of other staff too.

Of course her colleagues were concerned.

The mood was sombre and assaults on staff were not good for morale.

'Here.' Janet had fetched Adele's clothes from her locker and brought her a towel and the little overnight pack that Gladys and Phillip would be getting too.

It contained a tiny bar of soap, a minute tube of toothpaste, a toothbrush and a little plastic comb.

Adele freshened up and pulled on the tube skirt and top she had worn yesterday and slipped on shoes.

Zahir was waiting for her at the desk and speaking with Janet.

'I'm on my holidays!' Adele smiled. 'Do you think I'll pull?' And it made Janet laugh as she stood there with a huge black eye.

'Have a wonderful break, Adele,' Janet said, as Adele walked out in the clothes she had arrived in, trying not to be just a little more disillusioned with the world.

'Send us a postcard...'

They walked out and Adele winced at the bright morning sunlight.

'You're not very good at parking your car,' Adele commented, because it was over the line and at an angle.

He did not tell her the reason—that on hearing she had been injured he had hit the accelerator and when he had arrived he had practically run in to see how she was.

Instead, he held open the door for her.

Adele got in and a moment later he joined her.

'We meet again,' she said.

As he drove past the bus stop Zahir thought of all the times he had driven on, pretending not to have noticed her there.

And so did Adele.

She didn't understand why he briefly turned and smiled.

She didn't smile back.

'Are you sulking?' he asked.

'Yes, I'm sulking.'

'Are you warm enough?' he asked, because he had the air conditioner on up high.

'You can stop being nice now,' she said. 'I'm not your patient any more.'

'No, you're not. Adele, I have spoken with my

mother. If you are still interested, she would love you
to be her private nurse.'

'I don't need you feeling sorry for me, Zahir.'

'I spoke to her last night, before the incident.'

He had.

Zahir had thought long and hard about it.

He had been avoiding Adele for twelve months now
and it had got him precisely nowhere.

He wasn't used to avoiding anything, yet his feelings for Adele could challenge a lifetime of thinking
and centuries of tradition.

Wasn't he asking his father to do the same?

It was time to face things.

'On Monday she will fly home to Mamlakat Almas.
A car would collect you at six in the morning and you
would meet her at the airport…and you would return
to England on a commercial flight two weeks later.'

Adele frowned.

'You don't have to worry about a uniform or what to
wear, everything will be provided.'

She turned and looked at him and for the first time
since last night she properly smiled. 'What does that
even mean?'

'Just bring what you feel you want to. We are very
used to having guests in the palace and accommodat-
ing them.'

'Oh.'

'And if you are worried about something, there will
be someone who can advise you. It really will be relaxing and you need that. Especially after last night.'

Excitement started to ooze in, like jam squeezing out
a sandwich as you took a bite, but Adele did what she
could to rein it in for now as the car pulled up at her flat.

'I will do some studying up on hysterectomies…'

'Adele.' Zahir smiled. And in her direction too! 'It's a holiday. My mother will just need a little encouragement to walk, especially on the plane, and some reassurance, but we both know a private nurse is a touch unnecessary. She is, though, a queen. The second week would be yours to completely enjoy.'

'I want to see the desert,' Adele admitted.

'I'm sure it will be arranged.'

There was such energy between them, he knew that she felt it and how confused she must be by his cool treatment of her.

'You should go in,' he said, as still they sat outside her flat. 'Get some rest. You didn't sleep much last night.'

'I had Gladys singing and Phillip snoring.'

He said nothing, he was too deep in thought.

It was Adele who broke the silence.

'Thank you, Zahir. I know you didn't want me there but I really will take care of her.'

'I know you will. You will love my country. It really is magical.'

'I don't believe in magic,' Adele said. She had stopped believing in magic and miracles a very long time ago.

She had prayed so hard for her mother's recovery, and had later downgraded that plea to just the tiniest sign that her mother knew she was near.

Zahir looked at her bruise. 'You need to ice your eye.'

'I will.'

'And use some arnica cream.'

'Okay.'

For a second there she felt as if he was going to examine it again but though he raised his hand, he changed his mind.

And then, in that moment, she felt his resistance.

He hadn't been about to examine her.

Experience counted for nothing in this equation, for Adele had none, but she was quite sure then that she had been about to be kissed.

Maybe it was the knock to her head that was causing irrational thoughts.

Lack of sleep.

Too much want.

She needed to go, she knew, because she wanted to reach over and kiss him, and if she was reading things wrong she would never get over the shame.

She opened the car door and then, as she started to get out, she realised that she still had her seat belt on.

There could be no dignified exit, though, when there was a pulse beating between your legs.

She went to undo her belt.

He went to do the same.

For a year he had relied on self-control.

It was dissolving.

Zahir looked into the blue eyes he had wanted to explore since the very first day he had seen her.

She just stared back at him.

And then she remembered Bella, all beautiful and no doubt waiting in his home.

'How was the theatre?' she asked in a voice that was oddly high.

'Terrible,' Zahir said, though he knew what she meant. 'Bella and I broke up last night.'

'Because?' Adele asked.

'Because of this.'

Do what is essential, he had heard in the desert.

He had interpreted that as avoiding her, that it was

essential to resist her. Now, though, it was essential that they kiss.

For Adele, after such a horrible night, came the sweetest, most unexpected reward.

The feel of his lips on hers.

He kissed her softly and was careful of her sore face.

And as she moaned to the bliss, he slipped in his tongue and she tasted perfection. She discovered all that had been missing and why a kiss had never worked till now.

It had needed to be his.

There was silence in her mind and the sensual soothing of his tongue. Her hand went to the back of his head, and she felt that silk hair on her fingers.

There was utter relief as he kissed her, soon replaced by the yearning for more.

He kissed her deeper and his hand slid from her waist to the stomach he had touched last night.

And now there *was* tenderness as his hand slipped into her T-shirt and her skin was traced by him.

She knew then the hell he had gone through.

Trying to be friendly and to treat her as a patient.

And she knew now the reason for his seeming disdain.

His hand came up to her small breast and he stroked it through her bra and all this within a kiss.

'Does that explain things better?' he asked, as he moved his mouth a fraction away.

It did.

'Do you understand now why I didn't stop the car the other night?'

His hand was still on her breast and the ache between them could not be soothed by his soft caress.

'You should have,' she said.

'I would not have been tender then.'

'That would have been fine,' she said, and now she got the reward of his smile.

And always he was honest and upfront and explained to women that it could never come to anything.

It would possibly be fairer to say that now.

Yet he could not.

He removed his hand from her breast but hers was still on the back of his head and possibly it would require surgery to remove it, for she wanted to feel his lips again.

'Adele, this would be very much frowned upon back home.'

'I'm not going to tell your mum,' she teased, but now Zahir did not smile.

'I am returning home with the Queen.'

She swallowed and now she removed her hand and sat there and stared out of the window rather than at him. 'Because you don't trust me?'

'No,' Zahir said. 'I was always going to return with her. Do you see why I didn't want you there?'

She did.

'Why did you change your mind?' she asked.

'Because otherwise it would have been goodbye.'

She didn't understand.

'Go in,' he said.

'I don't want to.'

'Go in,' he said again. 'I will see you on Monday.'

'And?'

He didn't know.

All Zahir knew was...they had been awoken.

CHAPTER SEVEN

'READY FOR THE OFF?' Annie, her favourite nurse at the care home, asked on the night before Adele flew to Mamlakat Almas.

'I am!'

'You're eye's looking a lot better.'

Adele had been icing it regularly and using the arnica cream that Zahir had suggested. The spectacular purple bruise had now faded to pale yellow.

Sometimes she felt as if she had dreamt their kiss.

As if her mind, tired of nothing happening, had manufactured it.

Yet she knew it had been real and though the last few days had been busy she had dwelt on it regularly.

Hourly.

Maybe every five minutes or so!

Even though Zahir had said everything would be provided, she had spent a small fortune on underwear, nightdresses, dressing gowns and slippers in case she had to go the Queen at night.

It was very hard dressing for mother *and* son, Adele had thought as she'd closed her case on her hopefully subtly sexy lingerie.

But then she also knew there would be no furtive kisses or hot sensual Arabian nights.

She would be working and Zahir had told her anything more would be very much frowned on at his home.

And, from the little she knew, things were different there and her lovely new underwear had no hope of being seen.

Still, it was better to be safe than sorry!

'It will just be for two weeks,' she told her mum as she kissed her goodbye.

Yet it was about more than a two-week break. Adele knew that by taking this step she was if not cutting the cord then loosening it a touch.

Annie did too.

'You know we'll take good care of her.'

'I know that you will and I'll call every day.'

As she left the nursing home Adele felt different.

Of course she would be back and she would always visit but this was a huge step in reclaiming her life.

It was very hard to get to sleep and it felt that as soon as she did her alarm went off.

The car duly arrived and Adele was only too happy to close the door on the flatmates from hell.

She had bought some linen trousers and a long-sleeved top for the journey and then regretted it as her trousers had already crumpled while waiting for the car to arrive.

The driver made small talk as he drove her to Heathrow, but they took a different entrance from the main one. Soon she was in a very plush room and there was Leila but there was no sign of Zahir.

Leila had the pale, sickly pallor of someone who had spent time in hospital and indoors but apart from that she seemed well. 'I am so pleased to see you, Adele.' She beamed. 'This is Hannah, one of the nurses who has been taking care of me at the hotel.'

There was a detailed handover.

Leila had seen Mr Oman for a post-operative check-up the day before and Adele was told that he was very pleased with her progress.

'This is his phone number,' Hannah said, as she went through the file. 'You are to ring him if there are any concerns. Here is a course of antibiotics for Queen Leila, if he feels it necessary for her to take them. However, Mr Oman also said that he has full faith that the healers can care for her from this point on. He has written a letter for them. They can also contact him with any concerns that they might have.'

Hannah said goodbye and Adele looked out at the royal jet, scarcely able to believe that soon they would be boarding.

'I am so excited to be going home,' Leila said. 'Zahir and Dakan should be here soon.'

And here they were.

Always, *always*, he looked immaculate.

Just not today.

His suit looked a bit rumpled, as if he had slept in it, and he really needed to shave.

Oh, she hoped he didn't!

Adele hadn't seen or heard from Zahir since they had kissed, and she tried to remember how she used to greet him before...

That's right, she'd smile and he'd ignore her!

It had worked for twelve months and it worked now, for Adele smiled and Zahir duly ignored her.

It was Dakan who returned her smile.

In fact, he came over. 'My mother's ever so pleased that you're going home with her. I brought some antibiotics just in case they were required...'

'It's okay,' Adele said. 'Mr Oman has already taken care of that.'

'These are for you,' Dakan said, 'in case you need them. Are you allergic to anything?'

'No but—'

'Adele, believe me, you don't want to get ill there. I'm sure Zahir has got some with him but he may well be busy or away. Have these with you just in case.'

'Thank you.'

A flight steward came out to greet Leila and Dakan went over to his mother and they embraced.

Leila's eyes filled with tears and, though they spoke in Arabic, it was clear to Adele that Leila found it hard to say goodbye and that she wanted both of her sons home.

It was time to board and Leila did so without fuss, though she needed a little help with the steep stairs.

Adele felt dizzy with anticipation as she boarded the royal jet and Leila greeted the captain, co-pilot and the rest of the crew.

They greeted her so formally—even Hannah had called her Queen Leila—that Adele realised the great privilege it had been to talk to Leila so informally.

The Queen and Zahir sat in a lounge area and Adele did what she could to make Leila comfortable. She gave her a little cushion to put over her incision and helped her to strap in for take-off.

'Are you wearing your anti-embolism stockings?'

'I am.' Leila nodded, and lifted the bottom of her robe to show that she was.

'Good,' Adele said.

Adele was guided a little further back to a gorgeous leather seat that was set apart from the lounge, but she would be able to watch the Queen and would hear her if she called. She was told that her room was further down at the rear of the plane and she could sleep there later.

Adele had thought maybe it would be small jet, but it was huge, and lavishly furnished.

Still, she tried to focus on Leila.

It was the most rapid take off. Almost as soon as Adele sat down the plane started moving and before long they were levelling out. Adele looked down and saw they were already over water and when she noticed Zahir looking at her she gave him a small smile.

This was normal to him.

It was a huge adventure to her.

Once they were able to move around Adele found her room. It was small but there was a very comfortable-looking bed and a small shower. It was like first-class travel and this was just for the staff! There was a muslin nightdress laid out for her on the bed.

As well as that, hanging up was a coral-coloured robe and some pretty jewelled shoes.

She thought about what Zahir had said about everything being provided and it felt as if she had entered another world.

She came out and Zahir was on his computer and was chatting with his mother when the meals were served.

Adele took her cues from the flight stewards. She was seated to the rear and would take her meal there, whereas Zahir and Leila ate at a polished table.

Adele chose a lovely mint soup and a small bread roll for starters but her stomach was too tied in knots to have a main course.

Dessert was a light, pale custard with a rich rose-water syrup over it.

She saw that Zahir had declined dessert.

A foolish mistake, Adele thought, and closed her eyes in bliss at the taste and then opened them to see him.

He made her blush.

With one glance from Zahir she felt heat in her face.

Once the meals had been cleared away, Zahir declared he was going to bed.

He went into his suite, stripped off and showered.

He hadn't slept last night. He had gone out but had soon returned to his apartment and drunk cognac, wondering when, if and under what circumstances he might return to England.

He pulled on black silk lounge pants and closed his eyes but sleep would not come.

Zahir, in an attempt to drag his mind from Adele and those awful linen trousers, made a couple of phone calls to some architects and tried to line up some meetings.

One of them, Nira, sounded promising and she had some questions that she put to him.

Adele, on the other hand, tried not to think of Zahir asleep a matter of metres away as Leila took out her sewing.

'Come and see this, Adele,' Leila said.

'Oh!' Adele walked over and looked down, and saw that the Queen was embroidering a small square. The silks were so rich and the stitching so detailed it really was exquisite. 'It's beautiful. What are you making?'

'A blanket,' Leila told her. 'I have been making it for many, many years.' She took out a few squares from the sewing bag for Adele to see. They were all different, and each one was a work of art in itself. They ranged from flowers, to delicate letters, to beautiful coloured birds.

'These must take hours and hours.'

'They do,' Leila agreed. 'It is a stitching technique

that has been passed on through generations. Each square has a different symbol or flower…soon I shall put them all together. It has been a labour of love.'

Soon, though, Leila put away her embroidery and declared that she was very tired. 'I don't understand why, though, I slept well last night.'

'You were up early,' Adele pointed out.

'I am always up early.'

'It's your first proper outing since surgery, so being tired is to be expected,' Adele said.

'Well, I'm going to go to bed, if you could come and help me.'

'Of course, but you do need to walk around first.'

The Queen wasn't sitting in cramped economy class but she had just undergone abdominal surgery and that was a major risk factor for embolisms.

'You're bossy,' Leila moaned, and then she smiled at Zahir, who had come out of his room and was on his phone.

Of course, Leila didn't nearly faint at the sight of Zahir in black silk lounge pants and a naked torso.

That would be Adele.

And neither did Leila care that his hair was wet from the shower and that his feet were bare.

That would be Adele too.

Oh, she tried not to notice him speaking in Arabic into his phone as he opened up the laptop he had left in the lounge.

Finally Adele walked Leila to her room and it was Adele rather than Leila who breathed out a sigh of relief as she closed the door on Zahir.

It was as beautiful as any five-star hotel.

There was a large walnut dressing table and a pretty lemon-coloured bed, which had been turned back.

Adele helped Leila to change into a nightgown and then Leila sat on the edge of the bed and Adele helped her with her legs.

Really, she was unsure whether Leila could not manage or simply was not used to doing it herself.

'I'll come and wake you in a couple of hours so that you can do some leg exercises.'

'Very well. If I need you or I am concerned about something I shall have a stewardess alert you, but now it is time for you to get some rest too, Adele,' Leila said. She could be bossy too! 'There should be a robe for you to change into before we land. There will be more of a selection for you when we get to Mamlakat Almas. Could you please dim my light on your way out?'

Adele did so.

'Thank you,' Leila said. 'Now you go and relax.'

It was incredibly hard to, though, especially when she came out of the Queen's bedroom and saw that Zahir was still talking on the phone.

She went to sit on her allocated seat and then changed her mind and decided to head to her own room, but Zahir ended the call then.

'Adele, come and sit in the lounge.'

'No.' Adele shook her head. She was blushing, but not from embarrassment. She was heated and turned on just at the sight of him and the memory of their kiss. Sitting on a sofa with him dressed in next to nothing had no chance of ending well.

He knew what was on her mind.

'No staff will come unless they are summoned.'

'What if your mother gets up?'

He smiled.

'My mother doesn't get out of bed without the help of a maid. You'll know when she wants to get up! Come on.' He gestured with his head for her to join him. 'We need to talk.'

They did and so Adele went over.

She went to sit on a chair but he patted the seat on the sofa beside him and rather tentatively she sat down.

'I was just speaking with an architect and arranging to meet.' He pointed to his laptop screen and she saw building plans.

'I'm not returning to London, I haven't renewed my contract,' Zahir, rather bluntly, told her. 'I am hoping to bring about change to the health system...' He gave a small mirthless laugh. 'Actually, there *is* no real system.'

'None?'

'There is one small hospital but it is under-resourced and overstretched. Most doctors stay a month and leave and I don't blame them. My father is resistant to change.'

'When you say you're not coming back, for how long?'

'Maybe never.' And he was brutally honest then. 'I have long held off on marriage, but my father will insist on it if change gets under way.'

And just as that evening when she had seen the flowers, and had known they had not come from him, today she knew that marriage could not apply to her.

'There are many traditions and legends and rules in my land,' Zahir explained. 'I could take the whole flight to tell you about them and only then would we scratch the surface. The main thing I am trying to explain is that I cannot see my country accepting you. That is why I have done nothing about us.'

'Zahir, I don't want to live there,' Adele said. 'I would never leave my mother for a start, but we could have had a year, Zahir. A whole year of...'

And she felt like slapping his cheek for his restraint. 'Now you're leaving, just as I find out you wanted me all along. Why did you tell me all this now when there's nothing we can do? Why did you say to your mother I could come when you knew you were going to marry? Why kiss me…?'

'Would you prefer that I hadn't?' he asked. 'I could have left, and let you carry on assuming that I disliked you. You could have had your holiday in France and returned and found out I had gone…'

She tried to picture it and she didn't like what she saw.

'Perhaps I would have returned in a few years' time and by then I'd be married, perhaps you would be too.'

And she sat there.

'All I can tell you is that I was not ready to say good-bye and had you not come today, it would have been goodbye, Adele.'

'What happens now?'

He shrugged his broad shoulders.

'That's no answer.'

'Because I haven't been to the desert to ask for a solution.'

No, she did not understand their ways.

Neither, fully, did he.

He had sought solutions under the sun and the stars on many occasions.

The answers were always the same but in various orders.

Do what is essential.

Be patient.

In time the answers will unfold.

Yet they hadn't.

He did not want his father to die, yet that was the only solution that Zahir could see.

'Adele, it was either say goodbye in the car that morning and you would never know how I feel, or bring you to my home. I chose the latter.'

Adele looked into his beautiful eyes and she was now very glad that he had.

To have never known his kiss, to have never sat here looking him in the eye, as painful as it might prove, she was glad to be here.

There was an ache for contact and he solved that with his thumb, running it along her bottom lip.

'I want to kiss you,' he said, and he looked at her mouth as he spoke.

'Someone might come.'

'Not unless I summon them.'

And she looked at his mouth too.

'Leila might call. Anyway, I'm working.'

'If you are needed they will buzz through to your room.'

She half expected the oxygen masks to suddenly ping down, she felt so light-headed.

'This might be the last chance,' Zahir said, and he saw the struggle in her eyes.

'Just a kiss?' Adele checked, because just a kiss surely couldn't be wrong.

'Just that,' he said.

She stood on legs that felt unfamiliar and walked the length of the lounge and past the Queen's room.

There were no staff around, the only sounds the engines and her own pulse whooshing in her ears.

She stepped into the small bedroom and told herself that there was no chance they would be caught.

Yet she knew this was wrong.

Zahir came in then and turned the lock on the door.

All this for a kiss.

'One kiss,' Adele said, as he went for the drawstring of her linen pants.

'Just one,' Zahir said, and her thighs were shaking as she stepped out of her clothes.

She lifted her arms and he peeled off her top.

He unhooked her new and very lacy bra and peeled it down her arms and his eyes took in her small breasts and looked down at her stomach.

Her knickers were silver and tiny and he could see the dark blond hair peeking out the top.

And Adele could see him hard beneath black silk.

She looked at his solid chest and broad shoulders. With this kiss their skin would make first contact. She lowered her head to taste his broad muscled chest.

'Don't waste your one kiss there,' he said.

His voice was gravelly and thick with desire and Adele felt as if hands had closed around her throat because she was struggling to breathe.

He moved her so that her back was to the wall and as she went to reach for him he took her wrists and raised them so that they were above her head and then he held them against the wall. He looked at the lift of her breasts and how she was shaking with arousal.

'You're presumptuous,' Adele accused, and he smiled a slow smile.

'I am.'

He restrained her yet his own restraint was gone and he kissed her so hard that their teeth clashed.

One kiss, which made Adele twist against the restraint of his hands as she fought for her chance to hold him and drag him in.

He denied it.

One kiss, where their chests finally met, and she wanted to move her mouth just to taste his shoulder but that would break the deal of one kiss.

Her breasts flattened against him as he crushed her.

His erection slid against her stomach and she wanted it lower. He just bored into her and, with a craving for more contact, with nothing else for it, she attempted to hook her leg around him, but he widened his stance so that her foot dropped to the floor.

But now he was lower.

His tongue moved with the same motion as his groin and it was still one kiss but it had been spiced with dynamite.

Her jaw ached with tension and that tension slid to her neck and raced down her spine. Her thighs pressed together and Adele was rocking her groin into him. As she started to shudder he released her hands.

She held him between them as she came, and he felt the rip of tension and the stilling of her tongue, the slight squeal that he swallowed as she gripped him hard.

And it was still just one kiss as he silvered her palm and fingers and Adele felt him hot on her stomach as they pressed into each other.

Then he kissed her back but not to reality, for that was lost to her now.

And then he was gone.

CHAPTER EIGHT

ADELE SHOWERED AND put on the little muslin robe and, quite simply, she crashed.

She fell into a deep, dreamless sleep and yet woke with instant and absolute recall and with a curious absence of guilt.

She just lay listening to the hum of the plane and tried to understand how she was feeling.

It was disorientating.

Not just that she was on the way to a strange land but the might of his want and the rage of her desire.

There was no compass, no goalpost, no promises made, other than that he would ask the desert for solution.

Adele got out of bed and looked out of the window and there below her were the golden orange sands that Zahir would be communing with soon.

'I'd like the solution too,' she said, not quite tongue in cheek, because it was so vast and so endless that she first glimpsed its power.

She dressed in the pretty coral robe and put on her jewelled slippers and then looked at her reflection in the mirror on the door.

Adele barely recognised herself—not just her clothes, she should surely be on her knees in guilt and shame.

Yet she smiled.

Her intercom buzzed and she was informed that the Queen was awake and would like some assistance.

Adele knocked and went in and then blinked in surprise when she saw that Leila was in the bathroom, relaxing in a deep bath with taps made of gold.

There were bubbles up to her neck and she smiled as Adele came in.

'I didn't know you could have baths on a plane,' Adele admitted.

'You can have anything,' Leila said. 'The maid ran it for me, though I do need your help to get out.'

Adele helped her to step out and once Leila was dry Adele checked her wounds. There were three small ones from the laparoscopic procedure and all looked dry and healthy.

'I still have trouble with the stairs,' Leila admitted.

'It's quite a big operation,' Adele said. 'I think you're doing very well.'

'I am a bit nervous to go home,' Leila admitted as Adele helped her to dress. 'My husband has been so concerned. We've never been apart for so long and of course he is cross that I never told him I was having surgery. My husband is such a...' She stopped herself from saying anything more.

'You can talk to me,' Adele said. 'I would never break your confidence.'

'Even with Zahir?'

'Especially with Zahir,' Adele said. 'You're my patient and he's not your doctor, he's your son. If I have any concerns I would speak with Mr Oman.'

'My husband is very stubborn and Zahir wants to make changes,' Leila said. 'Maybe I am worrying over nothing. I am a bit weepy. It says in the leaflet to expect to be.'

She handed the leaflet to Adele and she read it as the Queen spoke.

'I don't have to worry about not doing housework or heavy lifting,' Leila said.

'And no intercourse for six weeks,' Adele added.

She would not avoid subjects just because Leila was a queen.

'Poor Fatiq.' Leila smiled and then she surprised Adele. 'Poor me. I do think six weeks is a bit excessive.'

Adele remembered her time in training and often the women would joke that they'd consider it a little holiday, or ask if the doctor could change it to ten weeks instead.

No wonder the Al Rahal brothers came with reputations. It would seem that the whole family was highly sexed.

'I hate sleeping alone.' Leila pouted.

'You can still share a bed.' Adele smiled but Leila shook her head.

'We have to sleep separately till I am healed. It was the same when I had my babies.'

Oh, no, Adele thought. At the time they must have needed each other most they had been apart.

'Once I am home I shall meet with the healer,' Leila told Adele. 'I'm sure I will feel brighter then.'

The Queen had selected a gown in a very deep shade of fuchsia and for someone who had just had surgery she looked stunning.

'I am going to do my make-up,' Leila told Adele, 'and then I'll be out.'

Adele sat in her seat and breakfast was served. She watched as Leila came out and took a seat at the gleaming table and then she turned her head and smiled.

And Adele fought not to.

It was Zahir.

As he walked past she quickly averted her eyes and looked out at the ocean.

He was wearing black robes and a *keffiyeh* that was tied with a rope of silver.

She looked again and saw that his feet were strapped in leather and that he was holding a scabbard that contained a long sword, which he put down on the sofa with the same ease Adele might put down her bag.

She had only ever seen him in a suit or scrubs, sometimes in jeans if he came in at night...

Adele had known the day they had met that he was a crown prince, but she had never really given it proper thought.

He had always been Zahir, Emergency Consultant, and the man she'd had a serious crush on.

Not any more.

Before her eyes he had become Crown Prince Sheikh Zahir Al Rahal, of Mamlakat Almas.

And that was scary at best.

Breakfast was cleared and they all took their seats.

Now the jet descended and to the right she could see a glittering ocean and then a palace. As beautiful as it was, Adele knew that soon, if they were discovered, she might not be welcome here.

As they landed she watched as he picked up the leather scabbard from the sofa and put it on.

The hilt of his sword was jewelled and for a brief second he looked up and their eyes met.

She was used to him flicking his gaze away.

Now she knew why.

Adele stood by Leila's side to help her down the steps as the cockpit door opened.

The Queen had wrapped a scarf around her head and over her mouth and Adele attempted to do the same with hers.

The wind gave her the first taste of the desert.

Her scarf slid straight down and the hot air burnt in her lungs and she thought of the traditions and legends that Zahir had touched upon.

She doubted the desert was welcoming her.

CHAPTER NINE

THEY WERE DRIVEN the short distance from the runway to the palace.

As the car slowed to a halt Adele was pleasantly surprised when the door opened and she realised that it was Fatiq who had rushed to help his wife out of the car.

Leila gave a small cry of delight when she saw him and he was clearly pleased to see his wife and greeted her warmly.

For a moment Adele relaxed and she almost forgot he was a king.

But then she saw the look he shot at Zahir and she would never forget again.

They came into the entrance and Leila smiled at Adele. 'I am going to go up to my suite. You will be taken care of.'

'Thank you. Would you like me to help you up the stairs?' Adele offered.

'I will be fine.'

As Fatiq helped Leila up the steps she paused and held onto her stomach midway and bent over a little and he looked down at Zahir again.

Zahir stared back and Adele could feel the stand-off between the two men and it gave her goosebumps.

'Samina will take care of you from now,' Zahir informed her, and he walked off. She watched as guards opened two large engraved doors, which he went through.

The palace was splendid, and Adele had only seen the entrance.

There was a gentle, cool breeze and tiny humming-birds were taking nectar from flowers even though they were inside. She looked at the dark staircase and ancient walls and heard the delicate sound of fountains.

She was shown to her suite and, as Leila had said, there was a stunning array of gowns for her to choose from.

Samina gave her some lessons, such as how to tie a scarf so it did not slide down and how to greet the King or Queen if they passed in the corridor.

'We have a system,' Samina explained. 'If Queen Leila needs you, she will summon you with this...' There was a small tablet by the bed. 'If you are not in your suite the message will go directly to your phone.'

It was a surprisingly modern system, yet there was nothing modern about her suite which was beautiful.

There was a velvet rope above her bed, which Adele was told she was to use to summon meals. There was a carved stone stairway that led down to her own beach and, as she walked through the large lounge, Samina opened some shutters and Adele looked down at a stunning mosaic pool below that was hers to enjoy.

'It is very private,' Samina explained. 'You can swim and if you want refreshments brought out to you, just pull the bell on the wall there.' She pointed down to it. 'Would you like supper here in your suite or down by the pool?'

Adele chose the pool.

It was so tranquil.

Even here tiny hummingbirds hovered and sipped nectar from the flowers, yet despite the gorgeous surroundings Leila couldn't quite relax.

She had seen the look Fatiq had given his son. He blamed Zahir for his wife having surgery.

Adele was starting to understand just how resistant the King was to change.

And that left her and Zahir nowhere.

She called the nursing home and was told that her mother appeared comfortable and that there was no change.

There never was.

Later, Leila paged her and said that the palace healer would like to meet with her.

Samina took Adele through to the King and Queen's wing and showed her to Leila's room.

Outside was a robed man, who followed Leila inside.

He was introduced to her as the palace healer. Adele gave him the letter that Mr Oman had written and he read it and then spoke a little with Leila.

After he had gone she and Leila enjoyed a gentle stroll around the gardens. The sun was starting to set and there was the lovely sweet fragrance of jasmine.

'Is it good to be home?' Adele asked.

'So good,' Leila said. 'I will enjoy the peace for now. Things are going to get very busy soon now that Zahir is back. My husband wants to move ahead with a selection ceremony so that Zahir can choose his bride, but I have said I am too weak for that just now. In a month's time perhaps.'

And, yes, as much as it had hurt to hear it from Zahir, she was glad he had warned her so that she did not hear it first from his mother.

* * *

In the first few days, while Adele had worried she might be unnecessary, blissful as it was to mainly relax, she realised that Leila had been right to request a nurse to care for her in her home.

The Queen had some minor post-operative problems, which Adele was pleased to reassure her often happened.

'I shall call Mr Oman and see if you need antibiotics.'

'I want to speak with the palace healer also.'

Leila had seen him on the day she had arrived home but it had been a brief visit.

This was a more comprehensive consultation. He came to the Queen's chambers and they spoke at length. Leila translated what was said.

'He suggests that, starting tomorrow, I walk barefoot on the sand and that shall help my genitals and get me grounded.'

Adele blinked.

'He wants me to take a course in the healing baths. I have to have another woman come with me. That will be you. He is also going to speak with the *attar* and have him prepare a remedy.' Leila spoke with him again but they both were looking at Adele. 'He says you carry too much tension in your solar plexus.' Leila gave her a smile. 'I agree.'

Adele nodded yet she was troubled, especially when a maid came to her room the following morning with a muslin bathing dress that she was to wear under her robe and also a slender vial from the *attar*.

'This is for the Queen?' Adele checked, deciding that she would call Mr Oman before she administered it.

'No,' the maid said. 'The Queen already has her remedy. This has been prepared for you. You are to keep it at body temperature and carry it in your robe, and take a sip morning and night.'

'For me? But what's in it?'

The maid didn't answer and, troubled about what the Queen had been given, Adele decided to call Mr Oman. She was surprised to find he had already had a long conversation with the healer.

'Yes, he discussed it with me,' Mr Oman said. 'I agree that Leila should be out in the sun and the herbs he recommends are an excellent choice. Make sure she completes the antibiotics.'

They had a gorgeous morning, walking barefoot on the beach, and then Adele helped Leila down some stones steps. The healing baths were cut into rocks and filled by the ocean, and they took off their robes and got in.

It was bliss.

Unlike the ocean, here the water was calm and there was just the occasional gentle lulling wave.

'I needed this.' Leila closed her eyes and lay on her back and Adele found she was soon doing the same. 'The nurse at the hospital put salt in my bath, but of course it cannot match the magic of the ocean.'

Colour was returning to Leila's face and as the days passed, Adele realised just how tense she herself had been because she was starting to unwind.

Maybe she should try the remedy.

Adele didn't know why, all she knew was that she felt relaxed here.

That afternoon, when Leila had gone for a rest, instead of walking towards the beach, as she did most afternoons, Adele headed to the desert-facing side of the palace.

And it was there, for the first time since arriving, that she saw him.

Zahir was driving out through his own private exit when he saw Adele.

Her hair was blonder from swimming in the ocean and her cheeks were pinker. She looked very beautiful in a lilac robe and silver scarf.

He slowed the car to a stop and got out and she walked towards him.

'Am I not supposed to be here?' Adele checked.

'You can walk anywhere,' he said, 'unless it is gated. Don't worry, you cannot accidentally access the royal beach or gardens, they are all guarded. Just wander as you please.'

'I shall, then.'

He looked amazing in his robes and the *keffiyeh* brought out the silver in his eyes. He no longer had stubble on his jaw, it was way more than that, and he was simply beautiful.

'How has your time here been?' he asked her.

'Amazing,' Adele said. 'I can't say I've really been working...'

'My mother is very pleased that you are here. She said you have been liaising with Mr Oman.'

Adele nodded.

'And she says that the healer prescribed you a remedy.'

'He did,' Adele said. 'I don't know whether I should take it. I don't know what's in it.'

Zahir smiled and when he did, her stomach turned

into a gymnast, because it didn't just somersault, it felt as it was tumbling over and over.

'Do you have it with you?' he asked, for he knew how things worked and that a potion should be carried by the recipient and kept at body temperature.

She nodded and went into her robe and handed over the vial.

He read the intricate writing that she could not understand.

'It's fine to drink, though just a sip morning and night,' Zahir told her. 'Do you know, my father and I were just talking and he pointed out that both Dakan and I have never been ill? He is right. I remember when I was studying medicine and I joined the rugby team. I strained my shoulder. I was new in London and I was surprised that they strapped it and suggested pain and anti-inflammatory medication. I ended up at a Chinese herbalist.'

'Did it help?'

'Yes,' Zahir said. 'It did.'

He had returned to Mamlakat Almas so gung-ho and demanding yet he could see the rapid improvement in his mother and he was quietly pleased that the healer had taken some time for Adele also.

She carried pain.

Emotional pain.

It was something he could both see and feel and something modern medicine had little room for.

He had seen it when he had shone the torch into her eyes, but he had expected to see it then. She had been hit after all. But the pain he had seen wasn't acute.

It was chronic.

Layer upon layer of pain.

He could only imagine his colleagues' reactions if he had written that in his notes.

'I am just going to look at the site for the new hospital.'

'Are the plans going well?'

'No,' Zahir admitted. 'Would you like to join me?'

'Is it allowed?'

'Of course,' he said. 'If the hospital goes ahead we would need nurses. Why wouldn't I seek your opinion?'

He was giving her the same explanation he would give his father. The truth was, he wanted some time with her.

It had been a long week, knowing that she was here and wondering how she was doing but being unable to enquire.

It was lovely to be out with Zahir.

He drove the car through ancient, dusty streets and then through a very modern city, at least in part.

There was an eclectic mix of ancient and modern. The most fashionable boutiques were housed in ancient buildings and there were locals and tourists, bikes and old cars along with sports cars and stretch limousines. Then there were towering modern hotels.

'We have everything but a workable health system,' Zahir told her. 'We have a good education system yet our best brains travel overseas to study medicine and few want to work back here once they have.'

They drove a little further and came to a small, run-down-looking building.

'This is the medical centre,' he explained.

They walked in and he spoke with a nervous receptionist who quickly summoned someone, a young woman, who showed them through the facility.

There was some very basic equipment and an occasional gleaming piece of machinery.

'Dakan and I bought these defibrillators last year. The trouble is, we need to train people in their use. It is a multi-faceted problem. This is the theatre...'

They stepped in and Adele could see why the Queen would seek treatment elsewhere.

'What do you see happening?' Adele asked. 'Tear it down and start again?'

'No.' He shook his head. 'This building should be the gateway to the new, though that is not my idea...' He led her through and they walked outside. The heat hit them like an open oven door and, in contrast to the busy street at the front, to the rear there was a vast expanse of nothing and they looked out to the desert.

'Like most cities, it is overcrowded and there is a clamour for space, yet this land had been held back for generations. The architects and advisors of the time knew that the city would one day need more room. I cannot build anything, though, without the King's approval. I want a facility that incorporates both traditional and modern medicine. I want them combined.'

'It would be amazing,' Adele said. 'What about the healers? Would they agree?'

'We are all healers,' Zahir said. 'It is time to put ego aside and to exchange knowledge and respect each other's ways. It was the palace healer who suggested my mother seek treatment elsewhere.'

They walked through the building and out to the car.

'I should get you back,' Zahir said.

He made absolutely no reference to the two of them and she looked out of the car window at a large sun in a pink sky. 'I'd love to see the desert.'

'I will see that it is arranged,' Zahir said.

They both knew that it wasn't what she had meant.
She'd wanted to know if he had sought solutions
about them, but more than that she wanted to go to the
desert with him.

CHAPTER TEN

IT REALLY WAS a wonderful, relaxing time.

In the morning Adele and Leila would swim gently and then lie on their backs in the healing water and talk.

Adele was now taking the tonic that the *attar* had prepared and she had never slept better. She was starting to awake refreshed, instead of wanting to pull the covers over her head and go back to sleep.

Sometimes she would see Zahir and they would walk on the beach or go for a drive.

They spoke about things but not about them, and though she ached to know if there was any progress or hope for them, she was also grateful that they didn't discuss it. It meant she could meet Leila's eyes when she returned.

One afternoon, as she and Zahir walked on the beach, Adele looked over at the glittering palace.

'How come it's called Diamond Palace when there are so many other stones?'

He didn't answer her.

'Zahir?'

'When you're ready to know, you shall.'

Zahir asked about the car accident she had been involved in.

'Did you see my notes?'

'Yes...' he nodded '...and also I heard Janet tell Helene.'

'I don't really like to talk about it.' If he could simply choose not to answer then so could she!

They walked in silence for a moment and she looked at the sparkling water and at the gorgeous palace ahead and wished she could stay here for ever.

It was Zahir who broke the silence.

'Do you know, I was going to buy you a car for helping my mother?'

Adele smiled. 'It wouldn't have been appreciated. I can't drive. I was only learning when it happened.'

'I could give you lessons,' he offered. 'I taught Dakan to drive when he first came to London. He's rather arrogant...'

'Like you.'

'Of course, and I doubted he would pay much attention to a driving instructor. I would be very patient with you, Adele.'

'I know you would,' she said, and she thought about it. He was very calm and controlled and if there was anyone who could teach her to drive it would be him, but she shook her head.

'After the accident I promised I would never get behind the wheel of a car again. I meant it. I just don't want to.'

'Fair enough.'

She liked it that he accepted her decision and didn't try to dissuade her.

And, Adele realised, she could tell him what had happened that day.

She wanted to.

For the first time she wanted to tell someone who

wasn't a lawyer or a police officer or an insurance representative.

'I'd only had a few lessons,' Adele said. 'I was on a main road and trying to turn into a street against oncoming traffic,' Adele said. 'I'd done it at the same spot the previous week, except this time it was rush hour and there was this wall of traffic coming towards me.'

She stopped walking and so did Zahir.

Adele couldn't both walk and talk as she recalled that day.

'I kept missing the gap in the traffic and realising afterwards that I should have gone then. I was starting to panic and the cars behind me were getting impatient and sounding their horns.'

He saw unshed tears but today he was grateful that they did not fall, for it might kill him to listen to this and watch her weep and do nothing. Given they were in view of the palace, he was very glad that Adele didn't cry as she told her tale.

'Mum suddenly said "Go..." and even as I went, even as I put my foot down, I knew that I'd made a terrible mistake. She said, "To hell!" and everything went slowly. I knew then that she had been telling the drivers who were sounding their horns to go to hell. I sent her there, though...'

'And yourself.'

Adele nodded.

'It was an accident, Adele. A terrible accident.'

'I know,' she agreed. 'And for the most part I've forgiven myself. I just...'

'Say it.'

She couldn't.

'You can say it to me,' he offered more gently.

'I think it would have been easier if she'd died.'

And she looked up into silver-grey eyes and they accepted her terrible truth.

'It would have been harder for you at first,' Zahir said, 'but, yes, easier on you in the end.'

'I don't know how to move on.'

'You already are,' he said. 'Moving on is just about going forward, not necessarily pulling away.'

And they started to walk again.

Slowly she started to heal.

The evenings were hers for relaxation and enjoyment and at night she would check on Leila's wounds and give her her tonic.

It was blissful.

A bliss Adele never wanted to end, but time was starting to run out and on her last Friday she and Leila lay on their backs in the salty sea water and Adele closed her eyes against the sun and just floated.

Leila was pensive beside her.

'My husband has to go on a royal visit to Ashla—a neighbouring country—tomorrow,' Leila said. 'I am thinking of joining him.'

Adele turned her head in the water. 'Will there be a lot of formal duties?'

'Not for me,' Leila said. 'Just one dinner on the Sunday night. I like visiting Ashla, we always have a nice time when we go there. We would return on Monday morning.'

That was when Adele flew home.

Her time here had raced by but now it was ending. Oh, it would be wonderful to see another country, but she loved her mornings in the healing baths and the occasional time spent with Zahir.

It was dawning on Adele that she might not see him after today and nothing had been solved.

Not a thing.

There was no solution.

'When would we leave?' Adele asked.

'Oh, no.' Leila shook her head. 'I do not need you to come with me. You can have the holiday you so deserve. I think a couple of days away with Fatiq are in order. Things are very strained between us.'

It was a huge admission and when Leila finally made it Adele gave it the attention it deserved and stood up in the water.

'Leila?'

'I love him very much. Today, though, is a difficult day and the build-up to it has been harder than usual.'

Adele remembered what had been said the afternoon Leila had collapsed. 'Is today Aafaq's birthday?' she checked, and Leila nodded, and then she too stood in the water and told Adele something that perhaps she should not.

Yet she could no longer hold it in.

'Things are very tense between Fatiq and me, Adele.'

'Birthdays and anniversaries are the worst. Well, I haven't lost a child and my mother's still alive but I know how much they hurt,' Adele said.

Indeed they did.

'Separate rooms aren't helping matters,' the Queen admitted.

'Does that have to be adhered to?' Adele gently enquired.

'I don't know.' Leila gave a helpless shake of her head.

'What about when you go away?'

'Oh, it will be separate apartments there,' Leila said. 'I cry every night.'

Adele was worried, not just for Leila but for Fatiq too.

They were grieving for their son but not together, and the rules kept them apart at a time when they needed to hold each other most.

And Leila spoke then about her tiny son, and how his little feet and toes had been just the same as his brothers. How hard he had fought to live. 'He wanted to live, just as much as I wanted him to live,' she said. 'I want his life to have meant something wonderful— instead, year by year, it is proving to be the death of our marriage.'

Adele didn't know what to say.

'Oh, we would never break up but we are growing further apart and this operation hasn't helped. Maybe I should have carried on with the healer.'

'Leila,' Adele said, 'you collapsed. And am I right in guessing that it wasn't the first time?'

'You are right.'

'You needed the surgery. I am so sorry you are hurting so badly today.'

'I will miss Aafaq for ever,' Leila told her.

'Of course you will.'

'It has helped to speak of him on his birthday. Usually I just deal with it alone and so does Fatiq. One day I hope we can speak of him but I can't see it happening. This evening Zahir is taking me to the desert so that I can visit Aafaq's grave. Usually I go by myself.'

'What about Fatiq?' Adele asked, and then corrected herself. 'I mean, the King. Does he go and visit the grave?'

'He went this morning.' Leila said. 'Alone. He's so...'

Her face twisted in suppressed anger and Adele watched as she fought to check it.

'He's grieving,' Adele said. 'It manifests in different ways.'

There was a sad atmosphere back at the palace and, late afternoon, as Adele lay by the pool, she looked up and saw a helicopter. She guessed it was the Queen and Zahir.

It was.

He held his mother's hand as they were taken deep into the desert and he held her shoulders as she stood dry-eyed and pale at her son's grave.

Zahir looked at the small stone his father must have placed there earlier today.

'I wish we could celebrate his life,' Leila said. 'Yet all it does is tear us apart.'

Zahir knew his mother was referring to her marriage.

'Adele says that he is grieving,' Leila continued. 'That it manifests in different ways. I just thought he was angry with me.'

'He is grieving,' Zahir said, and he was glad that his mother had had Adele to talk to.

But soon she would be gone.

Now that he had seen a photo of Aafaq, now that he had spoken with his mother, it hurt even more to be here, and yet he would work through it.

Zahir prayed for his brother, for the tiny Prince who had never had a chance to serve his people.

He himself, on the other hand, did have a chance, yet it was being denied to him.

Still there was no hint of solutions.

He knelt in prayer and every fibre in his body strained for a sign, for a glimpse as to what he should do.

Be patient.

Do what is essential.

In time the answers will unfold.

Yet *still* they hadn't.

He picked up sand from his brother's grave and pocketed it.

And then he put his arm around his mother and walked her back to the helicopter.

She was drained and tired and Zahir was again glad that Adele was at the palace because she greeted the Queen with a gentle smile and he knew that his mother was in good hands.

Adele walked up the many stairs with Leila and on the way she saw Fatiq and lowered her head as she had been instructed to.

'Fatiq,' Leila called to her husband, and there was a plea in her voice. Adele would happily melt away if only these two would talk, would embrace, but then the King spoke.

'Layla sa y da.'

Goodnight.

Adele checked Leila's wounds and they had all healed. She gave her her potion and Leila lay in the vast bed and looked so alone.

'You're going to cry when I go, aren't you?' Adele said.

Leila nodded.

'Would you like to cry with me?'

And she did. She cried for her tiny son who should be a man and her husband who seemed to be moving further away from her every day.

And Zahir heard it.

Walking in the grounds, he heard his mother weeping and he wanted to go upstairs and shake his father.

There must be change.

He was no longer patient.

CHAPTER ELEVEN

LEILA SEEMED MUCH better in the morning.

'Look,' she said to Adele when she came in to check on her.

They would not go to the healing baths today as the King and Queen were flying off and Leila was preparing for her trip.

She held out a small square of fabric to Adele. 'I made this last night.'

There were tiny rows of gold and reds and above dark navy and dots of stars and there in the centre was a small silver heart.

'Where the earth and sky meet.' Adele smiled. 'For Aafaq.'

'It is beautiful, isn't it?' Leila said. 'I put all my love into it.'

Her maid came in to dress her and Adele witnessed a very regal Leila. She wore a cream gown with a sash and when they went downstairs Fatiq was wearing a military uniform.

All the staff lined up to formally bid them farewell as it was official business they were leaving on.

'I will be back on Monday morning,' Leila said to Adele, 'in time to say goodbye. You are to enjoy your days off. Do you have plans?'

'I want to go to the souqs and to see the desert,' Adele admitted.

'Well, there is a driver at your disposal, just take some time for yourself.'

'You do the same,' Adele said.

Fatiq went to his office to say goodbye to his son. 'You are now ruling.'

'Not really,' Zahir said. 'If I make any changes over the weekend, you will simply veto them on your return.'

'Then don't make changes,' Fatiq said, and turned to leave.

'Father...' Zahir called him back, not as a king but as a father. 'Please go gently on my mother. She is recovering from surgery...'

'She is recovering from an unnecessary procedure. She left the palace laughing and smiling, yet she has returned unable to climb the stairs unaided and she weeps each night. Now, with the help of the *attar* and the healing baths, she is slowly starting to recover. It does little to enamour me to your modern ways. However, I do think, on my return, we could consider plans for a birthing suite at the hospital.'

It was the tiniest concession but a possible step forward.

Zahir didn't trust that it would transpire.

'As well as that,' the King said, 'I think we should hold the selection ceremony soon. I was going to invite Princess Kumu...'

'Don't extend any invitations,' Zahir said. 'Not without my consent, for it would not look good if Princess Kumu and her family came to the palace and I was not here.'

Zahir had fired a warning shot and he watched the clench of his father's jaw.

Yes, he was warning that he might leave.

The King did not respond to the threat from his son, just walked out of the office, and Zahir followed him.

They bade farewell and Zahir stood there as his parents were driven to the airstrip.

He watched them take off.

Zahir was now the ruler.

There was no point working on the hospital in his father's absence, he knew that.

Yet change would be implemented.

'Ask Adele to come and speak with me in my office,' Zahir said to Bashir, a royal aide.

His office looked out over the desert and he put his hand deep in his pocket and felt the sand he had taken from his brother's grave.

'You asked to see me?' Adele said, and the sound of her voice lifted his soul and he knew he was right to do what he was about to.

He nodded and turned.

'How about I show you the desert?'

'Is it allowed?'

'I am the ruler,' Zahir said. It didn't fully answer the question. 'If you want to call the nursing home and enquire about your mother, you should do so now, because there will be no reception out in the desert.'

'How long will we be there?'

Zahir didn't answer.

'Should I bring anything?'

'No.'

She called the nursing home and spoke to Annie. 'How is she?'

'She's the same. When are you back?'

'On Monday.' Adele hesitated. 'Annie, I'm going into the desert, I'm going to be out of range…'

And she thought of Zahir's words and she told herself that she was simply moving forward, not pulling away.

'We'll take care of her, Adele,' Annie said. 'You go and have a wonderful trip. Time in the desert, out of range, sounds magical to me.'

It was the most exciting adventure of her life.

Adele sat next to Zahir in the helicopter and they put on headphones; she was lifted into the sky and for a moment felt as free as a bird.

The palace was on the edge of the desert and soon all that was beneath them were golden sands.

'It's amazing,' Adele said into her mouthpiece. 'Just miles and miles of nothing.'

'No,' Zahir said, 'there is so much more to see.'

She just drank it in but Zahir was right—there was more.

The helicopter hovered and descended and she looked down at the sand dunes and saw a caravan of camels and their long shadows. It was truly mind-blowing to think that in this huge expanse there were people surviving and going about their business.

They flew over vast canyons and then the helicopter hovered as Adele took in a sight she had never thought she would—a desert oasis.

It was the most wonderful thing she had ever seen.

'There is a hot spring there.' Zahir's voice came through the headphones. 'Birds gather and drop seeds…'

It *was* magical.

Adele was starting to believe in magic again.

'And people live there?' she asked, because there was an array of white tents set beside the hot springs lake.

'That is the royal desert abode. Would you like to see it from the ground?'

She nodded.

The closer they got the more Adele's excitement grew.

The helicopter landed and they ran under the rotors but soon the sand gave way to a rich lush moss that surrounded the water.

It was nothing like she had ever seen or imagined.

She had thought the desert abode was a tent in the middle of nowhere; instead there were trees, delicate flowers and the lake was a dazzling azure.

It was paradise.

'Do you miss coming here when you're away?'

'I do,' Zahir admitted. 'I miss home all the time, but not the politics.'

There was a herd of white Arab horses and they were magnificent.

'Do you ride?' Zahir asked.

'Very well,' Adele said, and then laughed at her own joke. 'That's a lie. I've never even been on a horse.'

He pointed to a large tent by the lake and told her it was the royal one.

'So who lives in the other tents?'

'There are maids and the horsemen and a falconer.'

'Where's your harem?' Adele teased.

'Over there.' Zahir pointed as they walked towards the main tent. 'There is a tunnel from their tent that leads to the royal suite.'

'Are you serious?'

'Yes?'

'And do you…?'

'I came of age in the desert, Adele.'

She was sulking as they reached the royal abode. Or

she was trying to, but it was so beautiful that she forgot to be cross as she removed her shoes. The floors were covered with Arabian rugs and the walls and ceilings were lined with cascading white silk.

She took out her phone and Zahir smiled.

'Are you so bored on our date that you are checking your phone? I don't think that's a good sign.'

'Did your mother tell you about my date with Paul?' Adele laughed. 'Well, I'm actually checking for reception.'

There was none.

And her phone didn't tell her the time either.

'There are no clocks…'

'We go by the sun and the stars,' Zahir explained. 'The main reason for coming here is to get away from all things modern. I agree with my father on that point. Here is for introspection and to seek guidance. It is a haven from the modern world.'

'It's actually quite freeing,' Adele admitted.

It was and she told him why.

'You know, I always have this knot of dread—what if I miss a call and it's about my mother? The first thing I do is check my phone, yet while I've been here…' she shook her head unsure she could explain, '…it doesn't matter.'

'Tell me.'

'Well, I've always put off having a holiday. I convinced myself I'd panic all the time in case something happened and I couldn't get to her.'

'You know, if there was any change then I would get you straight home.'

'I know.' Adele nodded. 'But, rather than panicking, I've found…' She didn't know how best to explain it. 'I'm ten hours away at best. It's actually nice to know if something happens I won't have to deal with it. I now understand why people kept suggesting that I take a proper break.'

'Good for you.'

'Anything could happen,' Adele said, 'and we wouldn't know.'

And then she met his eyes and they told him that anything could happen and she wouldn't mind at all.

She wandered around. There was the royal suite with cascades of crimson silk and on one wall a red velvet curtain. Above the bed was a velvet rope.

'I doubt that summons breakfast,' Adele said.

'It doesn't.'

'Does that ring in the harem?'

'It does,' Zahir said.

She was tempted to pull it just to see some sultry beauty come through the curtain.

Adele did so and Zahir smiled and put her out of her misery. 'The harem was disbanded before my parents married. I believe it was a condition she insisted upon when she attended the selection ceremony.'

And she remembered Leila tapping at her ruby and telling Adele that she had made demands of her own.

Now she understood the demands Leila had made had not been about keeping her in splendour.

'Good for her.' Adele smiled.

And she thought of Fatiq, who really loved his wife. She just wished she could help there, but knew that there was nothing she could do.

A maid served them some tea and pastries and they sat on cushions. They were alone, finally alone, and she never wanted it to end. 'When do we have to go back?'

'When we choose to,' Zahir said. 'Would you like to

go riding? It will be sunset soon. I can have them prepare a gentle horse.'

'That sounds amazing.'

It was.

They went on a slow walk along the dunes and a huge orange sun turned the sands and the sky to molten gold. The colours meant it was like being in the middle of a furnace, yet with the setting sun a soft wind circled them.

The sky darkened and the first stars started to appear as the air cooled. Adele wanted more of the desert.

She wanted more of Zahir.

'Will Leila know...' Adele asked '...if we stay here tonight?'

'The staff are discreet. It might eventually filter back but you will be long gone by then. But I think she will understand when I tell her I have feelings for you. Deep ones.' He was honest. 'I can barely get my father to agree to an X-ray machine, I very much doubt he would allow you to be my bride.'

'I could never leave my mother.'

'I know,' Zahir said. 'So for now all we have is this time.'

'For now?'

'I told you, I have asked the desert for a solution.'

Which didn't seem a lot to hang hope on, Adele thought.

Perhaps she'd sighed because Zahir looked at her and smiled.

They arrived back at the oasis and when she'd thought there could be no more surprises she watched the steam rise from the hot waters as it hit the cold night air.

'Do you want to go in?' Zahir asked.

Often, too often, Adele had wondered how it might happen—a kiss that grew out of hand, as had been the case on the plane, or he might sneak her to join him in the royal suite. Never had she envisaged the absolutely certain, almost calm way he dismounted and held out his hand to help her down.

And she knew this was it.

They had withheld and resisted but finally they were alone and there was nothing now that could stop them.

Though there was one thing perhaps, Adele thought as he lifted her down and for a slow, sensual moment her body slid over his.

If Adele told him this was her first time, she knew Zahir might well reconsider.

And she didn't want that.

He held her against him and she could feel that muscular body and the roughness of his robe.

'You're sure?' he checked.

'Very.'

He turned her around and undid the zipper of her robe and it slipped to the ground.

A nearly full moon lit them and Adele could feel his eyes on her as she took off her underwear.

'It's cold,' Adele said.

'Then get into the warm water.'

The water came up to her shoulders and she stood and watched Zahir undress.

First he removed the scabbard that held his sword and dropped it to the ground, and then he disrobed and removed the leather straps from his feet. And then as he stood and she saw that magnificent body fully naked he strode with purpose to the waterside. She wondered if perhaps she ought to tell him.

No.

She lay on her back in the water and gave him full view of her body, and as he stared down she parted her legs and she felt her stomach tighten as he stared.

It was too late to be shy, she decided, and she would never regret this magical night in the desert.

He joined her in the water and Adele stood. They faced each other for a moment and then he reached over and she slid through the water to the demand of his hands.

The air was cold above the water but their kiss was warm and deep and his beard was rough and sexy.

His hands were over her skin, feeling her breasts, cupping them, and then teasing her nipples. Then down to her waist and then to her buttocks. All this as her arms wrapped around his neck. His mouth was so beautiful and she explored it. The steam had made their faces damp and their mouths slid easily.

She could feel him nudging at her stomach and one hand moved from his neck just to hold him again.

He lifted her so that her legs wrapped around his waist and she could feel the nudge of him at her centre and held him there. It made her kiss him harder as his hand slid to her sex and he felt her warm and slick.

And then they stopped kissing and she stared deep into his eyes, and they were back to their first meeting.

Somehow they had known even then that they were meant to be.

Their kiss was deep and her body pliant. Her arms were loose enough around his neck that he could guide her.

He positioned himself, one hand at the base of her spine and the other around himself so he could take her fast and deep, and she now stared into his eyes.

No kissing.

Just watching and waiting for him.

Yet he did not slide inside her easily, as he had planned to.

Adele made throaty noise at the bliss of intimate pain.

And Zahir realised that this was her first time as he seared into her, and though she moaned in pain she ground down in acceptance.

She was tight and the pleasure for him was intense. He felt her mouth bite his shoulder and he held her hips and thrust in hard. He knew from her moans that she gladly suffered an erotic mix of pain and bliss.

He was not gentle, he was rough, delivering the pleasure that made her thighs shake and her calves ache as they gripped him.

Her cold mouth came up to his and her tense lips were on his as he took her ever more deeply.

He angled himself and she stiffened at the new sensations he aroused and then she moaned because he stroked her inside so exquisitely.

They were surrounded by stars; they were there when she looked up and they were reflected on the water as she rested her head on his shoulder as he took her faster. They were bathing in the sky, that was how it felt; they were two stars locked now in eternal orbit.

Adele felt the swell and the hot rush of him deep inside and he moved her as she pulsed around him.

They were sweating in the cold air and heat below and she took every drop he delivered and then he stilled her with his hands and they kissed until she again rested her head on his shoulder.

'Why didn't you tell me?' he asked, still inside her.

'You might have said no.'

Zahir shook his head. 'Never.'

CHAPTER TWELVE

'I HEAR ABOUT you going out on dates?'

They were back in the tent, lying on the opulent bed and still wet from the hot water. She could see the bruise her teeth had made on his shoulder and she felt sore but sated.

'Yes, I've had many first dates.' Adele smiled.

He didn't ask about her being on the Pill and she remembered telling him that she was when she'd been hit.

She knew she had missed taking a couple of them. When she had stayed overnight at the hospital and possibly the day after that she hadn't taken it.

There was no point saying anything yet, though.

There wasn't exactly a glut of pharmacies in Mamlakat Almas.

She would deal with that later.

Adele had everything she wanted in this moment and many more times throughout the night.

She came to his hand and he came to her mouth.

They spent the night making love rather than waste a moment sleeping. Together they made up for lost time.

But all too soon morning started to creep in.

Zahir pulled back a drape and he dressed in his robe and left the tent as Adele lay there, watching the stars disappear and the day invading in a glorious riot of yellows and pinks.

'We'll leave soon,' he said when he returned from wherever he had been.

She didn't want to leave.

She had never felt more at peace than here in the desert.

'Are you looking forward to going home tomorrow?' Zahir asked.

'I'm…' Adele couldn't answer. She wanted to see that her mother was okay but she wasn't looking forward to it as such. And she wanted to sort out where she lived. She loved her career but just couldn't quite envisage Zahir not being there.

No, she couldn't answer honestly because the truth was that she wanted to be here, sharing his bed.

He saved her from lying with a kiss but she could hear the maids setting up for breakfast in the lounge and she pulled back.

'Where did you go?' Adele asked.

'To visit my brother's grave. I always do when I am here. I finally spoke with my mother about all that happened.'

'That's good.'

'I can see now that she had pre-eclampsia,' Zahir said.

'I'm sorry that I couldn't tell you.'

'No, I respect that you didn't,' Zahir said. 'I know that you think my father must be mad but…'

'It must be so difficult for him,' Adele broke in.

Her response surprised Zahir but Adele had given it a lot of thought. 'The one time your mother stepped outside tradition he lost his son.'

He thought about that as Adele went to bathe.

She came back pink and dressed in a silver robe and neither wanted to leave, so they lingered over breakfast.

She drank a lovely infusion of hot lemon and mint and they ate sweet cakes and he saw that she was holding back tears.

'It isn't over,' he said. 'We have tonight. You will be in my bed back at the palace.'

She shook her head.

'The staff aren't going to say anything. They are good people and we will be discreet. My parents won't find out for ages and I am fully prepared for that.'

It wasn't that so much that troubled her.

It was the next day when she went home.

CHAPTER THIRTEEN

FOR LEILA THE hope that a weekend break might help her marriage soon faded.

And being away from home had been more tiring than she had anticipated.

In the morning, unable to face another day and night smiling and being gracious, she asked Fatiq to make their excuses and to fly them home.

'That is impolite,' Fatiq told her.

'I don't care,' she said.

Leila was through with being polite.

Fatiq had strode into the palace, not best pleased.

'Inform Zahir that I am back.'

And Bashir knew, because whispers had swirled through the palace, that Zahir was not here and neither was Adele.

Neither was the pilot who had taken them into the desert yesterday afternoon.

'I believe that Zahir is out,' Bashir said.

'Where is he?' Fatiq demanded.

Bashir did not answer.

Leila certainly did not need to know where their son was—he was a man after all.

'I am going to have some tea and then lie down,' she

said. 'Bashir, would you have Samina disturb Adele and ask her to come and see me.'

Leila had the most terrible headache and it had been a strained time away with Fatiq.

'Of course,' Bashir said.

Oh, they delayed and played for time, and by the time the Queen had taken some morning tea and was slowly climbing the stairs, Samina came to her with the answer.

'Your Highness, Adele is not in her wing.'

'Where is…?'

And the Queen stopped herself from asking the question when she saw the conflict in Samina's eyes.

'Actually, don't trouble Adele.' She knew. 'I gave her the weekend off.'

'Where is the nurse?' Fatiq was coming up the stairs behind his wife.

'She likes to walk on the beach,' Bashir said.

Poor Bashir did his best too.

But the King was no fool. He climbed the stairs right up to the turret and looked out at the splendid view and then came back down.

'Where is the Crown Prince?' Fatiq asked. 'He needs to be informed that I am back.'

Bashir was sweating and Samina's eyes were wide as he answered the King.

'I believe that Zahir has gone to the desert abode.'

'Fetch Queen Leila's nurse,' the King said in a voice that had even the little hummingbird hovering at the fountain falter.

Oh, Leila would not be getting her lie-down!

'You are dismissed for now,' she said to Bashir, rather than have him answer that Adele too was at the desert abode, and she followed her husband back down and into his office.

'He took her to the desert!' an enraged Fatiq said to his wife as soon as they were alone.

'Adele always said that she wanted to see it. Perhaps he is giving her a tour. There might have been a sandstorm.'

The King gave a derisive snort, which told Leila what he thought of that. 'The palace staff are embarrassed. Thanks to your nurse—'

'My nurse,' Leila interrupted, 'saved *me* from embarrassment.'

She was angry too but she was also conflicted.

Zahir always kept to the rules.

Now, were it Dakan who was home she might have been better prepared for such goings-on.

But Zahir?

A short while later there was the sound of the helicopter and they stood at the window and watched it descend.

Leila watched the helicopter land on the lawn and saw Zahir and Adele disembark.

They were relaxed and laughing and there had been no sandstorm, neither had this been an innocent tour.

They were lovers, she could see that it was so, and so too could Fatiq.

And then Zahir must have seen the royal jet for he stilled and put a protective arm around Adele.

The King sucked in his breath at the public display of affection.

Leila watched as Adele startled and turned as if to run.

'My parents are here,' Zahir told her.

'They can't find out.'

He looked up at the office window.

They already have.' He took charge immediately.

'Come. We will go in by my private entrance and I shall take you this morning to the airport myself. You don't have to face them.'

Adele had never even set foot in his wing.

And now she sat on his bed with her head in her hands and she felt mortified.

'Can you say we got stranded, or that we slept apart…?'

'I'm not going to lie, Adele,' Zahir said. 'My only regret about what went on is that it now makes things difficult for you.'

'And impossible for us,' she said.

'Not necessarily.'

'Somehow I don't think there's going to be a solution here,' she said, and it was a jibe at the faith he had that things would turn around.

But he remained calm.

'Adele, it is better they know. Not yet, of course, but in the long run it is better than doing and saying nothing and marrying a neighbouring princess simply to appease him. I am not going to apologise for last night.'

His only regret was that Adele would be embarrassed and he would now do his best to handle that.

He left her on his bed and walked down the stairs towards his father's office. He nodded to Samina, who was crying, and he gave a small nod to Bashir. He knew they would have done their best to cover for him and Adele.

One of the guards gave him a small grim smile of quiet support as he opened the door and admitted Zahir to face a very angry king and a rather strained queen.

Zahir returned the guard's smile.

And then he stepped in and took charge.

'We shall speak later,' Zahir informed them by way

of greeting. 'Right now I am going to take Adele to the airport. Clearly it will be uncomfortable for her to remain here.'

'You don't even try to hide it,' the King shouted in exasperation. 'You don't even attempt to come up with a polite excuse!'

Zahir's response was calm. 'I refuse to hide any more that I have feelings for Adele. I have been doing just that for the past year and it has got me nowhere. I have driven past her, drenched in a storm at a bus stop, and told myself I was right to do that, that it was essential to keep my emotions in check. I have ignored her, I have tried to remove myself from her and I refuse to do so any more.'

'You have free rein in England,' the King retorted angrily. 'And I know full well that you and Dakan use every inch of it. You know not to bring those ways here.' He looked at Leila and of course he now made it her fault. 'Now, if there were still a harem none of this would have happened...'

'This isn't about sex!' Zahir said.

And Leila blinked in confusion, not at what Zahir had just said but at his words before.

'Zahir, I don't understand,' she admitted. 'Why did you drive past her when she was drenched from a storm? I taught you better than that.'

He did not answer and Leila's heart broke for her son as she realised the reason was a love that could never be.

Never, because she looked at Fatiq and he had become a stranger.

'We shall leave by my private exit,' Zahir said to his father. 'There is no need for Adele to receive your disdain.'

He walked out.

'I expected better from Zahir,' Fatiq said.

'Why?' Leila retorted. 'He is his father's son. Re-member how you used Bashir's ladder to come to me after the selection ceremony because you could not wait for the wedding night?'

The King said nothing.

'We had the biggest premature baby that this king-dom has ever seen,' Leila now shouted. 'Zahir's shoul-ders nearly killed me and we had to smile and pretend he was small.'

'At least we were betrothed.'

'Barely,' Leila snarled.

It had been the night of the selection ceremony that they had first made love and she had told him that night that if he wanted her then the harem was to be gone.

Fatiq had readily agreed.

They had known on sight they were in love, Leila thought.

Look at them now.

Oh, she ached for her son and Adele.

And she ached for herself and her husband too.

Zahir spoke with Samina and told her to pack Adele's things and then to arrange to have them put in his car. He told Bashir to move Adele's flight forward by a day.

Then he headed to his suite.

'Should I go down and apologise?' Adele asked.

'No,' he said. 'You have nothing to apologise for.'

'I'm her nurse!'

'Adele, we didn't exactly do it in a cupboard while she was breathing with the aid of a ventilator.'

That made her smile.

'No,' she admitted.

'You were on holiday by then and she was away in

another country, trying to sort out the disaster of her own relationship while I was working on mine.'

And he acknowledged then to Adele that he knew the trouble his parents' marriage was in.

'He's so stubborn, so set in his ways...'

'You're not,' Adele said. She had thought Zahir was at first, but she had seen how open he was to discussion and change and how calm he was under pressure and she loved him so very much.

'I don't know how to help them,' Zahir said. 'Every time I bring up change he gets angrier...'

'Maybe he's scared to be proved wrong.'

Zahir dismissed that.

'He's not scared of anything. Come on,' he said. 'We shall leave by my private exit.'

Except it was not so easy to leave quietly.

Samina came and informed Zahir that the Queen had requested that the car be bought to the main entrance and that the Queen wished to bid farewell to Adele herself.

'Don't apologise,' Zahir told Adele again. 'Not just because you have done nothing wrong but because it would acknowledge that something occurred.'

He saw her frown.

And now he smiled.

'Just wish her well.'

Oh, Adele did.

She loved Leila very much; she was so much more than a patient to her.

If ever there was a walk of shame, though, this was one, Adele thought as she went down the palace steps with Zahir by her side.

The King was nowhere to be seen but a strained-looking Leila stood at the bottom of the stairs to say goodbye to her guest.

She was supposed to have helped her to feel better; instead, Adele could see the tension in her features and she could not meet her eyes.

'Zahir,' Leila said, 'perhaps you could wait for Adele in the car.'

Adele screwed her eyes closed and pressed her lips together because she wanted to say how sorry she was yet Zahir had told her not to apologise.

'Thank you for the care you have given to me,' Leila said.

Adele's cheeks were on fire and still she could not bring herself to meet the Queen's eyes.

'I am going to miss our lovely walk and talks,' Leila said.

'So am I,' Adele said. Oh, how she would!

'I have a small gift for you,' Leila told her, and her voice was a little shaky but she remained dignified as she handed Adele an intricately engraved wooden box. 'Please open it.'

'I don't think I deserve a gift,' Adele said.

'You do.'

'No,' Adele said, 'I don't.'

'How could I be cross with you for loving my son?' Leila whispered, and then spoke in a clearer tone. 'Please accept my gift.'

Adele opened the box and was dazzled. A stunning sapphire that was beyond anything she had ever seen, let alone touched, was being given to her.

'It comes from the palace wall, from the same guest room where you stayed,' Leila explained. 'In a few weeks' time a ceremony will take place and the hole where your stone was will be filled with a diamond. One day, generations from now, the *qasr*, I mean the palace, will live up to its original name. The only requirement to accept this gift is discretion. We don't need the world to know or understand our ways. Adele, please accept it and I trust you to keep the spirit in which it was given.'

'I shall,' Adele said. 'Thank you.'

It was agony to get in the car.

Adele didn't want to go home, she simply didn't want to ever leave, but she climbed in and Zahir was silent as he drove off. He looked down at the box she held in her hands.

'You understand what the gift means?'

'I do.' Adele nodded. 'What happens in the palace stays in the palace.'

Zahir gave a small smile at her interpretation and nodded. 'Pretty much.'

Through dusty ancient streets he navigated the vehicle and she looked at the glittering city skyline that was so modern in comparison with the villages she had seen from the sky. And she remembered the comments she had read about Mamlakat Almas and the suggestion that it was best not to get sick here.

'I don't know how long I shall be,' Zahir said, 'but know this isn't the end.'

And she looked out of the car and at a city that needed a hospital and a modern health care system to be implemented. Zahir had a fight on his hands to do that.

'It has to be the end.'

'I know you don't share my faith but I have asked for a solution.'

'There isn't one.'

She would not cry when she said goodbye.

And she didn't.

'Can I ask that you don't call me?' Adele said.

'I need to know that you get home okay.'

'Well, turn on the news tonight and if there haven't been any plane crashes, you can assume that I did.'

'I will be back in London at some point.'

'And very possibly married.'

'No.'

'Zahir, you know there are going to be repercussions. This country needs to change and your father will use anything he has at his disposal and so will you…'

Would he?

Could he turn his back on Adele and take a wife if it meant better care for his people?

'I shall address things with my father.'

'Why?' Adele said. 'I can't come here. I'm not leaving my mother.' And it wasn't just that. 'After this morning I could never face your parents again.'

It was impossible, and safer to end it.

'I've had the most wonderful time of my life,' Adele said.

'I'll see you in London.'

'I shan't be your mistress, Zahir.'

'Liar.' He smiled. 'I might have to reinstate the harem and keep you there.'

How could he make her smile even now?

Yet he did.

There could be no kiss or embrace for they were in public and so she walked off and went straight through customs and she did not turn around.

And still she did not cry.

Not on the plane because it would be so loud that they would have had to divert to the nearest airport as she wailed.

And not even when she landed.

To terrible news.

CHAPTER FOURTEEN

LANDING IN LONDON, Adele told herself that she should be looking forward to seeing her mother; instead, she was resisting listening to a message that Zahir had left on her phone.

There was also one from the estate agent, informing her that the flat was hers.

That call she returned.

And then, before she went to the underground to take the tube home, she rang the nursing home and told them that she was home.

'Hi, Adele,' Annie said. 'We weren't expecting you back till tomorrow. How was your holiday?'

'It was wonderful, thank you,' Adele said. 'How's Mum?'

And she waited for the familiar answer—that she was comfortable and that there was no change. Instead there was a pause.

'You need to come in, Adele.'

No, her mother wasn't dead, but there was something that Annie needed to discuss and not over the phone.

Adele went straight there.

She didn't even stop to drop her suitcase back at the flat and she sat with it beside her in the nurses' office.

'When she had her hair washed last week, the nurse

noticed a lump on her neck. We spoke with her GP and a biopsy was done. Adele, we did discuss telling you...'

'I understand why you didn't.' Adele said. She was grateful for the thought they had put into it. Of course she would have rushed back and for what? To sit by her mother's bed and await results.

She wouldn't have had the time with Zahir, even if it had come to such an embarrassing end.

'When do the results come in?'

'Dr Edwards expects to have them back tomorrow when he does his rounds.'

Adele sat by her mother's bed and held her hand.

'I'm back,' she said, but of course there was no response.

There never had been since day one.

And then, only then, did Adele allow herself the bliss of listening to Zahir's voice as she turned on the message he had left on her phone.

'Call me when you land,' he said in his lovely deep voice that felt like a caress. 'Let me know how you are.'

She didn't, because she needed him so much now and it would not be fair to tell him so, knowing there was nothing he could do.

No, she had no faith in the desert offering a solution.

And she sat by her mother's bed.

'Call me when you land... Let me know how you are.'

She played it over and over and over some more.

And the next day, after picking up the keys to her new home and signing the lease, she listened to it again before she went back to the nursing home for Dr Edwards's round.

'It isn't good news, Adele.'

He was terribly kind and as Adele sat in the office

he gently explained that it would be wrong to send her mother for invasive tests and treatment.

Nature would take its course.

'I want her to have pain medication,' Adele said.

'Of course.'

'I want to be sure that she's not in any pain.'

'We'll do all we can to ensure she's comfortable.'

It was Adele who was the one in pain. There was a wash of guilty relief that finally there was an end in sight and that was so abhorrent to her that she was propelled to her feet.

'I'm going to go and sit with her,' she said.

And as she did she held her phone to her ear.

'Call me when you land,' Zahir said in his lovely deep voice that felt like a caress. 'Let me know how you are.'

Adele hit delete.

And then she gave her mother a kiss and headed out to the office. 'Annie, I need to update my contact details.'

She had deleted his number and blocked him and by tomorrow she would be at a different address.

And the day after that she would be back at work.

'Wow!' Helene said as a suntanned Adele came into the changing room. 'How was Paris?'

'Fantastic.' Adele smiled.

'Good God, how hot was it?' Janet said as she took in Adele's sun-bleached hair and brown limbs.

'Pretty warm?'

'Are they having a heatwave?'

'I think they were.'

'Where's our postcard?' Janet checked.

'It must be on its way.'

She didn't tell them about her mother and she certainly didn't tell them she had been in Mamlakat Almas.

Instead she was brought up to date.

'Zahir didn't renew his contract,' Janet informed her as they walked around to the nurses' station, 'so we're rather short-staffed, though what's new?'

Everything, Adele thought.

The place felt different without him, though her home life was better, of course, now that she lived alone.

The days just seemed to limp by, though.

For Zahir they did too.

She had been gone almost a month and there was no progress that Zahir could see.

In any direction.

He was working with Nira, the architect, and she had some wonderful suggestions but his father just knocked back every one and it incensed Zahir.

'Why are you so opposed to this?' he demanded of the King.

'Our scholars are the basis of your system. We were the forerunners, and that wisdom I refuse to lose. I consult with the Bedouins and the elders, not with you.'

Zahir walked out.

His father was right. His culture had contributed so much to modern medicine. Surely they could marry ancient and modern. Other countries managed it and yet his father blocked him at every turn.

He found himself on the beach, and he strode in the pristine white sand and looked out to the stunning gulf and he did not know the solution.

He looked up at the palace and saw that a long ladder was resting against the wall that led to the suite where Adele had resided.

Up the ladder a man went, and beneath it were the elders, all watching as the small ceremony occurred.

From early times the elders, with little evidence, had believed that Mamlakat Almas was a land of diamonds. Rubies and other precious stones had been panned from the rivers and later mined. So convinced were they, despite evidence to the contrary, that the kingdom held the most precious stones, that when the palace had been built it had been named Diamond Palace. Its walls had been dotted with precious stones with the promise that one day diamonds would be discovered. They had been and now, when a guest stayed at the palace, they were presented with a stone from the wall and it was replaced with a diamond.

There were rare exceptions.

On the night of the selection ceremony the Sheikh Prince would meet with the elders and the King. A diamond would represent each bride and when the Sheikh Prince had made his selection he would hold the diamond in his palm and show his choice to the King. If the King endorsed the decision he would place his palm over the chosen stone and it would then be presented to the future bride.

That should be Adele's stone.

Zahir strode over, and his shout halted proceedings and he told them to hand over the stone.

Adele's stone.

The elders frowned and tried to argue with him but Zahir was having none of that.

'I am the Crown Prince of Mamlakat Almas,' he reminded them. Not that it counted for much as his father had the final word after all, but for now he put his hand on the hilt of his sword. 'You can take it up with him later, but for now you are to give me the stone.'

They did so.

He put it into his deep pocket.

He made his way back to the palace and he saw his mother sitting in the lounge, taking tea.

Leila was doing her sewing and, despite the tension in the palace, she was looking forward to tonight. It had been six weeks since her surgery and she and Fatiq had a romantic meal planned.

Maybe when they shared a bed again it would be easier to communicate and his mood would improve.

All was seemingly well and yet she could not relax. She looked up when she heard Zahir stride through.

'Zahir?'

'I am going into speak with the King.'

And her heart sank because she had dreaded this moment and yet she had anticipated its arrival.

Two proud, immutable men, both of whom thought they were right.

And she loved them both.

The huge wooden doors to the study were closed and the guards were outside and she gave them a look that told them they had better not attempt to halt her.

One bowed and opened the door and she stepped into a heated exchange and listened as his son stated his case.

'Even the healer has opened his mind. He and the *attar* have liaised with Mr Oman and they have worked well together to return the Queen to full health.'

'She wouldn't have been so ill were it not for the surgeon. You have never had a day's ill health in your life,' the King again pointed out.

He refused to understand and Zahir shook his head. 'I will not sit back and do nothing. If you refuse to implement the changes I have suggested then I am returning to London. At least in England I can save lives. I will return when you either give me the authority I need, or on your death...'

'Zahir,' Leila said in a shocked tone, and he turned and looked at his mother.

'Tell me another choice,' Zahir said.

Leila had spent many nights awake, trying to come up with one, and she gave a sad shake of her head.

Zahir had not finished, though.

'I shall be taking this stone and asking Adele to marry me.' He held out his palm to his father, who should now place his palm over the stone, in acceptance of Zahir's choice.

Fatiq did not.

'Adele would make a wonderful queen.' Zahir fought for her, for them.

'She brings nothing,' Fatiq said.

'Adele was like a breath of fresh air to this palace,' Zahir countered. 'She has emotional charity and that is a rare gift indeed.'

'I will never endorse that marriage.'

'Well, I don't need you to.' He did not look at his father as he answered; instead, he turned to his mother when she asked him a question,

'You love her, don't you?'

'Very much,' Zahir said. 'And she loves me.'

The King had other ideas, though. 'Adele only wants you for your riches. She persists because...'

Zahir closed his eyes and still did not turn as he spoke.

'Adele does not persist. She has cut off all contact. She has blocked me from calling her. I had somebody go to her home but she has moved. Anyway, her mother is very sick so she cannot be here.'

'So this is just an excuse for you to turn your back on your people?' Fatiq said.

Leila addressed her husband then.

'Zahir has never made an excuse in his life,' Leila told him, and she gave her son a small smile.

'Is that why you did not stop for her when you were driving because you knew where it might lead?'

Not just bed, Zahir could have handled that. It had been more that it would lead to this.

To standing in his father's office and being told he could not marry the woman he loved.

'I loved her then,' he said to his mother.

'And is this love the reason you did not want her to come here and be my nurse?'

Zahir nodded. 'It was. But I have found out that she is essential to me.'

And they were the words from the desert.

Zahir was so angry at his father but as he went to walk out he remembered what Adele had said, and the sympathy she had shown for his father.

'I spoke to Adele about Aafaq,' Zahir told his mother and he saw her face flinch.

'I told Adele it was not to be discussed with you,' Leila said.

'She did not tell me anything. When I asked her a question she said I should speak with you, and I did. And when I visited my brother's grave, as I do every time I return to the desert, I again sought a solution. When I returned to the tent I said how angry I was about the health system here and how frustrated I was by the complete lack of progress. Adele said that she understood my father's plight.'

Now he turned around.

'This is not to be discussed,' the King warned.

'Then we won't discuss it,' Zahir said, 'but you will listen.'

'No, I saw what your machines did to my son.'

'They kept him alive till you got there,' Zahir said, and he now fought to be gentle for he could see his father's pain. 'My mother had a condition called pre-eclampsia. The only treatment is delivery. That is it. They can try to hold off delivery for a few days, but by the time she arrived at the hospital it was too late for that.'

'Zahir,' Leila said, 'please don't.'

'Yes,' Zahir said. 'He needs to hear this. Had she got there earlier they would have given my mother steroids in the hope of maturing the baby's lungs and they would have given her treatment to bring her blood pressure down to avoid her having a stroke. And though my mother cannot remember much more about what happened, I know that had the pregnancy continued she would have had a stroke or a seizure. I know, from all I have studied, that had my mother been here she would have died. She would have been buried in the desert with her son in her womb. I *know* that. You would have lost them both,' Zahir said. 'You would have lost your Queen.'

'I don't believe that,' Fatiq said.

'Then I can't help my people. I shall return when my hands are untied.'

He put the stone into his pocket. He felt the sand from the desert and, as had been promised, yet not in neat order, the answers came to him.

He thought of Adele and what she had said, that maybe his father was scared to be wrong.

For if he was wrong, didn't that then mean his pride had killed his own son?

'Father, I don't believe modern medicine could have

saved Aafaq back then. Maybe now, twenty-five years on, he might have stood a better chance. I have seen the photo of him, and from my mother's dates most babies born at that stage died back then.'

Fatiq said nothing.

'You could make Aafaq's death mean something. He could be the catalyst for change—'

'Go,' the King interrupted. 'Go to the woman who you put before your people.'

'If that is your opinion then you don't know me.'

Zahir was done.

Fatiq remained in his office, but Leila walked with her son to the royal jet.

'It had to be said,' Zahir told his mother, and he put his arm around her as they walked.

'I know it did,' Leila agreed. 'I have been trying to keep the peace and it has got us nowhere.'

'You'll come and see me in London?' Zahir checked.

'Of course I shall.' Leila smiled. 'Give my love to Adele.'

'I will.' He looked at his mother. 'You'll be okay?'

'Zahir, I am not scared of your father. The only thing I fear is that I have lost him. I love him so much. I am angry at his resistance to change, but now maybe I can see why he resists. Your father and I need to talk about Aafaq, and you need now to be with Adele.'

Zahir nodded.

He did.

Finally his patience had run out.

There was no answer, he could not fight for a solution any more.

He looked down at the desert as he flew over it. He wished he were down there, just for one more day.

There was so much guidance he needed and now

he had his parents' marriage to add to an increasingly growing list.

And his upcoming marriage.

He reached into his robe and took out Adele's stone.

There was but one regret with Adele.

The night he had left her alone in a storm.

It had gone against everything he believed in.

How he wished he could take that night back.

And yet, would she have been ready for the strength of his desire?

At least then, by the time his mother had fainted, they might have faced the upcoming problems as a couple.

Then again, things had unfolded in time.

A word came to him.

Resolution.

There could be resolution at least for him and Adele.

He would focus on that for now.

CHAPTER FIFTEEN

ADELE SAT BY her mother's bed and held her hand.

The room was silent and, apart from the diagnosis, nothing had changed.

Yet everything had.

'You're going to be a grandmother,' Adele told Lorna. 'I found out this morning...'

She wanted to cry.

Yet she was scared to.

She was terrified to break down only to have no reaction from her mother. She was scared that Lorna might fail the final test Adele had set long ago—that desperate tears might awaken her.

She didn't want to know the answer and yet she couldn't hold it in any more.

She started to cry from the bottom of her soul and she rested her head on her mother's chest and held her hand as she wept.

There was no reaction from her mother, no arms went around Adele, and there was no attempt to reach out to her daughter in her plight, no tiny squeeze of her hand.

Adele lifted her head and watched her own tears splash on her mother's face and crying brought her no comfort.

None at all.

So she stopped.

'I'm going to be okay,' she said to her mum. 'I know that I shall be. It's good news really...'

It was.

A baby was good news.

Yet it was so scary too and she did not know how to tell Zahir.

She simply did not know.

It was a rainy summer day and she got off the bus and went into work to start her late shift.

The department felt different without Zahir there. It just did. Adele put her bag in her locker and closed it and then rested her head on the cool metal. She straightened up when Helene came in.

'I've lost my pen,' Helene said.

'Here.' Adele handed her one.

'How did Hayden do on his driving test?' she asked, because she had heard Helene saying he'd taken it yesterday but she had stopped talking when she'd seen Adele.

'He passed.'

'That's good.'

They had avoided the subject and sort of danced around it but Adele refused to play life like that any more.

And she was healing because as she walked around with Helene Adele felt her warped humour seeping back.

'Hey, Helene,' she said. 'Now that Hayden's passed, would you maybe give me some lessons?'

And she watched Helene's slight bulge of the eyes at

the thought of Adele behind the wheel and then Adele laughed.

'You're wicked.' Helene smiled.

'I am.'

'Oh, by the way,' Helene said, 'Zahir called this morning. He wanted to speak to you.'

'Probably something about his mother.' Adele shrugged and feigned nonchalance but her cheeks went bright pink.

She couldn't hide for ever, but she did not want him calling her at work and if he did so again Adele would tell him not to.

Before or after she told him that she was pregnant?

Maybe she would be his London love after all, she thought.

She just could not see any other solution.

Zahir could.

To Dakan's utter shock.

Zahir had just come back from Admin, having signed a new six-month contract, and they sat in the canteen of the hospital and Dakan shook his head as Zahir spoke.

'You can deal with it if you so choose,' Zahir said. 'I have an architect lined up. Her name is Nira and you are to meet with her next week.' He looked at his brother's taut features. 'Or not.'

'Why not you?'

'I am tired of speaking with architects, only to have every suggestion they make knocked back by our father.' Then he told his brother what he had done. 'I will no longer be returning to cover any royal duties. Not until our father backs down. I have told him that that role now falls to you.'

'I have a life here.'

'Your duty is back there,' Zahir said calmly. 'I have always returned at short notice, but no more. You will now fill that role.'

'I never thought you would turn your back on our people,' Dakan said.

'And I never would,' Zahir replied. 'I shall rule when it is my time but until then it falls to you, or not...' He would wait this out, Zahir had decided. His silence and removal would hopefully force change. Dakan was the royal rebel, charming, funny and yet, Zahir knew, more than capable of filling the role of Crown Prince in his absence.

'You can't just swan in here, meet me for coffee and tell me...' Dakan started, but then halted as they heard the emergency chimes.

'Major incident. Could all emergency staff and the trauma team make their way to Emergency.'

It went on repeat and Zahir stood.

'You don't work here.'

'As of half an hour ago,' Zahir corrected him, 'I do.'

He strode down the corridor, and ambulances were already pulling up and patients were being wheeled in.

Most of them were crying children.

He headed straight into Resus, where Janet was busily setting up.

'What's coming in?'

'I'm not sure. We've been told it was a car versus school bus,' Janet explained. 'We haven't got a clear idea of the number of injuries or their severity yet, but given that it's a school bus I didn't want to wait and see.'

'Good call,' Zahir said as he put on a paper gown.

'You're back?'

'I just signed my contract. I'm fine to be here.'

Janet didn't really care right now whether or not he

had signed it. Zahir's hands were more than welcome, today especially.

The driver of the car arrived and she was extremely agitated and distressed,

'Try and stay calm,' Zahir said, but the woman kept crying and trying to sit up despite the fact she was wearing a hard cervical collar.

'Adele.' Janet called for Adele to come in and take over as she needed to be out there, triaging.

Adele walked into the resuscitation area and she saw him, his shoulders too wide for the paper gown. He looked up and just for a second their eyes met and this time he smiled and greeted her.

'Adele.'

And she wanted to run to him, to ask how and why he was there, but right now the patient was the priority and required all her attention.

The rest would all simply have to wait.

'I don't know what happened...' The driver was sobbing. 'A school bus. Oh, my God— oh, my God...'

'You're going to be okay,' Adele told her, and asked her name.

'Esther!' she said through chattering teeth, but it was an irrelevant detail to her right now. 'How badly are they hurt?' she begged. 'Please tell me how many are hurt?'

'We don't have that information, Esther,' Adele said. 'We're taking care of you.' She started to undress the woman. 'Zahir...' Adele said as she undid Esther's jeans.

Esther had wet herself.

'Can you open your mouth for me?' Zahir said, and he shone a torch inside. 'She has bitten her tongue. Esther?' he said in that lovely calm voice. 'Do you suffer with seizures?'

'No,' Esther said. 'Please can someone find out how many are hurt…?' And then she stopped begging for information and gave an odd, terrified scream, which Zahir recognised. Patients often experienced an aura before a seizure. It might be a terrible smell, at other times a feeling of impending death and fear, and often they let out a scream as they dropped, though Esther was already lying down.

'Help me roll her onto her side,' Zahir said.

And they did just that as Esther started to seize.

They hadn't worked together often, Zahir had made sure of that, but he found out now that they worked together very well.

He suctioned the airway as Adele pulled up drugs and soon Esther was postictal and snoring loudly while being closely watched.

And information was starting to emerge.

Paul, the paramedic, came in.

'We've just brought in the passenger. Apparently she and Esther were chatting when she let out a scream and started to fit.'

'Thank you,' Zahir said.

And other information was revealed.

He saw a worried look on Adele's face when the radiographer stated the usual—that if anyone was pregnant they should step outside.

And he thought of a night in a desert and of the magic the desert had made, whether you believed or not, and of course there might be consequences.

'Adele,' he said. 'I'll stay with Esther.'

Zahir was here and though there was no time to

catch up or to ask how or why, her world just felt better knowing he was near.

And later, Adele sat with Esther, who was awake now, distressed and crying.

'I don't know what happened,' she said. 'I need to know how the children are.'

'I honestly don't know,' Adele said. It was the truth. Janet had said she was to stay with Esther. She hadn't sought information; truly it was easier not to know what was going on than to have to withhold it from her patient.

It sounded as if the department was calming down.

There had been the sounds of crying and frantic parents arriving but the only person who had been bought into Resus since Esther's admission was a cardiac patient not related to the accident.

It could be good, or there could be other hospitals dealing with injuries.

For now, Adele focused on Esther.

Her toxicology screen was back. It would seem no drugs and certainly no alcohol had been involved.

Sometimes accidents happened.

Terrible, terrible things happened and there wasn't always someone to hang the blame on.

Except ourselves.

She thought of Fatiq and was quite certain now that he blamed himself for the death of his son.

For years she had beaten herself up over what had happened with her mother.

Now she ached for Esther.

One of the security guards called out that the news cameras had arrived and Esther closed her eyes in dread and fear.

'I can't face this...'

'You can,' Adele said.

She had.

Adele remembered seeing the images of her accident on the evening news as she'd sat waiting to find out if her mother would make it through surgery.

'Four members of a family have been taken to hospital and another woman is in a critical condition after a learner driver...'

Adele went with Esther while she had an EEG and she sat with her for a long time until finally she fell asleep.

Janet left her alone.

She was a healer too and knew Adele needed this.

Later, much later, Adele heard the sounds of police radios and them asking Zahir if they could speak with the driver now.

'Adele.' Janet put her head around the curtain.

'It's time to go home.'

Adele shook her head.

'Yes, Adele, it's time to go home.'

Esther opened her eyes as Adele stood.

'I have to leave now,' Adele said. 'But I'll come and see you in the morning.'

Moving forward didn't necessarily mean pulling away.

Whatever the outcome.

Tomorrow Esther would know a friendly face.

CHAPTER SIXTEEN

ADELE STOOD IN the summer rain at the bus stop and waited.

Not for the bus.

She let two go past.

It was like standing in a warm shower and she was drenched right down to her underwear.

But finally she saw his silver car indicate and turn and Zahir drove towards her. She hung off the bus stop and swung her bag.

She saw the whiteness of his smile and then he slowed down and stopped. The window slid down and she walked over and stood there.

'Get in.' he said, as he had wanted to for so long.

She lowered her head and peered into his lovely plush car and then at the lovely, sultry man.

'You might not be able to afford me,' Adele said.

'Get in,' he said again.

She did.

And the world, and all that was going on in it, could wait for now.

This was about them.

About two stars who belonged, who connected, and together they shone brighter.

She was soaking wet and her clothes clung to her

and he undid his seat belt and kissed her hard against the soft leather.

She dripped water all over him and the windows steamed up.

His hands roamed over her breasts and went up her wet skirt and between her legs. Then he peeled her wet body from his and started the car.

'That's what would have happened had I stopped that night.'

'Pity you didn't,' she retorted.

They drove through wet streets and the air was thick and potent. She asked no questions so he could tell her no lies.

Adele didn't want to know about the palace just yet and she didn't want to speak of her mum, or find out about Esther.

Tonight had been waiting so long.

And he asked no questions either.

Zahir had only one thing on his mind.

She discovered his home was a very plush apartment and she sat in the passenger seat as he got out. She wondered how he might have explained her arrival that wet, stormy night.

Zahir, she soon found out, explained himself to no one.

He greeted the doorman and told him that the keys were in the ignition and would he please park his car. He walked a very bedraggled Adele through the foyer.

There was another couple in the lift, and he wished them goodnight as they got out at the fifth floor. He pressed the button again for the eighth floor, the only sign of his impatience for he had pressed it once already.

He opened the door to his apartment but as they stepped in he asked but one question.

'Would you still be here now had I stopped the car that night?'

He deserved an honest response.

'I'd have been on my knees by now.'

For being so crude she was hauled over his shoulder and marched through his apartment and thrown onto his vast bed.

He removed her knickers and skirt and kissed her up her thigh with a rough unshaven jaw. Adele dealt with her top half herself. He kissed her very deeply, and there were a couple of fingers there too as he explored her intimately and so *thoroughly* that her feet pressed into his shoulders.

And she thought of that night and that he had not stopped and she shouted it this time.

'Pity you didn't,' she sobbed.

He kissed her again and when she came to his mouth he made her his again, and not gently.

Jacket on, tie on, he just unbuckled and unzipped and took her hard. He was fully dressed, she was naked and it was utterly divine.

There was not a thought in her head except how she loved this man and how the world could disappear when it was just them.

Zahir got up on his elbows and thrust faster and she moaned and held his face in her hands, just because she had to. His hips thrust harder and he moved into that delicious point of no return and she watched his grimace and felt the rush of his release. She was rigid to the very soles of her feet as she came.

He did not collapse onto her afterwards, he just stared deep into her eyes. Sometimes she felt as if he was looking deep into her soul.

He was.

There was pain there still, but there was the shine of fresh happiness and a little ray of hope.

And he would make it grow.

'You haven't paid me,' she teased as he stood and zipped up.

'Here.' He went in his pocket and tossed her a diamond. If it had come from anyone other than Zahir she would have known it was false.

She slipped between the covers and sat there examining it, too stunned for words. He went out for a few moments and returned with two very welcome mugs of coffee.

'I really am getting the royal treatment,' she said, as he put a mug down by what was now her side of the bed and he undressed and joined her in it.

'We're getting married,' Zahir said.

'Has your father given his permission?'

He shook his head.

'We can't, then...'

'We can. I'm going to be here with you in England. I've signed a new contract.'

'No...' It was Adele who now shook her head. 'You belong there.'

'And one day I shall be, but for now I will do what I must do and that is to marry you. I can't live in a jewelled palace and live a charmed life when I cannot help my people. I shall return when I am able to do so and I hope that when I return it will be with you as my Queen.'

It had become, to Zahir, as simple as that.

He would do what he felt was essential and trust that patience would serve him well and that the answers would unfold in time.

'Dakan can fill in for me until then. I am prepared to wait it out. I was speaking to him at the hospital today just as the alert came. He's not best pleased.'

And the rest of the world trickled in.

'How's Esther?'

'She's doing well. It would seem it was her first epileptic seizure. Thankfully there was no one seriously injured...'

He watched as she closed her eyes in relief and knew that today would have brought up a lot for her.

'How is your mother?' he asked, and he expected to hear that there had been no change.

'She's dying,' Adele told him. 'And please don't say sorry because I don't deserve it. To be honest, I feel a bit relieved.'

It was the most terrible admission and she felt his hand take hers.

'Who do you feel relieved for?'

'Myself,' and then she thought harder. 'I feel relieved for her too. She's had no life since the accident.'

He took her in his arms and his hand explored her flat stomach. It was wonderful to think there was a life starting in there.

'Did you tell your mother she was going to be a grandmother?'

'How do you know?' She turned in his arms. 'I think I forgot to take my Pill when I got hit—'

'Adele,' he interrupted, 'I took you to the fertile waters by the royal tent...' He smiled. 'No Pill was going to save you.'

'Were you trying to get me pregnant?'

'Truth?' He looked at her. 'That night there was nothing on my mind but you.' He kissed her long and slow.

'But, yes, in taking you to the desert I knew one way or other that it would bring things to a head.'

'You're okay with it.'

'I am thrilled,' he said, and he kissed her again.

'Did I tell you how much I love you?' he asked. 'And how much I always will?'

He didn't have to.

She already knew.

Zahir took the stone and held it in his palm. 'In my country, when the choice is made, the Prince holds the chosen diamond in his palm. The King is supposed to place his palm over the stone.' He held out his hand. 'I don't need his acceptance, Adele, just yours.'

It was overwhelming.

Centuries of tradition she could wipe away with a sweep of her hand. But then she looked from the stone into his silver-grey eyes.

Zahir was better than that. Even now, loving her, he was preparing to one day return to his people, but with her by his side.

'I thought the desert hated me when I arrived,' Adele admitted. 'I felt, if it found out about us…'

'We made love in the desert, Adele, and it has given us the greatest gift.'

She looked up and smiled.

'I'm not just talking about the baby, Adele. We returned and we were caught, yet our night together confirmed our love. There's no need to be scared for the future.'

She wasn't now.

There was hope and there was excitement and there was a love that had proved to be undeniable so she lifted her hand and placed her palm over Zahir's.

They were together now.

'You don't belong on the palace wall.' He told her what he had been thinking that day as they had walked on the beach. 'You belong on the inside, as my Queen.'

And one day you will be, Zahir hoped.

CHAPTER SEVENTEEN

IT WAS TO be the tiniest of weddings.

The staff at the nursing home would be their witnesses and Adele and Zahir would marry by Lorna's bedside.

When Zahir made a decision, it was made, and he wanted Adele as his wife. The problems that the marriage might create he would deal with in the fullness of time.

Right now all he wanted was for their union to be official.

He had informed his father, who had terminated the call, as Zahir had expected him to. The formal invitation that Zahir had had delivered to the palace would have been torn up, he was quite sure.

He pulled up outside the nursing home at ten to two in the afternoon and was told by a smiling Annie that Adele wouldn't be long and that the photographer was already there.

They had worked so hard to ensure that even though this wedding was small it was beautiful.

Lorna's hair was back to brunette and her nails had been done and she was wearing a gorgeous nightdress. The room was decorated with flowers and after the brief service there would a lavish meal for the nursing-home staff and guests.

And, whatever the consequences, it would be done. As was right.

'Lorna's ready to be mother of the bride,' Annie said.

'Could I speak with her, please?' Zahir asked, and Annie nodded and pulled the curtains around them.

Zahir sat down by Lorna's bed. He understood how poor her condition was yet he understood Adele a little better because he spoke to Lorna as if she could hear him.

Just in case she could.

'Today I am marrying Adele,' Zahir said. 'I know that you must have your reservations, as at some point I will be a king and there will be many demands on both myself and Adele. I want you to know that I will do everything I can to support your daughter with that transition. I know that she will be a wonderful queen. I want you to know that I am not taking her from you. You need your daughter now and Adele needs to be here with you. We are so looking forward to the baby's arrival. Know that I shall take the best care of them.'

And Zahir understood Adele a little better still.

There was no response, no flicker of the eyes, no squeeze of the hand to say that she understood.

Poor Adele, Zahir thought, and poor Lorna.

'You have my word that I shall take care of her,' Zahir said.

And his word was worth a lot.

He came out from behind the curtains and startled, for there, instead of his bride, stood two very unexpected guests.

His mother and father had come.

Not to protest, Zahir quickly realised, for his father was wearing a suit and his mother embraced him.

They had heard all that he had just said to Lorna.

'Adele is pregnant! That is so wonderful!' Leila was beaming and always she surprised Zahir, because in her own way she fought for change. Her acceptance of the news made her husband step forward and shake his son's hand.

'We want to show that you have our support,' the King explained. 'And you do.' The King looked at his son. 'It is time for change.'

He had waited so many years to hear those words yet right now Adele was his top priority.

'I cannot come back just yet,' Zahir explained. 'Adele's mother is very ill.'

'We heard. Tomorrow an announcement will go out that you have married and that there will be a formal celebration back home, when the time is right...' Leila said.

'Who is in residence?' Zahir frowned, because his mind never moved far from duty. 'Is Bashir acting...?'

'No, Dakan is in residence,' Leila said. 'And he has full rule. Your father and I are taking a holiday together. Our first... I remember saying to Adele that I hadn't had one.'

And then Leila stopped talking as the bride arrived.

She wore a slip dress in pale ivory and flat shoes, and she was carrying a bunch of jasmine that Zahir had had sent for her from his home. She was a bride fit for a king.

'Leila!' Adele said. 'Fatiq!'

Oh, she broke with protocol, she was so grateful to them for being here.

Her eyes filled with tears as Leila embraced her and

congratulated her on the wonderful news that she was expecting a baby and Fatiq, handsome in a suit, smiled too.

'I hope it's a girl,' Leila said. 'A boy would be wonderful but I love to shop for girls.

And, in her own unique way, Leila had removed any pressure on Adele to produce a suitable heir.

'Our people will be very surprised,' Leila said, 'but they will be happy.'

'Our people will be surprised too,' Adele said, and Zahir smiled.

They hadn't told anyone at work.

That news would be shared on Monday and she could not wait to see Janet's expression when she explained the need for a new name badge.

Yet she wouldn't have to wait, for there were two more guests at this very special wedding.

Janet and Helene, dressed to the nines, had just arrived too.

'They worked it out,' Zahir said.

'Of course we did.' Janet smiled at Adele. Then she went to see Lorna, who she had nursed on such a black day.

Leila clapped her hands to get things under way. 'I have brought a gift for your mother, and also something that you should wear on your wedding day,' Leila said. 'There are certain traditions that must be upheld.'

And it would seem there was going to be a delay, as the bride, according to Queen Leila, was not quite ready.

Adele went back, with the Queen, to the room she had dressed in.

'I can't believe that you're here,' Adele said, as Leila took out a sheer veil and started to arrange it.

'I can,' Leila answered. 'Believe me, Adele, I choose my battles wisely.'

'Battles?'

'There are some advantages to being a queen. When I get angry, I get very, very angry, and I told Fatiq that things were finally changing, that I never thought that I would see the day that I was absent from my son's wedding, that I had played by the rules but no more, that I had collapsed and still he would not consider a modern health system.'

'And he listened?'

'Not at first,' Leila said.

'But Zahir had spoken to him about Aafaq. Adele, he blamed himself, he was holding onto so much guilt and grief. We cried together for the first time and I think he came to understand that he would have lost us both and it was not his fault that Aafaq died. But, Adele, he is a very proud man—he had to be the one to make the decision and yet he is stubborn. I wanted my family to be together again so I decided to move things along.' Leila smiled a secret smile. 'Do you want to be my nurse for two more minutes?'

Adele frowned.

'You said I could confide in my nurse.'

'I'd love to be your nurse for two more minutes.' Adele smiled.

Leila nodded. She would say this once and once only. 'The day Zahir left was six weeks after my surgery. We had a romantic dinner planned but of course I was very upset that night. Well, six weeks turned into seven...'

Adele let out a gurgle of laughter.

'And if you ever say that to Zahir...'

'Oh, I never shall,' Adele said.

'Well, Fatiq asked if there was anything I could think

of that might help me to feel better. I had just turned to my sewing and remained in my own room at night. I said perhaps a cruise, some time away, and that maybe a little romance might help me to return to my once happy self. But, of course, Zahir had gone and Dakan said he would only step in if he had free rein with the hospital. And then seven weeks turned to eight and the King suggested that maybe Dakan should take over, maybe a new system was in order! It had to be his idea, of course.' Leila rolled her eyes and then smiled. 'And now here we are and we are about to take a long over-due honeymoon!'

Adele was delighted. Leila had gone on a sex strike, and it was perhaps the funniest thing she had ever heard.

'You are no longer my nurse now,' Leila warned.

There would be no more confiding but Adele felt as light as a feather as she set to join a wonderful family, one with a very powerful queen!

Leila laughed too but then she became serious.

'I will do all I can to guide you too,' she said. 'I have never had a daughter and my mother did little to pre-pare me for the role. I shall not let that happen to you.'

It meant so much to hear that.

'Are you going on honeymoon too?' Leila asked.

'Not yet,' Adele said. 'I don't have any annual leave until September and Zahir has only just come back, but anyway...'

'You have this time with your mother,' Leila said. 'I have a gift for her. One thing you must understand is that when a favour is done or something precious is given...' She faltered. 'You are a precious gift to our family, Adele.'

'I see,' Adele said, though she didn't.

Leila left her then and Adele took a moment to breathe.

Their parents were here, together, to witness this day, and she felt as if the earth had moved just for her. And her friends were here too.

She walked out and her eyes should have first gone to Zahir but they were drawn to her mother's bed. The quilt that Leila had been working on for so many years, each stitch created with love, was over her mother's bed. The gorgeous silks, the complex beauty, and Adele knew that Lorna was wrapped in love for ever.

Adele wore a veil when she hadn't expected to and as she stood before Zahir and he pulled it back, her smile was wide.

There was love and peace in this room and she felt it all around.

She looked into Zahir's eyes as he made his vows in English. He more than met her gaze now.

He held it and it felt like a caress as he told her he loved her.

'I will do all I can to provide for your heart and to hold your trust as we share the journey ahead.'

He looked deep in her eyes and saw there was still pain, but he was patient and would work to see it lessen.

And Adele made her vows to him.

'You made me believe in love at first sight.' She believed in magic too now, for how could she not? 'I have and always shall love you.'

And that was it. They were husband and wife and Zahir, very thoroughly, kissed his bride.

They posed for official portraits and Adele knew they were important ones. Without the King smiling at their side, it would have sent a message of disapproval to his people.

Oh, Fatiq smiled beside his wife.

They were *finally* off on their honeymoon tonight!

There was a little party afterwards, and the oldies put on some music. Annie had hung up a disco ball so that light bounced off the walls.

Janet and Helene sat on Lorna's bed and told her about the magic being made.

The King and Queen were dancing dreamily, and a few of the residents too.

And, of course, Adele and Zahir danced.

The lights flickered and they felt again as if they were bathing in the sky.

Two stars locked in eternal orbit.

They were simply meant to be.

EPILOGUE

LORNA HAD DIED soon after the wedding.

There was no sense of relief for Adele.

She didn't even know how to cry.

Lorna had been buried wrapped in the blanket but still Adele had not been able to cry.

A month later they had returned to Mamlakat Almas for a formal celeration to mark their marriage and then come back to London so that Zahir could complete his contract.

The baby would be born in England.

When Adele was six months pregnant they went back for a flying visit. Even though they would be there for just one night, Zahir had made sure that there was the necessary equipment and staff on hand should something happen.

It was supposed to be a brief visit, a duty visit, but just before they returned to the UK Adele had finally broken down.

This time, she had arms to hold her as she cried, but not with remorse or guilt. She simply wept for the mother she had lost.

It has been a long time coming and the grief did not fade with her tears.

The flight was delayed, of course, and Adele lay on

their bed and tried to fathom that she was going to be a mother and that hers was gone.

Zahir was patient.

Yet his concern was deep and so was his love.

The *attar* prescribed a blend of herbs to nurture both baby and mother and also a slight calmative, and that helped a little.

On the morning that they were due to fly back to London they lay in bed and Zahir stared out at the desert, feeling the kicks of their baby beneath his hand when Adele stirred.

'Adele,' Zahir asked, 'are you looking forward to going home?'

Half-asleep, she answered him honestly.

'This is home.'

She loved England and would always go back to visit friends but Mamlakat Almas felt like home.

She stretched and turned to face him and, more awake now, she smiled, still unable to believe that she could wake up with him every morning. 'What time do we leave?'

And Zahir had come to a decision—the choice would be Adele's.

Dakan had moved mountains, his goal to get the birthing suite ready should Adele need it.

Zahir could feel how much more relaxed she was here.

'Do you want to stay?'

'Stay?' Adele checked. The baby was due in eight weeks and soon it would be too late to fly.

'Maja is a good obstetrician, she is one of the best...'

Dakan had made sure of that and Zahir would not even consider it if he did not trust Maja.

'We could have the baby here?' Adele checked.

'If that is what you want,' he agreed.

And Adele thought about it and realised she very much did.

It was the most wonderful time. Mornings were spent in the healing baths with Leila.

They spoke about Aafaq, yet Adele still couldn't speak about Lorna. Sometimes they just floated in silence. Adele, who had been without a mother for so long, loved that she had guidance and support from Leila.

Afternoons she would walk barefoot on the sands with Zahir and at night she would lie in his arms and try to comprehend how far they had come.

It was peaceful, it was gentle, it was bliss.

And then, two weeks before her due date, Adele woke up and looked out at a red desert sky.

'What time is Maja coming to see you?' Zahir asked.

'At midday,' Adele answered, but then she asked him something. 'Do you think she knew I was having a baby?'

All those hours, all the years talking to her mother without so much as a sign that Lorna could hear and yet she asked him now.

'I do.'

'You're just saying that.'

'No.' Zahir shook his head. 'Did you tell her about me...?'

'You were all I spoke about for a year.' Adele gave a soft laugh but then it changed. 'I miss that.'

It had seemed agony at the time but Adele now missed those times with her mum.

'Of course you do,' he said. 'I spoke to her on our wedding day and just like you had said there was no response, no sign she understood, yet she held on until she knew you were okay...'

'I don't know.'

Adele didn't know what to think.

'Talk to her again,' Zahir said. 'Maybe in your head. Have those conversations that you miss.'

Adele did.

She walked on the beach and in her head she chatted to her mum and told her how much she loved her.

How sorry she was.

And some tears fell and then she smiled. 'You'll be pleased to know I have a driver now.'

Zahir was right.

It helped to talk to her mother again. For years there had been no response but now she could feel the breeze on her face and the sand at her feet and she could talk to her whenever she wanted to.

Then Adele saw Leila walking towards her and she always made her smile.

Leila had nearly finished the blanket for the baby.

It was complete, save for one square, and she was trying to squeeze the baby's name out of Adele.

Adele wasn't telling; instead, they chatted about Maja's visit today.

'She thinks it might be wise if I deliver soon, given that the baby is so big.'

'Good,' Leila said. 'Hopefully you will be prescribed more time in the healing baths after you have the baby. I was there for weeks afterwards. You know how I suffered in my labours. Both Zahir's and Dakan's shoulders...' And then she hesitated but a little too late, for Adele had frowned.

'I thought that Zahir was premature?'

'He had very big shoulders,' Leila said quickly. 'Even at seven months.'

Then she looked up at the palace and saw the ladder against the wall and she smiled at the memory of Fatiq climbing up it to be by her side.

'This is the stone I received the night after the bridal selection,' Leila said, and she pointed to the ruby that she wore around her neck for Adele to admire.

And she gave a tiny, almost imperceptible wink.

Yes, what happened in the palace stayed in the palace, but those last tweaks of regret about her walk of shame left Adele then as she realised she that Zahir hadn't been premature in the least.

They laughed.

Zahir was working in his office when he took a moment to enjoy the lovely view and saw his mother and Adele walking on the beach.

He loved his country.

Always.

And he loved the changes that had been made and the care that had been taken of Adele. He could see her calm and relaxed and happy and walking with his mother.

He watched as Adele and his mother stopped walking and started to laugh.

Adele was doubled over with laughing and it was nice to see.

Leila carried on walking and talking and then turned as Adele failed to catch up.

He watched his mother walk back towards Adele.

That was all Zahir saw.

He swiftly made his way through the palace and down to the beach.

'I'm here,' he said, and then he stopped talking as Adele looked up and smiled in relief.

They shared a gentle kiss on the beach where she had first told him all that had happened and as they looked at each other he could see in her shining eyes the healing that had taken place.

And he knew then that they had been right to stay.

Samina helped Adele into a fresh gown and Zahir walked her down the palace stairs. When she bent over midway, Adele remembered the glare that had passed between father and son when Leila had doubled over.

Things were so different now.

The birthing centre was beautiful and the bliss of an epidural could not be overstated.

'Adele,' Maja told her, 'you need to have a Caesarean.'

She had come to realise that and so too had Adele and Zahir after a lot of very unproductive pushing.

It had always been a real possibility.

Adele was slight and Zahir was not and this was rather a large baby.

She thought of Queen Leila and what she had gone through and was so grateful for all that had changed.

Adele stared at the ceiling as she was moved through to the theatre and Zahir was by her side.

'The staff are praying for a calm and wonderful delivery,' a nurse explained, 'and then they will come in.'

Their ways really were beautiful, Adele thought.

Zahir was utterly calm and sat by her head and held her hand. He chatted as if they were sitting at a bus stop, rather than about to become first-time parents.

He calmed her in a way no one else ever could.

And she loved his patience and also his occasional

impatience when a solution wasn't forthcoming at his pace and he pushed things along.

She loved his almost unwavering belief that the answers would unfold in time.

And she loved, most of all, how essential she was to him.

As he was to her.

It was a moment like no other.

She heard the gurgle of the suction machine and felt the odd sensation of tugging and then heard the sound of tears.

Lusty, healthy tears and they were gifted with a small glimpse of their son.

He had thick black hair and was a big, angry baby indeed. Adele laughed when she saw him and knew, as fact, the Caesarean had been necessary.

'Go over to him,' Adele said to Zahir, and he gave her a kiss and then did so.

The staff were a little nervous as Zahir approached.

He was not only a doctor but would one day be king and so too would his new son.

'He is beautiful, Your Highness,' Maja said. It was the proudest moment in her career to have delivered the future king. She was so pleased that he had been born safely here in Mamlakat Almas.

He was crying very loudly and a nurse was wrapping him up and preparing to take him over to Adele.

'Can I take him?' Zahir asked her.

That would be a yes.

He took his baby and rested him in his arm. He looked down at his son, who stared back and calmed in such a firm hold.

Zahir went over to Adele and sat on the stool, putting the baby's head by hers and watching them meet.

And he saw tears flow freely from Adele's eyes.

He was the most beautiful baby, with navy eyes and thick black lashes and he didn't look like a newborn. He was stunning and he had her heart just like that.

And the name they had chosen was absolutely right, Adele thought as she felt his little fat hand reach out for his mother.

'Azzam...' Adele said, and she kissed him.

And later, much later, sitting in bed, holding her baby with Zahir by her side, the baby was introduced to his family and Leila finally got to know his name.

Azzam.

Royal Prince Sheikh Azzam Al Rahal, of Mamlakat Almas.

It would be stitched onto a little square tonight and placed in the centre of his blanket.

The palace healer also came to visit Adele and he thought she might need at least eight weeks of the healing baths.

'Maybe ten,' he said, and gave Adele a smile.

'Your mother will be delighted,' Adele said to her husband when the healer had left.

They were breaking one old tradition, though, and Adele would be back in Zahir's bed on her first night home.

'Once you have finished your course in the healing baths, we shall have to see about a honeymoon.'

'Where?' Adele said.

'You choose.'

And she thought of an oasis in the desert but she would not be forgetting to take her Pill this time.

She could not have been happier.

Neither could Zahir.

And later, after she had fed him and Zahir was settling him down, she called Janet to share the happy news.

'It's a beautiful name,' Janet said. 'What does it
mean?'

'It means determined,' Adele said, and then Zahir
smiled at her and she met his gaze. He walked to Adele
and sat on the bed, took her hand as she explained further.

'Resolved.'

* * * * *

CHALLENGING
THE DOCTOR
SHEIKH

AMALIE BERLIN

Dedicated to Mr John Bradbury, one of my junior high teachers, for his support and encouragement, and for the awesomeness of having a reading nook with a big comfy lounging pillow in the corner of his classroom.

Also really hoping he doesn't read past the dedication page…the idea of it gives me a wiggins…

CHAPTER ONE

THE HEAT PRINCE DAKAN AL RAHAL had been used to in his youth blistered the back of his neck as he prowled away from the new high-rise apartment building in the heart of his kingdom's capital. Only a few days as ruler-in-residence since the king had flown to England to attend the impromptu wedding of his eldest son, and already Dakan couldn't remember ever having a worse mood.

It also made him aware of just how practical the traditional white robes would've been to wear, not that practicality would change his mind about wearing them. He liked the clean lines of his dark suits, he just liked them better on soggy winter days in England. What he wouldn't give for a brittle autumn wind right now. For just one overcast gray afternoon, he might even be convinced to wear the sword tradition dictated for the ruler in residence.

But until either the King or Dakan's elder brother Zahir—the true heir—deigned to return to Mamlakat Almas, he was stuck.

And if he was stuck, the architect Zahir had hired would damned well be stuck too—right in the flat where she was supposed to be working.

Planning the new hospital as part of the overhaul to finally bring their medical system into the twenty-first century was the one bright spot on his calendar for the foreseeable future, made bearable all the bureaucratic nonsense he had put up with every other hour of the day so far. The hospital was the only thing he could get excited about. But the day he'd finally gotten time to come and plan with her, she'd gone sightseeing.

Typical.

Traffic stopped at the light, and Dakan took off, as fast as he could weave through the waiting cars and trucks, counting on the three royal guards behind him to keep up. Back on the walkway, his feet ate up the decorative tile expanse separating him from the bazaar blocks away.

At least something had changed since his last time on foot in the capital. The cobblestones were gone. The highly trafficked pedestrian walkways had transitioned to decorative tiles in different shades of sand—something he might've appreciated if he'd only been seeing it in a photo. But here every time his foot touched the walk his frustration increased. Even his fingernails felt tense as he dug them into his palms.

It wasn't just having to fetch the person he'd come to meet that had him wanting to ring one of the jets to go somewhere twenty degrees cooler, it was that he was there at all.

England could be cold in the winter, but at this time of year it was downright pleasant. Additionally, he went where he wanted, never had guards trailing after him, dated whomever struck his fancy, and he drove. He had everything there, most important of all freedom.

Since his residency had ended and he'd earned his license, Dakan had snagged a sweet ride, a flat that made panties hit the floor, and had started shopping around established practices to decide where he'd like to begin the career he'd worked years for. That's what doctors did when their education was finished—opened or joined a practice—but before he'd gotten to see even a single patient he could call his own he'd been summoned home.

All damned fine reasons to wake up irritated.

Another block and the decorative tile walk opened up to a wide lane lined with stalls on either side, sprawling out from one of the oldest buildings in the city—a holdout built by imported Byzantine craftsman. It had been made entirely too well to do the sensible thing and fall in to make way for a new era, an era that required more than a single clogged lane for people doing their daily shopping like that which faced him now.

It would be just as crowded inside—merchants waited years to get to move into the old building. Even with it practically butting up against the impressive modern towers built in the last decade—luxury dwellings, businesses, and prosperity on display two short blocks away—people still had to crowd through open-air shops to buy their groceries and necessities.

As much as Dakan loved his father, when it came to the way he ruled, the way he kept things always the same—as if it'd been so much better back then—made Dakan want to shake him. Or lead a revolt and then leave Zahir to rule, thus freeing Dakan to return to England.

Just find her and make sure to get her number so he could just call her next time she skipped out as if she was here on a tourist visa. Then maybe make a note to have the clerk write her a stuffy memo about the dossiers of royal contractors out there waiting to take her place should they need to.

What did she even look like?

She was British, so fair probably. Maybe dark hair but pale skin. Look for the tourists.

Scratch that. Look for the guard sent to accompany her. Or ring the guard. By all that was holy, he was losing his mind.

"Figure out who her escort is and call him," he said to his men, leaving them to it and moving into the crowd. He stood taller than most and that helped. It also helped that as people caught sight of him they moved as much as they could to give him room to pass.

But none of these people were the ones he was looking for. A sea of bodies, and none bearing royal colors.

By the time he reached the large arch leading inside, he'd started to sweat.

"They're in the third arcade, Your Highness," said a voice at his shoulder and Dakan nodded, yanking off his dark glasses and stashing them so he could see in the much lower lighting as he picked up the pace.

By the time he'd entered the ancient third arcade, he'd caught sight of the colors he'd been looking for. From there, he looked to the side for the woman.

There was a woman on his left, a simple green scarf covering her head. Was that her? Some tourists and those who worked in the country covered their heads out of deference to their customs…

Whatever, she was British so the same rules didn't apply.

He reached for her elbow to turn her toward him. Wide and startled pale green eyes fixed on him, a boost of the exotic amid the warm tan skin that greeted him. Exotic, but not.

This wasn't her.

He might get away with touching a foreign woman, but he'd never put his hands on a female citizen unbidden. And this woman was definitely a citizen. Damn.

Nira Hathaway stared up at broad shoulders and tousled black hair framing the most startlingly attractive male face she'd ever seen. When she'd zeroed in on his dark brown eyes a weird heaviness had hit her chest and her knees had given the sort of twinge no doubt designed to remind her they could bend in the middle. And that they might do so whether she wanted them to or not.

The man snatched his hand back and bowed, his Arabic flowing like music to her ears. "Forgive me, I thought you were someone else." When he straightened he started to frown and she hadn't even said anything yet.

"It's all right, sir. Though I must ask, who did you think I was?" Her Arabic, though better than it'd been a few weeks ago when she'd really started to pour on the effort, still sounded mechanical and sloppy even to her amateur ear, but it was good enough to muddle by.

Since her arrival in Mamlakat Almas, very few people had spoken to her, the only thing she was actually ready for. She'd been learning Arabic for months because she'd wanted to learn it since childhood, but that didn't mean she spoke to anyone outside of her instructors, who were expecting her to sound somewhat silly. Starting the program as a working adult also meant she didn't give it as much time as she would've liked to. Or hadn't until the last few weeks.

Normally she'd never have asked Mr. Universe for clarification, but he'd thought she was someone else. That meant she looked like someone he'd expected to find, someone who *belonged*.

The dark brown eyes with thick black lashes she could've been convinced to murder for drifted back to her from her escort, eyes sharpening in focus.

Clearly there was something going on she didn't get. Something other than her having a possible backside doppelganger roaming the city.

"Are you Nira Hathaway?" the beautiful man asked, switching to English.

She nodded and switched too. She wasn't going to flirt with the regrettably handsome man. Flirting would be a dumb idea for a number of reasons, not the least of which being her cluelessness about how it'd be looked upon in this country. Women probably didn't just date in Mamlakat Almas or pick up random men at the market.

"I am. You are...?"

"Dakan Al Rahal," he said, dark brows pinching together to make a slash across his forehead.

Her stomach soured.

As soon as she heard his name, the resemblance to Zahir came into focus. Same height, same jaw, hair color...she should've recognized him. What kind of respectable professional woman became stupid just because a man was...exceedingly handsome?

Though Dakan had a roguish quality to his appearance that probably instilled this reaction in everyone who saw him. And he was a doctor too, like his brother, that much she knew. Doctor. Prince. Adonis in a superbly cut charcoal suit.

There were probably words he expected her to say now. Think of words. Any words. English words even.

I'm Nira and I like long walks on the beach and...

Not those words.

"I didn't know we were meeting today, Prince Dakan." There. Words. Should she have said "Your Highness?" That probably was one of the things she should've learned when preparing for the trip, but Zahir had just gone by his name, never once using his title. But here among the magnificent ogival arches and vaulted ceilings? It felt wrong to call this man Dakan, and Mr. Al Rahal wasn't any better than Mr. Universe.

But his collar, with two buttons open, displayed the kind of wide muscled neck that let you know his shoulders and chest would have the same definition... Mr. Universe probably suited him.

"I suppose it was incorrect to expect you'd be waiting there for me to get round to meeting you. Aren't you on the clock, Ms. Hathaway?" Unconcealed exasperation rang in his tone, even here among the now unnervingly quiet area of the arcade. It helped clear her fuzzy head. Being falsely accused was so rarely a turn-on.

"Oh, no. I'm not on the clock. I'd never charge a client

billable hours without working. My firm only charges billable hours, not days, and only when someone is actively working on a project. The first days I was here I organized the workspace and all the equipment, got everything set up within the system to make sure the backups happened, but today I ran out of things to do. I've done some light sketching out of ideas, but—"

"Let's go back to the flat where we can speak without stopping commerce," he cut in, bidding Nira to look around them with a simple glance. Practically everyone in the arcade stood watching them, a sea of wide eyes, alert to the point of horror. Which explained the quietness.

They might not understand what was being said— she honestly had no idea how many everyday citizens in Mamlakat Almas would know enough English to translate this conversation—but tone was universally understood. She'd angered the Prince. Nothing good ever came from angering a prince in his own country. Never mind how wrong it felt to be anything even resembling rude or disrespectful. She'd be horrified on her behalf too if she weren't already horrified.

"Of course, yes, I'm sorry. You're right." She gestured for him to go as he wished, shifted her bag of purchases to her other shoulder and fell into step behind him as he wound through the opening crowds.

Some combination of height, shoulders, and *royalty* was what made him imposing. These were his subjects, that's why everyone moved. And he was possibly her employer while the project continued, so that explained why she felt a bit...off now too.

It had nothing to do with the expanse of his shoulders. Besides, no way were they that wide anyway, the suit jacket only made them seem so formidable and square that it added to all the other authority rolling off the man.

They stepped out into the sunshine and the thick scent of spices and incense dispersed with the normal city smells and another low odor she couldn't put her finger on. She'd been smelling it since she'd arrived, something earthy and warm. It wasn't the sea, though she smelled the fresh salt air too. Mamlakat Almas was a coastal city ringed by rugged desert and mountainous terrain. Maybe it was the desert. Did sand have a smell?

She tried to keep her eyes down as they hurried back to her lavish—and temporary—penthouse flat. Not because she didn't want to look around, really there was little Nira wanted more than to look around. And not because she felt intimidated, although having her possible new boss angry with her didn't make her feel like singing.

It was a way of making herself invisible. There was power in eye contact, and this country—as much as she wanted to be here—still felt foreign to her. Being able to blend in was a kind of social invisibility she'd long coveted. The ability to not stand out. She could do that here if she figured out what was socially and culturally expected of her. Blending in wasn't something she'd ever really done at home. She'd always looked different, felt different.

By the time they got inside, Nira had picked up more of the Prince's frustration, but the beautiful interior of the building helped her at least.

Speaking might just help them both. Heavy silences made everything worse.

"I love this building. It's like they plucked the interior of some glorious old nineteen-twenties New York building and encased it in glass. I expected the flat to carry on the same style, but it's completely modern. Floor-to-ceiling windows, clean, straight lines—gorgeous, but two completely different styles blended together."

Dakan stopped in front of the lift, pressed the button, then folded his arms. In the polished brass on the lift doors she met his reflected gaze and did the only sensible thing she could think of—she continued babbling.

Maybe he just needed more encouragement to break the ice.

"Take this lift door, for example. It's definitely art nouveau." She reached out to trace her fingers along the polished brass design, tracing the flowing curlicues symbolic of peacock feathers, "and I'd say it's actually from the period—not a replica. The way the design is incised into the metal like a patterned window screen."

She looked directly at him again, and her stomach bottomed out once more as if she were in the lift already, all hope that he'd take the hint diminishing.

Nothing but a slight lift of his dark brows came in response. Was that a sign of interest for her to continue, or some kind of hint for her to shut up?

Probably to shut up.

He checked that the button to summon the lift was still lit.

Definitely to shut up.

Had she really made him so angry by not waiting around, doing nothing, with no idea of when he might swing by? She'd left *once* to go to the bazaar close by, it wasn't like she'd taken a desert trek by camel to skinny-dip at some oasis. And she wasn't on the clock anyway. Her company had no billable code for sitting around, doing nothing.

She should probably shut up.

In a moment.

"I've seen those cut screens in all of the admittedly few places I've been to here. The bedroom in the flat has the eastern wall of windows with these pliable die-cut screens that roll down from the ceiling like you might expect a window blind to do. It makes waking up a pleasure, softens the sunshine into little patches of light to ease you into the brightness of the day."

A bell pinged and the lift doors slid open.

Still no response. And that was top-notch architectural

geekery too, completely wasted on this man. Everyone at her firm would've been interested in her description of the building details. In fact, her fellow architect geeks had already flooded her daily social media posts with pictures of the building or skyline, always asking for more detail. Because it was interesting. And beautiful. And unexpected.

He stepped into the lift, and she and her escort followed.

Give it up. He was angry, and that was all there was to it. Once they got up there she was definitely going to be shouted at. She should probably be glad he hadn't deigned to dress her down in public.

She settled in between the men, far enough from each to avoid accidentally touching either, and folded her hands.

Zahir was more personable.

He probably would've liked her architectural geekery too.

The lift stopped and as they exited, the flat door swung open, as if someone was simply standing there, waiting for his return. Probably the kind of deference the Princely One expected, for people to wait around to do things for him.

If she wanted this job—and she really did—she had probably better figure out how to do that without screaming at him or stabbing him with her 9H pencils. She could sharpen those suckers to a deadly point, and they didn't wear down fast. That made for the potential of lots of stabbing between sharpenings, so very few billable hours would need to be devoted to it. Was there a code for Stabbing the Client? She'd just have to use the handy old 999-MISC.

Dakan strode through the monochrome penthouse, his black suit and shiny shoes perfectly complementing the gunmetal gray tile floors, pale gray walls, and the black and white accents. He stopped when he'd reached the work area she'd spent days rearranging while waiting for him to get there.

Where the heck had Zahir gone?

She trailed to the desk and opened her laptop. Might as well get this over with. She could at least have something to work on and he could leave her to it. Then she could schedule her hours off—one couldn't work twenty-four hours a day—explore the city to satisfy her need to know, and still have a well-filled-in time sheet to show him later with far more than eight hours per day anyway.

"I don't know what instructions Prince Zahir gave—"

"He didn't give me instructions. That's not how we operate," Dakan said finally, as he grabbed a chair from the other side of the desk and joined her where he could best view the laptop.

The laptop and the photo of her parents.

Given the way their meeting had gone so far, providing him a hint she was in the country for more than professional reasons might be a mistake. She discreetly laid the frame down to cover their faces and went on.

"Okay, then I don't know what he told you about how we'd been working. I had done some proposals and pitched other ideas with rough sketches or animations—"

"We're starting over." Dakan cut off her explanation as he settled behind her—which was at least better than him looming over her shoulder.

Starting over. Right. She went about finding and opening the file for the rough animation she'd first thrown together for Zahir and opened it.

"We started by talking time lines and construction methods so he could have some ideas on how long it'd take to have a fully functioning hospital with the different means of construction. There are a couple of ways to do this and I've prepared a sample time line for each."

"I want the shortest time."

Impatient. She fixed her eyes on the screen precisely because she wanted to turn around and speak to him.

"The shortest time line to get full use of the building, of course, would be to build it all and then open it. But there's an alternative, which would allow you to start getting use out of it much sooner but at a limited capacity. Given the current need, it might be worthwhile to have a staged opening."

"Staged?" Dakan said, and in his reflection she saw him shed his jacket and drop it on the table before leaning forward, elbows on knees. "Open different parts at different times?"

"Yes." The animation started to play as she spoke. "In a staged opening you start with one department—and here I started the animation with the original hospital because it's already there. But basically you build one section at a time and finish it for use before moving on to the next part of the facility. That way you can open and just keep tacking on expansions as they become available.

"They do this in smaller communities usually to make medical care available locally at the earliest possible time and start with, say, doctors' offices. Open those and start seeing patients while they build the next section and maybe add an emergency department. Then testing facilities and outpatient surgery, then open fully with a number of beds and a children's ward, add a proper obstetrics and surgical department, then add more beds. Like that."

Reflected Dakan nodded as he sat back. "I like that idea. Do that. But we don't really have the number of doctors required to staff a building of offices yet. I'd rather start with two different departments at a reduced scale that can be expanded on each side. The biggest part would be the emergency department with some very basic diagnostic equipment—X-ray and a lab—and then have a smaller area to the side where a couple of GPs could have offices in the guise of urgent care for less-than-life-threatening illnesses that still require immediate treatment."

As the conversation and planning started, the tension she'd felt in him drained away. He definitely seemed as eager to get started as Zahir had been, and as he spoke, the irritation that had saturated his voice during the bazaar confrontation earlier ebbed away.

She could work with this man. It'd be different, but he was a doctor too. They had the same goal: get a facility up and running for the people.

"We could do two different reduced-size units. Any time you split your building efforts, construction slows. So unless the extensions are staggered from one side to the other, you're going to slow progress to open new units. Unless you really expand the crew."

"The size of the crew won't be a problem. Will you be designing as we go too? Is that possible? I know it will take a long time to finish a full design, and I'd rather they break ground and get going sooner than later."

Nira gave up looking at his reflection and spun in her chair to face him, her eyes finding his immediately. He was still leaning forward, maybe that was why it suddenly felt so intimate. Even just talking shop, their eyes instantly connected and held just a beat too long for her comfort.

Nira would never call herself shy, but this was all new terrain for her, and she didn't want to make another mistake already. She shifted her gaze to the safety of the middle distance, a thinking point to keep her thoughts on track.

She probably should put off some of her exploring until they got the first unit under way, devote as much time to this as she could now, show Dakan that his goal was her goal. Reflecting well on her firm and gaining a happy client who might ask for her again for later construction efforts would be a great thing for her career.

Her quest could wait.

She could wait.

She'd waited twenty-six years to fill that void, and another few weeks wouldn't kill her.

CHAPTER TWO

"I HADN'T CONSIDERED designing as we go," Nira said. It seemed rude to sit with her back to him when she had no real reason to do so, aside from avoiding looking like a sex-crazed royal fan, which her reaction to him was starting to feel like.

He might be a prince, but he was a prince who had not even responded slightly to her geekery. Being attracted to him—while entirely understandable—would be a really stupid idea to entertain.

Keeping her goals in mind? Much more sensible than some overdeveloped Cinderella story. One-sided attraction should always be ignored, especially when the other side was a freaking prince. Stupid. Understandable, but stupid.

There were other aspects of her heritage to explore without adding "Explore Arabic sensuality" to her list. Besides, Mum had already done that, with disastrous effects. *Focus.*

"I suppose I could design in stages to an extent, but I'd need to block out the entire footprint first. You know—the general layout, decide the square footage of each department and the best flow of one department to another before I got started. But otherwise I don't see why we couldn't go in stages with the proper planning. It'll be trickier, but designs are always done with specifications and constraints, so not that much trickier."

And by doing it in stages, she'd actually get to be here for part of the construction! She'd get to see the first building rise that truly came from her ideas. It made the whole job even more exciting for her.

He gestured to a writing tablet lying at her side and Nira slid it over to him with a pen. "Okay, then, you'll start with the split building we talked about. I'll get someone else working on selecting good equipment so you'll have equipment dimensions to work with in your plans."

Nira leaned slightly to get a glimpse of his writing. Not the chicken scratch she'd expected. "Did you take drafting classes?"

"Drafting?" He stopped, an odd lift to his brows. "That's not part of a medical curriculum."

"You write like you've done hours of board lettering."

Silence hung after her words, and suddenly Nira was reminded of the elevator. She'd said something wrong again. It wasn't a stupid question—lots of people took drafting classes in secondary school. Probably. If they wanted to…draw things.

Light crinkles appeared in the corners of his eyes just before he chuckled. "I have no idea what that means. Board lettering sounds like writing on wood." Her shoulders relaxed when he laughed, and a dimple appeared in his left cheek that completely wiped the notion of royalty from his persona.

"It's a way of writing, back to Ye Olde Days of drafting when they tried to make everyone's writing standardized so it would be universally legible. Most computers have a hackneyed font called Draft-something-or-other now approximating the style. I just meant your writing is very neat and uniform. I thought doctors were all scribblers."

"My first education was to write from right to left. When I learned English, it was hard to remember at first, so I learned to take care with my…lettering, was it? I want to be understood."

"Of course. I didn't think about that. I should've, though. My attempts at writing anything in Arabic have been laughable. I drag my hand in the ink and smear it, or I drag my hand on the pencil and smear it. We won't even talk about calligraphy nibs..." She shrugged and gestured back to the tablet. Stop derailing things. The man might be a doctor when he's not prince-ing, but right now he was her client, and clients deserved not to be interrupted by nervous women trying not to notice how their dimple contrasts delightfully with their square jaw.

"I need to know patient volumes we're designing for. Do you want to start small until you get people used to the idea of the hospital?"

He took the redirection with ease, not commenting on her failure not to smear her practice writing. Thank God.

"No. I want to go big. Big enough it's impossible for people to ignore it. Big and shiny enough to draw attention and bring people in. Starting small just means staying small. It will get the use it needs if we make it important by making it big."

That was a new tactic. Her career experience wasn't yet expansive, but everyone she'd worked with had worked within a budget. But when your client ruled a country, he could probably do whatever he wanted with the budget.

"I still need a target number of patients, because my idea of big and yours might be two different things. And I hate to ask this since I know how fast you want me to get started, but it would really be beneficial to me to see what sort of facilities people are currently using."

He laid the pen down and leaned back in his chair. "You want to go to the hospital? It's barely functional. I'm not sure what you could get from going there besides tetanus. Though, on the upside, as far as hospital infections go, I doubt you could get MRSA."

"I'd like to avoid tetanus, so I won't touch anything.

I don't know what MRSA is, so I'll just be glad I can't get it."

"Methicillin-resistant Staphylococcus aureus. It's like staph on steroids, resistant to most antibiotics, really hard to get rid of. But since antibiotics so rarely make it to Mamlakat Almas, anyone who has it would likely have caught it from someone coming into the country. So, probably right before they died, or healed it themselves."

"Right. I'd like to avoid that."

Maybe going to the current treacherous hospital wasn't the best idea. Except...

"But we're leaving the current building and adding on? Blending the old and new?"

That was why Zahir had hired her specifically, even without a CV loaded with practical experience. Also it was why the animation had started with the old building.

Dakan scribbled a few more notes on the pad, then leaned back again. "No. It's on a large piece of land. As we're going to do it staged, we'll leave the old hospital up and functioning—such as it is—and begin construction for the new facility in another area of the property. Maybe right beside it, then tear down the old when the new is up and running."

Definitely not blending the old with the new that way, not that the current hospital was exactly old—it had been built in the twentieth century if the old blueprints were accurate. He was probably exaggerating. Still, she could work with that. And who wouldn't want a shiny new facility? But she had a point about visiting the hospital besides seeing what she was adding to.

"It's nothing to me if the old building is razed after the first unit is completed, but I still need to see the facility or visit a healing center. Zahir—I mean Prince Zahir—said there were a few bigger healing centers within the country. I need to see how the waiting and reception areas function, see what people expect so I can make sure the building feels familiar enough to be welcoming."

He fixed his gaze on her, and for a moment she thought he might finally yell at her, as she'd been expecting him to do in the lobby. But instead he paused for a considered moment and said calmly, "I know blending the old and the new is what you and Zahir discussed, but I really have no interest in that, Miss Hathaway."

With her not knowing what to call him, every time he said her name it made her a little more aware of their different positions. She'd address that first. "Please call me Nira. I don't mind."

"All right, Nira. I've inherited the hospital project, and since I've had a few more days to think about it, I've decided to go a different route from Zahir's old plans. I want a thoroughly modern hospital. None of that modern on the outside and quaint and nostalgic on the inside nonsense either. Modern. Something that would look at home if it was plunked in the middle of London, Sydney, or New York."

"Prince Dakan." She used his title again, since he'd made no overture that she could go without it. "Your brother was quite adamant the king wouldn't accept such a facility any of the times he's presented any plans. He batted back all our proposals already too, before we any got further than conceptuals."

The only reason she had the job was the years of study—or some might say *obsession*—with studying ancient Middle Eastern architecture. She'd only been in the country three days. Prior to that, she'd simply been emailing Zahir proposals, which the King had constantly knocked back. She had loads of ideas, doodles, and even a few sheets of paper with what could almost pass for sketches, but no idea if any of it would work.

"Three days, sitting in a fancy flat in your kingdom, isn't enough to get what I need to design anything properly. All I've seen, aside from a fantastic skyline, has been the bazaar today and the airport the other day."

"My father isn't here," Dakan reminded her, then moved to her drafting table, where he began riffling through the dotted newsprint paper sketches she'd used to think on. "He won't be involved in the design."

"But isn't he coming back?"

"I certainly hope so," he murmured, stopping at the conceptual fountain she was most proud of, and giving it a good look.

"Water makes for a soothing environment. It's good for waiting areas," she explained, trying not to sell the idea too hard. She liked it too much to risk so bold an opening maneuver.

"It's also good at slowing down progress. The objective is to open as soon as possible. Embellishments will come later."

"The footprint, the basic layout, needs to be present for later, though. And there are structural issues—like plumbing and power—that need to be accounted for in the building stage, or you'll just end up having to rip up what we've already built."

"Fine, then put what is required for the fountain in the foundation so it can be added in later. Then put a floor over it and make it useful."

At least he seemed to like it.

"Please don't take offense at this, but I really need to see what is expected now. I don't even know if the waiting rooms can be together, or if they need to be segregated by class or gender or some other classifier. You can thank the internet that last week I learned how to tie a scarf and also that henna is amazing but far too hard for me to do on myself no matter how much I like to draw or doodle. I may know Middle Eastern architecture and art back to ancient times, yes, and I've been learning Arabic for about eighteen months, but pretty much every other aspect of your culture is still very foreign to me. I don't want to mess it up, and waste time and money as I struggle to get it right."

"Aren't your parents immigrants? Or your mother at least?"

Her mother? Maybe hiding the picture wouldn't save her from this discussion.

"My mother is British. Ginger, even," Nira murmured, wariness seeping into her belly. How had they gotten round to this subject? "I know I look like I should know these things, but I grew up in a tiny village in the north of England, where everyone looked like she did, and no one looked like I...like *we* do."

"Your father?"

Her father. Or the mystery that was her father. The wariness turned to lead. "I don't know."

Nira knew exactly three things about her father: what he looked like in the one and only picture she'd ever seen of him, currently face down beside her laptop; that he was from the Middle East somewhere; and that her mother refused to ever answer any questions about him. She had never allowed Nira to explore those aspects of her heritage.

She'd surmised their relationship had ended badly. But she wouldn't be ashamed about it. So what if she didn't know her father? Plenty of people didn't.

Lifting her chin, she made herself look him in the eye. Being illegitimate was probably heavily frowned on here, and he could disapprove all he liked. Whatever nonsense had gone on with her parents had nothing to do with her capabilities.

"My point is I need information or the building will be as culturally clueless as I am. You want people to use the facility when it's open, and so do I. The best way to ensure that is to make them feel at home there."

The Prince nodded too slowly for her to read the meaning behind it, those dark eyes giving no hint of his opinion on her parentage. "We're not so different here. People are still people, Nira. It doesn't matter what they look like, or where they grew up."

So maybe he didn't care? Not that she should care either way, but right now navigating this place required she do a lot of guessing and reading between the lines. But his reaction was far enough from her expectations that she couldn't decide if it could give her any clues for future interactions with other people here.

"They need to feel like they've not been tucked away somewhere and forgotten in a little waiting room, and they need to not feel like they're lost in the crowd of a big waiting room." He grabbed the pad of paper again, thought for a moment and then scribbled down some numbers beside a list of prioritized departments. "Use these numbers to rough out your footprint. I'll get someone working on the equipment, hunt up a firm to handle the interior, and get some examples of facilities I like and want you to aim for. I'll be back in two days."

Two days. Nira nodded mutely. What else could she do?

He picked up his jacket and swung it on as he strode for the door.

She looked at all he'd written down—numbers, departments with arrows linking them up, which she could only interpret as clues as to where to locate them. One department was missing.

She called after him, "What about healers? Will they have their own department?"

"No healers. Doctors!" he answered, not even breaking stride.

Two days later a very tired Nira stood at the massive plotter and sorted out the drawings that had already fallen into the bin.

Any second now Dakan would blow in and she'd find

out whether or not he thought she could handle the job, whether her ideas were up to snuff.

She shuffled another print to the drafting table and smoothed it out, trying to uncurl the sheet as the last drawing rolled off the plotter.

"You're still wearing it?" Dakan said from behind her, chuckling as he made his way in.

"Wearing what?"

"The scarf." He nodded to her head. "I figured you'd have abandoned it by now."

Nira reached up and touched the colorful silk carefully. The housekeeper, Tahira, had helped her with her technique in the days since she'd seen him last. "I thought it would be respectful to your ways for me to wear a scarf. And…well, I just want to."

"They're not exactly my ways. My ways are a little more complicated, and honestly I miss England. Working with a British woman is a perk for me. Aside from that, we're indoors now in your home, out of public view."

"But you're a stranger," Nira countered. Anyone would hear the *Gotcha!* in her tone. She knew that much at least—a scarf should be worn in public or with strangers.

"Am I?" The shock in his voice couldn't be anything but an act, but it still made her smile. "I'll have to do something about that, then. You can get to know me over dinner, and tomorrow you won't have that argument. And then you can tell me why you want to wear the scarf when you're at home."

With their rocky start, she'd assumed that same general tension would permeate all their interactions, but his mood had drastically improved today. He might even be flirting with her—how weird would that be?

"Call me Dakan because we're friends now, at least in private. Right?"

Setting the colorful silk and clips on the side table, she

smoothed her hands over her hair to make sure it wasn't sticking up absurdly.

He smiled then, flashing that dastardly little dimple pitting his left cheek—undoubtedly designed to make her heart stutter.

Good grief, the man was still beautiful, and she'd spent a large part of the last two days trying to convince herself she'd just been fooled by her memory—it was pretty much all she'd been able to talk to herself about. And she'd been terribly convincing. Up to ten minutes ago she'd have sworn he'd only been that handsome in hindsight, and maybe through some kind of Cinderella story memory filter. But here he was, in the flesh, making her insides quiver...

And judging by the twinkle in his eye as he smiled, he was used to knocking women's feet out from under them.

Well, her feet could just get back under her, charming, beautiful man or not. Her goals still mattered, and one of them was not to go to a foreign country and have an ill-advised romance. Those always ended badly, or, if she listened to Mum, sometimes worse than that.

He summoned Tahira, ordered dinner to be prepared, and then turned back to her drawings.

For the next hour they went over the different layouts she'd come up with—high-rises versus sprawling facilities with clusters of smaller buildings and parking structures. And finally settled on a layout that combined the best of both.

"Did you bring the examples you talked about?" she asked, after shuffling off the printouts that had been rejected and leaving his choices on the drafting table. "I'd like to look at them and get started."

"After dinner."

"Or during. We could have a working dinner, look at what you've brought." She looked around him, expecting to see a bundle of prints somewhere. "Where are they?"

Dakan fished a DVD out of his jacket pocket, bumped the button on her laptop and loaded it into the tray. "I don't want a working dinner. But I'll set this up…" His words dried up as he caught sight of the framed photo beside her computer.

Attractive couple. Fair, freckled woman with red hair. Man with dark hair and tanned skin.

He picked it up to examine the photo more closely, and found himself looking at the frame, which was constructed of tiny gray bricks and mortar.

It was very well made, and obviously done by hand— there were just enough irregularities in the bricks to see small fingers had formed and smoothed them. The architect had spent hours constructing it to fit the photo—the one personal item on her desk.

"Are these your parents?" he asked, looking back at her as he did so.

There was wariness in her gaze again, like that he'd seen in her the other day when they'd spoken of her father.

The father she'd claimed to not know.

"I thought you didn't know who your father was?"

"I don't. Not his name or where he's from—aside from a Middle Eastern country. All I have is this one picture."

She carefully extracted the photo from his hand as if he might break it. Or like she'd saved that photo from being destroyed in the past…and now protected it with tiny bricks she'd made herself.

"He looks…" Familiar.

Familiar but grainy—the photo was old enough that he couldn't be certain.

How likely was it for him to know her father anyway? Millions of people lived in "a Middle Eastern country…"

CHAPTER THREE

"Happy," Dakan said instead. "They both look happy. I'm guessing things went downhill after that picture if your mother isn't giving you other information."

"That's my guess as well."

His Big Emotion warning system started to become more insistent. She wouldn't carry around her unidentified father's picture for no reason, but continuing to poke at this situation—when he already knew nothing he could say would make it better for her—was a bad idea.

But the familiarity of the man bugged him.

"Do you know where that was taken?"

"No. She never told me what country she was in. I assume it was his country, but I really don't know. Maybe he was living abroad."

"So she came here somewhere, had a fling, got pregnant, and went home?"

"I guess."

She grew stiffer the longer they spoke about it, no trace evident of the smile she'd returned earlier when he'd found himself flirting. Instead, her shoulders stretched this way and that as she spoke, trying to dispel tension.

"I'd like to tell you more, but I really don't know anything." She placed the photo back on the desk, though a little further back this time. "I used to ask her all the time, but she'd never answer. And she always shut down any attempts I made to learn about that aspect of my heritage when I was growing up. Burned a book or two, even! One was from the library…"

The housekeeper informed them dinner was ready, and Nira gestured to the guest bathroom. "Would you like to meet in the dining room?" She darted off like someone wanting to escape.

He really shouldn't pry into her background. He liked people. He was good with people. But big, sticky emotions weren't really his thing. Definitely Zahir's territory. He'd know what to say to her to make her feel better—good leaders were like that—but *he* just didn't.

There was one thing he could do very well, which he was pretty sure would make her feel better. Kissing her had been in his mind since he'd dragged her out of the market and marched her back home. Which was weird, and probably some kind of side-effect of being stuck where he usually avoided showing interest in women out of fear his father would start beating the marriage drum again. She might be British, but she looked like those princesses he and Zahir had been threatened with for years. So, exactly opposite from his type.

Dakan went for pretty much anything he could only really get abroad—blond or red hair, pale skin, pale eyes…

She had the eyes. Green and gorgeous, they stood out—not that she wouldn't have otherwise. One thing the scarf always did wonderfully was focus attention on a woman's face. Even without the long silky dark hair she'd been hiding, she was something to look at.

She didn't belong in Mamlakat Almas, and theirs was a progressive kingdom if you ignored the archaic medical system.

When Zahir had rebelled and gone back to England to marry Adele, it'd been because of their father's refusal to change, but somehow their father had given permission for the hospital project to continue as they desired—something he hadn't even mustered the energy to ask about when he'd heard. He was still more than half-certain that whatever work they did on the hospital would be for nothing once the King strapped the sword back on. Another reason he needed Zahir to come home and take over, because if *he* managed to get a system set up that allowed for healers and then left his father to run it? Bad things would happen.

He was probably doing this all wrong anyway, but the project had been passed and even if he wasn't the one born to lead, he had to make an effort. Taking his frustration and questions to Zahir would not only put pressure on his brother to come home and get on with leading before Dakan lost his mind, but it would also upset his brother's newfound marital bliss and further prompt the King to start foisting brides and selection ceremonies onto *him*.

His problems couldn't be fixed any time soon. Nira didn't know how lucky she was with her background, despite feeling the absence of her father's presence in her life. Dakan knew all about feeling trapped. Freedom was important, people often didn't realize just how important it was until they no longer had it. And the only place he had it was in her country.

They both emerged from washing up at the same time and he waited for her to sit before joining her. "So, how is it you've become an expert in our architecture at your age when your mother burned your books?"

"She ignored the books on art and architecture, or maybe she didn't realize they'd have chapters devoted to Middle Eastern art and architecture. Plus, they were from the library. After she had to replace that one book, she got a lot less fire-happy."

He shouldn't smile at that—really, who burned books these days? But the phrase "fire-happy" tickled him. "That's the contraband you smuggled into your house as a teenager? Art books?"

"What did you smuggle in? Page Threes?"

Flirting. Sexy teasing, he loved sexy teasing, and the innocent look she gave him over her water glass brought an urge to escalate it. "I didn't have to smuggle in anything. I was at an all-boys school. Others smuggled. I just enjoyed the fruits of their labor."

"Lazy."

"Smart," Dakan countered. He could hardly keep from staring at the sexy architect but he forced his mind to focus. Stick with the facts. "Is your mother still living?"

She didn't quite flinch, but a fleeting grimace told him the situation wasn't good, whatever it was.

"She's alive. Healthy. Very unhappy that I'm here."

"Is she ringing you daily and demanding you come home?" He would be.

"We've moved past Official Anger Level. We're now at the Not Speaking stage. I never pressed her too hard for information about my father—she didn't want to talk about him and I knew it hurt her. But I haven't had that same consideration from her. I email her daily so she knows I'm still alive—she has wild theories that I'll be kidnapped and sold into some kind of sex slavery here. She probably thinks... Wait a minute, do you have a harem?" Her voice went up so comically at the end Dakan had to concentrate not to choke on his drink.

"It was disbanded before my mother and father married. One of mother's stipulations to agree to the betrothal."

"Good for her!" Nira relaxed after her near shout hadn't drawn the servants, and settled down again. "But, sorry, no, we don't actually exchange words."

"Are you emailing pictures?"

"There's a thought, but my emails or texts all say 'Still alive.' Probably pretty bratty of me to phrase it that way, but I'm kind of out of words where the situation is concerned."

No matter the snappy way she described it, he could see the situation bothered her immensely. She fidgeted with her cutlery, pushed food around her plate... "Does she know you'd been learning Arabic prior to coming here?"

"She knows now. I didn't tell her at the time."

"More smuggled textbooks?"

Her smile returned, though only at half-strength, and she shook her head. "I only started learning Arabic after I left university, about a year and a half ago. I bought all the units of an immersion language system, but turns out it takes a long time to do a unit. You can't just sit down and become fluent in a weekend."

He switched over to his native tongue, testing her. "So you've learned how to say hello and ask for directions?"

She'd just taken a bite, but paused to listen as he spoke, not even allowing herself to chew before he'd finished speaking. Still at the extreme-attention-paying stage.

Her response was stilted, with many pauses and errors in pronunciation here and there that reminded him of the way children started learning to make certain sounds. They continued at a slow pace, but she mostly answered him in Arabic, with short dips into English when words failed her.

She wanted to explore her heritage, hence enjoying the scarves, and that's what she'd do more of when the project was really going and it wouldn't slow progress.

He felt a twinge of guilt. Time off was important, and no one knew that better than a doctor just finishing residency. "I know most people work about one-third of the day, and I'm asking more of you. You should really take some time to move around. There's probably a gym somewhere in the building—I have no idea. But if not, I can have a machine of your choosing sent up. Sitting is the new cancer."

"Do you just have equipment lying about?" The question went from Arabic to English then back again, but she had a solid enough foundation to leave him confident she'd get better the more she practiced.

"There's a well-stocked gym at the palace. I can send over whatever you like, then take it back after you're finished with it."

"Elliptical?" English.

He nodded. "Done. And after we get going—after there is a plan in place for the initial building—I'll make sure you get some time off to explore. Perhaps Dubai?"

"Why not here?"

"No reason. Though if you get hurt in Dubai, there are better medical facilities available. Did Zahir have you bring antibiotics with you?"

"No, but he said if I got sick to call him first."

"Call me first."

"Are the healers so bad? It seems like you would have a...low..." Again she paused. Her Arabic wasn't bad, but she'd gotten to the point it wouldn't improve if she didn't force it to with conversation. "Low...number of people... alive...if they did not offer some good?"

"Population." Dakan filled in the word she'd been unable to find. "The healers do some good, but the problem is they often don't realize their limits. My mother's healer realized..." He stopped himself before he really got going. The Queen wouldn't thank him for spreading her business around, but it had somehow started to come out. "They don't do well with infections, for instance. And anything that requires surgery."

He couldn't explain about his mother's medical condition, or the terrible birth he knew she'd suffered with his younger brother all those years ago, that was all too personal to lay out. Not only for the sake of his mother's privacy but because he hadn't yet forgiven his father for putting her into that position.

The question in her eyes made him want to tell her. He and Zahir had spoken briefly, but as much as he loved his brother Dakan was all too aware that they weren't equals. Always aware of it. Which was a good part of why he wanted to be anywhere but home right now.

"Is she all right now? Your mother?"

The question made him focus and Dakan nodded. "Two months ago she had to go to England to have surgery she should've had ages ago, but couldn't because of the way things are here. After years of quiet illness…"

Absolute sympathy shone in those lovely green eyes. "Is she still there?"

"No. She and my father went away on holiday together. Somewhere. I have no idea where. She's much better now than she had been before. For years. One thing I can say for her healer, he eventually realized the need for surgery, but he's exceptionally progressive compared to other healers. And my father…"

He didn't even really know what to say about that. He probably, in fact, shouldn't say anything about his father, but if anyone would understand family drama it would be this woman, who had spoken so openly about her past. Even now, he saw only concern in her eyes and unasked questions. He wanted to explain.

He switched back to English, not only to aid her understanding but also to make it less likely the housekeeper or any of the guards would understand if they happened to overhear. "The reason I said no healers before is because I don't want them getting in the way. If I give them too much room now that the King has apparently decided he'll give a new hospital a chance, I can see the system being easily corrupted and the doctors pushed into a secondary role once I'm gone and it's all running—which would probably make me put my fist through something." Or borrow weapons from the hall of armaments and do something else violent. "Forgive me. I'm…"

"Passionate about this. I understand. You should be.

Though I don't really understand what healers do. Is it homeopathic remedies?"

"The healers and *attars* work together, diagnosing and brewing tonics and other treatments. But their decoctions have actual measurable amounts of different ingredients—herbs, minerals, food, oils, spices. Most with medicinal qualities. They also try to treat the whole body, not just the particular injured part. Homeopaths focus on distillations of different kinds, taking ingredients down to one part in millions, and largely rely on placebo effect to treat their patients."

"No love for the homeopathic medicine, I see." Her flirting smile returned, and somehow the situation seemed a little less dark suddenly.

"No."

"But treating the whole body sounds like a good thing."

"It's not a bad thing. It's just about them knowing their limits."

She considered his words for a long moment and then tilted her head at him. "So, you want to guard against the King undoing your hard work, but you don't know how they will respond to your decision to change their plans?"

"If Zahir wants healers, he can come back here and handle the hospital project himself."

And, Lord, did he hope Zahir came to the same decision.

Zahir's plan wasn't exactly wrong—it would still be great for their people—but he wasn't only doing things this way to make his brother come home and free Dakan to return to England. Even if that was also a fine reason to do whatever he wanted. Not that he usually needed a reason to do what he wanted.

What he really wanted right now was to make Nira Hathaway smile at him again, something he could do just fine on his own.

"Before you start thinking I'm not up to the task of

building this hospital," Dakan said, affecting his most serious frown as he spoke, "I'll have you know I built the biggest Lego playhouse you've never seen when I was growing up. I was a Lego master. Everything I built had perfect right angles and I didn't even try. I didn't even have to use a…a…" The frown cracked when he couldn't think of the right word and used one from her professional vocabulary. "A protractor?"

Though he could see the spark of amusement-tinged exasperation in her eyes—he was, after all, going to make her work on something that might very well be overruled when the King returned and found what he'd been getting up to—she played along. "I don't know, that sounds like a challenge. Do you still have that playhouse? And just for future reference, the word you were looking for is a set square. You use a set square to make things square."

"A set square? Really?"

She nodded.

"Okay, noted for any future Lego house stories. But, no, I don't still have it," Dakan said, returning to his serious expression. "It got blown up."

Her amusement disappeared just as fast as it had arrived. "Someone bombed your Lego house?"

He held her wide, startled gaze for several long, somber heartbeats, and then let himself smile. "You fell for that so easily, Nira. Not all Middle Eastern countries are riddled with war and violence."

A mutinous wrinkle formed on the bridge of her nose, and she turned her gaze to every item on the table.

The woman was going to throw something at him! Food? Something breakable?

She reached for the bread.

"Wait…" The temptation was there to arm himself for a food fight, but that might've been a step too far even for him.

Her hand closed on the still-warm flatbread and she ripped off a chunk.

"Zahir and I stole a trebuchet when I got tired of the little house, made the servants help us move everything to the beach, and obliterated it with a barrage of the biggest rocks we could carry."

There.

A bright, musical peel of laughter erupted from her even as she turned her head and gave him the most dubious sidelong look.

"I'm fairly certain if you look long enough, you can still find Lego blocks on the beach by the palace."

"Okay, you're forgiven for being a dork. And you're lucky you don't have that Lego any more. I might have to challenge you to a Lego battle, which would mess with our hospital timeline."

"Can't have that."

"Would be a tragedy."

"Or we could go for a Lego hospital instead, scrap all this planning nonsense. Cheerful red, blue and yellow bricks. Green roof. Easy snap assembly."

She pretended to consider his suggestion, nodding as she munched on the bread. "I have to ask: where in the world did you find a trebuchet? And how did you steal one, for goodness' sake? How old were you when you got tired of your Lego playhouse, twenty?" Then she did chuck a small bit of bread at him, bouncing it off his chest.

He picked it up and ate the evidence before the housekeeper could catch them. "I was six. Zahir was almost twelve. It was a very small working model from the Hall of Armaments at the palace. One of our ancestors had built this small trebuchet a few centuries back for some reason, I have no idea why. It's perfectly preserved, still in working order, and has since been chained to the floor. We took off with it. Then we both got punished, Zahir more than me because I was six. Big lecture about responsibility and being good leaders, which I've come to believe he took far too seriously."

Talking and laughing with her was enough that Dakan could almost forget where he was and where he had to return to when he left the penthouse.

In the palace and on duty, he had to be serious. He had to be what was expected of him, or at least try to be. He had to be post-trebuchet Zahir, and he sucked at being any version of Zahir—even his crappy knock-off attempt chafed terribly.

Something he couldn't fix right now. It was better to try and fix Nira's problems than his own. And he was starting to think he could. The more he spoke with her, the more he became convinced he'd seen her father some-where. Not just seen but spoken with. She had manner-isms he'd have sworn were learned but which seemed to have been inherited.

He'd definitely seen that sideways look before. At some point in his life. Here, maybe. Maybe in a neighboring country he'd visited for some reason. It hadn't been in England, and as little time as he'd spent in Mamlakat Almas since going away to school young, it shouldn't be too hard to revisit those short months per year and what he'd gotten up to during holidays.

He'd have to sneak in and get a shot of that photo of her parents when she wasn't looking, so he could have some time to really study it, perhaps jog his memory.

It was in there somewhere, buried, but it would be cruel to get her hopes up if he couldn't produce the information.

"Now, back to Arabic. You want to become fluent so you must practice. Now, which famous ancient buildings did you reconstruct with your Lego?"

CHAPTER FOUR

THE NEXT DAY Dakan sat in his father's study, signing the daily papers staff brought him, when his mobile rang.

Nira?

He dropped his pen and hurried across the study to where he'd set his mobile phone charging earlier. He'd given her his number in the hope she'd call—not that he wanted her to have trouble with the examples he'd given her, but talking to her was the highlight of his days in residence. He wanted to make her misbehave a little, a desire she already harbored, or she wouldn't have reacted to his flirting in a way that had made him flirt with her even more, a way that made him want to throw off his responsibilities and hers and spend the day just talking. Playing.

Their verbal sparring was the closest thing to play he could remember having had at home since the trebuchet incident.

He lifted the phone and turned to look at the display. Not Nira. But it was the next best thing.

"Zahir. I'm running amok, you really should get back here and stop me."

"Good morning to you too, Dakan." His brother, ever able to recover smoothly from whatever Dakan threw at him. "Have you reinstated the harem?"

"No, but now that you mention it…" he returned to the

seat and leaned back "...I like that architect you hired. I think she'd look fantastic in something sheer and dirty."

"It would be Mother you'd have to fear if you tried it. Besides, Nira works for you. Don't go putting your cheesy moves on her."

"Too late." Come on, Zahir, be the responsible one. Dakan hated being the responsible one.

"You're lying."

Dakan tsked. "I'm the ruler in residence so don't start flinging insults. I may have to...figure out some kind of... diplomatic something. Sanction. That's the word. Or sentence you to hard labor. Here. In the palace."

"I thought you liked Nira. It's such a chore, working with her?"

"It's not her, believe me. She's gorgeous and mysterious. And a little bit weird."

"Just like you like them."

Dakan laughed this time. "Yes. Somehow, despite not being my type, she sort of is my type. How's Adele? Missing the palace? Let me talk to her. I bet she'd like to come and visit for a few decades."

"Adele's pregnant."

Dakan's stomach bottomed out from those two simple words. "That was quick."

And that was the wrong reaction...

"Yes." Zahir let the word hang and Dakan didn't even have to ask what it meant.

Zahir wasn't coming home. No way would he let her deliver here, with the medical system being what it was.

"Congratulations." There it was, the right response, even if he had to strain to get it out.

Zahir let the pause extend for a moment, no doubt searching for the right thing to say to Dakan. "It's only forty weeks. Less now, since it's been a few weeks already."

"Right." The filler word squeaked past his lips, just because he needed something to say.

Plans dashed. Would anything be able to shorten his stay now?

"Father and Mother will be back before then. A couple more weeks," the voice said down the line.

But the hospital would still need to be Dakan's job. He couldn't just up and leave as soon as their parents returned, though that was how things had always gone for Zahir: live in London and come home only when he was needed. Hospitals took a long time to build, more than a year. Probably a couple of years. Stuck.

But a birthing center... That he might be able to get done in a few months.

It'd been two days since she'd last seen Dakan, and Nira had spent most of that time working. In between viewing the examples he'd had compiled, she'd spent too much time mentally replaying their dinner and the thrill that had rushed through her with every playful word and flirting smile. But the rest was about proper working, still a lot of work between spells of idiocy.

The only other time away from her workstation was to tend to necessities, so her timecard—not that Dakan had made a single other mention of the thing—was so filled it shouldn't be legal in a civilized society.

Today she'd even showered and put on lounging pajamas to work in. The dresses she'd taken to wearing since she'd arrived were largely comfortable but light in color and they all had sleeves. Sleeves hindered her board work and invariably ended up smudged all around the elbow with fresh graphite—but the pajama top was sleeveless.

Besides, it was just her and Tahira. The guards she had stay outside the flat and downstairs, aside from their hourly checks, so they probably saw her bare arms from the back a time or two when they peeked in and she sat bent over the drafting table, her hair twisted into a sloppy knot on top of her head and secured by pencils.

"Good afternoon."

Dakan's voice rumbled down her spine, and she suddenly wished she'd worn sleeves to hide the wash of goose-bumps racing over her skin.

Thank goodness she'd had the forethought to put on a bra.

Pencil in hand, she turned on her stool and smiled so brightly she hoped it would drown out all other aspects of her appearance.

"Not good?" he corrected. "Well, I'm about to make it more interesting."

She looked at what he carried. Tucked under one arm he had a bundle of blueprints, and in his hand a couple more disks for her. "More examples?"

"Yes. And no. Here, these are all the plans of the hospital that's there now." He didn't say anything about her appearance, but here she stood in the presence of a gorgeous prince, at best disheveled and without a drop of make-up. Her bun felt loose and baggy too, she just knew it was hanging to the side as if she'd had her hair done by a drunken five-year-old.

Lifting one hand, she felt for the pencils and surreptitiously slid them free so she could unwind the still-damp mass of hair. At least that was somewhat concealing, even if it was the sloppiest mess of waves and tangled curls he had probably ever seen. To his credit, although he stopped unrolling the prints and shuffling papers around to look at her, he said nothing.

"Oh, well, that'll be helpful so I can see how it's working now. I just had a footprint of it before."

"That's not why I brought them." He spun her chair, urged her to sit with one hand and then rounded the table to sit opposite her. "We've got a slight change in plans."

"Change? Okay. What kind of change?"

"We're not working on the hospital any more right now."

Nira squinted at the plans he'd unrolled. "But this is the hospital."

"Yes, I mean I want you to stop working on the new hospital designs for the time being. There are bigger worries."

"New project?"

"Old building, new project. So I guess it's still the same project, but we're shifting priorities. We need to remodel the old theater and add a small addition to the building there. The surgical theater there isn't only underused, it's horrifying. I've liaised with the neighboring kingdoms and their hospitals are ready to receive any surgical patients we have for the next couple of months. And when I say remodeled, I mean gutted. Completely redone. And I want a tiny wing added to the side with a nursery to accommodate twins…"

"Who's having a baby?"

"Zahir and his wife."

Nira had to smile at that. She didn't know Zahir was married, but a new baby was always welcome news. "And you want to get the hospital ready for the birth of the new babies."

"It's only one so far as I know, but I'd rather prepare for twins and have it only be one than prepare for one and need incubators and the like for two."

"Got it." She flipped through the prints to find the one for the theater layout. "So, all new everything, plumbing and electrical included?"

"Yes."

"And a small addition with a nice patient room for the mother, a nursery with both beds and incubators, along with storage required for whatever babies would need.

I'll need some specs. Bathrooms, and…?" She reached for her pad and made some notes. "How far along is she?"

"Still first trimester. We have some time, but I want it sorted as quickly as possible so they can visit. As soon as you get those designs, I'll hand them over to a contractor and crew for them to get started, and we'll move back to designing the hospital."

A challenge. She liked challenges, but even if her brain still wanted to focus on the hospital, she'd take some time and do this first. He was the boss. Plus, she wanted the baby to be safely born here too.

They discussed further specifications and Nira gave up making notes on her pad and instead plucked up the copy of the blueprint and went to the copier to make something she could write on. "So, am I right in guessing they won't return and relieve you of your obligation to remain here if there's nowhere safe for the baby to be born?"

"You are correct."

"So you're no longer worried about making Zahir come back and do things himself if he wants them a certain way?"

Dakan leaned back in his chair and watched her at the machine, lining up the wide paper and feeding it into the machine. Finally going to address that, it seemed.

"That doesn't change what I want."

"Why not? If you're wanting him to take over, wouldn't you want it to be something we won't have to rip up and start over again? Not that I don't want to stick around here and design for however long I'm needed, but I really don't like wasted efforts. If he's going to just want to rip things up and start over, I'd rather be going in his direction from the start."

"But you work for me, and I don't want to go in his direction. Not only because I want him to come do it himself but because I don't think it's the right way to go. It would be okay, but it leaves too much wiggle room for the system to revert to the old ways. We talked about this."

"I know we did, but it seems a bit…out on a limb with a saw? Have you and Zahir talked about this?"

"Nira. Stop. Don't worry about it. You work for me. I've thought this through."

"I know I work for you, I'm just trying to understand the logic. I like logic, it offsets my more random instincts."

Dakan sighed inwardly. This whole situation was convoluted. She wasn't wrong that this could backfire, or at least get very messy—both his intended direction and his reasons for bucking the direction Zahir had expected him to go. And the feelings stirring within him for the unexpectedly beautiful architect could also lead to something messy. Very messy.

Yes, she worked for him, and as much as he told Zahir he was going to enjoy himself with her, the idea of taking full advantage didn't sit right. Which meant he had to make sure she was on the same page with him. Be temptation. Show *her* what temptation looked like, because he already knew. Those flowing pajamas let him see every curve and every jiggle as she moved around the workspace. They didn't even have to be transparent. Pair them with a skimpier top and she'd be harem-ready.

"I see your point, but even if it chafes you to have to rip up more work at the behest of the Al Rahals, I prefer to overwork you than to provide a substandard corruptible system for my people."

Which probably surprised him more than anything. His first instinct had been to be a massive pain in the butt so Zahir would come back and be the leader. *He* was supposed to just be the follower when in Mamlakat Almas. But those early lessons about duty must have stuck, or maybe duty had become real in medical school when he'd begun to realize the gravity of duty to those you cared for.

"It's okay. I figure you're not used to being questioned.

Mild temper tantrums are probably to be expected." She delivered the words so gently and levelly that had it not been for the twinkle he spotted in her eye when she looked at him on her way back to the table with her new copies of the pages he might have wondered if he'd misheard her.

"Temper tantrums are a little louder. This was just me being an arrogant know-it-all. Get it right."

Bending over the table, she began drawing and making notes directly onto the sheet, and her loose hair fell like a curtain, concealing her face from him. Was she smiling? He couldn't tell. Every now and then she'd tuck the locks behind one ear, ask him a question and go back to her notes, but the heavy wavy locks always slipped free of her little ear and fell forward again.

"Why did you take the pencils out of your hair?"

Nira lifted her head and he saw a tiny blush blossom on her cheeks.

"Because it probably looked worse than it does down."

It did. Her hair down made him want to put his hands in it, feel the texture and the weight of it. Made him want to nuzzle in and breathe her scent.

He couldn't say that, so he shrugged. "Kept it out of your eyes, though."

"I'll put it up…"

"No. It's fine with me as it is. I was just talking when I should probably leave and let you work."

"Don't go yet. I have a few more questions."

"Okay." He pulled his phone out and made as if he was checking notes, then wandered around the workstation to where her laptop sat. The photo was there, and she had her back turned. He took advantage of her distraction and snapped a couple of quick shots of the photo, then returned to the drafting table to see what she'd been feverishly working on before he'd arrived to derail her.

Little slips of graph paper had been cut into different-sized rectangles, and each one was labeled with one of the departments he'd requested. She still had one marked "Healers."

He flipped through her sketchbook, looking at what could only be configurations for those departments. "Healers" was always included, but with a dotted line rather than a solid one. She expected him to change his mind, and already planned for it, at least at this stage where it was all boxes doodled on paper.

He'd let her keep on with it for now.

Although she claimed to be a classicist with regard to architecture, some of the concepts she'd doodled were daring and unique, something Dakan always appreciated. He liked buildings that didn't look precisely like buildings. Who needed tall square structures when they could have curves and elegance that stood out from the city while blending in with natural shapes?

"What did you work on for your firm before coming here?"

"Whatever they told me to work on. I didn't lead projects. This is my first time leading. I usually get shuffled into whatever team needs me, and whatever they were working on."

"So how did Zahir find you?"

"He hired my firm, told them what he wanted—as blend of old and new. And they suggested me to him. I interned where I work now, and my supervisor witnessed some of the projects for my last couple of years in university. They all were just that, a blend of different kinds of Arabic architecture. Even some white-walled Moroccan styles. Though I knew that wasn't where I came from, I still like it. I took a holiday in the south of Spain just to visit the Alhambra and soak in its style. It was the closest thing I could get away with before coming here. They still actually have a fair amount of Moorish influence visible throughout the country."

"Moors are a bit different."

"I know, but the styles blend."

"So you really do like this building, you weren't just trying to make me stop scowling at you that first day."

"I really do like this building," she confirmed. "It's unexpected. Do you hate it so much?"

Dakan shrugged and went to sit down again. It was more entertaining to watch her than to look at her doodled boxes. "It is unexpected, and I can see the appeal of the contrast, but it's also misleading. You said you expected the flat to be that old, heavy style, and it wasn't."

"That's true, but I guess I like that mix. Not out of sentimentality either. Although there is a bit of that, I'm not sure how I can have nostalgia for something that happened before I was ever born, but I kind of do. Then again, a lot of architecture affects me that way. I love it. It... I don't know how to explain without sounding crazy."

Dakan watched her small delicate hands move over the paper, sweeping lines and text, feverishly moving until she suddenly stopped dead, stood straighter, and brought the blunt end of the pencil to her mouth and tapped it on her lower lip thoughtfully.

Drawing attention to the soft curve of her lower lip did things to his breathing. Made him need to look somewhere else, but he couldn't bring himself to. Instead, he said, "I'm sure it won't sound crazy. Tell me."

Distract me.

Maybe crazy would take away some of the appeal.

"Don't be so sure," she muttered, but didn't look away from the copy of the print she was marking up.

"Tell me," he repeated, taking a cue from her and chucking a nearby eraser at her.

The bit of white rubber bounced off her hip and she did finally look at him. A sigh and she bent to retrieve it from the floor, sat and focused back on the print.

"I already told you some of it. I had one outlet. I didn't know, well, I *don't* know anything about my family on his side. If I even have a family on his side. Architecture was the one thing I could learn and study that made me feel connected to him. To them. It's a feeling... I can't describe it. I felt it the other day in the bazaar when I first got there, but it sounds strange. Like those people who fall in love with inanimate objects."

Dakan had been expecting some quirky story about inspiration, about building things that lasted. But this was something else. Her voice started to wobble a little just as she stopped talking. Vulnerability.

He leaned forward, not sure whether or not he should ask for clarification.

Vulnerability was Big Emotion territory. And it might interfere with his plan. "You mean..." What was it called? "Objectophilia?"

"Objectophilia? That sounds like a sexual deviant word of some kind. Like necrophilia..."

"It's feelings of love, commitment, and even sexual attraction to objects."

"No. It's not like that." She stopped with another sigh, and though she still looked at the print she worried the pencil between her fingers and tap-tap-tapped the tip in a tight cluster on the print. "The books became like family albums, that's the closest I can describe it. Architecture affects me. I feel something when I see these things with my own eyes now, and I know it sounds weird." She waved a hand, affecting a slight change in her voice as she announced, *"Oh, I feel like this ogival arch is my cousin, and that barrel vault is my sister. Domes... My father is a dome."* She didn't look at him the whole time, and she didn't now, just repeated in a softer voice, "I'm not explaining this well. I know how it sounds. I *hear* how it sounds."

Dakan didn't know what to say to her, but understanding burned down his throat.

He'd thought she'd just wanted to learn, scratch that

itch to know where she'd came from. That this was something she'd be able to let go of once she had experienced the region for herself. But it was more than that. This wasn't a whim.

Nira swiveled in her chair and rolled to the laptop to open some program, self-comforting by distraction. Use busyness to distract from emotions.

He could see the wound now. Old, but still raw. And he didn't know how to help her.

She'd been assigning emotion to pictures in books since childhood, probably long before she'd had that photo of her father to shift her emotion to.

Pulling himself from the chair, he stepped up behind hers and began to gather the long damp locks back.

It was an excuse to touch her when all he really wanted to do in that moment was hug her and say whatever would act as some kind of balm. An action he couldn't run with any more than he could his last reaction—the desire to kiss her.

She froze in her seat, her head very still as the long, heavy strands slid through his fingers.

"What are you doing?"

"Putting it back up for you."

Without any direction for him to stop, Dakan slowed down and combed his fingers through her hair, taking his time. A fragrant cloud of her scent mixed with fruity-smelling shampoo, he wanted to bury his face in her hair and breathe. But that would be even more intimate than kissing her. At the slide of her hair through his fingers, cool and sleek, his chest tingled with the imagined weight of the damp locks draped across his bare flesh.

Sweet mercy, he had to just finish the task, get her hair up before he had to tear himself away and make it seem like he was just playing with her hair.

"I don't think you're weird," he said with some effort, though he'd already told Zahir he thought she was a little weird. With the bunch gathered in one hand, he slowly twisted it to wrap around on itself. "It's understandable, you filled a need in whatever way you could." Everyone did things to try and heal themselves. He understood, even if it broke his heart a little.

"I don't know why I even told you all that." She didn't sound as vulnerable then, mostly dismayed and a little breathless.

"I made you tell me. And you probably needed to say it to someone." He eyed the pencils on the desk. Securing the somewhat neater bun with them was definitely outside his ability. "You're going to have to put the pencils back into it. I've no idea how."

Quietly, she reached up to transfer the bun from his hand to hers in a way that didn't let it unwind, then worked pencils into it in some snaking fashion that somehow held it.

"You say it's not weird, but I bet you don't have any similar eccentricities."

"I'm sure I do. I just can't think of any right now."

"If you did, they'd stand out. There's nothing strange enough if you don't at least lightly question your sanity over it."

One thing stood out, he just didn't want to examine it. Self-awareness was overrated, and definitely more Zahir's territory. His own territory was keeping so busy he didn't have time to become bogged down by things he couldn't change.

He changed the subject.

"Tomorrow we're going to the hospital so you can see what you have to work with."

She spun in the chair and the smile she gave him was a tiny thing but very welcome.

"And I'll make sure you get to see whatever you want to see. You have my word. Domes. Arches. Vaulted ceilings. Mosaics. The royal oasis... Whatever you want."

"After the new project gets going." Nira stood and although she maintained a good centimeter of space between them, she leaned up to press a little kiss to his cheek.

Dakan shoved his hands into his pockets to keep from reaching for her, nodded, and then stepped away to make his exit. "I'll be here to collect you at eight. Wear something sensible and hard to stain."

CHAPTER FIVE

NIRA STOOD AT the wide bank of windows in the penthouse flat, waiting for Dakan in her favorite fashion: while looking out over the city.

Her building wasn't the tallest, though it was close, but the top-floor views let her see almost everything in the city. Without even turning her head, she could see glass towers, squat, ancient brick buildings, and two gorgeous mosques—one built within the last fifty years and another centuries old with a massive white dome.

My father is a dome.

Why had she said that to him? She'd never felt a genuine need to say anything like that to anyone else.

The best architects straddled a line between practicality and imagination, and in the tradition of accepting artists, people usually forgave their eccentricities. Her fascination with everything Persian, Ottoman, and Byzantine had been considered a quirk by nearly everyone she'd met, and she had never expounded further.

But Dakan she'd told the truth, or something like the truth. She'd have told a more accurate truth if she could've defined it better.

Maybe he was right. Maybe she just wanted to tell someone, wanted someone to really understand how it affected her. She had a feeling she couldn't quite name. Not lust. Not some deviant kind of animism—she knew mo-

saics and arches weren't alive—though she might argue
some old buildings seemed to have a soul.

But the emotion was real. Something more than being
moved by beauty. A connection she couldn't adequately
describe but which comforted her even as it awed her.

Yes, still sounded weird. Even to her.

It was probably good her first official authorized outing would be to a hospital. That couldn't do anything for
her nameless woo-woo emotion, surely. But it would get
her out of the flat, and on the drive there she'd get to see
the city closer but in a way that passed by too quickly for
her to become overwhelmed by it. She hoped.

The hospital was a safe outing. Safe. Safe. Safe.

"I said wear something that wouldn't easily stain."

And Dakan had once again snuck in while she stood
looking out the window.

"I don't have anything dark colored. When you go to
a hot, desert country you wear light colors. So I just went
with the most..." she turned back to look at him, and after
a glance down her dress found an adjective "...plain. If it
stains, at least it's not the prettiest." And she wasn't going
out in one of the dresses with graphite elbows and fore-
arms, even if they couldn't be further ruined.

He was dressed in a sharp suit—precisely as he had
been every other time she'd seen him.

But there was one strange accessory now.

"Why are you wearing a sword? You said it was icky
there, not dangerous."

Dakan made a low disgruntled sound in his throat,
"Father's advisors have been demanding I wear the traditional attire—robes and the sword. Zahir always wears
it, so why won't I wear it? I got tired of listening to the
same comments on repeat daily, so I'm wearing the sword
as a compromise."

"Are the robes white or black?"

"White."

"They might be more comfortable."

"Trust me, they're annoying to move about in, though I'll concede they probably have better airflow. It's not that I don't like them for other people, but I feel ridiculous in them. Like some pretender, walking around in Zahir's outgrown clothes and big clown shoes."

She fetched her bag, checked her passport's security, and tried not to look at him. The word *pretender* stuck in her mind, a little clue that everything wasn't right between Dakan and his brother. But pointing it out right now seemed wrong, like taking advantage or poking at a wound. So instead she opted to go the lighter route. "Like you ever wore hand-me-downs in your life. And, just so you know, you stand out regardless of who's around or what you wear."

He escorted her to the door with a light touch to her back, the touch making her all too aware of the size of his hand and the placement of the tip of each finger through the simple cream-colored dress.

Of course she was hyper-aware of him. He stood out—tall, broad, and impossibly handsome, with his nearly black hair a little too long so it looked artfully messy, like he'd been caught in the wind, or more likely some woman had just been running her fingers through it...

It was probably silky and soft too. And she already knew he smelled too good to be real.

He was probably an alien. A beautiful alien with just enough hidden vulnerability to make her question the vow of chastity she'd taken when she'd started down this path to learn about her heritage. Six feet two inches of temptation to repeat Mum's mistakes.

The idea of coming to live in a Middle Eastern country as a woman alone was scarier if she tried to do it with an eye toward dating or romance, another good reason for the vow. But Dakan tempted her to chuck that vow out the window she now stared through to the wall of blurring landscape.

Those sexy smiles... He was probably an amazing kisser. Soft lips, the light scrape of his perpetual three-day beard. Those shoulders.

Fifteen breathless minutes later they got out of the car at the hospital and Nira immediately refocused on the enormity of their problem. The building was small, even though it had been situated on a vast empty lot in the middle of a city where land would not be cheap.

Even from the outside, she could tell she didn't want to be treated there.

"Wow. You know, you look at plans and you think, 'It's probably bigger than I'm imagining it.' But it's actually smaller."

Dakan offered an elbow, and she shifted her notebook to the other hand to take it, and climbed the few steps to the main entrance, only to be left there.

A few moments with the harried receptionist and Dakan returned to fetch her.

"Maintenance is in right now, but no other surgeries today. Feel up to going in while they're working?"

"Sure. Construction doesn't bother me."

"Good."

She followed him across the lobby and down a short hall to the theater.

Dakan warned as he held the door, "They did a procedure in here earlier, so it might be a little less clean than normal."

That stopped her. Nira stood in the doorway, looking about for red. "Why wouldn't they clean it before Maintenance came in?"

"I'm sure they cleaned it up some, but since they'll have to clean it again as soon as he's done, it's possible it didn't get the attention it deserves. If you see anything wet, don't touch it. That's the first thing you learn in medical school: if it's wet, and it's not yours, don't touch it."

"That's descriptive. And...it's not going to be a problem. I'd rather get plaster in my hair and coughing fits from the dust than touch something wet that's not mine."

The inside of the theater was also worse than she'd imagined, but she didn't immediately see anything that screamed viscera to her.

"It's a decent size," she murmured, half to herself, carefully navigating around the table. Once on the other side, she could see a tall ladder set up and a maintenance man up to his waist in an open grid space for dropped ceiling tiles, replacing them. Some fifteen feet up, she'd wager. Very high. Though the dropped aspect of the ceiling would've given them about twelve to thirteen feet at the finished height rather than the ten research specified.

Hearing them speaking, he leaned back on the ladder, far enough to bend double and peer out of the tiles. He said something, but she only made out a couple of words and irritation in his voice. He wanted them gone. But when Dakan answered—giving his identity and telling the man to carry on—he struggled to right himself back up within the ceiling. The ladder wobbled back and forth a few times, and without a word or another thought Nira darted the few feet over to grab the ladder and steady it.

When it ceased moving he managed to get straightened and back up in there. It was probably not every day a prince came around while he was working, so she could sympathize.

She tried to redirect Dakan's attention, but he'd already focused on her. "Fast thinking. Thank you, I didn't even notice until you were in motion."

"I've seen my share of construction accidents," Nira said, but since everything seemed steady now, she checked the bottom of the ladder for slip guards, and, finding none, let go of the ladder to begin circling the surgery for something to do the job and still carry on the conversation with Dakan. "Thought it'd be smaller given the size of the building, but it's actually okay. I'm going to want to take it down to the wires, and actually I want to take out the wires too. Run new electrical, update the grid and plumbing. Rebuild from the joists up, including a plain painted ceiling. Normally it would be a bit lower than it is—the only ones with this kind of height I've seen in my research have observation galleries, like in teaching hospitals. But here it's just dead space. You might consider adding something."

Not that that was the most important thing she should be telling him right now.

"We'll talk about that later. Right now, I have to say I can't believe they put a drop ceiling in here. Those things give off dust all the time, no matter how new they are. I can't imagine they allow for a sterile environment. They're porous, dusty, and vermin like to nest in them. Replacing them with the same thing is—"

"A very bad idea," he finished, following her gaze up again. "I didn't realize they did that. I've been told that sometimes the surgeons set up an awning over the table, but I thought it was just since the tiles began crumbling—which was why I'd ordered them replaced."

"They're never going to be safe, really, even when they're not crumbling. Bare wires and open joists would be better than those. Also, he really should be working with a partner, for safety's sake. You saw the ladder."

"You're right," Dakan muttered, swearing quietly. "I'm going to leave you to speak to the administrator and start sending surgical patients to our neighbors now rather than during the reconstruction. This isn't going to be a quick repair."

"If he had help it could be done in a day, but there would need to be some intensive cleaning after that, which would probably take longer."

"No, I'm going to shut surgery down until we have a proper theater." The disgust in his voice was impossible to miss. He switched languages, calling up to the man working, "Stop what you're doing and come down."

The man, who'd already looked nervous before, jerked his hands away from the tiles like they'd begun conducting current. When he twisted back to speak to Dakan, the ladder rocked again, but they were both across the room from him.

Coldness hit her gut as she realized the rocking of the ladder had reached the point where it couldn't be righted. The man seemed to feel it at exactly the same second—with one hand holding the ladder, he lashed out with the other and grabbed the rickety frame of the drop ceiling to try and settle himself, but gravity had him. The frame snapped and the ceiling opened above him, tiles breaking and falling as he fell in slow motion. All Nira could do was stare, watching the moment stretch out far enough it would seem she could've gotten to him, but she never could have this time.

Dust kicked up in the theater, but Dakan had started moving. He reached the tiles and bent to fling them back. "Nira, find someone, get a gurney and an emergency team."

"Is he okay?"

"Now!"

She'd spent all that time looking at the prints yesterday and pulled the image to mind. If she went back the way they'd come, it would take longer than if she left the theater and went the other direction, which should lead to the emergency department.

When she'd managed to traverse the debris and exit the theater, she turned left down the corridor and ran until she saw someone in a uniform. Words—maybe not the right words but words that got her message across—came so quickly she'd have felt proud of herself in any other situation. Within two minutes of the man falling, the team Dakan had ordered ran back ahead of her, rolling a gurney and carrying oxygen and a cervical collar.

It would already be crowded in the theater, so she stayed outside in the hallway, trying not to panic, though she still felt trapped and helpless in that eternal second where the man had been falling, wondering if he'd hurt anything vital on the way down and cursing herself for ever letting go of the ladder, or not demanding he come down straight away the first time it had rocked off balance.

Another couple terribly long minutes, and they wheeled him out and back the way she'd gone to find help. There was blood on him and the arm he'd grabbed the ceiling with had a terrible gash on it. What could've cut him?

Once they were out, she got a better view—broken bone stuck out of the wound. The bone cut it, so he must've hit something very hard.

Dakan had his suit jacket off already, but as he walked past her he stopped and pulled off the sword and belt to hand to her. "I need you to hold the sword. It will only get in the way until I'm done. Go back to the lobby and wait for me. I have to see to him." His dark eyes locked to hers and she could see a spark there she didn't normally see. Depth. Something...

She nodded, taking the sword and reaching for his jacket.

"It's bloody," he said, pulling the jacket back from her reach.

So was Dakan's well-tailored shirt. So much for not touching stuff that was wet and not yours.

"Go. Hope he's okay."

He held her gaze a moment longer, nodded, and jogged to catch up.

Once they'd all rounded the corner, and she had nothing else to do but leave and wait, Nira stepped carefully back into the theater and looked up. Ripping the ceiling down was half-done now...though not the way she'd have seen it happen. Above she could see evidence of some kind of infestation, and some mystery conduit she couldn't identify along with wiring haphazardly strewn everywhere. Might've been better before the ceiling had fallen, but now...

Right. Not the time. She stepped carefully back out and went to the lobby to wait, just as she'd promised. The lobby and waiting rooms had been her initial reason for wanting to come to the hospital, before things had gotten switched up and they'd begun planning for a royal birth.

Reception had a desk with an attendant to sign people in, a triage area, where presumably they spoke to a nurse and went into a queue to be seen, and seating. It was remarkably similar to how hospitals of that era had been designed at home too, outside of those dreadful ceiling tiles that littered the facility.

Thinking about the tiles brought that icy lance of fear back to her middle, and she forced herself to find a seat, then laid the sword protectively across her thighs. Just observe, don't think about that poor man, and learn all she could while Dakan helped him.

Seeing all this live made it easier to understand why he'd been in such a hurry to tear it down, but there were still good bones here, even if the inside had been poorly done when it had been new. It could be remodeled to the point people would never know it was an older building. New insides. Maybe a new facade outside. Repurposing the old, not exactly blending them together, but other than the bones she couldn't see anything worth salvaging here either.

He could die from that wound. Nira knew very little about medicine, but even she knew an open fracture was massively in danger of infection. And Dakan had said they weren't good at treating infection in this country. Closing the surgery probably meant he'd have to go to another hospital with better facilities, which might just save his life.

Nira retrieved her mobile phone and sent her mother a text while she waited for Dakan.

Still alive.

It was in her to say more, but what could she say that wouldn't make this fight they were locked in worse?

I'm just sitting here, hoping a man I saw with a horrific injury doesn't die from infection or blood loss.

I'm doing something good to help these people.

Neither of those would help. There were always other architects who could take her place. She wasn't integral to the completion of this project, she just happened to be the architect under contract for Dakan to use.

She thought a moment and then simply sent: Love you.

A moment later her phone pinged.

Are you all right? What happened?

The first response. If they could each just give a little, but Nira didn't know how to in this instance. It meant too much to her to be there. And to Mum it meant unfathomable danger to her to be there. Hard to compromise on those kinds of emotions. Just talking would be a start, if she knew somewhere less flammable to begin.

Nothing. I'm okay. Just needed to say it.

Another couple minutes passed, and Nira had started to think that the conversation was over when her phone pinged again.

Love you too. Come home appeared on her screen.

Fight still not over. Neither of them were willing to budge. She didn't need to say that, and she didn't have anything else to say that would offer comfort or clear the air. So she just put her phone back into her pocket and waited for Dakan.

By the time they got the man settled on the helicopter, Dakan could only pray it was in time to save his life. The best they'd been able to do for him had been to clean the wound, dress it, and arrange a lifesaving flight, hoping it was enough to tide him over. Hope and prayer—he sounded like the healers.

Hope and prayer never worked. Any times he'd heard differently, it had always been anecdotal. He'd never seen someone healed because another man had said words over him, had never read it in a chart.

He'd shed his jacket at some point, and now the previously crisp shirt he wore was stained with blood too. He fished his personal items out of the jacket, stuffed them into his trouser pockets and his jacket into the bin for medical waste.

When he'd sent Nira out to wait for him, she'd been as white as the traditional robes he still didn't want to wear. White enough he was faintly surprised to see her still upright when he got to her side forty-five minutes after the situation had started. White enough for him to hope it had wiped that earlier confession from her mind. The woman was too easy to talk to, he should take better care of his words.

"Is he okay? Is he alive?" she asked, standing as he approached and offering the sword back to him.

Well, he didn't want to wear it. Grabbing it by the scabbard, he tucked it under one arm. The car wasn't far away.

"He was when the helicopter left. And we're past anything that can be done from our end."

"Where is he going?"

"Dubai, since we can do nothing for him here. Their best trauma center has agreed to take our overflow, but the other needed surgeries will be shunted to different hospitals in different countries, decided by urgency and diagnosis. But trauma will always go to Dubai. Let's hope we don't have too much of it."

This ugliness was another thing that made him prefer England. Today there had been very little he could do for the injured man, and that helpless feeling made being home worse. There were always the other aspects, the family stuff—him never saying what he felt, doing what he felt, only what was expected of the younger brother—but this was worse because he should've been able to avoid it. The other stuff he was used to.

He'd long ago accepted he'd never be important to his country, not really. The only thing that could make him so was something he never wanted to see—something happening to Zahir. Freedom to live his life as he saw fit was the only really acceptable exchange in his mind, something he didn't have here. He didn't want to be the eternal follower. Even now, without Zahir or his father in the country, the hospital project was the only place he felt he could make his own decisions, rather than just sticking to the pattern set by others, and that might change at any minute.

"Let's go. I need to get out of this shirt."

His hands were clean, and he took her hand to walk to the car. Propriety be damned. She felt good, and he needed something good right now—something that felt real, and good. Maybe it was just how good it felt to be with someone he could relax around, or simple base attraction.

He led her to the car and got into the back, letting go of her hand so he could start unfastening his shirt, something else he could do around her.

"I wish I could've done that inside the hospital. It

should be burned. Everything is practically medical waste here."

Stuffing the shirt under the seat, he tilted his head to catch the gaze of the driver in his rearview mirror, and redirected him. "Palace."

CHAPTER SIX

Dakan had said "palace."

They were going to the palace.

Nira settled in the back beside him and tried not to look at the extremely nice naked male torso on display beside her. Remember that shirt was soaked with blood—he probably had blood on his skin too if she looked too closely. A good reason not to look.

He was in such a mood she didn't even know if she could even be excited about going to the palace. From a run-down hospital to a freaking palace.

Play it cool. Pretend her stomach didn't swirl with excitement at the prospect.

"We can't stay long. But I can't very well go around the city in bloody clothes, and I don't have anything to change into at your place." He reached over and took her hand again, and the excited swirling in her tummy moved up her torso to collide with the sizzle running up her arm.

When he'd taken her hand to walk to the car, she'd put it down to the idea that he wanted to go quickly and keep track of her. Something besides wanting to touch her. But now…there was nothing to keep track of.

Unable to help herself, she turned to look where their hands joined and up his arm—over the dusting of dark hair on tan skin, over the definition of muscle at the upper arm, to a shoulder she could sink her teeth into. That was the best muscle. She didn't have one really on top of her shoulder, at least nothing noticeable, but that smooth, developed cap of muscle made her keep looking.

Oh, God, she was going to be stupid. He was holding her hand, she was ogling his body…and they were going to what was effectively his place. If she made a pass at this man right now he'd take her to his room. Chamber. Wing. Place where he kept his bed.

Which would mean she…

"Nira?"

She was yanked from the mental acrobatics it took to try and figure out why she shouldn't make a pass at him.

"I'm sorry, what did you say?"

"I asked if you'd mind waiting for an official tour later." Tour?

"Oh. I… I…don't…ah…"

God. She wiggled her fingers and firmly extracted her hand from his. When she had it safely in her lap again and her eyes forward, it became possible to think.

"I'm fine. Later. I'm fine with another later tour."

It was now possible to think, just not easy yet.

"I mean to say I know we're in a hurry and I should get back to the flat so I can start on the new project." There. Complete sentences and everything. "So, yes, another time."

And while he went to change, she had her sketchbook and her phone so she could maybe get some pictures for later gazing. She could make do with one room. For this visit.

Change the subject.

"You're a proper doctor, right? Done with schooling?"

"I am. Fully licensed. In the UK."

"What kind of doctor are you? You seemed pretty at home in the emergency."

Yes. The emergency. Think about the blood, not about half-naked Dakan…

"I'm not big on emergency. That's Zahir's territory. Initially I trained as a doctor so I could help overhaul the medical system, but then I actually found I liked it. Hospitals aren't my thing. I want to take care of people, have patients I can come to know and keep healthy."

"So you're training to be a GP?"

"Yes."

"You seem like you'd be into something…"

"Flashier? More high profile?"

"I guess I would've thought you'd like that kind of adrenalin-rush medical practice."

The smile in his voice registered, and when she glanced at him, the dimple in his cheek confirmed it.

"Not really. It's valuable, I get that. It's actively saving lives. In big facilities, emergency consultants can often say they saved a life on their shift or maybe several. I just like helping people more than life saving. I like kids and old people. Seeing the same patient year in and year out, watching kids grow up. I like that more. I like knowing I can help someone's life be better. I never get that chance when I'm here. Born to follow, my father said that once. He said Zahir was born to lead, and I was born to follow."

As he spoke, it became impossible for Nira not to look at him. It didn't seem to fit at first, not with what she saw of him. She'd always thought of GPs as more for jumpers and button-downs. When she thought of Dakan as a doctor, in her imaginings he wore scrubs. And she'd never seen him in anything but a suit.

Before she could process this new piece of the Dakan puzzle, before she could even figure out what to say to him, he shook his head. "I don't know why I told you that. I don't even know why I thought it, really. Just thinking about…" He stopped and focused again out his window.

Her gaze followed as the palace came into view.

"You were talking about never getting to help people have a better life here," she prompted, trying to split her attention between Dakan and the palace. What he was saying sounded important to him.

"Right." He nodded, "I guess that's what makes the hospital project special. I'll be able to help all of my countrymen have better lives in one fell swoop so we won't have any days in the future like today."

Nira looked at the hand she'd escaped earlier, and slipped her own back into it.

Dakan turned back to her from the window, smiled, some of the tension in his brow diminishing. "Would you like me to roll down the window so you can see better?"

"I was trying not to geek out and ask. Really, I thought about opening the sun roof and standing up... Your window is probably the more sensible option."

He pressed a button and let it slide down, then tugged her a little closer to him so her view would be less obstructed.

"It's so sparkly..."

"It's Qasr Almas."

Diamond Palace. Palace of Diamonds...

"I know, but photos I looked at online never really did it justice. The camera always caught some sparkle, but compared to this it just looked like some kind of lame photo effect. Click the 'add sparkle' button."

She was supposed to be keeping her cool!

"It's strange, but beautiful. I can't even imagine someone building with that sort of mindset in this century. I'm still surprised any time a new building has a dome, and I love them. You have..." she paused to count and shook her head "...seven domes..."

"Seven is a holy number," he murmured, and then added, "You'll be able to see the large dome from the inside when we get there.

Seven domes.

And a beach that probably still had Lego lost in the sand.

And a magnificent prince who had depth, layers that

surprised her, and who couldn't go a single visit without flashing that freaking adorable dimple in his charming left cheek.

"I have no idea when my parents will be returning, but with my luck today, if we stick around more than a few minutes, they'll come strolling in while I'm half-clothed with you, then the lectures will begin."

The car stopped and Nira scrambled out so she could get a close-up look at the exterior stones and the precious stones set into the whole wall. Colored stones—sapphires, emeralds, rubies, and some other stones she couldn't identify. Much fewer diamonds than she'd expected, considering the name.

It sparkled almost as much as the man himself.

Her hand still tucked in his, she kept up, not asking a single one of the millions of questions swarming her mind. Let him change and clean up, she'd have time to unleash the barrage on the drive back to her place.

Vaguely aware there were other people there, Nira tried to look the grand entranceway over quickly before they moved on. Minimal attention to people was about all she could manage right now, in the presence of gilded opulence, the high vaulted ceiling of the entryway—a half-dome in its own right—and the carved doors she'd barely gotten a look at.

Alarmed voices dragged her attention back to the living, but it still took her a few seconds to concentrate enough that she could understand what they were saying.

Dakan was shirtless.

Dakan had blood on him.

Dakan held the hand of a strange woman.

Despite the impropriety of pretty much everything surrounding the two of them at the moment, Dakan answered smoothly, first assuring them the blood was not his, and going from there.

She'd forgotten it all in the narrow and extreme focus

that had overtaken her the instant she'd stepped out of the car. She'd even somehow forgotten he was shirtless.

He gestured the people out of the way and began walking again, and it took her only a heartbeat to get moving too.

Marble floors, several different minerals visible along with gold veining that looked... "That gold veining isn't natural, is it?"

"No. Impressive eye." Dakan stopped as she stopped, continuing to hold her hand as she bent over to look more closely at the contrast of pale pinks intermingled with at least three shades of sand.

"Why is it there?"

"The marble is beautiful, but fragile. Anywhere a pre-existing crack or seam opens, it is repaired with some process that uses gold. An idea pilfered from the Far East by my great-great-grandfather as a young man while on a diplomatic visit. It preserves centuries-old marble while increasing the beauty and interest."

"I've never seen that done before..."

She wanted to lie on the floor with a magnifying glass and study the surface, see how it had been worked in. With her free hand, she pressed her fingertips to the seam and ran them along where the thin golden vein was sealed to the marble. Perfectly level. It felt as smooth, as if cut by modern diamond saws. Could they just melt gold and pour it in there? Marble cracks further with extreme heat...

"Nira?"

"Sorry..." Nira stood back up and they resumed walking. Although the floor had been repaired in an admittedly fascinating manner that was entirely new to her, she wasn't here to see the floors. It was all about the dome.

They walked through another set of doors she'd like to study, and Dakan let go of her hand. "I'll be back in a few minutes."

A meager nod was all she could muster as her eyes tracked upwards.

Not an inch of it didn't shriek color or pattern. The stone walls were carved in high relief, and transitioned to blue and gold tilework laid in a pattern so intricate the only thing her mind could compare it to was a kaleidoscope.

Her vision swam and when the colors blurred together she looked down long enough to swipe at her eyes, but the tightness didn't leave her chest so quickly. She hadn't even looked at the freaking dome yet...

And she'd thought all architecture affected her. The repaired gold marble floors were beautiful—as beautiful as the mosaic—but they had only inspired fascination in her. Not this... There wasn't even a word in her for it.

Love was the word she'd use, but it kind of offended her to think of it that way.

Awe was utterly unequal to the feeling.

Wonder came close.

Reverence came closer.

Connected... Moved...

She finally allowed herself to look up at the dome.

Where the walls started to round into the dome, there sat a short span of stone carved in a band of words circling the base of the dome. Above, the tile resumed, right up to the oculus. So many shades of blue—from the pale light of a morning sky to the darkest blues of twilight—mixed in with shades of sand.

After several minutes, having her head tilted back, the room began to spin. If she didn't right herself soon she'd probably pass out. But she hadn't finished looking.

Not caring if anyone lingered who might notice her strange behavior, Nira moved directly under the center of the dome and lay down on the floor on her back for the best view.

Nothing she could've imagined could compare to it.

And the people who lived there probably never really even saw it any more. They were probably so used to it that it blended into the background, so they missed how beautiful it was, how meaningful. Taken for granted, like family—so at least there was that commonality to make her feel slightly less sensitive...

She had no idea how long she lay there, anyone could've come and gone without her knowledge. Anyone but Dakan. He'd never allow himself to be ignored for the sake of a pretty ceiling.

Not a sound registered with her as he approached, he was just suddenly in her vision, standing over her—unattainable perfection with the curve of beautiful color behind his head

"It's so beautiful..." she whispered up to him, glad she'd finally stopped dribbling tears after the rush of it had finally subsided.

Dakan offered a hand to her, nodding but not saying anything, helped her to her feet and waited for her to get her balance.

"I know you think I'm silly."

"I don't."

"Do you even see it?"

"I do see it," he said softly, keeping her hand and leading her from the domed chamber, back the way they'd entered. "I just see as much value in the modern. Today, what happened at the hospital? That kind of thing colors my ability to love the history—especially history not allowed to slip into the past."

Too soon they were back in the car, the soiled shirt now cleared away, and soon the palace stood behind them.

"I hope your perspective changes when the hospital is done. Even if you go back to London. One day, your kids will want to see all this. Trust me." And what he'd said to her about being destined to be a follower, never able to really help his people, came back to her. "We're coming at it from two different sides of the same coin."

"What coin is that?"

"We most want what was kept from us as children." She reached out and took his hand this time. "I want to know all of this, see all this, experience everything that was denied me. You want to do what you feel has been denied you."

He listened—that was something else that made the man so attractive to her. He listened to everything she said to him. She'd spent so much of her life having her thoughts silenced, on this matter at least, but Dakan listened and didn't seem to judge. Granted, she'd been able to get rid of the sneaky tears before he'd got back to witness them, but she'd pretty well bared this weirdness of hers to him and he hadn't said one single harsh word about it.

"That's not what I want most right now," Dakan said, his thumb starting to stroke the side of her hand from wrist to thumbnail, back and forth in a slow, thorough caress that sent a shiver up her arm. Something in the air changed, and the gentle and somewhat companionable way he'd held her hand became something that heated her insides and messed with her breathing.

He pressed a button and a darkened window slid up between them and the driver, but he never took his eyes off her.

"What do you want?" She asked the question, knowing the answer. He wanted the same damned thing she wanted—to be really, really stupid.

In answer, he released her hand and his arm slid around her until his long fingers wrapped over her hip. Supple black leather caressed her body as he slid her to him.

Her throat went instantly dry, and she couldn't think of a single thing to say. She couldn't even figure out whether or not she should kiss the man. This morning, even after the hospital, she'd would've been tempted, but she could've resisted. But something about his unexpected confession moved her. Something about the way he accepted this feeling she couldn't name, didn't comment when it overcame her...moved her.

If she kissed him now, it would be all over. She'd be tearing the man's clothes off the second they were through the door of the flat.

Leaning back, she blinked up at him, eyes wide, shaking her head. "We can't. I can't..."

"You want me to kiss you, Nira."

"I do," she admitted, then followed quickly, "And I don't. I don't want you to kiss me. We can't. I can't."

"You can. No one will see us." The hand on her hip firmed up, curling her in against him even as she tilted her head back.

Oh, he smelled good. And after the cold marble floor at her back he felt even better. Warm. Firm. Strong.

"I can't because I want to. Because it can't go any further and there's something really horrible about this level of chemistry. It's like a trap. And you've been..." Less confessing would be good. Playful. Playful flirting was easier to say no to than this intensity threatening to swallow all her good intentions and every shred of reason. "You're seducing me with your sexy architecture!"

There. That was...well, pretty stupid. Not exactly flirty.

He leaned forward until the tip of his nose touched her cheek, and she could feel his breath fanning her skin. "I thought you said your feelings about architecture weren't sexually deviant."

"It's not..."

"So you mean I'm just here to tempt you like some sexy architecture-owning beast?"

"Yes," she lied. Going along with his interpretation was pretty much all she had going for her right now.

His lips brushed the sensitive strip where jaw blended

to chin. Technically, not a kiss. Just some maddening feather-light caress as he spoke.

"You are temptation personified." That was the truth at least. She turned her head so they were nose to nose, before he actually kissed her neck or her ear in some dastardly sexy checkmate. That'd be worse than kissing her lips.

"Because you want to be a good girl," he said, his voice still low, a deep throaty timbre that summoned an ache low in her belly, his lips barely touching hers as he spoke. "You turned your mouth to mine. Does that mean you want me to kiss you now, *ya amar*?"

Ya amar. Speaking Arabic to her when she could barely think in English.

"No." *Yes.*

Her heart hammered in her chest, but she balled her hands into fists so they wouldn't do anything impetuous, like reach for him.

His words finally translated in the fog of her mind and she asked, "Like the moon?"

"Beautiful." He whispered the explanation, stroking her ego in one word, but calling her on her lie with his next words. "You want me to kiss you despite all your denials. Take the choice away."

And it was a strike against her willpower and her devotion to the rights of women that he was right.

Her stay in Mamlakat Almas was supposed to be a guidepost to help her figure herself out, in order to explore what she might've been had she been raised here. Even counting out the track record Hathaway women had with Middle Eastern men, she shouldn't sleep with him—embracing what she might've been meant wrestling with the idea of chastity. Even if it was a little late for that, technically. She couldn't go abandoning her admittedly possibly temporary principles over pure lust.

But in the back of her mind, if he kissed her, as the instigator, he absolved her from blame. Like that was even minutely acceptable!

Whoops, went to a foreign country and the sexiest prince in existence ravished me in the back of a limo. Rascally Prince. What can you do?

"That's unfortunate," he said, letting go of her abruptly as he drew back. "Because I'm not going to do that. I'm not going to kiss you until you're begging for it." The car rolled to a stop and she realized only when he opened the door and got out that they'd arrived. Her workspace waited for her.

On quivering legs, she managed to crawl out behind him and stand, but Dakan blocked her in against the car, holding the door with one hand as the other went to her hip. Still with that low seductive purr, he whispered at her ear.

"And you will beg me for it, *habibi*. Because you're not going to be able to think of anything but the way my mouth would feel on yours, on your skin, at your breast. You want me as much as I want you. The sooner you come around to admitting it, the happier we'll both be."

He squeezed her hip and let go of her, stepping back so that the door was clear.

She searched for something to say—anything to say—but came up blank. A girl could fantasize her whole life about someone throwing down such a sexy gauntlet, and in every fantasy she'd have a saucy comeback.

Nira had no saucy comeback.

All she managed to do was nod, and mutter, "Okay."

Walking took almost as much concentration, and she was glad he got back into the car and it pulled away so he wouldn't see her wobbling her way into the building.

Him leaving was probably all that saved her from begging right then.

CHAPTER SEVEN

FOR THE NEXT WEEK, Nira didn't see Dakan once. He phoned every couple of days to check she didn't need anything, letting her work and stew in her own confusion.

Or maybe it was some other reason. Maybe he'd thought better of his sexy gauntlet. That would be a good reason to stay away. It's not like there weren't a billion women in the world who would love to pick up his sexy gauntlet. But she might very well be the only one within driving distance, unless he was looking for a wife, and something told her he wasn't.

The only part of her mind able to achieve any kind of clarity was the part that got absorbed in the work. And that had been sadly waning since she'd shipped the theater plans off to her firm to check a couple of days ago.

Now, while waiting, she alternated between working on the wing addition and re-re-re-checking the changes she'd made. Remodels were always harder to work out than fresh builds and she didn't want something to slip through.

Equipment specs she'd been given all fit within the new footprint in a workable order, so was wheeled equipment that could be moved to the table.

The new electrical grid gave extra room for demands that might arise in the future, and had been double-checked before she'd sent the plans in for approval.

Dakan probably wouldn't mind her knocking out a wall to make the theater include a small scrub bay that should've always been there. But who knew what Dakan was thinking? She'd had him pegged for a sexy charmer used to getting his way, but that confession... It didn't seem like he got his way much here.

These alternating opinions were going to make her seasick.

Her email pinged with the plans being sent back to her. Nira opened to check for notes and, finding none, reached for her phone.

Nira had not once called Dakan yet. She'd worked as much as possible because during the moments when her mind became quiet she had a hard time ignoring his prediction. If that's why he'd stayed away, it was dastardly cunning.

She'd never begged for a kiss in her life—let alone for sex—but the pendulum of her opinion swung between certainty all would be well if she did exactly what he said, and certainty she'd end up way over her head. The shadow of her birth and the ghost of her mother's heartache had left a mark on her.

Mum hurt twenty-seven years later. The love she'd felt had twisted into something closer to hate, but that pain never went away.

Nira couldn't even predict how she might react in her mother's shoes, only that if she fell for him it'd mean heartache. This was a culture of arranged marriages, and she was no one. She had no auspicious background or elite family history. She didn't even really understand the culture beyond snapshots, generalizations, and probably the occasional accidental stereotype.

This wasn't going to get her anywhere. She wasn't looking for a husband right now anyway. She had yet to meet New Future Nira—whoever she'd be when she filled in the missing pieces—before she could even think about her future.

Just call him, already. If it's for work it doesn't count.

She dialed.

A moment later, he answered, *"Hal tashtaaqo lii?"* *Do you miss me?*

Yes, she bloody well did miss him. More than that, the sound of his voice sent a thrill through her that could only be fueled by the probability she was about to make a very stupid decision.

"I have approved plans ready for the theater. Do you want me to print them out and make copies for your contractor?"

"What about the royal wing addition?" He flowed with the way she steered the conversation, though a hint of amusement hung in his tone.

"Not done yet, but it's coming along. I expect to have new plans ready to send to home for review by the end of the week."

"So in three or four days?"

"I hope to send it on Friday so it can be reviewed on Monday and Tuesday in the respective meetings," she answered, then leaned back in her chair, chewing her lower lip. "So do you want the prints?"

"Yes," he answered. "Why don't you get them ready and I'll come for dinner?"

No. Say no. Fake a headache.

No. He'd want to diagnose that.

Tell him she was going to bed early.

God, no, don't bring up beds.

But hadn't she just been thinking about how he never got his way in things?

Keeping her tone light, so it didn't sound like a rejection, Nira said, "You may be the ruler-in-residence, but I think I'm still the one who is supposed to invite you over."

"You wish to invite me over? Very well! I graciously

accept. I'll even bring dinner if you don't want to tax the housekeeper with a last-minute dinner."

Maybe he did get his way sometimes, probably by doing exactly this. Because it worked. He made it hard to say no to him. Not just his stubbornness, but he made her not want to say no to him. Made it hard not to want to play this ill-advised game.

"Her name is Tahira, and she's actually already cooking and always makes way more than I can eat. So, yes, you may come over."

For once, Dakan knocked.

Nira heard the rap on the door and it took her a moment to realize what it was. He never knocked. She called, so Tahira didn't go scrambling for the door, "I'll get it."

When she opened the door, he was smiling, "Oh, wearing trousers. Scandalous," he said, winking as he slipped around her and waited for her to close the door. He'd ditched his usual suit for once and the flowing linen tunic and trousers looked even better on the man. So unfair. The clean whiteness made his usual scruff that much darker, and set off the polished bronze of his skin. The fact that he looked so happy probably also added to his aura of beauty.

Obviously he hadn't suffered a moment of doubt or confusion for the past week. He'd probably slept like a baby every night.

"You're in a very good mood."

"Of course I am. I'm here to get plans that will facilitate me returning to my life, and also? I believe I'm getting kissed."

Nira's heart gave a little flip when he said "kissed." "I didn't say that."

He offered his elbow, and she stared at it a beat too long before slipping her hand through it.

"We can talk about that later. For now, I have some

news I thought you'd be interested in. Want the good news first, or the really good news?"

Bypassing the desk and seating, Dakan guided her to the stunning floor-to-ceiling windows. The early evening sky had started to change color; soon the sun would be going down, and all the windows in the city reflected a hazy shade of rose.

"The good news, I guess."

"I just came from the hospital. The man we sent to Dubai? He's home. He got back today and I went to see him and what they sent back. He's doing very well."

That might explain the lightness in his step, attire, and demeanor. "That's wonderful news. You sure that's not the really good news?"

"I don't know. I lied, I couldn't decide which was better so I prioritized the one that'll make your life easiest and most interesting."

"Okay. Let me have it," Nira said. "Unless it's that you've found a more experienced hospital designer. Don't think I want to hear that even if it'd make my life easier and more interesting."

"Your job's safe. For now," he said, dragging her in front of him so she stood sandwiched between his firm heat and inches from the hard, bright window.

The instant she felt his chest against her back, the decision was made. She was going to kiss him, at the very least. Something else might happen but, smug or not of him to think so, he was right.

His hands slipped onto her hips and then around her waist to link loosely at her belly. Yes. Definitely completely at ease with the situation.

Would he have even a drop of hesitation about this? If she could get a peek at his pros and cons list about kissing her—or sleeping with her—would there even be anything in the cons column?

"You were right about the hospital. It looks like the

royal wing will be finished in time for the baby, and the operating theater remodeled. It'd be foolish of me to continue going down a different road from the one Zahir and my father agreed on if I still plan on handing it back later. And, look, I've come to the conclusion before you got back to working on those plans."

"That's good news," Nira murmured, but her thoughts or interest just weren't on the hospital. Meeting his gaze in the reflection on the window, the need to know took over her mouth. "Do you have any reservations about this? About something happening with us? I don't even know what's going to happen and I'm very conflicted, but you just don't seem to—"

He stopped her by sliding his hands back to her hips and stepping back enough to turn her to face him.

"Of course I have reservations," he said, brows drawing together above those deep brown eyes. "Not about whether I'd enjoy it, not about whether you would either. But one reservation is the possibility we'll get too involved in bed. I only get a few hours a week to come here as it is, and if we spent all those hours in bed, that'd be detrimental to the project."

It made her feel better to know he had doubts. Doubts fueled her nearly twenty-four hours a day, so absolute confidence worried her.

"What else?"

"That you'll forget where I stand and get hurt like your mother was hurt. Not pregnant, but just hurt. You don't have anyone but me in Mamlakat Almas."

"I don't really know where you stand, so that's a valid worry." She stepped to the side, as facing him in that narrow space between him and the windows was too much. "Never mind, this is too weird. Let's just have a nice dinner and not worry about that."

"No."

She'd stepped past him when he stopped her by catching her wrist, and once more sensation radiated from where he touched her. These kinds of reactions were the problem. Couldn't they make some kind of pill to turn that off?

"If you don't know where I stand, that needs to be remedied. I'll be clear. I like you. I think you're funny and clever, I think you're kind of strange in your devotion to living a lifestyle you have no idea how to live, but it makes you interesting. I also think you're beautiful and sexy, and before long I'll be gone from here, but you'll still be here, working with my brother."

"So, where you stand is...you like hanging around with me while you're here, but after you're gone, that's it."

For the first time since he'd arrived, Dakan frowned, but he didn't deny it. He nodded even as his thumb once more began that maddening stroking over her skin, though it wasn't an unconscious thing. She recognized it now as an attempt at comfort. He knew how it sounded, he knew it sat wrong with her, and wanted to make it all right.

"I doubt your mother was afforded that level of clarity. The kind of heartbreak you spoke of—that could only come from being blindsided and feeling betrayed. I can't betray you if you know at the start I'm going to be gone in a couple of months."

"Okay. I know where you stand now."

She already knew that, but maybe he already felt important to her because she was so isolated here. She needed to make some friends not obligated to be nice to her to protect their livelihood.

His words came back to her then and she tilted her head to look up at him. "Is this why my life is going to be more interesting?"

He let go of her hand, allowing her to put a little more space between them. Her arms felt shaky, so did her knees. She still wanted to kiss him. Okay, one more step back...

"We're going to visit a few healing facilities in the

country. I'm hesitant to call them facilities or centers. That makes it sound more organized than it is. But there are places with healers and different sorts of healing baths and treatments. They are like a strange mix of a spa and a doctor's office."

"We're going to go together? I get to go?"

"You get to go. I need you to see what they do so we can try and replicate some of it here."

She felt the smile blooming from her belly before it ever reached her face. Somewhere outside the city, somewhere she'd probably find a more authentic location to what she would've had had her parents not split up—something more everyday than penthouses and palaces studded with precious stones.

If she hadn't wanted to kiss him before... Her gaze drifted to his mouth.

One of them had to go before she threw herself at him.

Staying away for a week had been hard. Dakan's mood had been so black prior to today that Bashir—his father's aide—had constantly sent the *attar* to him to try and get him to drink a potion to help. It wasn't until today and hearing his first official patient was returning that he'd found something to smile about. Nira's call had come right when it could make the day good enough to wash away the previous seven.

He still needed to kiss her and wasn't keen to examine why just yet. The way she looked at his mouth made the perfect excuse to forget his challenge.

He leaned down to her ear and whispered, "Kiss me, woman, or make a liar of me. I'm pretty damned sure I don't care any more if you beg or not, just kiss me."

The breath that stuttered out of her open mouth sounded like a plea and then like a lament.

"I can't." She shook her head, stepping away, pausing to judge the distance between them, and then moving another meter away. "I'm not going to sleep with you. I can't do that and then travel around the country with you. Everyone would be able to look at me and see we were lovers. I want to kiss you. I want more than to kiss you, but…could you stop with a kiss tonight?"

Could he stop at one kiss?

Dakan watched her chest rise and fall far too rapidly for anything but excitement, fear, or both—considering the situation.

His mind was made up before he started moving, "Let's find out."

Three short strides and he reached her. She didn't move away again; she didn't ask for more assurances or answers. His hand slid into her hair to cradle her head and he pulled her to him.

His lips touched hers and the fire that had been threatening to eat through his will exploded in his belly, met by an equal hunger in her kiss. She slid her arms free of his waist to wrap them around his shoulders, leaning into him as she held him curled down to meet her, pressing every inch of her body against him that she could.

Her mouth opened and Dakan took the invitation to take the kiss as deep as he'd been dying to since that first day he'd met her.

It wasn't enough.

He wanted greater contact, to mash himself against her the way her whole body invited him to.

When his lungs began demanding air he still wasn't ready to stop. Breaking from the sweet mouth that held him captive, he trailed kisses across her cheek and down the side of her neck, letting his hands roam her body to settle beneath the cheeks of the plump swell of flesh that had jiggled so temptingly at him when he'd caught her working in her pajamas. He squeezed, pulling her hips against his.

A stuttering breath and a groan preceded the softly whispered, "Stop. We have to stop…"

He stopped kissing, but didn't release her yet.

The urge was there to convince her otherwise, but she said to stop.

Reluctantly, he let go of her bottom and moved away. The linen trousers, which had seemed so comfortable and casual, now might as well be a spotlight to the effect she had on him.

"I'm sorry," she said, but made a point of not looking down. "I just can't."

"So you said." Another deep breath and he got his pulse slowed down, then broke away to head for her desk area. She had plans for him, he'd get those at least before leaving.

"Do you want to stay for dinner?"

It was the apology he still heard in her voice that helped his frustration subside somewhat, that and the breathless quality that at least confirmed that she was as affected as he was. "No. I'll take the plans and go home. Let me know about the private wing, and I'll call you with our itinerary at the end of the week."

If he went straight home and into a cold shower, he might be ready to travel by next week. Or he might be wearing the robes for other reasons.

CHAPTER EIGHT

"TAKE THE LUGGAGE to my suite, along with the packages." The voice of Dakan's mother rang out from the front entrance, bright and happy.

They were home.

Dakan stood immediately and went to greet his parents. Or just his mother. The King was nowhere to be seen. "Welcome home, Mother. Did you have a good holiday?"

Ever the loving and affectionate parent, she hugged him hard and kissed both of his cheeks. "I had a wonderful holiday. Have you heard from Zahir? How is Adele?"

"Pregnant," Dakan answered, keeping an arm around his mother's shoulders as he steered her toward a settee.

"Yes, isn't it wonderful?"

"It is." For them. And it would be for his parents and the kingdom as well, just as soon as Dakan got the facilities up to date.

"Is the architect working on the hospital?"

Dakan stopped a moment and then nodded. "We've had to take small pause with that, but she's already gotten together plans for the surgery theater to be remodeled and modernized, and she's finalizing plans for a small wing off that short side of the hospital for family. It will be tight, but the contractor assures me that it's small enough to have finished by the time Adele delivers. After the plans are approved by her firm, the architect and I are taking a small trip around the kingdom to different healing centers to see how it can be incorporated into the hospital planning."

"Oh, that's wonderful. You've been busy."

Staff arrived and summoned them to a late lunch, and over the next hour he listened to his mother gush about the vacation and the different countries they'd visited.

Tabda Aljann.

The man in Nira's picture swam to the front of his mind along with the sudden certainty that he'd seen the man in Tabda Aljann as a child. One of the Al-Haaken family. Jibril? Maybe.

"Dakan?"

He forced himself to focus on his mother. "Forgive me, Mother. I got…a little distracted."

"Are you feeling all right? The color drained right out of your face. Should I send for the *attar*?"

"I don't need any tonics. I just remembered something." He fumbled for his phone and then flipped through until he found the photo of Nira's parents. Maybe it wasn't him. Mother had probably recently dined with the whole family, so if she knew him—and she'd known that family since she'd turned down their king's marriage proposal and married Dakan's father instead—she'd have seen him.

Damn. Showing his mother the photo might backfire on him and take the Nira situation out of his hands, but his memory wasn't good enough to proceed alone.

"Mother, do you recognize this man?" He handed the phone to her. "I know it's not the best quality."

"Oh, yes, this is Prince Jibril. We had dinner with his family when the yacht put in at one of their ports on our cruise. Who is this woman with him?"

Dakan eased the phone back and turned it off. He didn't want to lie to her, but he also didn't want to tell her that the architect was blood kin to the royals in a nearby country. Especially when he knew that dinner his parents had attended would've been tense already—things had never been what anyone sane would call friendly since that denied proposal, though they made a show of pretending they were.

"I don't know her name," he admitted.

"Where did you get the photo?"

"A friend." His mother would probably have better advice on how to handle this than anyone else in his family. At least she'd be sympathetic with Nira. Slowly, and minimizing the detail as much as he could, he told his mother the scant story of Nira's birth.

"She'll be very happy when you tell her you've found him."

"I don't know if I'm going to tell her."

"Why not?"

"Because she wants to know so badly she might hop on a jet, march up to the palace and demand to know if he's her father."

"You're afraid she might leave? Or that she might get hurt?"

"Both. She's got a good head for design, works fast and hard. Zahir did well in hiring her. But I've come to know her since she's been here and she could be very easily hurt if he responded in any way other than joy at seeing her. Something tells me he wouldn't be happy to see her, and neither would King Ahmad. Jibril's married, isn't he?"

"For a long time," Leila confirmed, then a little more slowly asked, "How old is she?"

"I don't know. Maybe a few years younger than me."

"His eldest son is Zahir's age."

He rubbed his head, an ache stabbing behind one eye suddenly. "I can't tell her. Not yet. Maybe in a while."

"Dakan, if she's of royal blood, even if she is illegitimate we can't have her living alone and going about alone in the city. It's just not acceptable."

"She's not living entirely alone. She's got a live-in

housekeeper and Zahir put guards on her to serve as her escorts."

"But she's still alone. She doesn't have anyone to look out for her well-being."

"She has me," Dakan said, then immediately regretted it as his mother's brows shot skyward. "She's my friend. I'll keep anything bad from happening to her."

"You know that's not proper. Your father will insist."

"Then don't tell him. We're going to go visiting some healing centers next week—that will give me some time to ease her into the whole thing."

"I won't lie to him."

"You don't have to lie. You just have to not mention it for a week or so."

He didn't want Nira living at the palace, and that's exactly what would happen the instant his father heard about this. He needed her in the penthouse, away from here. Somewhere they could be alone, yes, but not just because he lusted after her as if he'd never had a woman in his life. He needed to be alone with her, just talking with her and relaxing. She'd become his sanctuary, his Little London.

"You care for her."

He tried to think of what he could say to explain. His family loved him and he them, but he never truly felt understood when he was home. Which probably had something to do with his difficulty understanding himself sometimes. But Nira seemed to get him. Where words failed him, he simply nodded. "Yes. But don't go getting ideas."

"Who? Me? I have no ideas whatsoever. I'm sure the last idea I had was…in the nineties. And I'm far too tired to have ideas right now." She stood, bent and kissed the top of his head, and then wandered out of the room. "I think I'll have a nap. Then I need to get back to planning the party for Zahir and Adele, see where arrangements have been left. But first I'll send the *attar* to you with a tonic for your head."

"Why?"

"It's hurting. You always rub your forehead like that when your head hurts."

Maybe she did understand him better than he gave her credit for. She knew that much, at least. "Thank you, Mother. I'm glad you're home."

"Me too," she called, already out of the room.

The tour wouldn't take more than a few days, certainly not the whole week. He had until the last day at the latest to figure out how to tell Nira what he'd learned.

How did you tell someone they were very likely a royal bastard?

Nira dressed for practicality on the first day of their tour in loose-fitting linen trousers, a long tunic to cover her neck to wrists, and a matching scarf. The scarf still felt important to her. She wanted to belong, or at least feel like she could. Dressing correctly was an easy start, something she could control. And maybe people would see that she was trying, and give her a little more leeway if she did mess up or cause accidental offense. Kind of like an advance apology.

She heard the key in the lock and stood, grabbing the bag she'd packed with her sketchpad and pencils. They, together with her fully charged phone, would allow her to document anything she needed with sketches and or photos.

"Good morning," she said, her voice a little too chipper, but it morphed into surprise. Dakan wore robes, head to toe, he was like some exotic vision of a sexy lord of the desert.

He'd refused the robes every single other time she'd seen him, but now he was going to wear them? Even the brooding expression he wore couldn't detract from the effect he was having on her pulse.

"Did your advisors knock you down and change your clothes?"

"I'd actually even take that scenario." He placed two bags on the floor—one large canvas duffle bag and a suitcase. His hands free, he gathered up the yards of material of his robes, lifted them to show her the simple white linen trousers and T-shirt he wore beneath. "My parents returned from their holiday. The King insisted I wear robes since we're going out into the countryside in an official capacity. I'm stuck in them for the duration of the trip—which will actually be a little longer now."

"Why is that?"

"Tomorrow Father is sending me to the Immortal Fortress," Dakan answered. "Us, rather. I'll need entertainment, and I suppose this fits in with your desire to explore the culture. So you'll just be stuck with me for an extra day and we'll resume our trip on Wednesday and Thursday."

"What's the Immortal Fortress?"

"You don't know the story?"

"It's not one I'm familiar with."

"It's a fortress in the desert near the border. Very old, functionally abandoned until the yearly race. Traditionally, it's the King's duty, but since we were going to be out of the capital tomorrow, if he also goes into the desert, there are no Al Rahals within easy reach. There must always be a ruler in residence within easy reach. I'll tell you all about it tomorrow. We'll go and watch the race, crown the winner, and get back here for a relaxing evening."

A race didn't exactly sound like her kind of thing, but getting to experience anything in Mamlakat Almas besides work sounded like heaven. The fact that it was at an ancient fortress? Just amazing. Some opportunities only came once, how likely was it she'd get back there again?

"What's in the bags?"

"I may have failed to mention to them that we'll be returning to the city daily to sleep here. I'm taking the other bedroom. And the other is medical supplies. The helicopter is waiting for us on the roof."

He reached out and tested the weight of the material of her linen trousers. "This should do for now. Thursday's location's been getting enormous amounts of rain this season. We might end up canceling if it doesn't dry up—just so you're aware." He called to Tahira, who came out, instructed her to take the other bag to the second bedroom, when to expect their return, then held out his hand to Nira.

"Rainstorms and flooding in desert country?" she asked, "I bet they're enjoying that."

"It's rare, but there are stories of rains like that, just not within living memory."

Within minutes they'd boarded the helicopter, donned headphones and were whisked heavenward.

Dakan said nothing, just let her gaze out the window at the sand below, at the roll of early morning light casting perfect curving shadows off the dunes.

He'd taken her hand a few times when they'd been in public, and Nira had always assumed it was a protective thing—that she was out with him so he felt responsible for her safety. Then things had changed, and he'd begun taking her hand in the apartment when they were quite alone, and she knew the gesture had changed. It was just for the pleasure of touching.

But once they'd been seated in the helicopter, he'd taken it again, and sat now with their fingers intertwined, resting in his lap.

His thumb stroked the outside of her thumb, something he'd only done in private before now. Even in the back of the limo no one really had been able to see what had been going on, but here in the helicopter there were people sitting opposite them, and they'd definitely see.

Something was different.

The crew could hear anything she said to him, with everyone wearing the headphones with their mics. All she could do was peel her gaze from the landscape and look at him.

His eyes were closed, his head leaning back against the headrest, but he wasn't asleep.

Something was really wrong.

The only way she could think to get his attention was to squeeze his hand.

His eyes opened and he looked at her, brows up, questioning.

Nira silently mouthed, "What's wrong?"

Dakan shook his head, gave her hand another squeeze, and laid his head back again.

No "Tell you later" or indication that his reluctance to talk was because of their audience. He just didn't want to talk about it.

"Tomorrow we'll be flying further this way, and on Wednesday in the other direction over the royal desert abode. It's our oasis."

"You own an oasis?" As soon as the words were out, she felt dumb. Technically speaking, they kind of owned the country. "Why do you keep a desert abode? Isn't the desert harsh and somewhere you wouldn't want to live if you didn't have to?"

He shook his head. "You'll see tomorrow. The desert is harsh, but it's also beautiful."

"Can I see the royal abode? Is it another palace?"

"Tents. Massive luxurious tents. It actually looks more like a camp village—there are servants who live there year round, they have their own tents."

"On the way back on Wednesday can we stop and see it?"

"There won't be time. That flight is long."

The villages they were traveling to held no promise of

the architecture she loved, but they held the promise of glimpsing life for a normal person of Mamlakat Almas—something that would be closer to what he life could've been than what she experienced with Dakan. But the idea of a big luxurious tent? Man, she still wanted to see that. And an oasis in the desert? There were probably big palm trees and everything.

"Oh, well, it can't be that thrilling. Just green stuff amid the sand, right? No architecture."

"No domes," he confirmed with a tired smile, his head still back, his eyes still shut. His thumb resumed that rhythmic stroking, back and forth. It wasn't about pleasure. He was comforting her. Or maybe he was comforting himself.

Something was definitely wrong.

Little more than an hour later they landed a mile or so from a moderate-sized village she'd seen from above. A small clean car waited for them, and once the bags had been transferred, she and Dakan piled into the back seat.

Once again, within the confines of a vehicle, Dakan took her hand.

Two men sat in the front, and as one started driving toward the village, the other chattered away in such a fast, excited cadence that Nira only managed to catch a stray word here and there, but as they drove into the town, down the narrow streets bordered by squat clay-brick buildings, her excitement turned into something else. She realized how hard she'd begun to squeeze Dakan's hand only when he covered their clasped hands and rubbed.

The car rolled into what she could only assume was the market, which was a smaller version of the one Dakan had dragged her from on that first day they'd met.

"He says we're going to the big building on the left, and that we'll probably have a bit of a wait to meet with the healer."

"What language is he speaking?"

"It's Arabic, just a local dialect. You'll develop an ear for it by the end of the day. Listen for words you understand, and use them as guideposts to work out what the sounds would be normally."

Right. She couldn't even come up with words usually, figuring out what words these words sounded like? Pretty much the same skill.

Outside a squat, dusty-looking building the car stopped and their guide saw them inside.

"You wanted to see what would be familiar to people," he said, and she could feel the jerk smirking behind her as he spoke.

"Yes, I do want to see..."

The chattering man opened the door for them into a room choked with people. It couldn't have been more than four meters on any side, and there were only half as many chairs as were needed. People stood to wait, sat on the floor, sat together in one chair...

What could she do with this? She wanted to provide seating for anyone who had to wait at the hospital, not leave them to stand or sit on the floor.

Maybe low bench-style padded seats and creative use of the decor to build in places someone could perch... aside from chairs and couches.

Their talkative guide clapped his hands, getting everyone's attention, and then announced Dakan.

"That's not necessary," Dakan said, just a little too late. Immediately people began rising from the floor and their chairs, an offer of seats coming from all around the room.

"We're going to have to sit," Dakan murmured behind her, "They're offering hospitality. It'd be rude not to accept."

Nira nodded and though it felt wrong she followed Dakan to a single wide, armless chair and then squeezed onto it with him. She made her thanks, then met the kind gaze of an elderly woman to her left and smiled while Dakan began speaking to people to the right, telling them all the good things he'd heard about this healer. Probably lying to charm them—she knew he didn't really want to include the healers with the doctors, but he made a good show of it. It was a common political skill.

But Nira had become so attuned to Dakan and his ways in the time they had known each other that she saw the stiff formality in the way he addressed these people. Even though they might not notice that his usual charm wasn't up to snuff, she could even feel where their bodies touched that the usually relaxed Dakan had gone rigid.

He claimed to like people, but the prospect of speaking to all these people made him feel uncomfortable.

When there was a break in Dakan's conversation, the woman to her left spoke and it took Nira a moment to work out what she'd said. He was right, once she found her guideposts it became almost clear.

Was she a princess?

"No. I'm an architect," she said, speaking as slowly as she always did, with lots of pauses to try and recall words. But those nerves she normally felt when trying to speak the language weren't there. Their dialect was different, so if she made a mistake or pronounced something in a way that sounded silly or childlike, they probably wouldn't notice.

"The Prince hired me to design a new big healing facility for the capital. He brought me here so I could see a good one."

The woman smiled and nodded, and it presented Nira with the perfect opportunity. She fetched her sketchbook and a pencil and asked, "Would you mind giving me your advice?"

When the woman nodded and gestured for Nira to continue, she asked, "If you were designing a new room to wait in, what would you do differently?"

Informal polling method, to be sure, but effective. Once the woman answered, another woman a short distance away added to what was said. Before long, she was getting suggestions faster than her pencil could keep up with them.

They waited a good hour before Dakan got to go back with the healer, though it didn't seem like it with all the conversation happening around him.

Once Nira had asked for opinions and started taking notes—taking the people seriously—everyone wanted to give their ideas. He spent part of the time translating for her as they spoke too fast for her to understand much.

It started out being about the waiting room, then went from there to other aspects of the treatment. People weren't as averse to the idea of Western medicine as his father and that barely used hospital made it seem. Infections were a big worry to them.

Before he even got back to speak with the man he'd come to see, he had made a note to text Zahir that he was right about the blending, at least for now. If nothing else, it'd help the people migrate to the new system to have the healers they were used to there as well. He just wasn't convinced that their father wouldn't wrestle control back to the healers no matter how it started out.

Once Dakan fixed a problem, he liked it to stay fixed. That rarely happened in medicine, but with physical ailments there was always something tangible that could be done. There were defined steps to take—do this, if it doesn't work or the situation's too advanced for this, do that. Escalating plans of attack to defeat a physical foe—an ailment, disease, or injury, and people usually didn't fight treatment.

Emotions were harder to fix, the emotional landscape like constantly shifting sand.

He should probably stop thinking of the hospital as

something that would fix their problems. He couldn't guess what people—like Father—might do with it once they got it set up.

When the healer summoned him back, Dakan whispered in Nira's ear, "Will you be all right by yourself?"

She nodded and smiled over her shoulder at him, a peculiarly happy expression for someone talking about work. And chairs.

"If you need me, shout my name and I'll come." He kept his voice low, took his bag and rose, leaving Nira to fend for herself with the people in the waiting room.

Over the next half an hour he discussed ideas to incorporate doctors into the current system without overriding the healers and about building a new country-owned facility to take the place of the current building, allowing more room for treatment and patients and those who came with them.

By the time he returned to the waiting room he actually felt pretty positive about the whole thing.

He spotted Nira right where he'd left her, and she gestured him over as soon as their eyes met. With his much lighter bag on his shoulder, he approached and crouched down to listen as she began to gesture to a mother with her sick child beside her. The little girl, no more than five, lay limply against her mother's shoulder, her face flushed and her eyes showing the splotchy redness of recent tears.

An ear infection, Nira told him. Something they hadn't been able to shake.

Normally, he would've passed by, not inviting himself to minister to someone else's patient, but he couldn't turn down a direct plea for help. Especially when he had the antibiotics that would help.

Over the next quarter-hour he examined the child, administered a loading dose of antibiotics, spoke to the healer about irrigating the ear, and went over the importance of taking all the antibiotics just as he detailed.

It was routine, so routine that he could've done it in his sleep, but it still made him feel good. Useful. Helpful. And something else...an emotion he couldn't quite put his finger on and didn't want to examine.

By the time they left the building he was actually looking forward to the next facility visit, even if it would be more of the same.

"That was something to see," Nira said, cutting into his thoughts. "You're good with kids."

Their guide had gone to fetch the car, which left him a moment to let his guard down with her.

"I told you emergency medicine was Zahir's territory, and that mine was the land of the simple family doctor." He could say that to her, but it wasn't an accurate test. "Keep in mind, though, that was my *second* patient. It's probably easy to be good with kids when you only see one patient every few weeks."

"Your territory?" Nira said. "That's the second time you've used that word with reference to what you or Zahir do. You say it like that, it sounds like these old dogs our neighbor had when I was little. I can't even hear that word any more without hearing it in Mr. Benjamin's voice: 'Don't mind Chester—he's just marking his territory.' You talk about your territory and I immediately get the mental image of you and Zahir running all over, peeing on everything."

He laughed so loudly, so suddenly that he scared people walking out of the healer's building. It was probably against royal protocol, laughing and treating patients in public. He pulled his gaze to the sky, then the horizon, looking for neutral ground, but the smile stayed on his face.

"Sorry. Sometimes I say things and everybody regrets it."

"I don't regret it. I'm just glad you said it in English."

He laughed again, and their car pulled up so he opened the door for her. "Get in."

They climbed in and once they'd settled she turned to look at him again then reached up to adjust the hang of his *keffiyeh*, pushing back the white material that had fallen forward to conceal his face from her. "Did your talk with him go well?"

"It did, actually. And that sort of public meeting you held with the waiting room gave me a few more ideas. I'm going to run them by Zahir, but I think we've worked out some programs that will make things much better."

"Did he want to work with you?"

Dakan nodded. "Zahir was right, so long as it doesn't get corrupted and out of balance. Having both will be better."

CHAPTER NINE

THE MOMENT THEY stepped through the penthouse door that evening, Dakan pulled off the robe and *keffiyeh*. If he got to be here with her for a couple of days, he'd do it as freely as he could, squeeze every ounce of pleasure out of their time together, no room for the negatives that crept in when he was alone.

Once he told Nira about Prince Jibril, the peace he felt with her would come to an end. That idea ate at him, made him want to keep her close for as long as he could. Made him spend all day ignoring the ticking clock because he didn't like how it made him feel.

He hadn't been thinking about a long thing between them anyway. But he wasn't ready for it to end yet.

"Do you need Tahira to clean your robes for tomorrow?" Nira asked, eyeing his exceedingly rumpled casual outfit he'd been wearing beneath. "Looks more comfortable than your usual suit."

Hearing her name, the housekeeper appeared, informed them that dinner was nearly ready, and spirited away the discarded clothing to launder.

Dakan flopped onto the couch and leaned back, closing his eyes.

Tomorrow. He'd tell her tomorrow. Tonight he'd enjoy the bubble of peace in this place.

"You look like you've just run a marathon," she said

from very close by a short time later. "Or maybe like you're very drunk."

"Sleepy," he murmured, then opened his eyes to baggy green shorts and a T-shirt.

It wasn't revealing at all, but after spending so much time with her, and only seeing only her hands and face, the display of shapely tanned legs and the braless wonderland that was her chest… "You're the one dressed for bed."

"Yep," she said, sitting beside him, crawling under his arm and settling her cheek against his chest. "I need to ask you a question."

It was all very innocent, but it still made his mind race. She tucked her feet up under her and got comfortable.

"Ask away."

"You've been different today. I noticed it right away, and I thought at first maybe it was because you were sleepy, but it stayed with you all day. You're different when you're with people than you are with me. Actually, you're different with your patients too. Not just little kids, I don't think. I noticed it with the man at the hospital, but I didn't really put it together until I got to know you better."

He let his hand cup her shoulder, holding her there against him as they relaxed. "Different how?" He knew he behaved differently at different times, but he'd thought of the difference as upholding expectations—something everyone did.

"Stiff."

"With who?"

"Just with people you're interacting with. You even kind of do it here, not with me but with Tahira. You just suddenly stop being Dakan and become Prince Dakan. And then when you were with the little girl today you were Dr. Dakan, I guess. But he's more like regular Dakan than Prince Dakan. And when you were holding her and talking to her mother? It was really split. Your face changed, your voice changed—you were Prince Dakan from the neck up. The rest of your body was Regular Dakan, just a man comforting a child in distress. Like you carried and rocked sick children all the time."

"Prince Dakan is stiff? So I had a stiff head and a relaxed body?"

"Yes. You had a stiff head and voice and a relaxed body—what I could tell with the robes on. You hold your shoulders differently. I haven't seen that split personality thing happen before, but it definitely happened today." She tilted her head to look at him, then reached up and combed her fingers through his hair, which felt too nice to stop her from doing it, even if this cozy couch cuddle shouldn't be happening. "I thought you liked helping people have better lives."

"I do," he said quickly, and then paused to remember what he had been thinking at the time, but it was too much to think about when her fingers slid through his hair, soothing away the tension he'd carried today. "It was different today."

"Different how?"

"I feel obligated to be a certain way when I'm here, and I'm used to being another way when I treat patients— which I've only ever done in England. Here I've only ever been what was expected, or I tried to be within limits. I guess I don't know how to be both at once."

"Maybe you're just over-thinking it. Who says you have to be a certain way?"

"Everyone since I was small."

"I think, as a man, people will forgive you being a rascal more than they would a princess. You can rely on your cheeky charm with the masses, not just with people you speak with privately, or in other countries. You don't think they'd like the real Dakan?"

"I'm sure they would, but liking and respecting or following someone, feeling confident in their ability to lead your country? That's two different things. And I have to be ready to be…what I desperately don't want to be."

"Which is what?"

"Heir, should something happen to Zahir. People need to have confidence in me, just in case. When they don't, that leads to succession instability. The Al Rahal line is very old. We survived different empires as a sometimes puppet kingdom until the Ottomans began to branch into the area and our king made a stand to avoid being swallowed up again. Which is what the race is about tomorrow." He caught her wrist to pull her hand back to his chest. "You remember the story about the Lego house and the trebuchet?"

"How could I forget?"

"The part of that I didn't tell you was that it was my idea. Sort of. My actual idea was to use these old battle axes and chop it up. Zahir upped the game and went for the trebuchet."

"And got into trouble for it."

"We would've gotten into trouble for the axes too, but it wouldn't have been nearly as amazing as the trebuchet."

"So he made getting in trouble worth it?"

"He just did it better. I'm not saying that because I'm looking for sympathy. I know my limitations, and I think it works out well this way. There are things he's better at, and things I'm better at. So we have a wide range of stuff covered."

"Territory?" Nira mouthed the word up at him.

He squeezed her, groaning, "Would the word 'claim' make you happier?"

"Yes. It sounds like an old-fashioned gold prospector in a gold rush somewhere. I like it."

"Noted."

"But you're saying that being a prince is something that Zahir is better at?"

"Yes. Being a leader. Taking a tiny idea and making it

powerful, and having the ability to inspire people to follow him through it."

"But you don't like being a follower, and you don't want to be the leader."

He grimaced. "When you put it together like that, it sounds very egocentric and spoiled. Selfish. But maybe it's true. He's the leader, I'm the follower, and he should never let me lead him astray."

"And you wanting him to come back is noble, not just about freeing you to go back to England."

"See? You did it again. Made it sound bad. Maybe I shouldn't talk about this stuff. Better to not upset the status quo." Only he wasn't the one who'd upset the status quo. It was this showdown between Zahir and Father—which Zahir had apparently won, and yet *he* was still here.

She slipped her hand free of his and slid it up his chest, the good tingle left in the trail of her touch commanding him to open his eyes and look at her.

The sweetest eyes met his. Beautiful, yes, but they had the kind of warmth that made being seen by her feel tangible, made him want to stretch out and have her look at him whole.

"I'm asking you questions to make you think, not to criticize you. Because I want to stay here for as long as I can, and I want you to stay too. I also want you to be happy, but something is making you unhappy."

She did. He could see it in her eyes. The prospect of telling her about her father was making him unhappy right now, other than that he'd had a pretty good day. His position didn't really bother him, he was just trying to answer her questions. Answering them let him pretend he didn't have other important things to say that she'd spent her whole life desperate to hear—the dread that ate at him when he considered her future should Jibril acknowledge her and accept her as an Al-Haaken was hard to ignore.

Her hand slid from his chest to his cheek, and she

leaned up to press her lips to his brow. The soft, lingering kiss started there then wandered over his cheek and eventually settled on his mouth. Gentle, languid, it was as unhurried as it was thorough, kissing with no ulterior motives. His body reacted. He couldn't feel the slide of her tongue against his without wanting to take her to bed, but the slow, easy pace drained tension from his body, giving him comfort he'd needed all day.

By the time she lifted her head he didn't know whether to stretch out and cuddle her or take her to bed.

The second being the less likely option for now, he pushed her hair back, tucked it behind her ear and looked into her eyes again.

Peace won. He wrapped his arms around her, and once she'd settled against his chest they waited for dinner in easy silence.

The race to the Immortal Fortress was a morning affair, but even getting up to fly at first light couldn't put a damper on Nira's excitement.

Tents littered the desert all around the ruin, camps of families who'd come to enjoy the races, along with stables for the camels.

The helicopter touched down and an SUV waited to drive them the short distance to the ancient citadel. Today Nira couldn't touch Dakan—he was there on behalf of the King, and propriety wouldn't allow those little displays of affection, though she could sit with him to watch the race.

The fortress had one hole blasted in the wall facing the border, but the rest of it was remarkably intact. Stones that had fallen from the hole had long ago been moved to the side, though never carted away, the damage never repaired. The corridor and staircase up to the roof held firm. It was damaged, but it kept standing strong and true.

On the roof, a platform had been erected with two large ornate chairs—thrones, really—and a smaller, simpler chair facing them, all set beneath an awning to shield the royals from the sun.

Dakan took the larger chair, gestured for her to sit, and refreshments were immediately brought.

"Why are we on the roof?" she asked in a whisper when people had moved back enough that she didn't feel so conspicuous speaking to him.

"Because the King of Mamlakat Almas was on the roof, having his breakfast on that day. He'd sent his army to another part of the border to engage the Ottomans and hold them out. We'd have been happy as allies, but when did being conquered by anyone ever sit well with a small country, even one with shared faiths? The day before the battle, a messenger arrived at first light on camelback, scaled the wall, delivered word to the King, whom he'd seen on the battlements."

Nira sat, utterly absorbed by Dakan's story. She could see it all in her mind, and somehow felt so much more attached to it than she ever had to history classes at school.

"What did the King do?"

"Gave him food, water, a change of camel, and a message to summon his army to White Stone Castle." He pointed down to the building they sat upon. "The Ottoman army arrived ahead of his, but the King, his Queen, and all the people in the castle armed the cannons and fought with whatever they had. Hot oil they'd used for cooking."

"The Ottomans were the ones who blew a hole in the wall?"

"And the cries of the Almasian army behind them turned the battle around. There were terrible losses on both sides, but Suleiman the Great continued his march to the gulf, sidestepping Mamlakat Almas, and we've remained independent since. The third chair will be for the first racer to reach us and climb the rope."

"There's a rope?" She'd missed that part. "What do they win?"

"A fat purse of gold coins, and the opportunity to serve a year as the King's Messenger at functions in the city and small ceremonies—of which there are many—where they bring a message and read it out to whomever is in attendance."

"When did they start calling it the Immortal Fortress?"

"Not for another century, I don't think. They expected it to crumble in where the hole had been punched, but it never has. The desert tries to swallow it up now and then, they sweep out the sand a couple times per year, but it's still in great condition. The story now is that as long as it stands, the country will never be invaded from the north. The Kings began carrying out the race in the eighteenth century as a remembrance that the actions of one person can help the whole country."

As soon as he said the words, the smile he'd worn changed…like he'd only heard his own words after they were out of his mouth.

Nira reached over to touch his hand, even though she knew she shouldn't, and he squeezed her hand then let go abruptly and turned to the organizers. "Are we ready to begin the race?"

"All has been made ready, Highness. The racers are on standby."

Dakan nodded and gave word for the cannon to be fired.

By Thursday morning, Nira had recovered from their trip to the Immortal Fortress, and was over her excitement at traveling to far-flung villages.

Wednesday's trip had been long and exhausting, though when they'd flown over the oasis she had regretted that she hadn't been able to go there. Maybe she could convince him to take her once the hospital building began.

As a tour and a chance to see the country, it did not fail

to amaze her, but she didn't learn anything else on that visit that would help with the design.

Prince Dakan had kept busy, talking to people and trying to be whatever was expected of him, and she could clearly see the differences now that she was looking for them. Prince Dakan gave test vials to a man and ordered samples of the water taken from the therapeutic springs for testing. Regular Dakan would've gone into the springs himself to test them, or something else active. Prince Dakan didn't reek of vigor and activity like he did when no one but her was looking. He'd be easy to resist if she hadn't come to actually care about him enough to look beyond his royal persona.

He was still a puzzle, though.

He wanted to make the lives of his people better, and he didn't want anyone looking to him for leadership or decision-making, but he also didn't trust the decisions made by others.

The trebuchet incident kept coming up, and always with a different emotion attached to it. She wasn't sure whether it was a happy memory or a sad one any more.

All she knew for sure was that he was a man in conflict with himself, but she didn't know whether he ever expressed those conflicting opinions to his family. She'd never met the King, but intuition said he'd be domineering—that was perhaps what a king had to be. The idea of Dakan having any kind of discussion with his father, where he was actually listened to, seemed far-fetched. But Zahir had struck her as someone easy to talk to, and Dakan obviously loved his brother. He could talk to Zahir. They might not agree, but just talking things through resolved most problems.

Like with her mum. Nira wanted to talk about the situation with her father, she just didn't feel like she could. She didn't want to cause pain, but also she didn't want to deal with the frustration that came any time she tried. If they could just talk things through, if she could just understand...

"Nira?" Dakan said at her side, getting her attention.

She looked across the back seat to the open car door where he stood, bag in hand.

"We're here."

Facility number three. At least the geography was different here. Tuesday and Wednesday had been dry and sandy with little in the way of visible rocks. Today they'd made it to the area that had been experiencing lots of rain, but arrived right after the rain decided to move out and the ground had drained most of the water away.

The facility sat at the base of a rather steep cliff, which didn't seem safe. She grabbed her bag as she climbed out, and paused to look up. "Do they suffer from falling rocks?"

"The ground here is very stable. There hasn't been so much as a tremor in Mamlakat Almas for decades." He gestured for her to walk ahead of him. "Rain is even a rare event here. Except this season. But there's no rain today, and no signs of flooding. I think we're safe."

She stepped inside and moved in far enough to survey the room and let Dakan enter with his huge medical bag. There were fewer people in the waiting room than had been at the other two, and a number of chairs sat empty, perhaps due to the rains.

One empty seat was beside a very pregnant woman with a baby playing at her feet. He twisted to look as they came in, and started crawling toward them. Before the woman could catch him, his speed increased along with the volume of happy gurgling baby noises as he made a beeline right for them.

The alarmed woman scooted forward in her seat as she tried to find her center of balance so she could stand.

"Wait, I'll get him," Nira called to the woman, bending to scoop up the baby before he got trampled on in the close confines of the waiting area.

As soon as she had him in her arms, the baby immediately reached for her scarf and began tugging at it as Nira walked back to the distraught woman. "I believe this is yours." She tried to disentangle his fingers from the scarf, which now was horribly skewed on her head, and smiled despite the mess she knew she must look.

The woman reached for him, but it took both of them working together to get his little grabby hands unwound from the silk so Nira could put him down.

She chanced a look at Dakan, found him smirking and offering her no assistance, at least until the healer saw him and took him straight back.

"He is quite strong!" Nira said, when they finally got him back into his mother's arms.

"Forgive us, Princess. I think you must look like my sister to him," she explained.

Nira reached up to try and right the mess, but found it just wouldn't seat again. "There is nothing to forgive. And I'm no princess. The Prince hired me to design a hospital for the capital. We're touring places of healing so I can design the hospital well."

She made her way through what she wanted to say more easily than she had been doing, finding the words she wanted—or something very close to them—without long, tense silences. What she couldn't find was a way to tie the scarf appropriately again without the aid of a mirror.

Time to give up. She unpinned the colorful silk from where it covered her neck and unwound it. The best she could do on her own without a mirror was to drape it over her head and tie it under her hair so that her head was covered.

Smiling to smooth over any awkwardness, she began the same conversation she'd held at the first two facilities. This time she led with, "I was going to ask you what you'd change to improve the waiting room, but I think I have an idea. Somewhere for little ones to play safely?"

She reached for her bag to get out her sketchbook and pencil to take notes, and felt a rumble in her seat. The hair on the nape of her neck stood on end, brushing firmly against the knotted silk when she turned her head to look around for the sound.

Earthquake? Dakan said...

The sound of earth moving crashed outside, and she dropped her sketchbook. Everyone looked as alarmed as she felt, so this was definitely not a normal sound.

They should get away from the cliff, outside the building.

By the time the thought solidified, most of the other people had risen and rushed toward the door.

Yell if you need me, Dakan had said, as he always did.

Nira screamed his name, then pitched to her feet. Her legs felt encased in half-set concrete, but she was up.

Without a word, she took the baby from the woman's arms and anchored him to her chest. People piled out of the only exit; no one stopped to help them. She hooked her free arm under the woman's closest arm and strained to help her to her feet.

Something smashed into the outside of the side wall, then several more somethings followed in rapid succession, each issuing a resounding crack.

The baby screamed, and Nira did too as the surface of the wall bowed inward, cracks appearing from the center.

Behind her, she heard Dakan shout her name. As she looked back, the wall crashed in and the floor fell from beneath them.

Dakan felt the building shake, heard the rumble, and then screams came through the wall separating them from the waiting room.

The elderly healer, dumbstruck, gripped the frame of the window beside him and stared at the door.

Power surged through Dakan on a wave of fear, and he sprang from his chair. A moment later he had the door open to the waiting room. All he could see was dust in the air, and light behind it where there shouldn't be light.

"Nira!" he yelled, in time to see the other side of the building collapse and three silhouettes disappear.

It was her. He didn't have to see her clearly, he felt it in the roar ripping through his belly.

His lungs seized before he could call out again.

Dust. Cover your mouth.

Ripping the robes over his head, Dakan paused long enough to shred the shoulder seam of one arm, pulling it entirely free of the garment, and then tugging it over his head until it covered his face from his cheeks down.

Once out the door of the consultation room, the floor seemed intact to the front exit but looked dodgy. He tested it with one foot, but it bowed beneath the lightest pressure.

Their way was blocked.

Get the old man out; find Nira.

Grabbing his bag, Dakan used the hard bottom to push the glass out of the frame in the solitary window, then tossed the bag through.

"Come on, we have to get out," he said, offering a hand to the elder healer. It took both hands to ease the frail man through the window. A minute later he had the bag in one hand and the man's arm in the other, and was pulling him away from the broken building.

Outside, people had gathered, most of whom he recognized from his time in the waiting room.

His heart in his throat, he searched every grimy face for Nira's on the chance that she'd crawled out. Nothing.

All of his people were worth worrying about, and he was concerned for them too, but for Nira… Terror clawed at his guts.

The pregnant woman wasn't there either, or the baby.

Leaving the bag with the old man, Dakan rushed back to the front of the building to survey the damage. Big rocks. He'd told her they were safe.

They hadn't come through the roof, though.

To the left of the building he saw it, a slide of earth at the bottom of the cliff face behind another house that had been damaged, and a path leading from that mound of wet earth to the rocks piled against the side of the healing center.

A moment later he had his satellite phone out and was calling for the helicopter.

The call made, he began organizing people to take a head count, find out who else was still inside. And once that was done he doused his severed sleeve mask with water from his bag and put it back on, creating a slightly better filter.

He was going in.

Nira awoke to the sound of a baby crying in a high frantic keen that brought everything rushing back.

He lay face down across her belly. She could feel him there, angry, squirming and scared. His cries sounded wrong to her somehow, raspy and wet. Something else lay over one of her feet. Something soft and warm.

She opened her eyes, dust and dirt falling in and causing them to stream as she tried to see what was going on. Picking the baby up, she moved him so he lay down her chest with his head by hers in the vain hope that being face to face with her might comfort him.

That done, she curled forward, trying to look toward her feet, but another coughing fit took her, shaking her and the baby until she got past whatever threatened her airway.

He cried louder. She wanted to cry too, but she still had an inventory to take.

One more effort and she lifted herself enough to look

towards her feet. One of the woman's legs lay across hers, not moving.

Was she breathing? The view to the woman's torso was blocked by debris, and she couldn't hear the sound of breathing above the baby's labored, choking cries.

Dakan. Where was he? Was he down here too?

What was she supposed to do? Should she stay put and not collapse the rubble more, or just take a chance on getting herself out, regardless of what happened to the rest of the building if she went plowing through?

She laid her head back down, one arm still wrapped around the baby. She squeezed him enough to let him know she was there, then set to rubbing his back, trying to shush him as she took inventory on the room and tried to wake the woman.

She hadn't asked her name. What kind of person met someone and spoke with them but didn't ask their name?

"Hello?"

"Hi?"

"My friend?"

She tried several more greetings, trying to get some answer from the woman.

Nothing came. No movement.

Not far above her, maybe five feet, floor joists jutted from the part of the building still above ground. It wasn't deep enough to be a basement. Crawlspace of some kind? Some of the joists remained connected to the floor and angled down to touch the bare earth beneath. One lay across her other arm. She wriggled it free without too much trouble but it soon began to throb.

More dust and dirt showered down on them, and the baby's coughing cries began to sound like gasps for air.

"Nira?"

Dakan's voice, loud and rough with fear, carried through the opening above to her, even above the sound of the baby's cries. She patted his back, trying to get him to calm as she called back to Dakan.

"I'm okay, I think. But the baby can't breathe!"

"I hear him. Is your scarf still on?" he yelled back.

She squirmed to pull her other arm free from the tight space it was wedged into. When she did so, one of the joists directly above her, one that had one end planted to the right of her hip and the other still wedged against the remains of the flooring, fell a few inches.

"The floor is coming down!" she screamed, kicking her legs free from beneath the woman's and shooting her feet into the air to catch the bottom of the joist.

"Dakan!"

He didn't answer. God, where had he gone? He hadn't even finished his instructions about the baby.

He'd asked about her scarf. She pulled it off with her now free hand and shook it out as best she could, then put it around the baby's face, holding it with one hand as the other patted his back to try and help him clear his lungs. She didn't know what else to do.

Her mother had been right. She'd come to the Middle East, and now she was going to die here. Like stupid tourists who got stupid ideas about seeing exotic foreign lands and wound up being crushed by spontaneous building demolition.

The baby coughed hard once more and began to breathe more easily.

"Nira?"

He'd come back. He'd come back.

"He's a little better, I think," she called back. "But his mother hasn't moved. Or answered. And the floor! Dakan, the floor is going to fall if I let go…"

He called from above again, "I'm going to climb down to you. I found a way from the healer's consultation room."

The consultation room?

That was…

She looked through the dust-clogged shafts of light and got her bearings. She'd fallen straight down, so the consultation room Dakan where had gone was...on the other side the floor she was holding up.

"No! Dakan! No! Don't come that way!"

"There's no other way," he called back.

"Don't come that way. I can't hold more weight. Most of it's being transferred to the ground, but if the angle shifts, it's going to come down!"

She waited a few seconds, preparing to tense her legs for all she had. Was he going to do it anyway? Was he still up there?

The baby started screaming again in earnest now that he'd had a chance to catch his breath, and pushed at the scarf she kept pulled over his face.

"What should I do? Can you see another way?"

Nira lifted her head to look past the rubble and the dust.

"How much of the floor is intact in the waiting area?"

"It's not safe to walk on. I tested it."

"Get to the crawlspace. Find an access door. Or knock a hole in the foundation below the consult room and come in below the floor."

She patted the baby again and made a shushing sound. "Hurry!"

CHAPTER TEN

OUTSIDE THE HALF-COLLAPSED building men approached, running with tools in hand. When Dakan relayed Nira's suggestion to the men, they went round to the far end of the building to begin knocking a hole in the foundation.

Dakan left them to it and went to pack a small bag to take down with him. Face masks. Water. Small respirator. Bandages. His pathetic penlight, which seemed completely unequal to the task of lighting up a low, dusty basement. Crawlspace. Whatever she'd called it.

He made it back to the building in time for them to start pulling rocks out of the opening.

One large stone came, then some smaller ones. He couldn't even hear over the noise whether or not the floor was still up, whether Nira was calling for him, whether the baby was even still crying. Metal on stone, metal on stone...strike after strike until an opening big enough for him to squeeze through appeared.

"No one else come in until I say so," he instructed. It'd benefit no one to have more hurt if there was some way around it. Scout first. Make evacuation decisions after.

Dakan pulled a mask on and crawled through the hole and down to the packed earth floor about a meter below.

He immediately heard the crying baby.

When he'd slithered his legs through, he got back up and reached out for his bag.

He pulled the mask off his mouth so she could hear him. "Nira?"

"Please, hurry!" she called back immediately. He put the mask on and turned on his flashlight, then stood as much as he was able to move at a crouch to where the floor had fallen in.

The crawlspace wasn't a solid open rectangle—there was a corner in the earth, leading to what he imagined would appear L-shaped if viewed from above. Along the walls leading to the turn, there were shelves with jars, cans and dry goods...which meant there had to be stairs somewhere. He found them when he rounded the corner, still intact despite the floor above partially covering them, built into the side of what must have been a trapdoor concealed in the waiting room.

Just to the left, he saw the woman's head, then bent to crawl under wooden boards to reach her.

"I found her," he called to Nira, checking for a pulse and then listening to her labored breathing. "She's alive. Can you see her?"

"Her legs were on mine."

He dropped the awkward bag so he could crawl over the prone woman, where he found Nira on her back, her feet braced against a thick, precarious-looking board above her, and a screaming baby on her chest.

The air suddenly felt even denser than the dust, heavy and hard to breathe through. Every instinct told him to drag her and the baby out of the way and get them out of there. But the woman... There had to be a way to get them all.

"If I hold the floor, can you crawl out with him?"

"I don't think so. My arm hurts. Take him. Take him out and come back."

She was putting on a brave face, but he could hear fear making her voice wobble.

He couldn't look at her arm yet, not until he got back.

He also couldn't leave her here without any help. If nothing else, he could help her breathe better. He whisked his mask off, secured it over her mouth and tucked behind her ears.

"I think I saw a faster way to get the woman out. I'm going to get them to knock another hole in the foundations at the corner of the room right next to where the floor fell. Is that okay?"

She paused to think. Maybe it wasn't just his mind that had become sluggish… After a few long seconds of looking in the direction he'd mentioned, she nodded.

"Should be." Her words were muffled, but he could understand her. "Crawl over me with him, it'll be easier to get through that way than climbing over her. Don't put any weight on anything wooden."

"I'll be right back. Hold on a little longer," he said, swinging one leg over her and then the other, then picked the baby up from her chest, clamped him snugly to his chest with one arm, stuck the flashlight in his mouth, and crawled through with the still screaming baby, retrieving his bag along the way.

It felt like it took him a year to make it to where he could stand and walk at a crouch back to the opening.

Once there, he passed the screaming baby through, following it up with the bag, and directed the men to make another hole in the foundations at the back of the building, and gave the best location he could, along with another order to do it carefully because rocks tumbling in could hurt someone. The stairs would make it easier to carry the woman out without so much danger of dropping her.

When he finally made it back to Nira, her legs were shaking and she looked pale. He grabbed her wrist and checked her pulse. It was fast and her arm shook just as her legs did. "How do I brace the wood?" he asked, just as the sound of the pickaxes starting to attack the foundations came to them. It sounded like the right area at least.

Pushing the mask back, she got a deeper breath and said, "Big rock Plant it at the base where it touches earth."

"How big?"

"Like a bowling ball with angles instead of smooth."

"Okay." He'd seen them pulling stones like that out of the foundations. This sent him hurrying back to the opening once more.

He heard rocks falling in at the other site, but there wasn't anything he could do about it now. He gave instructions to the men still at the hole, and they produced three rocks that were almost the right size, but not quite.

Dakan took the two biggest and hurried back.

"There aren't any that big. These two were the biggest…"

She looked at them, considering. "Wedge the small one under the space between the wood and the dirt, then put the big one behind it. When you have it, tell me and we'll test it."

Dakan had to backtrack around her head to reach the end. He did as instructed, roughly shoving the rocks into the earth in the hope they'd slide slower.

"Take your feet away."

He tilted his head to get a visual of her and watched as she relaxed her legs but didn't remove them. The board started to slide again and her legs kicked back into position, taking the weight once more. Strain showed on her features and in her groans.

He pushed on the rocks. "It's not working."

"Step on it. Use your feet. Legs are stronger than arms."

That wobble of fear turned into a full voice tremor that shifted the sounds into some kind of wrongness that alarmed him further. He had to get her out of there.

Dakan braced himself against the intact rock foundation, one foot on the big rock he'd placed, and ground down with all his might.

The board actually slid in the other direction, enough to lift the tilted floor a few inches.

"Did you lift it?"

"Yes," he said, then, "Is that bad?"

"No. I'm letting go..."

Once again she relaxed her legs, but this time the boards didn't immediately start to fall.

"It's holding. Can you get up?"

He rounded the treacherous board, careful not to touch it, and reached for her unhurt arm to pull her through the hole to where the woman lay. Nira nodded toward the woman. "We should get her away from the—"

At that moment daylight spilled in through the foundations where the men were making their holes.

"I don't even have a neck brace for her," he muttered, shaking his head.

"Is the baby okay?"

"I don't know." He didn't know if either baby was okay, the one he'd carried out or the one still in the woman's womb. But they had a way out close by now. He climbed the stairs and helped shove the rocks outward. When the hole was big enough, he stepped down the few stairs, grabbed Nira and hustled her up to the hole. "You first."

"You need help with her. She's heavy."

"Your arm is hurt. Don't argue. The other men will come and help me move her."

He grabbed her hips and thrust her up and through the hole, and someone helped pull her through, then two men came down to help him with the pregnant woman. She still hadn't regained consciousness. He took out his stethoscope and listened to both mother and fetal heartbeats for a minute, counting. "Hers is a little slow, but the baby's holding on."

Within a quarter hour the helicopter lifted off with all his patients on board. Nira held fast to the baby even though her arm hurt. With some effort, she kept him from removing the makeshift hearing protection Dakan had fashioned with cotton, gauze pads, and tape. There was nothing else Dakan could do for anyone right now, but he'd get them to the trauma center in Dubai at least.

With one hand keeping the unconscious woman's pulse monitored, he watched Nira and the intensity with which she watched the baby in her arms. She'd swaddled him snugly enough to mostly immobilize his arms, and watched his chest move since the headphones muffled her ability to hear his breathing.

So much for his plan to tell her everything tonight. His family would just have to understand. Nira wasn't moving to the palace yet. Once the woman and baby were off to Dubai, he'd call his mother to let her know, then examine Nira's injuries.

No one could expect him to lay all that on her after the day they'd had.

Tomorrow would have to sort itself out.

The helicopter touched down at the airport and Nira had to turn the baby over to the crew so they could transport him and his pregnant mother to the hospital in Dubai. It'd taken Dakan promising to send the helicopter back to the village to fetch the father for her to let go of him.

The one bright spot from it all was that the injured woman had briefly roused during the flight to the capital, and now they'd both receive the kind of medical care in another country that they should've been able to get in their own.

When they were gone, Dakan put an arm around Nira and steered her toward a car that she hadn't even seen arrive. As soon as she'd climbed in, sleep overtook her and the next thing she knew, he was gently rousing her outside the dreadful hospital.

"What are they going to do here? I don't want to be treated here."

"I'm going to X-ray your arm." He swung the door open and clamped an arm around her waist to get her out with him.

She moved with him. It was too hard to put up any real resistance right now. "You said there wasn't an X-ray."

"I had a temporary set up until the hospital is finished, and imported a couple of technicians."

"I don't think it's broken."

"Good. Let's double check."

She didn't want to double check. She wanted to go back to the flat, run a hot bath, and soak away the pain and the grime she carried in equal measure. But she got out, because getting out and getting it done would get her to that hot bath faster. "Where did you put it?"

"Behind the building in a bus, like the mobile diagnostic clinics they take to the villages in the UK. We'll move it inside when the room for it is built."

Inside the lobby, her gaze naturally drifted in the direction of the current remodel. Long pieces of plastic sheeting had been secured to the ceiling and hung to the floor, discouraging people from going into the surgical theater and keeping the construction dust somewhat under control.

So it was really happening. Not that she could see much. Dakan led her the other way and soon she was in a curtained bay, being handed a gown.

"I don't need a gown for an X-ray."

Dakan continued to hold it out to her. "A building fell on you, Nira. You had a beam fall on your arm, and you used your legs to keep the ceiling from collapsing. Put the gown on so I can examine you. Unless you want the other doctor on duty to do it."

"I don't want another doctor to do it."

"Good, because I wouldn't allow it anyway."

"Can I get the X-ray done first?"

"I'm looking for other areas to screen."

Nira sighed and turned around, "Unzip me, then. But

I'm only stripping down to my underthings, then you'll look at me and I'll get dressed again before we go to the bus for an X-ray. I'm not walking around in a hospital gown with my bum on display."

"Fair enough," Dakan said. So obviously he could compromise a little.

She felt the zip slide down until his knuckle brushed the small of her back. It was the simplest touch, but a wash of awareness that hit her. He might as well have licked her.

It was the wrong time and place for that kind of reaction. They were destined to be together, for at least a time...and she wanted it. She just didn't want it in a hospital bay.

To hurry things along, she tugged on the shoulders of her dress to dislodge the garment and wrestle her arms out of it.

"Is it ill fitting?" she heard him ask from behind her. "You're jerking at that material like it's stuck to you with glue." His hands closed over hers and he took over, easing the material down much too slowly. She wanted this over with.

Princess seaming in the simple green dress allowed it to fall to the floor as soon as the zipper passed her waist and opened to the hips. She stepped out of it, picked it up, and faced Dakan.

No power on earth could make her look at him, though. She knew he wasn't looking at her like that right now, but the day had wiped out her confidence. Confidence required a steadier, calmer mind than she had right now. And probably a bath first.

She fixed her gaze on the ceiling and waited as he angled her toward the light. Even then she couldn't make her heart slow down, and with the feel of his hands on her body—even moving clinically as they were—it took all her concentration to try and breathe normally.

Carefully he ran his hands over her from her collarbone

down, skipping the breasts, but cupping his hands again around her ribs to continue feeling down her. He hit sore spots several times, and she was grateful for them. At least the soreness helped negate the tingling warmth that radiated from wherever his hands touched her.

A few questions, blessed yes or no answers, and he turned her around. "You have a lot of bruises but your sore arm is the worst of it. I'm not sure it's not fractured."

Now that he was behind her, it was safe to pull her gaze from the ceiling. She looked down her body and suddenly felt much worse. No wonder she was sore. "Please tell me some of that's dirt."

"Some of that's dirt," he obligingly repeated, whether he meant it or not. Then his hands were in her hair, brushing the back of her neck as he dragged the heavy mass over her shoulder. His fingers traced down her spine and that feeling raced back through her body, with goosebumps following closely behind.

That reaction was hard to miss, and he missed nothing. His hands slowed and his touch changed—instead of feeling with his palms and the tactile working side of his fingers, she felt the light bump of knuckles and then a soft, gentle smoothing of what could only be the backs of his fingers down the last portion of her spine.

"I need..." His voice sounded strangled and he took a breath, cleared his throat, and tried again. "I need you to lie down so I can examine your belly for signs of internal bleeding."

Was that some sign of desire? Or had he just inhaled too much dust in the rubble? "My belly doesn't hurt," she murmured weakly, not trusting her voice to remain steady.

"Please, Nira, I need to make sure you're all right."

Something in his voice made her look over her shoulder at him. He looked worried and more than a little upset, probably the only thing that could make her agree.

A moment later he'd helped her to the exam table and

was palpating her abdomen. The air between them had changed again, now somewhat awkward because of the sensuality clogging the air and his attempt to remain professional despite it.

Once satisfied, he picked up her dress and then helped her sit up, slipped it back over her head and helped her get into it fully.

"X-ray of arm," he said, and once again led her out of the curtained bay. "Then we'll go back to the penthouse and rest."

The penthouse had never looked so good to Nira. Tahira eyed them both worriedly, but spirited away the battered sketchbook they'd dug from the rubble.

Nira gave a slapdash attempt to wash her face, at least getting what was around her mouth clean, but she'd gotten into something sticky along the way and so when she returned and sat down to dinner it was with a still grimy face. Eating was likewise mechanical. She didn't taste a bite, but once she'd had enough and tried to rise, she really felt the soreness setting in.

A mildly frowning Dakan watched her as she rose, like she might fall at any second and he'd need to catch her.

She touched his shoulder as she passed but didn't say anything. If she wasted a drop of energy on words, she'd probably pass out and drown in the bath.

A few minutes later, when the water was adjusted as hot as she could stand it and she was ready to get out of the dress, she remembered the zip. Negotiating it with an injured—but thankfully not broken—arm was inconceivable.

She opened the door to call for Dakan, and nearly ran into him. "I was coming to ask you for help."

He gestured her back into the bathroom and once there moved her hair off her back again and unzipped the dress. This time he didn't let her do any of the work to take it off, just edged the sleeves back down her arms, and let the dress fall.

"Thank you," she said, her state of near nudity along with her conflicting emotions giving her enough nervous energy to speak. "I didn't say that earlier, did I?" She turned toward him and murmured, "If I had clothes on, I'd hug you. You didn't have to come in there after me. After us. You probably saved my life. Thank you."

She let herself look him in the eye, so he'd know she meant it. He'd risked himself and was still looking after her, and it wasn't just doctorly instincts. He cared.

That knowledge eased the worry from her mind and she stepped in to lean against him, taking whatever comfort and strength he offered.

When he'd appeared beside her in the rubble, all she'd been able to see had been his eyes above the material covering the lower half of his face—dark pools of worry and tension, and that look hadn't left him until after he'd examined her and been satisfied she wasn't badly injured.

Her relief had come while she'd still been under that beam, the moment she'd looked into his eyes. He hadn't left her down there. He'd risked himself to crawl into the dark insides of a collapsed building for her.

What she felt for him was real. It was love, and she knew it now as surely as she'd known he'd get them out of there. Her feelings were real, and so were his. It might not be love that he felt for her, but he'd put himself in jeopardy to protect her—and a man like that could never be a betrayer.

This wasn't the same as her mother's Middle Eastern folly. They might never have anything more than these few weeks together, but she'd take whatever she could and let it sustain her afterward, not tear her down. Nira was a builder, and all building required a leap of faith.

Dakan held her for a moment, then eased her around in his arms until her back touched his chest again, and he wrapped his arms back around her while burrowing his nose under her hair.

The same hands that had medically pressed and explored her belly not an hour ago now flattened out, fingers splayed, pressing her back against him.

"You don't have to thank me," he finally answered, his words caressing her ear, then nuzzled and kissed the back of her neck.

Immediately, goose-bumps returned, and she tilted her head slightly forward, giving him whatever access he wanted.

His hand slid up her belly, found the front hook of her bra and flicked it open, then let his hands slide up to cup and gently knead both breasts.

Needing to get rid of the rest of her clothes, she pulled her arms free of the bra straps. He released her and knelt to slide down to her knickers, finishing undressing her as he couldn't before.

When they touched the floor he turned her toward him again, at eye level with her sex. He pressed a quick kiss atop the small mound of flesh, rose and helped her into the hot steaming water.

This was happening. He needed her too, she could see it in the pained look in his eyes.

It only took him a moment to shed his ruined clothes, baring a body that was beyond perfection to her eyes. Tall and muscled, brown skin, fine black hair over his chest, and down over his belly, a slowly engorging manhood that left her feeling short of breath...

Dakan grabbed towels from a nearby closet and washcloths, and put them all within easy reach before stepping into the bath with her. "Lean forward, *habibi*."

He settled in behind her, and she turned toward him, tucking her nose under his chin as she snuggled in.

Gently, he stroked her hair away from her face and rested his chin on her head. Her dirty head...

This was definitely happening.

Nira would've never thought that having a man bathe her could be sexy, but the tenderness in his eyes confirmed all she believed to be true. It was love, though that sexy intensity he could flatten her with appeared when he helped rearrange her on his lap so that she straddled his thighs, and she saw a flash of something playful when he had to work to get off a particularly stubborn patch of sticky grime on her cheek.

When he'd rinsed her face clean, he took another cloth, scrubbed it over his face, wiped it clean, and then urged her back so she lay in the bath between his legs, him bent over to run his fingers through her hair.

Heavy sensuality blanketed every touch. He washed and rinsed her hair with care that left her feeling cherished. Sooner than she'd have liked, he'd washed them both clean and drained the tub.

"I don't want to get out yet."

"Neither do I." He turned the water back on as soon as the murky dregs drained away, adjusted the temperature, and set it to filling again with them in it. "I just want to be able to see through the water."

Before the water even reached her hips, he'd moved her higher on his lap, high enough that he could complete promises. His mouth dragged across her still damp skin, sucking, licking, nipping, but over any bruise he merely stopped to stroke his lips against the battered flesh.

Reverence and love, heat and need. It left her feeling breathless and aching, and it gave her strength to come together when her energy had long since left her.

CHAPTER ELEVEN

DAKAN HADN'T INTENDED on taking Nira to bed, or to bath.

Well, he had, but as soon as he'd learned who she was he'd tried to talk himself out of it and had stayed away as much as he could. It hadn't helped.

Dakan never deprived himself of whatever woman he wanted—he didn't know how.

It'd be too simple to blame some primitive need for conquest, like touching and tasting her was fun. But that's not how it was. The usual excitement paled before the hunger to consume her that ripped through him even while he wanted to walk away.

He leaned her back, turned the water off, and then pulled her more fully against him, letting his hands slide over her slickened skin to find and squeeze sweetly plump curves as he finally got her mouth to his.

Water sloshed in the tub as she leaned away, arching perfect breasts toward him, her green eyes dark and pleading, her fingers curled into the hair on the back of his head, urging him forward, her voice low and throaty. "Do you want me to beg?"

Dakan shook his head. "You don't have to ask for anything." He kissed his way to a taut nipple, then sucked it greedily into his mouth.

A tremor rattled her and she ground her sex against

his hardness so that he felt her heat, her wetness...slicker than the water.

Releasing her nipple, he pulled her back up against him and then flailed with one hand at the side of the tub. Where were his trousers?

"What are you looking for?"

"Condom," he panted, and she leaned out to find and pick up his discarded clothing. A moment later he had the foil package in hand but no dexterity. Wet fingers didn't want to open it up.

"Is it safe?" Nira asked breathlessly. "In the tub, I mean?'

Dakan thought for a moment, then, locking one arm around her, he dragged them both out of the bath. Her legs wrapped around his hips and gripped him, and he rolled her to the rug. Nira grabbed a towel, wiped her hands, and took the condom from him. A moment later, after employing her teeth to get the job done, she had it out and strong little hands unrolled it onto him.

It wasn't fun. It wasn't a game. The pleasure of her hand squeezing and stroking him was too much, too heavy, too raw. He pulled her hips back to his, and nudged his way into her. Not a virgin, thank merciful God. He didn't want to be the first. He wanted her to have memories of other men, in case this seared into her the way he felt it searing him. He didn't want her to love him.

"Is this all right?"

His voice sounded strangled even to his own ears. She nodded, grabbed his head and pulled his mouth back to hers, her soft body taking everything he gave her, returned every kiss, every thrust.

Not the first. And he prayed not the best even if he couldn't imagine anything better.

Don't love me. The words ran round and round in his head, in his heart, a silent prayer he let echo and repeat even as he wanted it ignored.

Don't love me.

Don't love me.

Don't love me.

He felt her tighten around him and then the blessed clenching that shredded the last of his self-control. He breathed in her every gasp and the words she whispered into his mouth. Words he'd ignore. Words he'd pretend not to have heard.

When the tide had passed, with what little strength remained in him Dakan rose with her still sealed to him and staggered to the bedroom. The bed bowed as he laid them both down and started all over again.

She couldn't mean it. It was just the emotion of the day. She didn't really love him.

Rapid, near-frantic knocking on the bedroom door pulled Dakan out of sleep. Nira, still groggy from all the sleeping they hadn't had, grumbled something and tucked her face back in against his chest.

That level of urgency at a bedroom door was always worrying.

Dakan reluctantly pulled himself from the bed, grabbed a discarded blanket from the floor and covered himself before opening the door. Tahira stood there, looking so wild-eyed he knew immediately what was wrong.

He hadn't taken Nira to the palace last night, and though the message he left had said as much, someone had come to collect them.

"Make tea," he said, just to give the frazzled-looking housekeeper a direction, then ducked into the second bedroom—never so thankful for a hallway in his life. Pajamas laid out for him the night before still lay on the bed. He grabbed the bottoms, tugged them on, and went to face the messenger after making certain Nira's bedroom door was closed.

So Mother had come to collect Nira. Could've been worse.

He rounded the corner and found his father standing at the wall of windows, overlooking the city.

"Father," he said, mentally scrambling to work out what to say. Something he could never do was speak candidly with the King, and it was probably that difference Nira saw in him from when he was a royal envoy to the times he could be himself. He could talk to his mother, be honest, but he always felt the weight of expectations in his father's presence. "I left a message. She was banged up pretty badly when the building collapsed on her."

The King turned and leveled a steely look at him. "And you needed to stay with her all night to monitor her health?"

He knew. So much for not speaking candidly. At least it'd be easier to know what to say if he didn't run his thoughts through that father-filter first.

"I just needed to stay with her. It was a bad day."

"You made her feel better, then?" the King asked, shaking his head. "I have come to bring her to the palace. Where is the maid?" His voice rose and Dakan felt that familiar headache blaze into existence—the one he always got when his father got demanding.

"I'll bring her later." He tried again.

Tahira came scurrying and bowed, and the King went on as if Dakan had said nothing. "Get the girl up. Get her dressed and presentable. Then pack her bags. She's coming with me."

"Father, please." Dakan held a hand out to Tahira. "She can't handle you swooping in on her today." He lowered his voice to a loud whisper. "I haven't even told her yet. Let me tell her first."

"Tell me what?" Nira's voice came from the hallway and he turned to see her peek around the corner, looking worried and exhausted.

Dakan immediately moved to guide her back down the hallway.

"Prince Dakan Al Rahal." His father's words stilled his feet as effectively as they caused his head to throb. "You will not be alone with her."

"I'm sorry," he whispered, taking her hand to bring her back into the sitting area, but in the next heartbeat all will to do as expected evaporated.

Anger rose and he faced his father. The man had never even met Nira before today. *He* was the one who knew what was best for her. "I will be alone with her. She doesn't need a royal audience for this—it's too much. I'm taking her to her bedroom to speak privately."

"I'm putting an end to this impropriety."

"Yes, you've made that perfectly clear," Dakan bit out. "All celebrate! We've reached the end of impropriety! But I'm still going in there with her. Unless you want to execute your wicked son today, stay here. What can you possibly think is going to happen if we're alone together? We just need to talk." Dakan didn't wait for an answer, just returned to Nira to guide her back to the bedroom, intent on ignoring his father if he shouted any argument.

Surprisingly, none came.

He closed the door, focusing on her extremely worried face.

"Am I being kicked out of the country because we spent the night together?"

"Of course not."

"He probably thinks I've got no morals now that we've…"

"Don't worry about him." Dakan urged her to sit on the edge of the bed and sat beside her, taking one of her hands in his. Speaking candidly with Nira had been easy from almost the beginning, but words that would hurt her didn't come easily. "Between the times we kissed, I realized I couldn't pursue you. Last night should've never happened because I know who you are."

"I'm no different from who I was when we met," she said, a frown line creasing her forehead. "What does that have to do with the King? And why does he want you to bring me somewhere?"

"He wants to take you to the palace and not as punishment. You didn't do anything wrong. It's about who you are. I know who your father is." He spilled the words in a rush.

All traces of anger left her face, and she went from tense and pained to every feature frozen with shock. He waited an eternity for some sign that what he'd said had sunk in.

When he saw hope bloom in her eyes, it made it everything harder.

"You think you know who he is, or you actually know him?"

He'd been unable to help himself last night, and he couldn't today—if she cried, he'd do whatever he could to stop her.

"He looked familiar when I first saw the photo, but I couldn't place him. The more we talked, the more convinced I became that I knew him, but I still couldn't remember from where."

"Why didn't you tell me?"

"I didn't want to get your hopes up. What if I couldn't ever remember? There was also the small matter of our project. I selfishly didn't want to distract you. We were making good progress."

"Who is he? Is he a bad person? Is that why you look so worried?"

"He's one of the younger brothers of the royal family of Tabda Aljann." Even saying the country's name made him want to grit his teeth. The rivalry was fairly petty, he had no real grudge against them other than disliking the knowledge that their king, Ahmad, had once wanted his mother— more than thirty years go. If he could've picked another family for Nira, he would have.

"He's a prince?"

Dakan reached for her other hand—she looked like she needed the support. "Yes." The closer he got to telling her everything he knew, the more he needed to touch her. As soon as the words were said—as soon as they themselves left the penthouse—she'd be completely untouchable to him.

"Seems like you can't swing a stick without hitting a prince around here. I want to meet him. What's his name?"

"His name is Jibril." That was at least easy to answer. The rest... "I don't know if you should meet him. You might not even want to. There's some things you should know first."

Some of the hope dimmed, and she turned her hands over so that she could curl her fingers around his in return, and nodded for him to continue.

"He's married, for one."

"Of course he is. It's been a long time. I wouldn't expect him to stay single all this time just because Mum did."

"No, *habibi*. He's long married."

"It's been a long time since they were together."

"His eldest son is the same age as Zahir."

He watched her slowly start putting it together. "Has he been married more than once?"

"No."

"So he was married when he was with my mother."

He nodded.

"He *cheated* on his *wife* with *my mother*?"

Dakan nodded again.

"Then he sent her away."

"I don't know the whole story, but that's my suspicion.

I haven't spoken to him. I'm not even certain how someone could diplomatically broach the subject with him."

"Maybe they found out she was pregnant, and he sent her away to protect her. To protect us," Nira said, though the look in her eye confirmed her words as a last desperate attempt to try and salvage something of the situation.

"Maybe." He said the word she wanted to hear, but from what he knew of Prince Jibril, Dakan doubted his intention had been so noble. And he knew for damned sure that his father's intentions were at least slightly skewed by her lineage. If she were an unacknowledged daughter from any other country, he wouldn't force her to move to the palace.

Nira fell silent as she worked through everything, but the look in her eyes made her seem lost, and in that moment all he wanted was to shove his father out the door—and do whatever else might give her the peace the past twenty-four hours had stolen.

But he couldn't do that.

"There's more…"

"I don't know if I want to hear more right now."

"I don't want to say it either," he admitted, releasing her hand to wrap his arm around her, and grudgingly added, "but I'm under royal order to do so."

She didn't say anything else, but both hands went to her face to scrub over her cheeks and eyes.

Get it all out. This piecing out business made it longer, and longer was worse.

"I figured out who he was when I was speaking to my mother. She was telling me about her trip, countries they'd visited, and when she mentioned Tabda Aljann, his name just sort of appeared in my mind. I remembered where we'd met and talking to him. My mother noticed me falter, that's why you can't stay here now."

"I still don't understand why the King wants me at the palace. I don't want to live there, I'll be a basket case twenty-four seven. You've seen how it hits me... Besides, my equipment is here. We can't go wheeling that monstrous plotter into the palace, it'd probably scuff something up."

"I don't want you there either, though I'm sure you can get used to being in the presence of your architectural family." He jostled her shoulders, then remembered she was still hurt when she winced. "Forgive me. I don't know how I forgot to be gentle with you today."

"It's okay. But I'm staying here. I need to work now before I lose track of the new ideas. Like a place for physical therapy in the future, which would be the perfect place for the therapeutic baths if that water composition can be manufactured. I'm ready to get back to work now."

"You don't have a choice, and you need to rest for a few days anyway."

She stood up suddenly and was back out the door, leaving Dakan to scramble after her.

"Nira..."

"Why do you want me there?" Nira asked as soon as his father came into view. "You don't even know me."

"You're a royal daughter of House Al-Haaken, even if you are unacknowledged. I won't have you living alone here in the capital. It's impossible."

Nira wasn't as hesitant to speak candidly to his father as Dakan was.

"I'm not going." She stepped back further, and it was then that he saw tears in her eyes.

"You're in Mamlakat Almas, I have ordered your relocation." His father's voice rose then and Dakan stepped between them, as if that could block the loudness of what would follow. "You cannot remain in a country and disobey her king. If you leave now, your contract will be voided and you'll never be allowed back within the borders of Mamlakat Almas."

"Father, I can handle this." Dakan shook his head, staring hard at his father. Dakan understood what this meant to Nira, and what it probably meant for her future.

She reached up and pushed her hair back from her face as if it were some spider web she'd just walked through, then stepped fully behind him. He felt her forehead impact the center of his bare back and her hands grip his sides.

"You should've told her earlier in the week, not put it off so you could bring her home and fornicate with her."

"I know! And that's not why I brought her home—that just happened. I was being selfish again, because that's what I do, right? Zahir's the generous one, and I'm his shadow. But the time I spend with Nira here is the only time I enjoy spending in the country. I knew as soon as I said these words all that would change."

He saw the spark of interest flare in his father's eyes and before he could say anything else, Dakan gave his head a sharp shake.

When the look stopped him saying anything marriage-related, Dakan turned to Nira and pulled her to him. "You'll be allowed to come during the day and work here. You're not going to be a prisoner, *habibi*. You're going to be an Al Rahal ward. So you'll have that tour of the palace finally, and you can look at as many domes as you want to for as long as you want to."

There was more, but he didn't think she could take any more right now.

He didn't have the heart to say it now anyway. He just hugged her and let himself smell her hair one last time, and then nodded to Tahira to take her to dress.

Without another word to his father, Dakan packed up Nira's laptop, sketchbook and pencils, and then went to change his clothes.

CHAPTER TWELVE

NIRA COULDN'T DECIDE whether to feel some kind of pride at the revelation of her birth, or terrified that people were now making decisions about where she could live and what she could do.

But in keeping with her desire not to get exiled from the country for disobeying the King, she rode along in the back of his car with the two Al Rahal men in a silence so heavy it could've made bricks and built the Hagia Sophia!

How different it felt from her first journey to Qasr Almas. She couldn't help but look at Dakan, and she knew he felt her gaze. The muscle at the corner of his ridiculously square jaw bunched harder when she looked at him for any length of time.

Just when she thought she might scream just to break the silence, they pulled onto the winding road that led to Qasr Almas, and she watched the Diamond Palace come into view.

This could be a massive mistake. The King had threatened to cancel her contract if she ran screaming for the airport now, but maybe that was the price of her freedom. She could find another job once she got home, probably. Though who knew the range of an angry king? She'd been hoping for positive references once this job was done, not for her client to send something scathing to her employer to follow her around until the only architecture job she could get would be designing garden sheds.

If she was honest, despite what Dakan had told her about her father, these people were the only ones willing to give her information. Maybe Mum would… *Oh, hell*. She'd have to tell her mum where she was living, if nothing else.

The car rolled to a stop, men opened the doors and the King exited on the side of the entrance. She and Dakan left via the opposite door, and he finally looked at her again as he extended a hand to help her from the car.

How many times had their hands linked in the past weeks? Even before last night, touching his hand had felt like an intimacy she'd never shared with someone else. Even before she'd known she loved him. But now he squeezed her hand, and the sorrow she saw in his eyes almost broke her down.

Carefully, he guided her hand to the crook of his elbow so material separated their skin and escorted her through the door.

A beautiful woman in flowing robes and glittering jewels came out of the palace, her arms open. The Queen she instantly recognized—Dakan had her eyes. She spoke Arabic to Nira straight away, and pulled her into a painful hug.

The Queen either didn't know about them, or she was very good at putting on a friendly face.

Either way, Nira wasn't going to bring it up. She returned the hug, then fumbled her way through the social gestures she'd have made with the royals of her own country—curtseying, inclining her head, pretending all was well and that nothing ugly lurked between the three.

"I shall show you to your suite personally. The healer is waiting for us there. Dakan said you had a building fall on you yesterday! I must say you look decidedly better than I feared you would. But you are stiff and sore, the healer will help." She gestured for Nira's bags to be brought. "I expect you and I will spend the next week in the healing baths."

"All day?" Nira asked. She hadn't subscribed to Dakan's idea that she needed time off—she was just playing along. "I need to work on the hospital." She glanced back, but Dakan was nowhere to be seen.

"Yes, Dakan said you are doing wonderful work. They're already building the suite for our Adele's coming birth, so you can have some time to recover. He said you saved a baby boy, landed with him on you to cushion him from the fall? Then held up a roof by yourself?"

Nira climbed the stairs as bidden, doing her level best not to look at anything but the next step. Getting distracted by the walls would be bad, or the carved balustrade running along her peripheral vision. She did break down and take hold of the rail about halfway up, slowing her pace somewhat and lengthening the likelihood that she might get overly emotional about the carvings and pillars dancing up the walls.

"I didn't so much plan the fall as that's how it happened. And it wasn't a roof, it was part of the floor. I really did very little. Dakan saved us. He got everyone out."

At the top of the stairs they turned down a short corridor, and she was shown into a suite that for the moment made her forget her pain and worry. There was no way to keep from looking. The bed was a platform built into the wall with a thick pillow-like mattress on top. There was a window with an arched top and deeply carved seat jutting from beneath where one could sit and gaze out at the sea…

What were they talking about? Work. She was talking about work. "I don't want to take time off." Right. Pay attention to the room later. Don't look right now.

She made herself focus on the Queen. "The tour gave me so many ideas, I don't want to forget anything."

Say something nice about the palace. "But if there was anywhere I needed to lie about and not do work, this would be the room for me. I don't suppose there exists any documentation about when the palace was constructed? Their methods or, well, anything that happened during its building?"

"There are scrolls. Your Arabic is very good, you should be able to read them."

As the bags had been dropped off, the healer motioned for the door to be closed and then he and a maid who introduced herself as Samina began to remove her clothing. Despite quiet protests, she was stripped down to her bra and knickers, and the healer began a careful inspection of her bruises.

"Dakan said nothing's broken. He made films of my arm. No internal injuries."

The man nodded. "But you are not well. Your muscle has been damaged, and you have need of soothing. It is right that you shouldn't work for a week, and you must take the healing baths daily. Wear no restrictive clothing. Will she be in robes, my Queen?" He directed the last question to Leila.

"Yes, there are many, and Adele's should fit her well enough. Their coloring is different, but they will serve until new ones arrive."

"New robes?" Nira asked, trying to keep up with the rapid Arabic. Hers was improving all the time, but she still could get very lost when overwhelmed. "May I sit?"

She had no idea what was expected of her, but standing there in bra and panties didn't help her keep focused on the words flying around.

The healer gave another order for the restrictive clothing to be removed, and gave instructions on tonics the *attar* would send and how to properly take them.

"Let Samina dress you and then you shall rest today. This afternoon, after the sun weakens, we shall go to the healing baths. Oh, Nira, I'm so glad you've come to stay with us. Dakan says you will want tutoring, and spoke of how much you loved the trip to the Immortal Fortress. I'm sure you'll find scrolls and books in our library to satisfy your every question. Perhaps we can visit a mosque when you're rested, or some of the other ancient buildings in the city."

Had Dakan already handed her off to his mother in that regard as well? Technically it would fulfill his promise to make sure she got the chance to explore when the project allowed, but before it had always sounded like something he'd participate in.

Samina led her to bed and she dutifully climbed in. She was tired. Maybe she could take some time to pursue her own goals finally. If Dakan came to yell at her to get back to work, at least she'd see him.

"Thank you, Your Highness. I'll try not to be too much trouble."

"You may call me Leila, Nira, though I'd still call Fatiq by his title. You are our guest and I'll not have you pinned down by a title when we shall talk so often." The woman went to look out the windows, and then gestured to the maid again, gave instructions for the windows to be opened and for Nira to be left to sleep until dinner. Then she turned back to Nira. "I'll leave you to your rest. Welcome to Qasr Almas."

Everyone filtered out of her suite and Nira got out of the bed to find her phone. She fumbled through her handbag, flicked it on and immediately texted Dakan.

Does your mother know? And can she not be told if not?

I don't know if she knows. Try to forget it.

Forget that they'd been caught, or forget what had happened?

She sat down on the bed again and tried to rewind what Dakan had said to her earlier.

"Last night should never have happened."

And "I can't be with you."

So it was over?

She lifted the phone again and texted.

Will you be at dinner?

No.

Breakfast?

I'm not going to be in the palace much. Rest. Work next week.

Or next month. I have access to a whole library here.

She waited for ten minutes for him to rise to her bait, but realized with a sinking feeling that he wasn't going to. Why did all her relationship arguments come down to texting?

Not trusting herself to stay calm if she rang Dakan, she walked back to the doorway and turned so she could get the whole room in an image. In an adjoining bathroom she took a photo of herself in robes that obviously didn't belong to her.

She sent both pictures to her mother with captions: *My bedroom. My new outfit...*

Then she dialed her mum's number. If that didn't make her pick up, nothing would.

She'd had enough of treading lightly.

* * *

The following Monday, having convinced the healer that she was fit enough to sit quietly at a desk and draw pictures, Nira let herself back into the penthouse. Tahira came in from the other room, and bowed upon seeing her.

"I'll be coming daily to work on the hospital," she said, moving directly to the desk so she could unload her laptop and sketchbook, all she'd had to work with since being moved to Qasr Almas.

Tahira offered tea in response, accepting without questions. At least that would be the same.

Speaking Arabic had started to feel normal. She no longer had to think in English then mentally translate to make herself understood. She could thank Dakan for that, if she ever saw him.

Not that she could count on that in the near future. Dakan was off doing medical system stuff. He no longer came strolling in whenever he liked, no matter how much she wished he would.

In the days since she'd been relocated, she'd occasionally seen him from a distance when the helicopter had picked him up or dropped him off. Texting him had worked that first day, but had garnered nothing but silence since then.

For the first time in her life Nira sympathized with her mother's romantic trauma. If this was how she'd felt...

She could ask her mum. Since she'd sent the photos, her calls were always answered. Her mother had even given a modest amount of information about Jibril. Apparently, knowing the man's name had been the key.

He was her father. Check.

He'd sent Mum home when he'd found out she was pregnant. Check.

They'd met in Tabda Aljann when she'd accepted a position as an air hostess on the royal family's new fleet of

jets. She'd fallen for him on a long flight she'd worked to
Australia. All that was new information.

Thanks to her studies, she knew Tabda Aljann meant
Paradise Begins in one of the local dialects. It didn't
sound like a bad place to go but she'd learned her lesson.
Just because something felt good, it didn't mean it was
good for her.

Mum had probably felt much worse.

Or maybe she'd felt better. She'd come away with Jibril's child, at least.

How would it feel to have Dakan's child?

Tears rushed to her eyes before she could banish the
thought.

What a stupid thing to ask herself.

She may understand her mother better now, but she
wouldn't become her. A broken heart could be mended,
or it could be left to putrefy.

Nira was a builder.

Inside, she might still feel like she was flat on her back
in that crawlspace, holding up floor joists with her feet,
but she wouldn't stay that way. She'd get out from under
it and rebuild, which was what she was doing now—getting on with life, designing a project that would advance
her career, laying a foundation for future projects to be
entrusted to her.

Foundations were never easy. To construct them properly you had to dig…and dig and dig and dig…until you
had blisters and raw, bloody hands. When you got far
enough down to know your building would be on steady
ground, only then could you start building.

She just hoped her heart would hurry through feeling
raw and blistered. A week had passed since she'd seen
Dakan, and she still felt she could barely take things hour
by hour, that some minutes were longer than days.

* * *

It had been just over a month since she'd come to Mamlakat Almas. Zahir and Adele had returned and the royal family had begun to ready itself for a celebration of their nuptials. Nira stayed in her room and made long, frequent visits to the penthouse. One future wing for the hospital had now been designed. She tried to deliver the plans to Dakan for approval, but he didn't answer her messages. After three visits to knock on the door of his suite in the hope that someone would drag him to the door, she'd finally given up and sent them via the servants. He signed them and send them back the next morning.

It was like she'd become completely invisible.

Leila, who Nira had figured out knew everything that had gone on with Dakan, still treated her with kindness, still welcomed her on the evenings Nira felt she could no longer avoid dining with them without appearing ungrateful and rude. The King was the one who didn't seem to know what to say to her. He'd ask the obligatory questions about the hospital, and once she'd answered he'd nod, make some sound of approval, and eat his dinner.

She made herself more scarce after their arrival.

The importance of the hospital made people excuse her workaholic approach to it. She actually wanted to meet Adele, but the idea of seeing someone in married bliss with one of the Al Rahal brothers...

Maybe she was becoming her mother after all.

They spoke daily now, and she couldn't tell if it was because of her new address and the fear it triggered, or because Nira's fresh, new heartache bonded them. Not that she discussed it much. It was her last bit of emotional currency, which she'd definitely need to get to the very bottom of her Father Mystery.

The morning of the fourth day since their arrival, Nira

was finishing tying her hair up in one of the many beautiful scarves Leila had provided, wanting to be out the palace door before everyone got up—as had become her practice—when a knock came on the door.

An inevitable thrill followed as with any knock—hope that it was Dakan. She wanted to run, her feet demanded speed, but she made herself walk. She knew better. Dakan didn't knock.

A pretty blonde woman stood there, smiling, on the other side.

Adele.

Cornered.

"Good morning. You must be Adele," Nira said, speaking English for the first time in weeks. For lack of any idea of how to greet the woman properly, she offered a handshake. "I'm sorry I haven't been around." The idea of having to explain made her eyes burn, and she gestured quickly to the room. "I've been working. Please, come in."

To have time for her emotions to calm, she walked across the room and opened the drapes then the windows.

"The mornings have nice breezes here," Adele said. "This was my room when I stayed as Leila's nurse."

Suddenly, Nira remembered Dakan saying that his mother had been ill, and it brought her a pang to think of their previous confidences, now a thing of the past. "I trust she's better now?"

"She is. Fully recovered." Adele perched on the window seat. "A selection of gowns is being brought to the palace today. Leila asked me to make sure you'd be here as you haven't anything to wear."

And just like that, her plans for the day changed. Breakfast with the Al Rahal women. Shopping. Maybe some studying later if she was lucky.

Adele had made it sound like a request, but it really wasn't one. It came from the Queen, and if the Queen wanted you to go shopping with her…

This was what Dakan complained about. Even if she still wanted to shake him for his utter abandonment of her, she'd begun to understand his feelings and they hadn't even asked all that much of her.

Dakan's itinerary for the day left him without anywhere to go to avoid the palace at noon when everyone would be milling about. He should've taken a car to his morning appointment. Then it might've taken the whole day.

The sound of women laughing caught his ear as he approached the garden, intent on getting to his wing before he was spotted. He recognized his mother's voice and who was probably Adele. Would Nira be with them?

A smart man would've kept walking, not stopped to try and see her. But, God help him, he wanted to see her.

He just didn't want her to see him.

Keeping close to tall bushy palms planted in artistic clumps and lines around the garden, Dakan stopped, ignoring instincts telling him to run.

The three women sat in an arc of three chairs and before them another woman held up a gown for their inspection.

His mother finally had a daughter to dress for parties. And also Nira—Mother probably already felt attached to her even without the bonds of matrimony to tie them.

Her dark hair hung over one shoulder, thick and braided with a ribbon woven through it to match her robe. Hair that soft should never be bound up.

Mother and Adele appeared to enjoy the dress viewing, but Nira sat with such a blank expression, despite the blistering noonday sun, he felt an unpleasant coldness seep into his limbs.

Of course she wasn't happy here—though he couldn't be sure whether it was due to her new constraints or because he'd disappeared from her life.

Right. Enough of this. He couldn't bring her more except further heartache by sticking around. If she saw him, it'd only reopen that wound.

He hurried to the exterior door of his wing and immediately went up the inside stairs and directly back out to the second-level battlements. He'd be able to see her from there. She'd never think to look up. He could look his fill, regain control, then get back to business tomorrow.

"Yes, Nira will try the green ones," his mother said, clapping her hands and gesturing to two different green gowns—one emerald and one pale green that reminded him of her eyes. She'd look magnificent in it. But then, she'd look magnificent in any of them.

Mechanically, Nira stood and held her arms out for the gowns. "I'll just go to my chamber."

"No…there is a screen behind us, use that."

Dakan looked down and that cold pit in his middle heated up. If he stayed there, he'd be able to see her changing.

A gentleman wouldn't spy on her like that.

A gentleman would walk away, or never have let it get this far to begin with.

She stood for a long moment after the gowns had been placed over her arms until his mother asked what was wrong. Nira finally asked for the lavender dress instead.

So her will was still there. He could take some comfort in that.

The gowns were swapped out and she trekked over to the screen, hung the dress on one section of it, and began stripping off her robe.

Look away. Now would be the time to look away.

He'd seen her before, of course, but…

The silk slid down her arms and past her hips to float to her feet in a puff.

The bruise on her arm had faded a lot. At least he could calm his mind with that knowledge. She was healing. He hadn't broken her body even if he was certain that he'd broken her heart.

She unzipped the gown and stepped into it. A moment later she had it on—save that zipper down the back. The memory of her zipper, the brush of her soft skin against his knuckles...

He was just torturing himself.

Rounding the screen with the back held together, she turned her back for Adele to zip and looked up. Their eyes locked over the short distance. Anyone else might've looked away from him, but Nira held his gaze. In her eyes he saw everything also currently churning through his insides. Desire. Sadness. Regret. Resignation. But something else—the way she held herself, the lift of her chin... Feelings he didn't feel right now. Strength. Determination.

She might sit quietly and do what she was told, but the woman had a steel core.

Adele finished with her zipper and bade her turn to face the Queen, and only then did she look away from him, turning her back on him as well she should. That was what he deserved, and what would be best for both of them.

He turned away as well, and went to lock himself inside until tomorrow came and another trip would rescue him from the lead deadening his own center.

He had to stay away, though he wanted to do something for her. Not an apology so much as give her something he knew she wanted.

Women in Mamlakat Almas enjoyed using henna for special occasions. All except Mother, who could never hold still long enough for the henna to settle, so she would never think to supply a henna artist to Nira. But Nira had mentioned loving the art. He could send her a henna artist without claiming the gift. Provide one last experience in her quest to discover her cultural heritage...anonymously.

She need never know it was from him.

CHAPTER THIRTEEN

DAKAN HAD DREADED the celebration since everything had happened with Nira, but was there any part of his life in Mamlakat Almas that he didn't dread now?

The medical care overhaul. He liked working on that. Having something useful and important to do was the only thing that kept him sane. Last month he could've said Nira, but in the past couple of weeks he'd felt dread for her every day. He dreaded what her life was shaping up to be, whether she'd caught onto it yet or not. He dreaded not seeing her, even as he did his best to avoid her.

The formal ceremonial acknowledgement of Zahir and Adele's union and prayers for blessings concluded, Dakan tugged the sleeves on his tux straight and walked into the ballroom for the private party with the family's closest couple hundred friendly dignitaries in attendance.

The Al Rahals, as hosts, were supposed to dress the part, but Dakan had resolved to stick with what he felt comfortable in, and to the burning sands with anyone who disagreed. The rebellion he'd avoided in his youth had finally caught up with him. There wasn't a single agreeable ounce left in him. No more acting simply to meet others' expectations. It had never served him in the past anyway.

He meandered to the side to an out-of-the-way spot where he could loiter and observe entering guests—and wait for Nira's father. One of the Al-Haaken would be there to represent their family. Mother had claimed not to know which, but he'd seen the lie in her eyes.

It'd definitely be Jibril, and Dakan was going to have a good long talk with him. He'd do what felt right. It started with the tux, and in the fairy-tale land of his mind ended with him and Nira hopping on a jet to London away from everyone who could cause them grief. Maybe there he could sort out relationships—how to have one. Probably not, but the fantasy was nice.

Nira came through the archway leading to the garden. Even with her head turned away from him and her hair covered, he knew it was her. She'd selected that lavender gown. The long sleeves and high neck may have hidden her skin, but it showed her shape. He didn't need to see her face, the hurt and determination he'd seen there the last time had burned into his mind.

The twinge in his chest had him turning away.

He stepped around a massive potted plant where she'd be less likely to see him, and refocused on the archway.

He couldn't undo his actions in the last weeks, but maybe he could prevent her father from doing further damage. Impress upon him the importance of civility with Nira, and disabuse him of any notion to abscond with her. He'd be civil but blunt. Not raise his voice. It was as far as his civility could extend in the matter.

"Why are you hiding in the bushes?"

Zahir.

Dakan cast an eye over his brother—the good one— regally clad in the expected robes.

"Plotting my escape," he murmured. He remembered the coffee in his hand and took a sip.

"I don't know about escape, but you're plotting something, by the look of you," Zahir said, moving to the other side of him and leaning one shoulder against the wall, demanding his attention but not quite blocking his view of the door.

"It's Nira's first big event. I don't want to take the fun out of it for her."

Zahir nodded slowly. "She sent me the plans for the hospital, what have been approved so far."

"They're rather remarkable, aren't they?" Dakan still pored over his set, even after he'd signed off on them. "You did well, hiring her."

"And you did too in actually carrying it out. I looked at the other proposals you wrote, for the Air Ambulance teams, traveling physicians, and the arrangements you made with Dubai and Qatar to use their hospitals during the build. Excellent ideas. Have you worked out proposed budgets for start-up and to maintain the service?"

Jibril swept in, blanking out everything Zahir had just said.

He needed to move if he was going to get to the man before Nira spotted him. Dakan turned back to Zahir and asked, "Can we talk about it later? It's your celebration. You should still be with your wife. It's her first big event too." He patted his brother's arm, and stepped around him to divert Jibril before he got too far into the crowd.

He intercepted him at the beverage bar and offered a hand. "Prince Jibril, I was hoping you'd be attending. Spare to spare, could I speak with you a moment?"

The man smiled at the greeting, and took Dakan's hand, just as he'd expected. The two families had been doing this dance long enough to know the steps.

Dakan shook his hand, though he wanted to break it. It might be jumping to conclusions, but that didn't mean the conclusions were wrong.

"It would be my pleasure."

They moved to a quiet area by the wall, and Dakan snatched his phone from his pocket, eager to get this over with.

"Do you remember this woman?" The photo of Nira's parents came up on the screen.

The man's eyes narrowed, all traces of the fake friendliness there vanishing. He twisted Dakan's cellphone so that the photo faced the floor, where people would not see it.

And looked angry.

"I see that you do. Were you aware your union produced a child?"

"What concern is this of yours?"

Now evading the question.

"Have you become entangled with this woman?" Jibril recovered his façade, but anger remained in his voice, his words. "This photograph is quite old, she is what the Westerners call a cougar now?"

Dakan didn't have the patience for this, but he wouldn't rise to the bait. He'd calmly deliver his message—a technique he'd been taught he actually approved of. The art of diplomacy didn't usually involve threats, but he'd learned how to modulate his voice during twenty-seven years of lessons.

"No, Al-Haaken, the child is my concern. Did you know about the child? She's here tonight. If you'd like to avoid her, it'd probably be a good idea if you left. That'd also be my preference in the matter. If you stay, you will address her respectfully. She looks like your family, so you wouldn't be able to miss her. Be a gentleman and we won't have any problems." He smiled, showing his teeth in the most socially appropriate manner possible.

Jibril knocked Dakan's phone out of his hand with a quick swipe. It hit the floor hard, and he made sure it was broken by slamming his heel down on it, shattering the screen.

"This is not your business, boy."

Clearly Jibril didn't appreciate Dakan's attempt at diplomacy.

He got exactly two steps away before Dakan was after him. Another three steps and they were at the beverage bar. As he rounded it, Dakan grabbed Jibril's wrist hard enough to spin him, but they'd kept things quiet enough so far that not many people in the room noticed their mild confrontation.

Jibril turned and Dakan stepped in, his hand still locked about the man's wrist. "You will only speak to her with cordial civility. Are. We. Clear, Prince Jibril?"

He could've just nodded, and that would've satisfied Dakan. There were a number of things he could've said without the situation escalating.

But Jibril's face turned red, his volume rocketing up so he all but shouted, "Unless you're the whore's son and not the good Queen's, leave it."

The sharply spoken words finally roused the interest of people in the ballroom, but all Dakan could really see was what might happen if they took Nira to Tabda Aljann. Was this kind of attitude the reason Mother had turned their king down? Did all the Al-Haaken men treat women that way?

If Jibril knew about the relationship between Nira and himself, would he call her a whore?

That was the thought that pushed him over the edge.

All the rage and helplessness that had been simmering in him since that morning she'd been denied him roared to life, and Dakan's fist flew.

No amount of warning him to be good to Nira would work. This was not a man who would even respect his own women.

He felt the impact and Jibril's head snapped back. As Jibril staggered backwards, pain streaked up Dakan's arm.

Not good enough. Jibril wasn't on the floor yet. And his hand could handle another round.

Dakan pursued him, fists balling.

Before that satisfying second crunch, something big and heavy impacted him from the side and he landed hard beneath the force of the tackle and the body that landed on top of him.

He twisted, shoving at his attacker. Another Al-Haaken?

No. Zahir.

"What are you doing?" Zahir bit out in a sharp whisper, one hand locking around Dakan's wrist in the same fashion as he'd detained Jibril.

"Fixing something," Dakan bit back.

"Guards!" *Well, damn. Father.* "Detain my younger son." Quietly angry again. The next thing he knew, several hands had him up and were marching him toward a side entrance.

Nira sought Adele at the start of the party, hoping to compare henna designs from the artist who'd shown up at the penthouse yesterday morning, only to find Adele entirely henna-free.

"But this is your wedding celebration. Everything I've read and watched online says you should have these for your wedding. I just thought that you and Leila had yours together and the artist came to the penthouse to find me."

"No, no one came yesterday. Did you have to sit still for hours while it dried?"

"Yes. But I really wanted to have it done sometime. It's so beautiful." She searched the ballroom, hoping to see Dakan. Would he have sent the artist to her? The man had been steadfastly avoiding her, other than the strange spying interlude. This didn't seem like the kind of thoughtful gesture a man who wanted nothing to do with her would make. She didn't even know where to file this memory aside from Sweet, Thoughtful, and Riddled with Mixed Signals.

If he'd sent the henna artist, it meant he remembered her very first tirade about how all she knew she'd learned online.

It meant he'd been thinking of her—which was at least something.

A man shouted, "Whore's son," and her thought train was derailed amid a ballroom full of gasps. She turned in time to see Zahir and Dakan go flying. Before she could even form the intention to approach them Dakan was marched out by guards.

The march took them directly past her, and Nira's heart banged out of rhythm as his dark eyes again met her own. He shook his head minutely and glanced back toward the rude man. What did that mean?

Leila fluttered toward the man Dakan had hit, ready to usher him out of the room. Damage control, no doubt. That's when she got a good look at him.

"Nira?"

Adele said her name, grabbing her arm. "You've gone as white as a sheet. Let's sit down."

She trailed where Adele led and sat like a sack of potatoes. Music that had gone quiet at some point resumed, and people began to mingle again.

"He shook his head at me," Nira said, looking at Adele. "Don't go over there. Don't speak to that man. I think that's what he meant."

"Well, that man was shouting very rude things," Adele began, but clearly didn't know the context.

She watched the door Leila and the man had passed through. "I think he's my father."

Dakan had punched her father in the face. After having been called a whore's son.

"Do you think he was calling the Queen that?"

"If he had been, Zahir would've leapt on him, not Dakan. He's the Prince you were telling me about?"

Nira nodded. It was him. He'd aged very well, although

it was now possible he'd return home with a different-shaped nose...

"Was he the one who had tried to marry Leila?" Adele asked.

"That was his king." She'd learned only enough of that to know there was a story: two men who had wanted the same woman and a rivalry birthed by the one who'd not been selected. "Dakan hit him. I think he hit him for me." She wanted to go and find where they'd dragged him off to but she wasn't family. "I think he meant my mum."

Adele motioned for a waiter, and soon a glass of juice was placed before Nira. "Drink this. You're still very pale."

Nira dutifully picked up the glass, as she'd been told. Her hand shook and the liquid sloshed about enough that she had to add her other hand to the glass to steady it enough to get to her mouth, and split her attention between drinking and answering Adele's questions about her blood sugar.

Had he sent her mother away? Maybe she'd seen this side of him and had left on her own. Maybe that was where his venom came from.

How dared he call her mum that vile word when he had been *married* while dallying with her?

Leila came back without Jibril, and straight back out the door Daken had been escorted through.

Adele came back and placed a plate with some nuts, fruit, and cheese on it in front of her. "Eat these."

"Will you take me to where Dakan is?" Nira wasn't interested in food.

"Not until you eat something."

All this being bossed around was getting really old. But Nira plucked up to cubes of cheese and popped them into her mouth, which turned out to be a lot of cheese to chew at once.

"Finish that small plate and then I'll take you."

* * *

"Every time I come here, I try to be what is expected of me. This was too important for me to just let someone else deal with it. I handled it as well as I could," Dakan said, his head now hurting almost as much as his hand. "Frankly, he needed a hell of a lot more than one punch."

"You try to be what's expected of you?" Mother repeated. "You usually aren't angry like this, so your cheek can be endearing. But when you turn violent toward a guest…"

"A guest who was invited why? You knew who he was. You knew *how* he was." Dakan shifted his attention to his father. "Who were you trying to provoke by inviting him? King Ahmad? Or me?"

"I wanted to confirm the link to Nira's mother," the King said. "It matters to her future and to yours. One of these days you will come to realize you wish to be with her, and that will not happen if she's in Tabda Aljann. But here, in Mamlakat Almas, we have the advantage."

"I'm not going to marry Nira." How many times did he have to say it?

"Why?" His long-silent brother finally broke in. "You love her. You don't deny you love her, you provoke international incidents because you love her, but you don't speak to her, you don't look at her. What is it you do wish from her?"

Dakan had been asking himself the same thing for weeks. He wanted to be with her, and he wanted to protect her, but it didn't feel like a right that belonged to him, even though he knew his aversion to the idea of marriage wasn't entirely rational. He couldn't even understand it himself, it was just there, part of a future that didn't feel like it belonged to him.

"I don't think I'd be a good husband, and likely a worse father—she's had enough experience with those.

As you've said, I've a number of character defects. It's better she finds that out before children get involved."

"Ridiculous," Zahir said. "And that still doesn't explain why you attacked Jibril. Tell us. What were you thinking?" It'd been years since he'd angered his brother enough to cause his spine to go rigid and that tone come to his voice. Zahir's disappointment bothered him more than their parents', but mostly what he felt in that moment was apathy for the entire situation. The fire that had blazed was...depleted.

"How about I just go to my suite and you all return to the party?" Which his little showdown with Jibril had interrupted. "I *am* sorry for disrupting your celebration."

"You're not forgiven," Zahir said hotly. "Name a reason. Give us something we can use to smooth this over without an explanation that would shame Nira and her mother publicly. Otherwise it will be time for grand gestures. If that punch was your way of telling her you love her because you're not man enough to say it directly, I don't know what we can do with you."

Dakan said the only thing he could—the truth. "I wanted to spare Nira further humiliation at the hands of Jibril after..."

"After what?"

"After I did to Nira what Jibril did to her mother." Dakan stood to face what must come. He knew what grand gestures meant: justice to the victim. Punishment.

"She's pregnant?" Fatiq asked.

"No. But I took her to bed knowing we'd never be what she wanted. When he called her mother a whore, I heard his words extending to Nira and saw red." Dakan drew a deep breath. He had no idea what else to say.

The door opened to the ballroom and Nira and Adele stepped through. He looked at her long enough to decide she hadn't been crying, so maybe Jibril had stayed away or left—the only positive he could take away from the evening.

Turning back to his family, he muttered, "I have no other explanations. Do what you will. Make your grand gesture."

"Grand gesture?" Nira's voice came from behind him, alarmed, but he didn't turn back, just waited for the pronouncement.

"Very well," Father said, his voice resigned, like he'd always expected things with Dakan to come to this. "Can Zahir continue the work you began from England?"

"It's all lined out in proposals. I've hired an agent here to organize the budgets and another…" Dakan stopped. He wasn't asking for details. "I have meticulous notes and two agents to help. They're very efficient. It can all be managed by phone or email."

Just get on with it.

This wasn't how he'd intended to get back to London, but it would serve. He'd have to hope Nira would reach the same point soon and return home to finish the plans. Maybe his sentence would provide initiative.

"Dakan Al Rahal, for breaching the sacred duty of hospitality and attacking our guest, you are exiled to the desert."

Dakan stilled. Those weren't the words he'd expected. A dressing down for improper behavior, yes, not a reminder that he'd violated ancient, even holy ways.

"Your passport is revoked. You will not leave our kingdom. You will not enter our cities. Until you can produce answers, you will not become a guest in another country, and you are no longer a prince of your own."

Nira's throat went as dry as that desert they were sending him into. What did banishment to the desert even mean? Was it a death sentence?

"Fatiq, that's too harsh," Leila said, stepping closer to Dakan.

Dakan put his arm around her shoulders and murmured something at her temple. Whatever he said, Nira could see the tension in his frame. Stiff Dakan, Prince Dakan. Not himself. Was he ever himself with them? She hadn't ever seen him do anything but argue with his father.

"The desert always has answers," Zahir said. "Meditate. Ask for guidance. I know you've never believed in it, but do it anyway."

"At least confine him until first light." Leila was the only other person in the room who seemed as bothered by this as Nira was. "He shouldn't travel in the desert at night."

The King nodded.

First light meant travel under the brutal sun. How was that better?

Dakan kissed the Queen's cheek, then turned and walked straight toward Nira.

Weeks with no contact, but simply seeing him walk toward her with that purposeful stride and determined glint in his dark eyes sent her still smoldering spark into a conflagration.

He didn't stop until he was chest to chest with her, his hands on her cheeks and his mouth sealed to hers. The kiss was so bare and pained, she felt drenched by it. He kissed her like a man who would never know pleasure or peace again.

Nira curled her hands into the lapels of his tux, keeping him there, taking all the feeling pouring through his kiss.

"Don't wait for me," he said against her lips when they both came up for air—exactly the opposite from what his kiss had said to her. "Go home. Be happy."

Other people pulled him from her. Once again, guards marched him away before she could think of a single thing to say that might make the situation better. Right after he'd told her not to wait for him seemed like the wrong time for a declaration of love.

As they approached a large archway on the other side of the atrium, he called over his shoulder in English, "Don't go near him, Nira. Don't talk to him. Don't go to Tabda Aljann. Don't go to him, do you hear me?" As they rounded the corner of the arch he met her gaze again and dug his feet in to make them pause.

Another story she didn't know about her father. The difference was that this time she'd seen enough to make the leap of faith. Between Mum's reaction to Jibril and Dakan's, all her questions had been effectively answered.

"I won't," she answered, saying the words he needed, though she probably would've agreed even if she hadn't meant it at that point.

He smiled, a subdued version of that grin that always made her heart melt, and then he was gone.

Tears threatened, but Nira wasn't about to cry in front of the King, who had banished him. For her, the party was over, but no excuses came to mind for her to make. She just curtsied, gathered the skirts of her expensive gown and muttered, "Please excuse me."

Once through the door, she skirted the ballroom, ignoring the curious looks from guests. Her mind swarmed with too many thoughts to focus on anything except what was essential to her sanity.

Get to the room.

Get her sketchbook.

Let her brain switch off.

CHAPTER FOURTEEN

IT WAS PART of Dakan's make-up to always test boundaries.

He'd been the child who would touch a bee after some-one had told him it would sting him, just to see for him-self.

Don't eat chocolate before bed or you'll be sick. He ate the chocolate.

Don't come back to the city until you sort yourself out.

Dakan wanted to go back to the city. He wanted to go to the penthouse, wait for Nira to come, and take an-other bath.

Meditate and ask the desert for answers? He'd fall asleep or die from some wasting sickness before the des-ert gave him any answers. He didn't even know the stu-pid question—which seemed the bare minimum to know when starting a quest for answers.

A week in, and out of things to do, Dakan gave in and called Zahir. How did someone seek answers in the desert?

An hour after the call ended, Dakan dressed and read-ied himself to walk in the desert, still with no idea about the question.

By late afternoon he'd found the grave of his baby brother, and sat there for a while, picturing what life would've been like with three of them and the Lego house at eleven, six and four.

Aafaq would've played inside with him—Zahir had been too old to get excited about the playhouse.

He would've been the middle brother. Would that have changed who he was the way Nira believed being kept from her heritage had changed her?

Dakan had never visited Aafaq's grave before, and he'd never meditated either.

Today he did both. A long talk he couldn't finish before he ran out of water and had to return to camp.

Before he'd even quenched his thirst, he knew he'd return the next day.

Zahir and Adele returned to England a week after their celebration, and Nira was tempted to go with them, but she wanted to be there when Dakan came back. The man had failed in his farewell attempt, but he could come back if he came up with whatever answers they wanted, so she waited, worked on the hospital, and walked on the beach with Leila—who was full of informative stories about the Al-Haaken brothers that explained everything she'd witnessed. Information Mum would probably like to know, just as soon as Nira worked out how to bring it up.

She and Adele had exchanged email addresses before they'd gone, and having someone else to talk to made things a little easier. But a half-pound less than unbearable was still a heavy load.

Nothing she did took Dakan from her mind. She didn't even know what he was supposed to be doing in the desert—how could sand tell him anything except that life was hard?

During the weeks since Dakan's exile to the desert, Nira and Leila had spoken daily, though not about Dakan, and because Nira knew it upset the Queen to think of Dakan out there, and because she was the Queen and this whole royalty thing still wigged Nira out a bit, she didn't force the subject. Leila wasn't her Mum, so she needed different tactics from shock and awe.

Into the third week, by the time their midweek beach prowl rolled around, Nira had reached her breaking point. She met Leila and immediately launched in. "I have to say this before I forget how I rehearsed it."

Leila nodded, her expression sharpening with focus.

"I want to go to Dakan, wherever he is. I think he needs someone to talk to. He doesn't like to talk about feelings or even think about them. If he's supposed to meditate and find answers, how is he going to do that when he doesn't even...?" *Hell, how did that part go?* "He doesn't even know himself. Do you know where he is? Can you help me get to him?"

Leila's smile was slow. "His life isn't in much danger there. He has been at our desert abode, he's not suffering as you think he is. At least not physically. Emotionally... Well, when there is nothing left for him to distract himself with, Dakan will listen to that quiet voice in his heart."

"So this is a thing he does?"

Leila shook her head and stepped in to put her arm around Nira's shoulders. "No. My youngest is very like me in that he has a great capacity to creatively amuse or distract himself. But he also has Fatiq's stubbornness."

"So what happens if he doesn't have some kind of epiphany when he's there? How long does his exile last?"

"It lasts until he can give a satisfactory response for the incident and his handling of this mess. Or perhaps until he simply gives in and does what Fatiq wishes."

"Marry me?"

Leila nodded.

"Oh, that's exactly what a woman wants to hear about her reluctant possible future husband. If it turns out he's the less stubborn of the two and gets bored, he might decide to marry me just so he can have electricity again."

"I don't think that will happen."

"I could help him, Leila. If we're alone, he'll talk to me. I know he will."

"Give him more time." Leila steered her toward the water. They always walked at the water's edge. It was no good to walk on the beach without getting your feet wet and feeling the sand between your toes.

Too much like walking in the desert.

When Nira got to the penthouse the next morning for work, Leila was sitting at her desk, waiting. The first thing that hit her was surprise, then fear.

"Has something happened to Dakan?"

The Queen rose. Behind her chair sat a medium-sized travel bag. "Dakan is fine. I'm here to help you, but only if you agree not to share your decision when I have finished saying what I came to say."

Keep her decision to herself? She could do that. "I agree."

"The day you came to us, Dakan asked me to protect your freedom. Yesterday my first instinct was to protect you physically, then I remembered his request. So here I am."

The conversation was quick, and Leila left as soon as it was over.

Two hours later the helicopter landed on the outside edge of the oasis, letting Nira off with her bag.

A man came out to meet her and Nira handed him an envelope Leila had given her, granting permission to be there.

With nothing to argue about, he gestured to the big tent—as if Nira could miss the thing—and left her to it.

Inside, she found layers of Arabian rugs, pillows for sitting on, cascades of white silk, intricate bronzed lanterns and a fire pit—though she couldn't imagine where wood to burn came from, or even if it was for burning wood.

It was so large there were rooms, separate tents connected together with enclosed passageways leading from one to the next.

In one, a bedroom, there was a massive four-poster bed and a thick velvet rope above it. Okay, that was a little weird.

She went through the whole complex, at least everywhere she could find, and Dakan wasn't there. But the massive bed looked comfortable, so she returned there and climbed up onto it. In the middle, she found an open notebook with an ink pen lying on the open page.

Left to right writing.

English.

She leaned over to peek at it, and the words "Dear Nira" stood out.

A letter to her.

She reached for the book.

As he now did every day, Dakan returned to the camp at dusk. Tonight, one of the groomsmen met him in front of the tent and held an envelope out to him. He found his mother's elegant script on the front, but it wasn't addressed to him. He stepped into the tent and removed his shoes to get a little more comfortable, lit a lantern and opened the envelope.

He hadn't expected to hear from her yet—Dakan knew by now that people watched him, and servants made reports. The family knew he was fine, aside from the headache that hadn't left him since he'd arrived. The one that had stayed so long he'd started to think he had a blasted brain tumor...

What he found inside the envelope sent a thrill through him, and left him feeling a little breathless. Dropping the letter, he picked up the lantern and went deeper into the tent.

Nira had permission to be there.

He found her in the harem room, a lantern hanging

nearby and his notebook open in her lap. If she'd read the whole thing, she'd never give up on him, even though she should. But he couldn't think about that now—he was so incredibly grateful to see her...

Her hair was down and she wore loose-fitting trousers and a T-shirt. Little bare feet wedged beneath each knee, she didn't seem to realize he was there.

"Why did you pick the harem room?" he asked, unable to help the smile that came when she lifted her eyes to him.

"Because I'm not a royal, and this is the royal abode. It seemed like the most appropriate room for me, class-wise."

"I'm not a royal either right now. Perhaps we should both join the harem."

She fidgeted with the corner of one page, nervously flicking it back and forth. "I think we're too well educated for that. Though I have to comment on this book. There are twelve letters addressed to me, their perforated edges still perfectly intact. When were you going to send them? The same day you decided to trim that beard, Wild Man?"

Her tease made him smile again, but his throat felt thick and his tongue sluggish. "I had no one to impress." He cleared his throat and walked fully into the tent to sit on the corner of the pillow-mattress. "I didn't intend to send them to you."

"Then why did you write them?"

"To try and make sense of things. I missed our conversations, so I wrote to you."

"Who is Aafaq?"

Dakan reached for the notebook, but she pulled it out of his reach.

"Aafaq was what they called my little brother. He was born too soon in order to save Mother's life. Zahir told me to talk to the desert, but that's just not me. If I'm going to sit in the desert and talk to anything, it'd be my little brother. His grave's nearby."

There it was again, that compassion in her eyes that felt like a caress.

"Is that where you were today? It can't be too close. The helicopter is loud."

"I heard it. Just decided it was Father, and he could wait. If I'd known it was you, I'd have come right away."

"You would've?" The sadness he'd inflicted on her pulled at her brows, still present even if she was happy to see him, and that light was there too. "You did a good job of avoiding me at the palace. You should know, I took a gamble coming here."

"What gamble?"

"If we don't talk through this and work things out, I'll be sent back to England and the project given to someone else."

Dakan lifted a hand to rub it over his face, and immediately knew how he must look. Dirty. Hairy. Not at all princely. But then, that was who she'd come to see. She didn't like it when he got stiff and princely.

"You shouldn't have come, then."

"It's too late now. If I leave, your people here will report to the palace that I was here. For better or worse, we need to work this out and I think we can."

"You continue to give me too much credit." He lay back on the bed and stared at the ceiling. "I thought you came to talk about your father. Have the Al-Haaken contacted Father?"

"I don't know, and I really don't care unless it's important to you." She scooted to his side, but didn't touch him. "I want to talk about the letters."

"The letters are me trying to explain what I'm thinking after my graveside chats with Aafaq."

She flipped through the pages, though he was certain she'd read it all before he'd returned. "I like the questions at the top of the pages. *How would I be different if Aafaq had lived? Why does it bother me to be labeled 'Born to Follow'?* She met his gaze, her brow lifted. "That's the first two pages devoted to relationships between brothers."

"Aafaq is my brother. I don't know the question to ask, so I just started the conversations thinking about what it means to be brothers. If I'd been second in line but not the youngest, would I be different? Would I have gravitated more toward Zahir's territory, been more like Prince Dakan—as you dubbed me—without forcing it?"

"Territory. If we were home, I'd make it a drinking game. Every time you said 'Zahir's territory,' you'd have to do a shot."

"Too bad we're not in England."

"If we were, we wouldn't talk. We'd just get drunk and then nakedness would inevitably follow."

Damned right it would. His willpower was shot.

"You frame it as relationships between brothers, but your brothers didn't cast your role. Your parents did that. The King—who I'm sure loves you in his authoritarian way—was the one who said you were born to follow. He probably didn't think about how that would stick with a child. And that would bother anyone, especially someone in your position. If someone told you that you were predetermined for greatness, that'd be a lot easier fate to embrace than being born to do whatever your brother told you. It's not about Zahir, it's about having your free will reined in before you could even understand what it meant."

Dakan really hated thinking about feelings, but he loved it that she was close enough to him now that he could touch her. She wouldn't let him take the notebook, so he reached for her hand again and let himself soak in the tangible physical relief he felt touching her.

His head instantly stopped aching.

She set the notebook on the bed beside her, freeing her other hand to reach for his. "What's wrong?"

"My head…feels so much better I'm a little light-headed."

He needed her around, even if it was an entirely selfish desire.

"Do you want me to stop?"

He shook his head. She wanted to talk, so he wanted to do whatever she wanted. Even if it was on unpleasant topics, he had missed their talks. He'd missed her voice. Her scent. Everything.

"When you're in London and you see Zahir, do you feel the need to be Prince Dakan?" Her thumbs began stroking his fingers.

"No."

"Then I don't think you're really talking about brother problems. It's not about Zahir. You can let go of that guilt." She momentarily pulled her hand away to flip the notebook pages and read back his words, "'I enjoy working on the hospital. It lets me do something important for my country —which is a new experience for me. I've never been important to the country, or felt I could be without something happening to Zahir, a thought that brings a mountain of guilt.'"

"I know what I wrote," he murmured, catching her free hand again. "Do you know the question?"

"I know the answer," she said softly, smiling in that soothing way.

She knew the answer? "What is it? Tell me and I'll come back."

"No. If I tell you what to think, it's never going to be real for either of us. If you ever decide you can have what we both want, even if you're uncertain about everything else in life, you have to be certain about us. I need you to know it like I know it, deep in your heart."

"If you tell me, I'll believe, *habibi*. I swear."

"I didn't come here to do your thinking for you." She lifted his dry, weathered hands and kissed the thumbs wrapped over her fingers. "I know you can do it. It's all in that notebook. Have you gone back and read it all together?"

"No."

"You should. Even if there's not one mention of territory in this book. All the times you've mentioned Zahir's territory in conversation points to it meaning something you haven't explored yet."

"All it means is that I'm better at different things than he is. I'm not him. If he's better at something, he should be the one doing it. People shouldn't expect me to be good at it too just because he is. We're different."

"Yes, you are. So different it looks contrived, like all those television shows and movies about opposites who live or work together, and the kooky shenanigans that ensue when they try to get along." She paused and pondered a moment before announcing, "The things you've said are Zahir's territory are emergency medicine and misbehaving in more satisfying ways, like bombing your Lego house rather than chopping it up. What else?"

"Nira."

"No, Nira is pretty much only Dakan's territory, whether he wants to claim it or not." She suddenly pulled her hands free of his, and he wanted to grab her and pull her to him again. "Read the letters with fresh eyes, as if I'd written them, without all your preconceived ideas about what you can and cannot do or what your place is." She leaned towards him and reached down to cup his scruffy cheeks. "And I don't care what answers your family want you to find. I only care about you."

He closed his eyes, nothing coming to him to say other than pleas for her to stay.

"I love you, and I know you love me. I even knew it

before I read it. And it's not the kind of love you can walk away from. I've seen up close the effects of twenty-seven years of heartbreak…always bitter and cold and broken. I don't know if he ever truly loved her—I hope he did before it got twisted—but I know she loved him. It never went away."

"Nira…how can I—?"

"Wait. There's one more thing I know. We are supposed to be together. And you're the only thing standing in our way." Her eyes welled up and she lowered her head until her smooth, cool forehead touched his, and her tears fell on the cheeks she held.

She let go and straightened. He couldn't tell whose tears were on his face any more.

"Find me when you're ready," she said, her voice shaking with effort, then turned and walked out of the tent.

Dakan reached for the notebook.

For the next two days they made love every night, and during the day he went to Aafaq, this time armed with the notebook Nira believed held the answers he needed, but the only questions he cared to have answered were: Why couldn't he have her? Where did this certainty that he couldn't come from?

On the third day he took extra water and food with him to Aafaq's grave, intent on staying until he'd sorted himself out. He had no idea why his father let her stay there without sending the helicopter to retrieve her. He had to sort it out before they took her away from him again, or before she lost faith and left him, even if he longed to spend every minute with her—every minute that twisted together paradise and agony.

Sometime in the middle of the third night Nira felt the bed give beside her and Dakan spooned up behind her. He'd warned before leaving that he wouldn't return until he had an answer, so she'd expected him to be away for days. Her heart immediately launched into a staggering rhythm before he'd even put his arms around her.

"You have answers?" she whispered, then squirmed around to face him. The lantern she kept lit cast a golden light over his tanned face, and she saw that light in his eyes for the first time in a long time, and the twinkle of mischief she'd so missed.

"You might kick me if I tell you."

"I'll definitely kick you if you don't tell me."

Tugging her beneath him, he rolled her onto her back and sought her mouth. Their kisses were always full of passion, but since that blessed building had swallowed her up they'd been full of love and urgency. The past few days' need had become longing tinged with heartache, and every touch of his lips had broken her heart.

But his kiss now held nothing but love, hope, and promises. He tasted like honey, heady and indolent, like he had all the time in the world.

When he finally lifted his head, she knew the wait was over. It was like peace flowed off him.

"Zahir will be King one day, and the King should always be treated with courtesy and respect," Dakan said softly, combing his fingers through her hair as he held her gaze, staying against her, his face inches away. "It would be disrespectful for me to be better at something than he is, or to even try to be. I'm the one who was born to follow, and I hate it being phrased that way. I didn't— I don't want to just follow. I want to do great things for our people too. So to reconcile those issues, whatever way Zahir went, I went in the other direction. I didn't even realize I was doing it."

Nira nodded, reaching for the buttons down his shirt. The talking would be more fulfilling if she could feel him down the entire length of her body, skin to skin. "Every page in your book led from one piece of the puzzle to the next, did you see it?"

"I saw it," he whispered, pulling the shirt off and helping rid them both of clothes before molding himself back to her.

"How does that explain punching Jibril? Did you work that out?"

"That was me after hitting my snapping point. It started at the penthouse when I defied my father for the first time ever—being directly disrespectful to the king."

"When he told you not to be alone with me?"

He nodded, his arms tightening. The time in the desert had made him a bit leaner, but his appeal was every bit as strong.

"After that, I fought with him on the beach about you. I think at that point I just said to hell with it, and let instinct drive me in matters I couldn't let my prince persona handle diplomatically. I didn't want to leave your future in my father's hands. I don't think he'd hurt you, but I just…couldn't let anyone else take care of you. I wanted it to be me, and it confused me. Plus, let's be real here, Jibril needed punching."

Nira could see the progression, one act of rebellion in a moment of stress, followed by another when the world hadn't imploded the first time. By the time he'd got to Jibril, everything had been so out of control it had probably felt like nothing could make things worse.

Then his words replayed in her mind and she asked, "You fought with the King a second time about me? This was after I moved to the palace?"

"The same day."

"What about?"

"I accused him of bringing you to the palace as leverage in this never-ending conflict with the Al-Haaken, and then refused to marry you. Not that I feel that way now."

"So the King had been trying to make you marry me for weeks?"

"You know, opinions formed by six-year-olds rarely work out well for grown men."

"You think?"

He grinned, and that dimple she'd so missed pitted his cheek again.

"I missed your dimple."

"I missed everything about you. We didn't even get a chance to laze about in bed that day, did we? The King arrived, it all went to hell, and I... Actually, that's the first day I started to really question what I wanted, because I knew I wanted you, even when I denied it to everyone else. I want you, Nira. I want to be with you, and I don't care where. I want you, and our children. I want to be there for you both, for you all, however many of you all there end up being."

She felt his breath fan her lips seconds before the first soft brush of his. Her mouth opened and he deepened the kiss, his body scorching the length of hers as he slid between her legs and set her on fire.

As they came together, peace fell over Nira with the certainty they'd found all their missing pieces. They'd roughed out the footprint and dug the foundations, and could start building a life, a family, a home...wherever they decided to put it. Solid. Beautiful. And built far too well to fall in a lifetime.

* * * * *

THE SHEIKH
DOCTOR'S
BRIDE

MEREDITH WEBBER

PROLOGUE

FAREED IBN JADYM IBN MUSTAFFAH FARUKE eyed the green country through which he travelled with distaste. Not that he didn't appreciate green. The shiny, almost luminous green of date-palm fronds around an oasis was always a welcome sight, and contrasted brilliantly with the red desert sand through which one had to travel to see them.

But green everywhere, everything green, apart from white paint splashed haphazardly on the fence posts lining the drive down which they now travelled.

Why, in the name of all that was holy, was his uncle coming to this run-down establishment, stuck out in a swathe of green, miles from the city in which they'd been staying?

So his uncle wanted to buy a horse—wanted him, Fareed, to see the horse before the purchase—but could not the horse have come to them? Ibrahim wasn't one to go out of his way for anything or anyone, however much he loved his horses.

But Fareed's apprehension about what was going on with his uncle went beyond this trip to a horse stud. Something was brewing in his uncle's devious mind, and Fareed had a disturbing suspicion that the 'something' was to do with him.

Why else would his uncle insist he take leave from the hospital to accompany him on this trip to Australia?

To buy a *horse*!

And why had Thalia, an old crone who lived somewhere in the palace compound and was said to read the future from marks in the sand, or oil poured on a cup of water, been spending so much time with his uncle prior to this trip? Thalia claimed she was a *kahin*, from a line of female fortune-tellers that went back into ancient times.

Surely his uncle, English educated, graduate of Oxford and with a further business degree from Harvard, didn't still believe in the words of a soothsayer?

Fareed shook his head, sorry he was in the lead of the four cars and couldn't ask his uncle these questions. Then something flashed past the window and soothsayers and his uncle's devious plans were forgotten.

The horse was a dark caramel in colour, its mane nearly white. It was pounding up the slight slope of a track on the other side of the fence, and on its back, her face alight with the joy of speed, sat a slim woman, taller than most jockeys but riding with her legs tucked up, her body bent along the horse's neck, flame-coloured hair flying out behind her—a woman at one with the animal.

A painting of the image might be called *Freedom*, and though Fareed yearned for freedom, duty was a stronger master. Oh, for a while he was okay, working in the hospital, doing what he enjoyed, feeling needed and appreciated, and although, when he *did* succeed his uncle to the Sultanate, he hoped to continue his medical career at least part-time, he knew his duty was to his people, and to helping them come to terms with the changing world in which they now lived.

But the beauty of the horse and its rider had eased some of Fareed's apprehension about this trip. Perhaps he should, as Ibrahim kept insisting, simply relax and enjoy the last few days of this break away from work. And, really, was green all that bad a colour?

* * *

The man Kate's mother was hoping would save the family's stables arrived in a fleet of long black limousines—if four exceedingly large vehicles could be called a fleet.

According to her mum, he was some kind of Eastern potentate—she read a lot, her mum!

The arrival of the sleek vehicles suggested he might be a very wealthy potentate, though no doubt a con man would have made an equally impressive arrival, Kate told herself.

Cynical?

Kate?

No more so than any other thirty-two-year-old woman who'd grown up with a dearly loved father who had always had a fortune waiting for him just around the next corner; no more so than any other woman who had recently been dumped by a long-term lover who couldn't believe she would go home to be with her mother after said father's death, instead of staying with him on the other side of the world.

She turned Marac and headed back to the stables. Mum would offer the potentate some tea so she, Kate, would have time to give the horse a good rub-down and settle him in his stall before the inspection party arrived.

Cantering back down the hill, watching the cars wending their way down the drive, she wondered about the future. *If* the potentate saved the stables, would she go back to the US, to Mark? Could she go back to a man with so little empathy?

She'd been home two months now, time enough to see the man she'd thought she loved through clearer eyes. No, going back to Mark was not an option.

But, then, if this potentate didn't buy Tippy, she wouldn't have to think about options.

Kate tried to see her home through the visitors' eyes: the lush paddocks shaded by wide spreading gum trees

and filled with spectacular horses; the green fields; the
placid stream running through the valley; the old stone
and bleached-wood stables; and, by the stream, the house,
built from stones hauled from the creek over a hundred
years ago...

Her mother's—no, in fact, it was Billy's heritage...

CHAPTER ONE

THE IMAGE OF the girl on the horse was still vivid in Fareed's mind as the vehicles rolled to a stop in a big paved area outside the stone-built house. A middle-aged woman had been waiting at the gate and she stepped forward as the entourage began to emerge from the vehicles.

And Fareed wondered again about his uncle's insistence on travelling everywhere with this entourage. Surely Ibrahim and the stud manager, with Fareed tagging along, could manage to buy a horse. But, no, a fleet of vehicles seemed to accompany them everywhere, with dour-faced palace guards, who probably hated green as much as he did, hovering protectively around his uncle at all times.

Preventing an attack from a rabid kangaroo?

The driver was already opening the door for Ibrahim, while the men in their unaccustomed garb of dark suits alighted from the other cars and stood erect, in a kind of deferential arc around where Ibrahim would appear.

Did he do it to impress people?

Fareed doubted that, for Ibrahim was the most modest of men, and rarely made a show of his position. No, there was definitely some hidden agenda in this trip to Australia, and he, Fareed, was completely in the dark about it. He stood beside his uncle as the woman approached, wishing he could read what was going on behind the bland but still charming smile.

'I'm Sally Walker. Welcome to Dancing Waters Stud. The river runs over rounded granite stones on the bend below the house and the waters seem to dance, which is where it got its name.'

She sounded nervous and her arm shook slightly as she offered her hand to Ibrahim. To Fareed's surprise, his uncle not only took it but raised it to his lips for a swift courtly kiss.

Sally Walker blushed a fiery red and Fareed felt a momentary pang of pity for her.

'Sultan Ibrahim ibn—' His uncle broke off the recitation of his name and smiled at her. 'You do not need to know the rest. We call ourselves son of our father—that is the "ibn"—then "ibn" again because he was the son of his father, and I could go on until next week just saying my name. You must call me Ibrahim.'

Hmm! Ibrahim at his most charming!

Fareed's suspicions grew.

'You would like tea or coffee, or a cool drink?' their hostess offered.

'Perhaps later, my dear,' Ibrahim said. 'But first the horses.'

The woman led the way to the stables, explaining as she went.

'The property was developed by my great-grandparents, and while their main interest was in breeding, my grandfather decided to try his hand at training and did very well. Not many horses, because the breeding side of the business was still important, but he found a special thrill in training his own horses, and that must have passed down in the blood to my father and myself.'

They reached the door of the long, low building, redolent of horse and hay and tack and polish. Some trick of the sun's position sent a beam of light into the dark shadows at the end, catching a slim, lithe woman bending and straightening as she brushed down the palomino Fareed had seen earlier. Caught in the ray of light, the pair took on a shining luminosity—something from a painting by an old master, Titian perhaps, given the colour of her hair coming alive in the light.

Fareed paused, riveted by the sight, while beside him Ibrahim seemed to suck in his breath. The girl straightened up and Fareed noticed Ibrahim nod to himself, as if satisfied about something—very satisfied...

The mystery of this trip to Australia deepened.

Damn, they were here before she'd finished. Never mind, she'd give Marac another rub this afternoon.

Kate straightened up, aware she'd have wisps of straw in her hair and smudges on her face and would smell of horse, but knowing she needed to be by her mother's side through this fraught process.

She led Marac into a stall, checked he had food and water, half shut his door, then rubbed her handkerchief over her face and hands and went to meet the visitors.

There was a phalanx of dark, swarthy men around a slightly shorter man. All wore immaculately tailored suits and stern expressions. Except for one, taller than the others—tall, dark and handsome personified, in fact—whose expression was more one of disdain. And his suit was better cut, though he didn't owe those broad shoulders to his tailor. She checked his face again and saw a classic profile—long, straight nose, broad forehead and a firm chin.

You missed the lips, a voice inside her head whispered, but she hadn't missed the lips, not in any way. In fact, it had been the lips that had drawn her attention...

He was still looking disdainful, she reminded herself.

Perhaps he felt visiting a small horse breeder's property was beneath him?

'This is my daughter, Kate,' Sally said. 'Kate, this is

Sultan Ibrahim and a lot of other names he says we needn't bother with.'

Kate approached the group and held out her hand to the sultan—didn't sultans wear golden turbans?—then remembered where she'd been and withdrew her hand.

'Sorry, I smell of horse. I really thought I'd be done earlier and cleaned up before you came, but Marac needed the extra run and it was such a beautiful morning, I couldn't resist.'

She smiled hopefully at the sultan, who not only returned her smile but didn't back away from her eau de horse.

'Well, don't let me keep you from your tour of inspection. I'll tag along behind in case Mum needs anything.'

She slid past the men, telling herself not to look at faces, but how could she not just sneak a peek now she was closer to Mr Handsome—fine-cut features, a long aquiline nose, cheekbones as sharp as razors, lips—best she didn't check out the lips…

She couldn't help glancing up as she passed him, drawn by something more than his expression. Drawn by something she didn't really understand, though it felt vaguely like attraction. Think about the disdain, she told herself, although perhaps it was disgust, not disdain, probably because of the pervading odour of horse that hung around her?

Could she dash up to the house and shower? So she wouldn't smell like horse if she was close to the man again? Was she mad? Attracted to a man like that? And, anyway, she couldn't leave the party now.

Not really, not if Mum might need her.

Or Billy.

Where *was* Billy?

The ache that rarely went away, tucked into a corner of her heart—the ache that was Billy, gentle, sensitive, slow-to-develop Billy— reminded her of the problems that lay ahead.

Face troubles when they come, girl, she remembered her father telling her, and although he always took the words a little too literally, she felt somehow comforted.

Ibrahim had paused by a half-open door and was talking quietly to the inquisitive gelding who'd poked his head out of his stall. As far as Kate could tell, the visitor wasn't speaking English but the horse seemed to understand him anyway and was nodding and holding his head sideways for a hard rub.

'Shamus is Tippy's—Dancing Tiptoes's—older brother— full brother, doing well in local two-year-olds' races.'

The young horse shifted his attention to Kate's mother and nuzzled her neck as she explained.

'You've tried him in the city?' asked one of the entourage—the taller one who'd failed to hide his disdain.

Sally Andrews shook her head.

'Since…'

She faltered and Kate, who knew exactly how huge a strain this meeting was on her mother, stepped in.

'Since my father died two months ago, my mother hasn't wanted to travel far,' she said, speaking directly to the man who'd asked the question, meeting the challenge in his eyes that seemed to peer right into her soul. 'And logistically it's difficult. One of our stable hands was killed in the same accident, so we're short-handed even with me here.'

The questioner's eyes, dark as obsidian, studied her intently.

Suspiciously?

She shook off the tremor of unease his look had caused and concentrated on the main man—Ibrahim.

'So, should I purchase Dancing Tiptoes and wish him to run in the best races, I will have to find another trainer?' Ibrahim asked.

He was standing so close to Sally he must have seen her reaction, and noticed Kate reach out to steady her mother.

Obsidian Eyes certainly had; he missed nothing.

Which might explain, Kate decided, why he, of all the entourage, made her feel so uncomfortable.

'Come and meet him,' she said, determined to ignore the stranger. 'There's no point in discussing training arrangements if you don't like the look of him.'

But who wouldn't? she thought, and her gut clenched as the ramifications of losing Tippy spun in her head.

It was inevitable that Billy would be down in the paddock with Tippy, running alongside him as if they were a pair of the same species.

'My son, Billy,' Sally said, and Ibrahim nodded.

Kate, whose eyes had gone to Ibrahim's face as soon as she saw Billy in the paddock, realised that the man had seen and understood a difference in Billy—seen, understood and accepted! An empathetic man!

Bother the man who was making her uncomfortable, Ibrahim was the boss. It was he who'd decide.

Sally's whistle had brought Tippy to the fence, Billy following more slowly, his natural caution with strangers holding him back.

Or did he understand more about Tippy's future than Kate and Sally realised?

Sally had thrust her hand into the capacious pockets of her trousers, but Ibrahim was faster, producing from the pocket in his immaculate pinstriped suit a small, rosy apple.

'I may?' he said to Sally, who nodded and tucked the sugar lumps back into her pocket.

Tippy studied the stranger almost as warily as Billy had, then threw his head back and snorted before lowering it to lip the apple delicately off the man's hand.

'He likes apples best of all.' Billy had come gradually

closer and now stood beside the horse, his too-thin face radiating the love he felt for the animal.

'I do, too,' Ibrahim said. 'Where I live it is hard to grow apples, so when I come to your country I eat as many as possible.'

'Where is it that you can't grow apples?'

'A place called Amberach, far across the sea. A very small place compared to Australia.'

'Did you come here in a plane?'

Kate was aware of her mother's tension returning. Once involved in a conversation, Billy could talk for hours. Should they cut him off?

She glanced at Ibrahim, who showed no sign of impatience—no sign of anything except, she rather thought, simple kindness.

'Yes, I came on a plane.'

'Next to horses I like planes best. Dad always said one day I could go on a plane with the horses, but Dad died, you know.'

'Yes, I did know that,' Ibrahim said gently, while Kate held her breath.

Please, don't offer him a plane ride, especially if you don't mean it.

But Ibrahim's attention was back on the horse—or was he diverting Billy?

'Would you run him again for me?' Ibrahim asked, and Billy whistled to Tippy and the pair took off, Billy understanding what was needed and circling in the middle while Tippy raced around the paddock, his delight in movement lending wings to his feet.

'A truly beautiful sight,' Ibrahim murmured. He turned to one of his men—not the tall, disdainful one. 'He is everything you said he was.'

The man nodded.

'Would you like a cool drink or a cup of tea or coffee?'

Kate offered, trying to hide the excitement she was feeling, although she knew her mother would be more apprehensive than excited.

Selling Tippy was one thing—the money from the sale would save the stables—but keeping him to train—her mother's long-held dream—was quite another.

'First we might walk around a little, see the other horses, the training track and the hill run I've heard about. Dancing Tiptoes was bred here—the mare is here?' Ibrahim replied.

'In foal again, and with the other mares,' Sally told him. 'When they're pregnant they seem to like the company. We'll walk this way.'

She led the party, Ibrahim close behind her, Kate and the entourage bringing up the rear.

'You'd already seen the horse?' she said to the man beside her—the one to whom Ibrahim had turned earlier.

'I was at your father's funeral, then came back here with others,' he said quietly. 'I know it is late to be offering condolences but I am sorry for your loss.'

Kate thanked him and lagged behind, caught off guard by his sudden kindness. She remembered little of that terrible day beyond a blur of cars and people and a need to be strong for both her mother and Billy, yet being uselessly emotional all day.

In fact, it had been Billy who'd been strong for her, and for their mother.

Maybe he would understand more than they thought if Tippy was sold and moved to another trainer. Maybe he'd transfer his love to a new foal—

'Ka-a-a-a-te!'

Her mother's anguished cry brought her out of her reverie. Looking up, she realised the entourage was now some way ahead of her. But instinct had her running down towards the brood mares' paddock, pushing through the phalanx of minders, seeing the taller man, eyes nearly swollen shut, red welts appearing on his face, pulling at his tie, his collar, trying to say something that sounded like 'knife'.

'He wants a knife,' one of the men said, while Kate grabbed the man, trying to ease him to the ground, issuing orders as she did it.

'Call an ambulance—emergency number is triple zero here—and you…' she pointed to the closest '…run up to the stables and get the first-aid box. One of the stable hands will find it for you.'

The stricken man was still struggling to talk, pointing at his throat and making gargling noises.

'What's his name?' she asked Ibrahim, who was looking so pale Kate feared she'd have two patients.

'Fareed,' Ibrahim whispered.

'Don't worry, he'll be all right,' Kate assured the older man, before turning back to her patient.

'Okay, Fareed, I need you to relax. Lie right back, you'll be all right.'

She'd fallen to her knees beside him as she spoke, straightening him out on the ground as best she could when he was still struggling, pushing at her and trying to talk.

'Lie still, you big lunk,' she yelled, and apparently shocked him into immobility. Seizing her chance, she tilted back his head in case CPR became necessary, automatically feeling for a pulse, counting his breaths, more gasps than breaths.

'He was waving his hands then started gasping,' Sally was explaining, but Kate had already found the tiny sting the bee had left behind, barely visible on the lobe of the man's right ear.

'It's anaphylactic shock,' she said as she pulled the sting out and felt in the man's pockets for a pen. 'Did any of you know he had allergies? That he was allergic to bee stings?'

The men looked blankly at her but there was no time to explain.

Tilting the patient's head farther back, she leaned forward, refusing to even consider the lips she was about to touch as anything other than an anonymous patient's. Although as she closed her mouth over his, breathing air into his lungs, trying to force it in through a passage she knew would be closing more and more, a shiver of something she couldn't understand ran down her spine.

Between breaths she reassured her patient, who was nearly comatose but still struggling, though feebly, against her.

It was Billy who brought the first-aid kit, and Kate, knowing an ambulance would take at least another twenty minutes to reach the property, didn't hesitate.

Opening the big case, she searched for the epinephrine injection she'd told her father to keep there. Either he hadn't bothered or it had been used, emptied and not replaced. She found a scalpel, still in its sterile wrapping, and a small roll of plastic tubing—heaven only knew its real use. Using scissors, she cut a small piece then pulled on gloves.

The skin on the man's neck was smooth and tanned, and her hand hesitated for a fraction of a second but she knew what had to be done.

She'd drawn the scalpel from its sheath and moved her hand towards that smooth, tanned skin, when one of the entourage stepped forward and, to her astonishment, pulled out a gun.

A small gun, but no less deadly than a big one would be, of that she was sure.

He muttered something at her in his own language and Kate turned to Ibrahim.

'His throat has swollen and he can't breathe—I need to make a hole and breathe into it for him until he can manage on his own. I am a doctor, I can do this.'

Ibrahim nodded and apparently translated but the gun didn't disappear back to wherever it had come from.

So if I do this wrong, he shoots me? Kate wondered in the distant part of her brain not focused on the job.

Feeling carefully, she found the space between his thyroid cartilage and the cricoid cartilage. The scalpel blade bit cleanly, a cut barely half an inch deep, and she slipped her finger into it to open it, before sliding the tube into place.

Ignoring the muttering going on around her and the distant yowling of an ambulance, she bent low and breathed into the tube. Two quick breaths, pause, another breath, pause...

The man's chest was rising so she'd got the tube in successfully, but he needed treatment—epinephrine to combat the shock, hospitalisation for at least twenty-four hours, and minor surgery to repair the gash she'd made in his throat.

Somehow she didn't think she'd have to worry about Billy missing Tippy. These people would want nothing more to do with the Andrews family.

The ambos, once they'd given the patient an epinephrine injection in his thigh, were audibly impressed by her efforts.

'Learnt about it, of course,' one said, 'but never had to do it.'

'I'm an ER doctor,' Kate explained, as they expertly attached monitors to their patient, then lifted him onto the stretcher. 'Though *I've* only had to do it once before so I was a bit shaky.'

'ER doc?' the second man said, when he'd strapped Fareed onto the stretcher. 'Don't suppose you'd come with us—sit with him just in case.'

'I think that would be an excellent idea,' Ibrahim said, and to emphasise the point he actually nodded towards the man who'd held the gun.

Or maybe that was her imagination running riot after the little bit of drama!

Whatever! Someone would have to sit with him to hold the plastic tube in place and it might as well be her. She climbed into the back of the ambulance beside Fareed, who was breathing, somewhat raspily, through the hole in his neck. His eyes opened, the drug taking almost immediate effect, and his hand lifted to feel his neck.

Kate caught the hand before he could dislodge the tube, and held it in hers so it could do no harm. It was a strong hand, with long, lean fingers that fought against her hold— a manly hand...

She put the distraction down to her own shock—*and* disappointment.

'You've suffered anaphylactic shock. You've got a tube in your throat so you can breathe and you've had an injection of epinephrine, which will combat the shock. Now you know you're allergic to bee stings, you should carry a pen with the drug in it wherever you go.'

The disdain she'd read in his eyes earlier returned, so blatant she wanted to turn away.

And let him get away with it?

'Not that I expect gratitude or anything for saving your life, but a smile wouldn't hurt!'

Fortunately, before she could let off any more steam, which she knew was nothing more than a release of her own tension, they drew up at the hospital.

A woman was beside him—a woman in big glasses and flaming red hair she hid in a plait, but nice skin—creamy skin, skin you'd like to touch but preferably when she wasn't going on and on at him. Fareed closed his eyes and tried to clear his head.

She was holding his hand.

He must know her.

She looked angry, but, then, he knew any number of angry women, though none he could remember with plaited hair. Her glasses magnified pale green eyes. Beautiful eyes, he rather thought—even angry, they were special. But the glasses were appalling, although the frames were the same colour as the little freckles sprinkled over her nose.

He was reasonably sure he didn't know any woman with freckles on her nose—well, not freckles that she left on show for everyone to see.

Men's voices and a door opening somewhere near his feet brought memory of what had happened rushing back. He tried again to feel his throat but the woman stopped him.

'You're at the hospital now. You'll be okay, you'll be fine. They'll want to keep you overnight, to check you haven't had a reaction to the drug, and they'll stitch up the hole I made in your neck, and—'

He freed his hand and put it up to touch her lips, to quiet her, then he smiled to show her he'd understood.

She looked so surprised—by his smile?—his next smile became a genuine one.

After all, she *had* saved his life!

Kate alighted from the ambulance, shaken by what was nothing more than a stranger's casual finger touching her lips. Before she could analyse the reaction, she realised that Ibrahim and his entourage were already there. The older man was watching anxiously as the ambulance men rolled the stretcher out, set it on its legs and began to wheel it away.

He walked beside it, talking to Fareed, obviously concerned about his health, asking questions of the nurse who appeared, giving orders to his men—a caring man.

A sultan?

The word was redolent of fairy stories from Kate's youth—men with golden turbans and casks of glowing jewellery. Did the world still have sultans?

Although it wasn't stature but money that had everyone running around after him, she decided less than an hour later when a specialist ear, nose and throat surgeon arrived from Sydney, helicoptered in to the helipad behind the hospital.

'I'm under orders to stay until the tube comes out and I'm sure he's breathing safely without it—which is now—and then to fix the hole you made,' the man said to Kate after he'd seen the patient. 'My mother could have fixed the hole with one of her embroidery needles. Who *is* this bloke?'

Kate shrugged.

'He came with Sultan Ibrahim to see one of my mother's horses, that's all I know. They must have got on to someone at their consulate and arranged to have you flown here.'

She hesitated, not sure whether to tell the surgeon about the gun. Decided not to. He'd see it for himself if he displeased the entourage in any way.

'Well, now you're here I'll leave him in your expert hands and go home,' she said, then smiled. 'A top ENT man sitting in a country hospital watching a patient recover from anaphylactic shock—that must be a change for you!'

He smiled back.

'Actually, it's all in a good cause. They bribed me with the offer of a very handsome donation to my favourite research programme.'

'Fair enough,' Kate said, aware the man had expected her to ask what it was and to stay for a chat, but she was suddenly overwhelmingly tired and had yet to work out how she was going to get home.

One of the sultan's men sorted that problem, emerging from one of the limos as she came down the hospital steps and opening the rear door for her to get in.

He's either going to kidnap me or take me home, and right now I'm too tired to care, she thought as she climbed into the luxury vehicle and sank back into the soft leather seat.

'Thank you,' she said, as the limo pulled away from the

hospital, then the build-up of stress she'd been feeling all day—apprehension about the important man's visit, worry over Billy should Tippy be sold, the medical drama and the strangely attractive disdainful man—seeped silently out of her body, and she rested her head back and closed her eyes.

CHAPTER TWO

KATE AND BILLY were clearing fallen branches from the top paddocks when the fleet of cars rolled back down the drive the next morning—three limos this time, not four.

Wet and filthy, Kate pushed her straggling hair back off her face and scowled as they passed.

'Mum's down in the bottom paddock,' Billy said, and Kate's scowl deepened.

Filthy or not, she'd have to greet the visitors.

Leaving Billy to finish the work, she climbed the fence and hurried down the drive behind the cars, arriving as Ibrahim's guard, as she thought of them now, formed around him.

'Sorry I'm such a mess—we had quite a storm last night—and Mum's down in the bottom paddock,' she said, aware she didn't sound the least bit sorry. 'If you want to wait inside I'll get her for you.'

Ibrahim waved away her apology and her offer.

'It is you I have come to see.' He spoke so formally Kate felt a whisper of apprehension slither down her spine. Studying him more closely, it seemed he'd aged since the previous day—grown weaker in some way. Shock over the bee-sting incident, or was the man not well? Could she enquire about his health, or would that be breaking some protocol she didn't understand?

'Let's sit on the deck,' she suggested, deciding to keep an

eye on him as they spoke. Maybe an opening would arise when she could ask him if he was all right.

Having decided this, she led him around the side of the house to the wide, paved deck that looked down towards the river. 'These chairs are used to work clothes.'

To Kate's surprise, only Ibrahim followed her; the other men remained by the cars, although the one who'd attended her father's funeral had peeled off from the group and was heading for the stables.

'Why—?' she began.

'He will find your mother and talk with her,' Ibrahim said, his smile allaying a little of her tension. 'You must not be alarmed.'

Kate found herself smiling right back. There was something about this man—the mix of old-world charm and courtly manners—that made her feel safe.

Safe from what?

She had no idea.

She led him up onto the terrace and waved him into a chair, then wondered about the propriety of offering a wet chair to a sultan.

'I think they're all dry but you'd better check,' she said. 'Sometimes a storm blows rain in under the roof.'

Ibrahim obediently felt his chair before sitting down, but now, seated herself, the safe feeling had gone and Kate was feeling *more* than a whisper of apprehension.

Had he decided it was easier to tell her rather than her mother that he wasn't buying Tippy?

What else could it be?

She was about to offer tea or coffee so she could get away for a few minutes and calm herself when he spoke.

'Firstly, I wish to thank you for what you did. Dr McLean tells me you saved Fareed's life and I am grateful, as would be my family and all my people for he is greatly loved. So here is where we are. I will buy your mother's horse, not out of gratitude but because I agree with my stud master that Dancing Tiptoe is a magnificent animal and will hopefully become a great racehorse.'

Kate's heart sank.

Stupid, really, when the sale meant her mother's breeding business would survive, and no doubt prosper, once word got around. But it was the training that her mother loved and to lose a horse with Tippy's potential…

Was she thinking this to stop herself thinking about Billy?

About what losing Tippy would do to Billy's fragile health?

His happiness?

Tippy was his life!

Ibrahim was still talking—she *had* to listen. Later she'd worry about Billy. He was saying…

Saying he'd leave the horse with her mother?

'You'd let her train him? Not take him away? Oh, thank you, Ibrahim, you have no idea how much that would mean to her.'

'And to your brother?'

Kate nodded.

'Yes, Billy and Tippy have been inseparable since Tippy was a foal. Billy has some kind of special bond with all the horses, but with Tippy it is so much more—as if he's found a soul mate.'

'I guessed as much,' Ibrahim said quietly, 'but, as I said earlier, there is a bargain attached. We love bargaining, we of ancient desert blood.'

Ah, the catch, Kate thought, tension building within her as she waited for the axe to drop on this dream result.

'I know our ways are different but they have proved successful over thousands of years. For a long time now I have been looking for a wife for my nephew, and in you

I believe I have found a person of strength and character who would be a perfect match for him.'

'I'm sorry? You want me to marry a total stranger because you think we'd be a perfect match? Ibrahim, I don't want to be rude, but that's ridiculous!'

Far from being offended, Ibrahim smiled calmly and continued as if she'd never spoken.

'I would not hold you to the marriage if, after a certain time, you both felt it was untenable, but I would like you to give it time, say a year. I realise this must seem strange to you—'

'Strange? It's beyond strange. Bizarre might come near but—'

She wasn't allowed to finish—not that she could think past the 'but'.

'To us it is a normal arrangement,' her guest said. 'You will have much in common, for you are both doctors and I believe your recent work has been in Emergency, which is where my nephew works in a new hospital purpose-built for such things. So you could work together, although, of course, you would not have to work unless you wished to.'

He had it all planned out, and he spoke as if this was a rational, reasonable conversation.

Which, of course, it wasn't! Not rational or reasonable at all! Totally unreasonable. Ridiculous, in fact! Although somewhere in the chaos in her head she remembered where this conversation had begun.

It was a bargain.

If she did this, he would not only buy Tippy but would allow her mother to train him.

Here, at the stud…

With Billy…

'And your nephew, what does he have to say to this?' she asked, squelching the questions that she really wanted answers to—why couldn't he find his own wife? Was he a five-foot-two moron with bad skin and a stutter?

Not that a five-foot-two moron with bad skin and a stutter couldn't be a wonderful man and a great husband, but—

'Fareed will accept I am acting in his best interests.'

'Fareed?' The name came out in a disbelieving squeak. 'The man whose throat I cut? That's the man you want me to marry?'

Settle down, Kate, breathe—but before she could obey this sensible order, another thought struck her.

'This isn't like some old Chinese proverb where, if you save a person's life you're responsible for them for ever, is it? I'm a doctor, it's my job—and think of all the doctors in the world who'd be burdened down with all those responsibilities. No, Ibrahim, it's impossible.'

Ibrahim regarded her, his face grave.

'I would not put responsibility for a life on anyone,' he said. 'In my position, I am only too aware of the burden of responsibility. I understand, as a doctor, you did what you had to do and as a result Fareed is alive. But this is a separate issue.'

He paused, looking out over the home paddock to the river, his face troubled by thoughts Kate couldn't guess at.

Not that she wanted to guess at anything—she was too busy trying to order her own thoughts.

Marry a man to save her family?

It was medieval!

But if she did it…

Ibrahim was talking again, and she forced herself to listen.

'I have been seeking a suitable wife for him for some time,' he said. 'He is thirty-seven and it is time he was married. It struck me yesterday that you would be a perfect match for him. You are strong, and resourceful, and caring of your family—this last is important to me because family is who we are.'

'But that's just it—family! *My* family!' Kate pointed out. 'I've come home to help Mum here at the stud, I can't go off and leave her now. She'll have more work than ever.'

Besides which she'd kill me if she thought I'd agree to such a stupid bargain for her sake.

Or Billy's...?

Ibrahim was talking again and Kate tried to concentrate, although the confusion in her mind was making it near impossible.

'I will provide the best available help for your mother,' he said firmly. 'An overseer, stable hands, new vehicles, whatever she will need.'

No confusion now! Kate closed her eyes and saw exactly how the stables could be—the way her mother had always dreamed they'd be, although somehow her father had always managed to lose whatever money they'd had before the dream could be realised.

Her mother would be in heaven.

And Billy would have Tippy.

But her mother would be horrified at the 'bargain'.

Not if she didn't know...

That last sneaky thought hit Kate like a sharp slap.

Was she actually considering Ibrahim's mad idea? Could she really deceive her mother?

She looked at the man who sat quietly beside her, gazing out at the green fields and river gums. Not the courtly gentleman she'd met the day before but someone older, more tired, somehow.

She dragged her mind back from the man to the question.

'But surely your nephew should marry someone from your own country. Someone who would know how—well, how to behave,' she offered desperately.

Ibrahim shook his head, but now he smiled.

'I have thought hard on it, and you would be my choice. Fareed is the son of my older brother so he is also my heir, and although he will be a wise and just ruler, he has ghosts in his life, ghosts I fear will stop him reaching his full potential.'

'So I'm not only supposed to marry this man but banish his demons, as well?' Kate demanded. 'Shouldn't you be calling an exorcist?'

She knew she was being flippant, but right now flippant was all she could manage. The turmoil inside her—the feeling of being torn in two—was just too much!

Ibrahim offered her a slight smile but obviously wasn't diverted from his course.

'I would not put such a burden on you, although I believe you could be the person to help him out of the past. It is why I have chosen you. And, as I said, I would not hold you to the marriage—divorce is simple in my country and should that happen, provided I believe you have behaved honourably, I will honour my agreement with your mother. That would be our bargain.'

Bargain!

The word brought her right back to where this bizarre conversation had started. Ibrahim would buy Tippy, have her mother train him, provide an overseer and stable help and the stables would not only survive but would undoubtedly thrive.

As would Billy!

And all she, Kate, had to do, was…

Marry the man with the disdainful yet seductively attractive face?

The words roared in her head, while a tremor of what she hoped was fear and not desire stirred inside her.

She tried desperately to pull herself together—to come

up with some sensible, solid, irrefutable reasoning against this ridiculous idea.

All she came up with was a question.

'I can work while I'm there?'

'Of course,' Ibrahim replied. 'We would really appreciate it if you did.'

'So you need doctors—or a doctor?'

He shook his head.

'Doctors we can buy.'

'And you can't buy wives?' The words were out before she'd thought them through, and as soon as they were hanging there, in the bright morning air, she realised her mistake.

'But, of course, that's what you're doing.'

Ibrahim studied her for a moment.

'We are traders back as far as our people go. Trade is give and take. It is bartering and making bargains, that is how we do things. You talk of buying as if it is a bribe, but if you could see it our way, maybe it would not look so ugly to you.'

'And Fareed? What does he think of this?'

Ibrahim's smile turned him back into the man she'd first met—the charming man her mother had introduced in the stables.

'He has no need to know who—it is enough that he knows he is to marry a woman I have chosen. He will meet you on his wedding night.'

'Wedding night?'

Kate's voice was back to squeaky—squeaky with disbelief.

'Our weddings are different. You will be married with the woman supporting you, and he with the men, so you will not meet until after the ceremony and feasting is over.'

It isn't that part of the 'wedding night' phrase that

worries me, Kate wanted to say, but somehow it didn't seem appropriate.

Not that any of this conversation had been particularly appropriate…

CHAPTER THREE

FAREED WAS PUZZLED when the limousine sent to collect him from the hospital didn't contain his uncle, and even more surprised when the driver announced they were going straight to the airport.

'The sultan is staying on for a few days but knows you wish to get back to work,' the driver informed him. 'His plane will take you home and return for him.'

Fareed wasn't entirely surprised. After his uncle had dropped his bombshell at the hospital, the evening after his allergic reaction to the bee, Ibrahim had avoided opportunities for further conversation—opportunities he couldn't have escaped if they'd flown home together.

That conversation had been startling, to say the least—shocking, in fact. He had known for some time that his days as a bachelor were numbered. Knew also that his uncle would be choosing his bride. After all, as Ibrahim had pointed out, he'd had plenty of time to find one for himself. And it was in keeping with the tradition of the family, and their people, so there was little point in arguing about it.

But the last thing Fareed had expected his uncle to announce on his hospital visit was a date for his wedding—a date within a fortnight of their return to Amberach.

Even more disturbing was his uncle's refusal to tell him the name of his bride-to-be. It would almost certainly be some distant cousin, someone Ibrahim had been secretly grooming—or having groomed—for the job. Because that's what it was—a job, a duty, preordained almost…

No, it was perfectly understandable that Ibrahim would be avoiding him!

Had she actually agreed?

That was Kate's first thought when, three days after Ibrahim's morning visit, Isaac, the man who'd first seen Tippy, arrived at the house, bringing with him a young stableboy, several mounds of luggage and an elegant leather folder, embossed in gold, with what must be the crest of Amberach and Kate's name.

It contained not only details of the flight she would take to Amberach with the sultan in two days' time but also coloured brochures about the country, its people and history right up to recent times, where a picture showed the sultan, in a long white robe and gold-edged headscarf, cutting the ribbon in front of the new emergency hospital.

A tall, distinguished-looking man, similarly dressed except for black edging on his headscarf, stood beside Ibrahim.

Fareed!

Kate peered at the photo—hoping to read something positive in the shadowed features?

He was as good looking as she'd first thought him, but good looks were usually way down on her list of important manly attributes.

Manly attributes?

What *was* she thinking?

'I do wish you hadn't made such a quick decision about going over there to work,' her mother said when she saw the documents, and Kate knew her mother suspected something.

Not a marriage something, that was for sure, but she knew something had gone on between Ibrahim and Kate.

'Mum, it's a brand-new hospital—look—and I'm only going for a year. It's not as if I haven't been away before, and think how exciting it will be. Look at the brochures Ibrahim has sent. What's more, you'll be so busy with training and getting the new staff into order, you won't even notice I'm gone.'

Sally smiled.

'It *is* good for us all, isn't it? Like a gift from heaven, to be able to keep Tippy here for Billy—'

'And for you to train him, Mum, to show what you can do with a really good horse! It's time to stop dreaming and get working.'

Sally hugged her hard and Kate swallowed the lump that had formed in her throat.

This is all for Mum and Billy, she reminded herself, *and for the future of this family*—my *family*.

Twelve months of her life was a small price to pay for the happiness she was bringing these two people, whom she loved with all her heart.

And there was no way she could think beyond that—except perhaps, from a purely selfish motive, it would offer a chance to put her life back together after Mark...

'Snow-capped mountains?'

Ibrahim smiled at the disbelief in Kate's voice.

'You did not expect them?'

'I saw the pictures in the brochures, but it still seems strange to see snow in a desert.'

Her host had spent most of the flight tucked away in what he called his mobile office, catching up on business and resting when he could. Perhaps he wasn't well, the kindly Ibrahim—could this be why he was so anxious to marry off his nephew?

You don't know enough about any of it, Kate told herself. *Just be glad you had a good sleep so you can face whatever lies ahead.* She felt fresh and rested, having lazed and slept in first-class luxury until a steward had brought breakfast and opened the blind for her to see Amberach for the first time.

Ibrahim had slid into the seat beside her as she'd blurted out her surprise.

'Amberach has everything,' he explained. 'It is winter now so there is more snow, but on the highest peaks a little snow remains all year round. It is the snow melt that makes the land around the base of the mountains fertile, and has provided a good living for our farmers throughout the ages. But the fertile plain is narrow and on two sides of my country the great desert has encroached more and more—right to the coast, where many of my people have lived on fishing and pearl diving for generations.'

'Do you still have a pearling industry?' Kate asked.

'I am trying to revive it, if only as an added incentive for tourists to visit my country,' Ibrahim said, as the plane swooped lower, over dark blue sea and yellow-gold sand. 'Once cultured pearls came on the market, our pearling fleets went out of business. Most turned to fishing, but the fisherman must go farther and farther from shore to get a good catch.'

Kate nodded, remembering the things she'd read, but the plane was coming in to land and a mixture of excitement and apprehension at what lay ahead held her silent.

The plane landed but no one moved and to Kate's surprise it was then towed into a huge hangar, sumptuously decorated in deep reds and purple and gold.

'The women of the family prefer to alight in privacy,' Ibrahim explained, 'although these days many of them, especially the younger ones, frequent the shopping malls and go with friends to the theatre.'

They disembarked, Ibrahim ushering Kate into yet another sleek black vehicle—into the front seat this time.

'I have asked Fareed to meet us here. He will take you for a short drive along the esplanade and past the old fort on the way to the palace. It will be an opportunity for the two of you to talk a little but remember, he knows nothing of the wedding plans. It is not necessary for him to know until the wedding night.'

Kate frowned at the man she'd discovered was so devious and felt her stomach knot at the thought of the deception she would have to play.

Or was it deception if Fareed didn't know?

She heard voices and looked up to see him striding into the hangar.

'Is this really necessary, Uncle?' he demanded. 'Do you not have enough lackeys that one couldn't be found to show Dr Andrews around this morning? I'm barely back at work and you call me away.'

His face might be a mask, but his eyes glittered with fury.

Kate tried to blend into the car, to pretend she wasn't there at all, but Ibrahim was unrelenting.

'It is a small thing I ask of you,' he was saying to Fareed. 'Dr Andrews is our guest and all I would wish of you is to show her a little hospitality. Perhaps as a mark of your gratitude…'

'In that great hulking limousine? If you want me to play tour guide she can ride with me in my car.'

Kate thought she detected a quick smirk on Ibrahim's face and wondered just how wide his manipulative streak might be.

'Well, come along!'

Fareed this time, the order curt.

She longed to rebel, to tell the pair of them she wasn't just a piece of meat to barter over, but she bit her tongue because, sadly, that was exactly what she was—Ibrahim's pawn.

She forced herself to think of the rewards of the position—the continued success of the family business, her mother's and Billy's happiness...

Billy! In her head she saw the tiny scrap of humanity that had been her longed-for baby brother, born twelve weeks early and looking like the living doll she'd been imagining. All tied up with wires, his little eyes taped shut, tiny hands and feet and tubes everywhere.

Billy, who'd fought to live, then battled through one illness after another to survive.

Billy, who'd only really come fully alive when Tippy had been born and the two of them had formed some magical bond.

She shut away the memories and followed meekly behind the angry man who so obviously didn't want to be stuck with her.

If he only knew...

Fareed's vehicle was a high-set SUV, black like most of the vehicles she'd seen these people use.

'Why are all the cars black?' she asked, as she clambered in, unaided by her husband-to-be.

'They aren't,' he replied—two crisp words cutting off any further conversation.

Kate studied his profile—more stern than arrogant—and shivered inside. Perhaps there was still time to pull out of this arrangement. She could speak to Ibrahim and ask if she could work for two years—even three—instead of marrying this man, but she knew she couldn't risk the happiness of the two people she loved best in all the world.

And yet if she *was* going to marry Fareed, shouldn't she at least attempt to get to know him?

'I'm sorry you were pulled away from your work. If I had known Ibrahim was going to interrupt your work to take care of me, I could have asked him to call me a cab.'

Fareed's reply was a derisive snort.

'Call a cab when he has a dozen vehicles at his disposal and probably twice as many drivers? I'm to take you to the palace where, no doubt, he'll be happy to organise a car and a driver to be put at your disposal for however long you are here.'

He turned to study her as the traffic slowed.

'It seems you have bewitched him.'

How to respond?

'Nonsense! He's asked me here as thanks for the bee episode and so I could see your country and perhaps work here for a while. I imagine, once I start work, I can live in at the hospital.'

Another snort.

Kate sighed.

If the man was like this when he thought her just a visitor, how much more awkward and dismissive would he be when he discovered she was to become his wife?

She should tell him —let him work it out with Ibrahim— but she had given her word she'd tell no one of the agreement. To all intents and purposes, she was coming here to work, full stop.

And as for seeing sights, so far all they'd seen was traffic. Was this Fareed's way of disobeying his uncle's orders? She'd have been better off being shown around by one of the camels wandering across the streets—the cause of the traffic chaos.

'Are they sacred animals that they are allowed right of way?' she asked, and Fareed, though he looked momentarily shocked that she had asked a question, did, finally, reply.

'No, just animals with minds of their own! But they

have been essential to the survival of my people for thousands of years, so no one would harm one. We will be out of this traffic soon.'

Kate turned her attention back to her surroundings.

Rows of small shops and businesses gave way to signs of development, boarded lots, some with massive cranes rising behind the fences, and beyond them the outlying residential area of a sparkling new city.

'How exciting it must be to be able to build a city from scratch,' Kate said. 'To try to get it right from the beginning.'

For a moment she thought Fareed wouldn't answer, but after a swift glance her way, he relented.

'This city is my uncle's dream. He had so many plans he needed teams of architects and engineers and builders to implement them. He drew the best from all over the world, told them what he wanted, then made sure he got it. He might appear a charming cosmopolitan man but he has the core of steel all our leaders had to keep the tribes alive in inhospitable places for thousands of years.'

Kate heard the words but also the love this man must feel for Ibrahim. Could a man who loved his uncle be all bad?

The vehicle left the city, the built and unbuilt bits of it, and swung onto a wide road that ran along the shoreline.

'Oh!'

Kate barely breathed the word, so astonished was she by the wide stretch of golden sound reaching out to the deep blue of a placid sea. Squat palm trees lined the landward side of the road and beyond them, green parklands stretched to the foothills of craggy red-grey mountains.

The road curved gently around the shallow bay, coming to a point where rugged cliffs met the sea, and perched atop the cliffs, like something formed from the land itself, there was a multi-towered building.

The old fort?

'How do you get to it?' Kate asked, staring up now at the sheer cliffs.

'There is a way from the inland side,' Fareed explained. 'And a secret way from the sea. Once it was a place of refuge for the fishermen who lived along the shore, but now it is deserted, except for the caretakers and some artisans who are restoring parts that have deteriorated.'

As they rounded the corner, Kate turned back to look again, marvelling at the beauty of the structure and wondering how on earth it had been built on such an impossible site.

But they were passing the fishing village now, the colourful boats tied up along the shore, and beyond the village high mud brick walls—

'Another fort?'

'The palace,' Fareed replied.

She was here!

In Amberach!

With her bridegroom?

CHAPTER FOUR

THE PLANS FOR the wedding were completely out of Kate's hands, and there were brief moments when she allowed herself to relax and enjoy her new surroundings, but the strain of deceiving her mother lived with her night and day.

Too afraid her mother would hear the anxiety in her voice, or that even talking to her mother—*lying* the way she was—would make her break down, Kate had used the time difference between the countries as an excuse to communicate through emails.

The pain of the deception stayed with her as she settled in the palace, in her own suite of rooms in the enormous, rambling, maze of a place.

In reality she'd had little time for worry or self-pity, with various female members of Ibrahim's family fluttering around her, helping her settle in, filling her so-called 'dressing-room' with garments and gowns she was sure she'd never wear, underwear so fine it looked as if it would fall apart if she breathed and nightgowns that made her blush.

In the bathroom she'd found perfumes, soaps, creams and various unguents she'd only sniffed at, filling an entire wall of shelves, while another cabinet carried an array of make-up from the top French cosmetic manufacturers.

The day before the wedding, she was escorted to a large reception area. It was magnificent, the floors covered in silk carpets woven in dazzling jewel colours, the walls carved with fanciful trees and flowers and painted, again in brilliant colour. Arched windows along one side of the room must look out into the big courtyard that Kate had been too timid to explore.

She only knew it was laid out in patterns similar to the carpets, with a fountain in the centre and trees and bushes cut into fantastic shapes. Not that she could see it now, for filmy silk curtains covered the windows, billowing slightly in the breeze.

Following her escorts, she was led to the far end of the room and seated on a low divan in the middle of a kind of dais, so she was raised above anyone coming into the room. Women began arriving—women she'd never met, although all of them appeared very excited to be meeting her. And all of them were beautifully dressed in designer fashions once they'd removed the black *abayas* that had covered their gowns.

They cooed and oohed and touched her clothes— a beautiful silk gown in palest lemon—and her hair—in its usual unruly plait down her back, and cooed and oohed again.

Several younger girls appeared, giggling and carrying pots of what looked like paste.

'This is your henna party,' one of them, who introduced herself as Farida, told her. 'We are to be your attendants today and tomorrow. We are cousins of Fareed. This is Suley and this is Mai.'

They set down the pots they carried, and beckoned an older woman towards them.

'Hayla is the best henna artist in the country. She will do a beautiful job. Your skin is so pale, the henna patterns will look stunning.'

Henna?

Artist?

Patterns?

Kate longed to ask for details but the girls were chattering excitedly amongst themselves and more and more women were arriving, introducing themselves and touching her, as if checking she was real.

The three handmaidens cleared everyone away, and the artist knelt in front of Kate, taking one of her feet in her hands and turning it this way and that.

She opened the lid on one of the pots and Kate realised what was happening. She'd seen pictures of women with their hands and feet decorated with the dark red-brown colour—henna.

Fascinated in spite of herself, she watched as a lacy pattern of vines and leaves began to show up on her foot. Thick heavy lines, although, as Farida explained, the thickness was there to dye the pattern into the skin and would later be washed away.

'But you must be very still,' Mai warned.

So Kate sat, looking out at the partying women, all eating now, maids circling the room with great platters of food.

And Fareed?

What would he be doing?

She pictured his face, trying to wipe off the disdain. He was certainly a handsome man, and well built—something she'd realised as she'd struggled to get him to relax after the bee sting.

But how the hell was he going to react when he realised who Ibrahim had chosen for his wife?

Fareed stalked through the hospital, his usual pleasure in the place he had created deadened by the dread of what was to occur tomorrow. The marrying part was all right—he'd known he had to marry, and soon—but he knew his uncle well enough to know the old man was plotting something—something Fareed guessed he would not enjoy.

He'd slept in his apartment at the palace the previous night, hoping to pick up some gossip about what lay ahead, but even his most devoted of servants were tight-lipped. Either that, or they, too, had been kept in the dark. He might as well return to his apartment here at the hospital tonight— one last night of freedom.

How bad could it be? he asked himself as he continued his patrol of the reception area, glaring at anyone unfortunate enough to cross his tracks. Apart from sleeping with the woman from time to time in order to produce some heirs, he need have nothing to do with her. Once the wedding month—which was, in fact, forty days—was over, she'd have her own apartment in the women's part of the palace and he need never see her, except in bed.

With the lights out!

He shuddered at the thought of having sex because it was his duty, not because he was attracted to a woman. Perhaps he wouldn't be able to perform?

He slammed a hand against his head and was glad when his pager called him to the emergency room, so he could concentrate on work to escape the wild imaginings running through his brain.

At least thinking about the wedding was distracting him from thinking about the woman who was supposed to be coming to work at the hospital—the woman with the flaming hair, at one with the horse she rode so expertly.

He knew she was staying at the palace, but as yet there'd been no mention of when she might deign to start work. He should probably have asked either her or Ibrahim but, as far as he was concerned, getting over the wedding was enough to be worrying about without having to consider a woman who, for reasons beyond his understanding, he found profoundly disturbing.

In fact, the longer she stayed away from the hospital, the happier he'd be,

* * *

Sitting still was hard, although Kate was fed tidbits by her new-found friends. Little morsels of delicious food, sips of brightly coloured fruit juices. And below her the party swirled, while beautiful women, tall and short, imperious looking or gently feminine, all clad in glorious gowns, came up onto the dais to check on the progress of the henna and to admire the patterns, most of them still touching her hair as they passed by.

'Are redheads so rare in Amberach,' she asked the girls, and they giggled behind their hands.

'Yes, but they say your colouring reminds them of Fareed's mother,' Mai added. 'Apparently, she, too, had red hair, though none of us ever saw her.'

Uh-oh! Kate thought as things began to click into place. Was this why Ibrahim had chosen her? Was Fareed's mother one of the ghosts he carried in his head? And, if so, what was she, Kate, supposed to do about it?

Icy dread crept through her veins. The moment he re-alised just who his bride was, Fareed would know just how badly Ibrahim had treated him—had tricked him.

And her!

She needed to know more about Fareed's family—his parents—and what had happened to them, but even after such a short stay in Amberach, she knew she couldn't ask. Questions about families were taboo.

Although she *could* ask Ibrahim!

With two feet and one hand painted?

No, she couldn't stop this process now, but she needed to speak to Ibrahim—to demand to know if he'd chosen her because she bore some curious resemblance to Fareed's mother.

She'd tell him…

What?

That she couldn't be part of a plan to deliberately hurt Fareed?

That she couldn't go through with the wedding?

And tell her mother and Billy what, when she returned home and Tippy was sent to another trainer?

She breathed deeply, hoping to calm her racing thoughts, but the coldness remained in her body, although in her heart she felt a spark of pity for the man she was pledged to marry.

The morning of the wedding arrived. Kate woke and stared in fascination at the intricate patterns decorating her hands and feet. The henna paste had been put on thickly and allowed to stay there for many hours before being washed off to leave the delicate pattern behind it.

The women she couldn't help thinking of as her handmaidens appeared in a welter of excitement, each bearing articles of clothing that appeared to be made out of spun gold. They shouted orders at the two servants, Mariam and Layla, who would appear from nowhere whenever Kate came to her room or woke from sleep.

'Cloth of gold out of one of the treasure chests, no doubt,' Kate muttered at Mariam, whom, she knew, spoke no English. Mariam was trying to remove Kate's pyjamas—old favourites she'd brought from home and refused to be parted from.

Dodging the ministrations of her helper, she grabbed Layla, whom she knew *did* speak English, and told her she would dress herself.

'But you must bathe, and be made up, and properly dressed from the skin out, for he will want to unwrap you like a precious parcel.'

The excitement in Layla's voice suggested this was the most momentous moment in a woman's life.

There'll be no unwrapping of this parcel, Kate told herself, although this time silently because making a mockery of the wedding in front of these women would be unkind, and probably go against her part of the bargain.

She and Fareed would sort out what happened after the wedding, and whatever they decided would be their business. And in spite of her nerves, she was fairly certain she could reach some arrangement with him—after all, she was probably the last woman on earth *he'd* want to marry. This was not an affair of the heart but a business arrangement and she could—she would—make it work.

So she went along with being bathed in water with rose petals floating in it, in being massaged with cream that made her skin feel like silk and being dressed in golden knickers and a golden bra, a long golden underskirt and a huge, all-encompassing golden gown on top of it all.

As if this was not enough, a golden shawl was draped across her hair, and a fine gold veil drawn down across her face.

At least she thought it was her face, although it, too, had been painted, her eyes outlined in thick, dark kohl, her eyebrows extended, so from behind the veil all that could be seen were dark, mysterious eyes.

Behind her geeky spectacles that she'd deliberately chosen after losing so many smaller, fashionable pairs, or broken them by sitting on them, or mutilated them in a dozen different ways.

'You *cannot* wear them,' Farida decreed, seizing them from Kate's hand and secreting them in a pocket in her gown. 'It spoils the whole look.'

'But I can't see where I'm going without them,' Kate protested.

The young women laughed.

'We are to escort you to your throne and you won't have to move from there until the party is over and the prince comes to claim his bride. Then he will guide you to the marriage chamber.'

'Marriage chamber?'

Kate's voice faltered over the words and the women laughed again, making jokes in their own language and dissolving into hilarity.

Think of it as part of the job, she told herself, *and just go along with it.*

She was led into a room full of women, maybe four hundred of them, with more coming in all the time. From her seat back on the dais she could see they entered with their black *abayas* covering their clothes, with evening scarves, although it was only mid-morning, covering their hair. Evening scarves, she'd learned, could be coloured and patterned and embroidered with bright thread and studded with jewels.

Even without her glasses, she realised the women were no sooner safe inside the room—a women's place—than they stripped off scarves and long black cloaks, revealing themselves in the brightest of gowns, floor-length ball-gowns mostly, their necks and arms adorned with brilliant jewellery.

It was a stunning mosaic of colour, swirling below her, voices rising higher and higher as friends and relatives greeted each other.

Farida, Suley and Mai stayed with her, lying against cushions near her feet, taking plates of food from the servants to offer her a taste of this or that, pouring cardamom-scented coffee for her.

But although she'd seen the local women eat and even drink behind their veils she had no idea how they did it, and, terrified of spilling something on the beautiful clothes, she did nothing more than sip a little water now and then.

From time to time she was conscious of a noise from outside the room.

'It's the men's party,' Suley explained. 'They chant as they do the old dances, and sing songs of the victories their tribes won many years ago.'

Would Fareed be dancing and singing?

Conjuring up his face, she doubted it. He didn't look like a man who'd give himself up to gaiety.

The day wore on, the women dancing now, their scarves tied around their hips to accentuate the movements of the dances. They danced alone, sometimes falling back to watch one person perform then joining in again so now it was a kaleidoscope of colour swirling in front of Kate as she sat and waited for what lay ahead.

Dreading it—not the marriage part, since surely in this day and age, two adults could sort that out—but Fareed's reaction to his uncle's choice…to her.

Finally a man appeared at one end of the room—a tall man, robed, like she was, but in pure white, with golden braid around the neck and sleeves, and a golden cord holding his headscarf in place.

A sudden hiatus in her heartbeats told her it was Fareed, although he was still too far away to recognise without her glasses.

Fareed had sat in solitary splendour on his dais in the men's room, while the celebrations of his wedding seethed below him. It was only when the dancing started that he was compelled to join in, linking arms with his uncle and one of many male cousins in the dance of the swords.

Why the dance of the swords was performed at weddings he had no idea, but he did know it was near the end of the celebrations. Soon his friends and relations would push him towards the women's room next door. He would have to pretend to struggle as he was thrust into the room full of women, most of whom would be struggling to pull their *abayas* over their fine clothes and cover their heads before he happened to see their hair.

He would have to walk through the crush, being examined as a fine camel was examined at the big sales, everything but his teeth checked out, mostly by strangers.

Once inside the room, he could see, at the far end, three young cousins on the dais with his gold-wrapped bride. At most of the weddings he'd attended recently, the bride had opted for western bridal gear—huge marshmallow-like white gowns with white veils covering their hair and faces.

But, probably due to Ibrahim's influence, this bride was a traditional 'parcel'—a blob of gold he was expected to unwrap, presumably with pleasure and excitement.

He felt neither, and for some unknown reason his mind threw up an image of the girl on the horse, back in the green valley in Australia. It must have been the freedom of the way she'd ridden that had made the image appear now, when he was about to lose his own freedom—or a greater part of it...

He stalked down the room, the women forming a passage for him, clustering closer, seemingly looking him over—judging him—until he reached the dais on which the mystery woman sat, hidden in the folds of gold.

His young cousins helped her stand, and as he drew close they handed her to him—just like a parcel, only one with legs. He took her hennaed hand, and led her through a curtain at the back of the room, the women whooping and hollering behind them.

Wedding night!

The two words were echoing in Kate's head as he drew her down a corridor she didn't know—well, thought she didn't know, from what she could see without glasses and from behind the veil.

And into a room dominated by a humungous bed with

a pure white silk coverlet, piled with pillows in the same white silk.

He let go her hand and turned towards her, saying something in his own language, talking, talking, asking something, she was sure.

She wished she could see his face more clearly but it was impossible, so she took a deep breath and spoke herself.

'Please, speak English. It's me, Kate... I thought Ibrahim would have told you.'

She was trying to untangle the veil and scarf as she spoke, so he could see as well as hear her, but it had been pinned in such a way that she was only making things worse.

She was about to ask him to help when she realised he'd stepped back as if he'd been shot.

In revulsion?

'Look, if you'd stop standing there like a dummy and help me out of this gear, I can explain everything.'

He moved, but not to help her. Instead, he turned away, pacing the room so through the golden veil he was a blur of white, stopping suddenly by the bed and ripping off his headdress, flinging it on the bed, stripping off his long cloak, his actions violent enough for Kate to make them out from behind her veil.

Then he paced again, bare chested now, with nothing but a long white piece of material covering his lower body. Barely covering, for even through the blur of gold silk she could see the flash of long tanned legs appearing and disappearing.

Totally disconcerted, and increasingly angry, she moved towards him.

'Will you stop the pacing and help me out of this get-up? And see if you can find what Farida did with my glasses? And then we could talk this through. Do you honestly believe I'd allow myself to be married to a total stranger if I didn't have a very good reason?'

'Money!'

Fareed spat the word at her, his fury so great he daren't go near her for fear he'd do her harm, preferably by strangling her so she'd shut up while he tried to think.

'Could you at least let me try to explain?' she was saying. 'Mind you, if you don't get me out of this tangle of veils I'm going to faint and, much as it might give your ego a boost to have your bride lying prostrate at your feet, I'd prefer to remain conscious.'

His ego?

What was she on about?

Surely she didn't think he had any intention of consummating this farcical marriage?

'Are you going to help or not, because if you're not I'm heading straight out the door—if I can find it—and I'm going to yell until someone does help.'

And have the whole palace know his bride had fled, screaming, from his bed? He'd be a laughing-stock—a joke—but surely that's what this was—a joke...

Ibrahim's joke!

She was stumbling in what she must have thought was the direction of the door when he caught her shoulders and spun her to face him.

Through the thin gauze covering her face he saw the kohl lining the pale green eyes he'd seen before in such a different context. Huge eyes looking up at him, a mix of fear and defiance in their depths.

And he could see this through the veil? his cynical self demanded.

But somewhere under there would be that hair—'golden' his mother had insisted he call the colour—because his uncle had played the ultimate deception. Not only had he married his nephew to a westerner but to a pale, mouthy parody of his mother.

Rage at this deception burning through his body, he ripped at the cloth that hid the woman so completely. Ignoring the look of shock on her suddenly revealed face, he tore off the outer cloak, hearing whatever hooks held it together rip from their anchors.

'Stop right now!'

Her voice was strong, though he was sure he detected a tremor of fear beneath the strength.

And well she might fear him, the barbarian inside him whispered.

But hadn't that barbarian been banished generations ago?

Maybe not, for his hands still held the cloth of gold, ready to rend it further—ready to render her naked.

'Fareed!' she said, her voice steady now, the green eyes hazy—desperate—as she looked directly into his. 'I know you must be angry, but we can sort this out. We're both mature adults—we can talk, work out a plan. Your uncle promised it did not have to be forever, nor did he say the marriage had to be consummated. I thought we could sort out some sensible living arrangements, preferably away from the palace, and work together as colleagues. Our private life is no one else's business.'

He stared at the half-naked woman in front of him, her milk-white skin reddened in places where he'd ripped cloth across it, flimsy strips of lacy gold underwear visible through the wreckage.

Was it because it was his wedding night that the sight of that underwear against the pale skin had his groin stirring, hardening?

He spun away from the sight of her. He was angry at his uncle's deception, but even more angry now with this woman who assumed she could take control of the situation, and was suggesting some half-baked plan for them moving forward from here.

Who the hell did she think she was, planning *his* future?

And how the hell could his body possibly have reacted to the sight of her? She was nothing more than a whore, just as his mother had been.

Kate could see the tension in his shoulders—anger, she guessed—and read disgust in his eyes as they scorched across her.

Who could blame him?

But somehow she had to make this work—to talk this man down from his anger, to sort out some arrangement he could live with, because if she failed, then all her hopes for Billy's future happiness—for her mother's future, too— would be lost.

So she had to reason with him, but not beg or plead. She knew instinctively that should she show a smidgen of weakness before this man he'd walk all over her.

'I'm sorry,' she said, trying to project calm, mature composure, while inside she felt more like unset jelly. 'I'm sure you were looking forward to what lay ahead—undoubtedly the opportunity to deflower whatever beautiful young virgin your uncle had chosen for you—and suddenly you're stuck with an ageing redhead that no number of fairy godmothers could turn into a beautiful princess. But it's only for a year. Can't we make it work?'

Had her voice wavered on that final plea so that he turned back towards her? No, it must have been her jibe about deflowering because fury flared from his eyes, as vivid as flames from a flamethrower.

'Why?' he demanded, a threat as deep as the ocean clear in his voice. 'Why should I even *try* to make it work? So you can squeeze more money from my uncle? Has he not already paid you well? I know all about greed—it is what kept my mother coming back—not me, or my father, but plain, simple greed.'

He took another turn around the room, while Kate tried to understand, not the words but the pain in his voice, but before she could feel too sorry for him he hit again with a new jibe.

'Well, go right ahead. Stretch out your grasping hands. He won't miss it, he has plenty, just don't expect me to play along with your little game. Am I supposed to get you pregnant, too? Provide him with another heir of mixed blood? Is that his little game?'

The disdain she'd first seen in his eyes back at the farm was replaced by disgust, and she wanted to cringe and fold the torn material of her gown around her, but she had her pride.

'I won't dignify that remark with a reply.'

'No?' He shot the word at her. 'You're only too happy to talk about me deflowering virgins but when I bring up a bit of reality you cringe!'

He stepped towards her and it was all she could do *not* to cringe. Instead, she straightened and looked him straight in the eye—blurrily.

'Will you just get over yourself? Okay, so you feel your uncle has cheated you—I agree. You should have been told—in fact, you should have been able to choose your own wife—but apparently things are done differently here and your uncle assured me that you were happy for him to do the choosing, so live with it.'

He stood before her so still she wondered if he was breathing. So close, she could feel the heat of his body, see, even without her glasses, the taut muscles beneath the tanned skin of his chest, the breadth of his bare shoulders, the power of his muscled arms.

The tension that had accompanied her through the day

intensified to the extent she could barely breathe herself, but she *had* to sort this out.

She would *not* burst into tears of frustration, neither could she show any sign of weakness in front of this man, for although she knew so little about him she did know that if she gave ground now he'd walk all over her and the whole situation would be lost.

Dragging air into her lungs, she tried again. Not moving back from him, though his presence—less than an arm's length away—had her nerves on fire, and was sending wayward messages through her body.

'We do not have to make it work as a conventional marriage,' she said, and inwardly marvelled that she could sound so calm. 'Surely we can treat it as a professional association. I'm a good doctor who's specialised in ER work, and you need ER doctors in your new hospital. Your private life can remain your own business. There must be accommodation at the hospital we can use to get us away from the gossiping tongues of the palace. We wouldn't need to see each other away from work—even at work if you can arrange the shifts so ours don't coincide. Would that be so very difficult?'

Fareed found himself frowning at this little bit of a woman, standing so upright in front of him, refusing to back away from his anger, pale as milk, eyes huge as she tried to see without her glasses, hair like fire in the desert, asking but not pleading for his co-operation.

From her side, it *had* to be money that had made her agree to the marriage, and, heaven knew, both he and his uncle had plenty, but why had his uncle *done* this?

Why had he chosen this particular woman?

This *red-headed* woman?

What deep game was *he* playing?

And how would he, Fareed, find out if he didn't play along, at least for a short time?

He must have been staring at her for too long for suddenly he realised the skin above her barely there brassiere was reddening.

Yet still she held her ground—her pride too strong to allow her to gather the bits of torn cloth around her.

And it suddenly occurred to him that not at any time in her pleas for him to keep up this pretence of marriage had she mentioned that he owed her—owed her his life, in fact.

He knew his frown would have deepened, yet still she stood, flushed white skin burned in places by his rage, other parts teasingly covered by scraps of golden cloth.

And the green eyes, huge and looking strangely lost…

'Get some clothes on. I'll find your glasses,' he said, turning away before she saw the effect she was having on his body. 'Is there anything else you need?'

To his surprise, she smiled, pale pink lips parting to reveal small, even, white teeth, like little pearls.

Somewhere inside his head he heard the groan from the cliché he'd just used, but the description had sprung to mind, possibly to divert him from thinking of those pearly teeth nibbling at his lips, his skin…

'Some food would be good,' she said. 'I was too terrified of spilling something on the clothes to eat anything earlier.'

Which made him frown yet again as he went to the door to order food and send someone in search of her glasses. Most women he knew might have refrained from eating because they refused to allow a square inch of fat to mar their beautiful bodies, but none would have admitted it and asked for food.

When he returned, with her glasses, she was sitting on a chair by the great arched window, wrapped in a voluminous towelling robe that would have been in the bathroom.

'I've no idea where my clothes are, or even where I am in the palace,' she said, as she slid the unattractive spectacles into place. 'When I arrived I had some rooms that led out onto a terrace and then into the garden, but I can't see anything but darkness from here.'

He felt behind the ornate Persian rug that decorated the wall beside the window and flicked a switch.

'Oh!'

The word was barely breathed, and when she turned towards him he couldn't help but read the wonder of what she was seeing in her eyes.

'But it's so beautiful,' she whispered. 'Like something from another time.'

'And you want us to go and live in a hospital apartment? They're much the same here as they are all over the world.'

'Of course they'd be the same, but we can't stay here,' she said, turning back to take in the beauty beyond the window once again.

He was looking at her looking out, looking at the long plait of red-gold hair lying against the white robe, hearing something a little like regret in her voice.

'Why not?' someone said, and he was reasonably sure it had been him.

Kate wrapped the robe more tightly around her body and stared out at the small courtyard beyond the window. Stairs from a wide terrace, overhung with vines of some kind, led down to a small swimming pool set in a garden of palms and flowering rose bushes.

Tucked in one corner was a small cabana with what looked like a spa beneath it and at the other end of the courtyard a small pergola. But it was the way the area was set out, like a pattern on one of the beautiful silk carpets that abounded in the palace, that had stolen her breath.

'My father had it built for my mother. It is completely private and the only access is through this suite of rooms, so you can use it at any time.'

She turned, looking up at Fareed, who stood behind her.

'Like now?'

He frowned but nodded, and because she was beginning to believe this was one of his few facial expressions—
disdain, disgust and frown—the frown didn't bother her.

She'd kept the bra and knickers on under the robe; she
could swim in them. Surely a quick swim would clear her
head.

'How do I get out there?'

Still frowning he showed her how the window was really a huge arched door, and even opened it for her.

Still in the robe, she slipped out into the rose-scented air,
across the terrace, down the steps, dropping the robe and
her glasses by the edge of the pool and diving in.

Fareed watched her swim up and back, her white arms
drawing her slim body through the water with surprising
speed, turning and swimming again, back and forth in the
small pool.

In all the times he'd been brought to visit his mother
in this suite of rooms he'd never seen her venture into the
courtyard, let alone swim, so the sight of the night swim-
mer held him transfixed.

A knock on the door told him the food he'd ordered had
arrived and he quickly gathered up the torn material of his
bride's gown and shoved it into the bathroom before opening the door. Palace servants had eyes like falcons and few
were loyal enough to keep all they saw to themselves.

The young woman who entered set the tray on the table,
bowed slightly and departed, her bare feet shuffling across
the carpet the only sound in the silent room.

He opened the door and stepped outside, intending to
call the woman—Kate, Katya in the marriage ceremony.
But beneath the vines that overhung the terrace was a small
table and two chairs and a sudden impulse made him carry
the tray of food outside.

'Here is food,' he said, loudly enough for her to break

her stroke, looking up at him with strands of her darkened hair clinging to her face and neck.

He should have turned away immediately, but couldn't, transfixed by the ease with which she pulled herself free of the water, rising almost straight out of it, like a mermaid from the depths.

Gold lace clung to her breasts—full but not too full—and hid her womanhood, but the shape of that white body, the slim waist, and rounded hips...

He turned way, more angry than ashamed, angry at the betrayal of his body.

'Aren't you hungry? Don't you want some food?' she called, and by the time he faced her she was once again enveloped in the too-big robe and was bent over, wringing water from her long plait.

Stupid, stupid, stupid, Kate! What had prompted her to ask that question? Why hadn't she kept her mouth shut and let him disappear to wherever he'd intended disappearing to?

She glanced up and saw he was standing by the table, as if uncertain she'd actually asked him to share the snack.

'Well, sit, why don't you,' she muttered at him as she came up the shallow steps. 'We're both adults, surely we can handle this.'

'I can handle it better when you've got clothes on,' he said, and the statement was so totally unexpected that Kate *had* to laugh.

'I won't take it as a compliment,' she said, still smiling. 'After all, it's a perfectly natural reaction for men to feel some kind of hormonal reaction to naked females, like dogs do to bitches in heat.'

CHAPTER FIVE

He sat—heaven only knew why, except he *was* hungry. He'd been too busy accepting congratulations—that was a joke—to eat much during the partying.

Kate—his wife—was studying the food rather cautiously, finally settling on a slice of melon that would do little to alleviate her hunger.

'Do you know what it all is?' he asked, mainly to divert himself from noticing the way delicate tendrils of hair were drying on her forehead and those teeth biting into the melon.

She glanced up at him.

'Some of it, although people have been very kind and mostly asking what I'd like to eat so I've stuck with things I know, like rice and fruit and vegetables.'

He felt a twinge of sympathy for her, quickly dismissed when he reminded himself she'd chosen to come here—to accept his uncle's bribe.

But she was right, they were both adults—they just had to work out a way out of this tangle. If he found out how much she expected from his uncle, he could offer her more to leave.

Now!

Well, soon…

So play nice!

He took a small china bowl and spooned rice into it, then added two little kofta and some nutty sauce.

'Try this,' he said, passing it to her, unable to stop himself noticing how small her hands were, with fine, delicate fingers, enhanced by the patterns of henna and tipped with pink, unvarnished nails. 'The kofta are little meatballs usually made with lamb or goat. In old times they could just as easily have been camel meat, although that was more usually used in dishes where the meat was cut into pieces and cooked over the fire for a long time.'

She waited politely until he'd finished speaking, then she dipped a little kofta into the sauce and ate it, nodding her appreciation and finishing the bowl.

'Oh, that was good, I'd like to have some more but I must try the other things first. That looks like eggplant.'

He gave its local name and spooned some into another dish, together with a mix of beans and spices that was his favourite.

She ate that as happily as she had the first dish, although she did pause halfway through.

'You're not eating?'

He could hardly tell her he'd been too busy studying the way *she* ate—with such enjoyment and delight. Poor woman must have been starving.

Poor woman indeed! Keep your mind on the job ahead! On the plan!

What plan?

Bribe her to go away?

He filled a bowl and began to eat, as she ventured to refill her own bowl with bits and pieces off the tray, pausing before she began on the mixture to say, 'Tell me about the hospital.'

He kept eating, surprised to find he'd be happy to talk about the hospital. He'd checked her out on the internet after her heroics at the horse stud and discovered she'd worked in some of the world's best emergency rooms, including a hospital in the US that had been the model for the one he'd set up—a hospital built primarily for emergency care.

'You worked at Goldsmith?'

Surprise flickered in her eyes.

'Internet, huh?'

'Well, we did have a fairly dramatic introduction.'

She put down her plate and studied him as he spoke.

'You would know Goldsmith was built as a purely ER hospital to divert emergency cases away from the bigger, mostly specialised, hospitals in the area—kind of like a tri-age hospital where patients were attended to and sent home or stabilised and sent to whichever hospital they needed.'

'Exactly.' She was nibbling on another piece of melon, tiny bites—small pearly teeth sinking into the creamy flesh...

Focus!

'We don't have big specialised hospitals, but the main hospital in town can handle most things. The problem was—' *keep your mind on work and you won't watch the teeth* '—that many of our people were intimidated by the size of the place, and they also felt that it was too—too important, if you can understand that—for them to visit with something trifling like a cut thumb, even if the thumb was hanging on by a thread.'

To his surprise she grinned at him.

'I do wish more people felt that way,' she said. 'Not the thumb hanging from a bit of skin but the people with the aches and pains who are lonely and just need someone to talk to. The good thing about Goldsmith was that we had people they *could* talk to, and psychologists to see the women who'd pop in to get a script for diazepam because they were stressed over their work, or kids, or husband, or whatever. Those people need more attention than we could ever give them in the hectic rush of a normal ER.'

The warmth in her voice and the faint flush on her cheeks told him even more than the words. This was a woman who not only enjoyed her work but understood what he wanted in *his* hospital—she'd be ideal.

That, of course, would have been in his devious uncle's head as he'd made this absurd plan. Fareed had complained to him too often about the difficulty in getting good staff—staff who cared.

Kate decided she'd look extremely greedy if she ate another piece of melon, but she had to do something because somehow she'd killed the conversation dead. Just when she was thinking maybe they *could* work out a way to survive a year of marriage, he'd cut himself off again.

All she could do was try again.

'The hospital?'

She'd barely said the words when a jangling from the bedroom behind them alerted them to a phone ringing somewhere.

'Mine,' he said, and stood up, striding back into the room.

Not knowing what to do with the tray of food, Kate left it there and followed, and once inside couldn't avoid hearing Fareed's end of the conversation, the questions he was firing into the phone making it obvious there was an emergency of some kind at the hospital.

Damn it all, her clothes had to be *somewhere*! If she went with him to the hospital to help out, proved herself as a doctor, it might put some of his aggravation to rest.

Still talking, he strode towards the wall at the end of the bed and pressed something that made a door appear. Hurrying after him, she tripped on the robe and fell into his back, all but knocking him flying, as well.

Somehow he turned and caught her, looking down into her flushed face.

'Chasing me into my dressing room?' he said, his voice lighter than she'd ever heard—almost teasingly light. 'I thought you said we didn't need to consummate this marriage.'

She fought the blush she knew was imminent and pushed herself away.

'If this is your dressing room, where's mine? Is there a problem at the hospital? I'll get dressed and come, too—there'll be *something* I can do to help.'

She was watching his face so saw the shadows of indecision and read them easily. An extra doctor would obviously be good, but her? If he'd checked her out on the internet it couldn't be he didn't trust her as a doctor, so was it because she was a woman he didn't want her there—or because she was his wife?

He nodded as if he'd come to a decision, although reluctantly, she guessed.

'On the other side of the bed there's a rose carved on the edge of the panelling. Give it a twist and the door will slide open.'

'Slept in the bridal bed before, have you?' she teased, and was answered with a glower—a much more recognisable expression on his face.

'You've got five minutes!' he growled, and she fled, knowing he'd leave without her if she wasn't ready.

Knowing also that she'd somehow snapped the slender thread of understanding they'd achieved as they'd talked about the hospital.

It had been her crack about the bridal suite—

Forget it and get ready!

Fortunately, all the clothes she'd brought with her when she'd come to Amberach had been moved into this room, in addition to the outfits she'd been given, which she thought of as costumes.

Pulling on jeans and a shirt over her damp underwear, she found a pair of sneakers, failed to find her socks, so put them on without. If she got blisters, she got blisters. What was a blister or two against showing this man she was as good a doctor as he was and as such should be treated with respect?

She was waiting by the door when he came out of his dressing room, dressed much the same as she was. Apparently her attire, or maybe her punctuality, met with his approval for he nodded briefly then led her through the maze of corridors to a rear entrance near the garages where a real fleet—more like forty-four than four—of vehicles was kept.

He opened the passenger door of the big black SUV and actually put a hand under her elbow to help her in. Her skin's reaction to the touch shocked her, and much as she tried to put it down to surprise that he'd be so polite she couldn't quite believe that excuse.

Being attracted to her husband would be a totally unnecessary complication, she told herself firmly as she strapped herself in. And wasn't she right off men after Mark?

But she couldn't help but watch as he strode with swift grace around the bonnet, then swung himself in beside her in one lithe, easy movement.

It had to be the wedding thing that sent a tiny shock along her nerves as once again they were in a car together.

'You knew about the wedding plans the day I drove you from the airport,' he said suddenly.

'I did, but I'd been instructed not to mention it to you.'

Kate squirmed with embarrassment as she admitted this, but Fareed's answer was a shout of laughter.

'Smart Ibrahim! He thought of everything. Swore you to secrecy then insisted I drive you to the palace. It is custom, you see, for the bride and groom to meet briefly before the wedding. In that way he acknowledged the custom without actually letting on what he was doing.'

He paused, turning to Kate.

'You didn't feel obliged to tell me?'

No laughter in his voice now, only a hard, keen edge.

'I believed I should. I felt most uncomfortable about it, in fact, but I'd given my word to Ibrahim—'

'And you didn't want to risk losing his largesse!'

I don't care that he thinks I'm a money-hungry bitch, Kate told herself, but his words, and the way he'd said them, cut deeply into her heart.

Desperate to change the subject, she turned the conversation.

'Where are we going?'

Would he reply?

She held her breath, only releasing it when he said, 'It's an accident in the mountains.'

'The snow-capped mountains? I saw them as we flew in.'

'Not those, but closer and still rugged mountains!' He was driving fast but competently—competently enough to take his eyes off the road and glance her way. 'Did you learn anything of my country before you came? Or since you've been here? Does it interest you at all?'

The disdain she'd seen too often in his eyes was now clear in his voice, and, tired of all the antagonism between them, Kate snapped.

'I had five days before I left home to sort out the work I'd been doing for Mum, update my passport and get a visa for Amberach, let Goldsmith know I wouldn't be back for a while, get some clothes together and reassure my brother I wouldn't be eaten by bears or any other wild animal that might live here.'

She paused for breath but wasn't finished.

'But, yes, I did read brochures Ibrahim provided, although reading about a place is not the same as seeing. And apart from the drive from the airport, since I've been here I've been immured in the palace with women who want to clothe me in ball gowns and silks and satins and paint my feet and hands and face and fuss over me to absolute distraction. Then I had to practise for the wedding, which, as it turned out, was to walk onto a dais and sit there like a big parcel for a day, while women all around me danced and sang and ate.'

Much to his surprise, Fareed felt a momentary sympathy for the woman, but quickly reminded himself she'd asked for whatever treatment she'd received. Although it was a pity she hadn't seen much of his beautiful country given he had every intention of sending her home as soon as possible.

'Tell me where we're going. What's happened in these mountains of yours? Oh!'

Her cry was so genuine he turned to look at her, and saw her staring out the window. They were beyond the range of city lights now, and in the moonlight the dunes of the desert rolled out in front of them, a sea of sand with ghostly shadows chasing down the hollows and shimmering highlights on the tops, where wind had carved shapes worthy of a Michelangelo.

'It's the desert!' The genuine awe and wonder in her voice made him warm to her again. Although surely anyone, he reminded himself, who wasn't soul dead would react the same way.

Her face was alight as she looked from side to side, peering out the window and windscreen as if to take it all in at once, then abruptly they were at the mountains—at the foot of the jagged range that rose from the desert plains so suddenly that you could have been in a different country.

The road wound steeply upward, hairpin bends testing the skill of any driver. She clung to the seat but still looked out, and up now, peering around as if she could absorb it all through her skin.

A vibrant, fascinated woman!

Fascinating, as well?

He slammed the thought back into whatever dark corner it had emerged from. The small bus, carrying tourists back from a visit to the old fort, had slid off on one of the deadliest curves on the road, and the flashing lights of ambulances ahead told him they were nearly there.

'I have begun to train some of our ambulance people as paramedics—not me personally but through an excellent tutor from England. But as yet, none have finished the course, although all have done their basic first-aid training required to work as attendants.'

He pulled up out of the way of the emergency vehicles, and Kate slid out.

'Tell me what you want me to do,' she said.

'I believe they've all been rescued from the vehicle as there were fears it would either burst into flames or go crashing into the ravine below, but the attendants have done little beyond the initial ABCs.'

Airways, breathing, circulation—the beginning of any emergency treatment.

'So, will you stabilise the worst cases and send them straight to hospital?' Kate asked.

They were striding towards the well-lit scene, where uniformed attendants mingled with battered, bewildered survivors—the walking wounded.

'We'll stabilise, as in stopping bleeding or giving CPR if it's necessary. The ambulance attendants will have hooked those in need up to oxygen. It's just a matter of checking and prioritising so those in most need get first use of the ambulance.'

'Basic triage?'

'Yes,' he said. 'If you could do the first check and call me to anyone with life-threatening injuries then I'll deal with him and send him on.' He hesitated before adding,

'That sounded bad, didn't it? As if I didn't trust you? But I believe it's the most efficient use of our time.'

They paused, taking in the scene, and Kate watched him as he spoke and thought she'd surprised what could almost have been a smile out of him as he'd made the apology.

Or it could have been an optical illusion.

She rather hoped so, because as he strode ahead of her again she realised she could find a smiling Fareed quite attractive.

Quite attractive?

He'd reached the first attendant and taken a sheaf of paper and a pen from the man.

'Jot down what you find and tuck it in the patient's shirt,' he said, passing her the paper. 'The attendants all speak English, so get them to help with the lesser injured until we have transport available.'

He walked off again while Kate took a pair of gloves from an attendant and knelt beside the first patient, a small man of Eastern appearance, grey of face, his leg twisted at an impossible angle. Morphine would help his pain, but if he had a head injury...

She examined him carefully but swiftly—breathing fine, heart rate steady, no blood that she could see and no outward sign of a head injury. His pupils responded to the light of a torch she'd borrowed from the attendant who hovered by her side.

Morphine could affect later examinations if the man had a head injury, but he needed pain relief...

'You have splints? Morphine?'

He nodded and went off to get what was needed, and Kate moved on.

The next patient was barely conscious and the rasping noises he was making suggested damage to a lung.

Kate quickly searched the man's chest for a puncture wound of some kind, but found nothing, although the man's gasp when she pressed gently against his ribs suggested one or more could be broken. She tipped the man's head back and saw the slight deviation in the line of his trachea, tapped his chest on the opposite side of the deviation, and heard a hollow drum sound.

'Get Dr Fareed,' she said to the attendant, who'd returned with a package of splint material and morphine.

Back at the first man, she gave him morphine to ease his pain, hoping it wouldn't interfere with any examination he would have at the hospital, then straightened his leg and was in the process of splinting it when Fareed arrived.

She pointed to her second patient.

'I'm thinking tension pneumothorax, so we'll need to release the trapped air and put in a chest drain but I don't know how much you do on site. I think—'

But Fareed was already inserting a needle between the man's ribs, into the pleural space where air, escaping from a damaged lung, was slowly compressing not only his lung but his heart, as well.

''That will relieve him for the moment, and we'll do the drain when he gets to hospital. Could you do a note to send with him and get him away?'

Kate jotted down what had been done for the man, checked the oxygen mask the attendants had in place, and handed him over.

Moving on, squatting, checking, speaking quietly to each patient, assuring and reassuring, hoping they'd understand her tone if not her words.

Fareed must have found more critically injured people because the four ambulances in attendance had already gone screaming down the dangerous road. She watched him move among the others, as reassuring as she was, always ready to listen, holding one man's hand as he tried to sit, patting his shoulder, speaking gently all the time.

All doctors are kind, she told herself as she returned

to her most worrisome patient—the man with the broken
femur. But the generalisation was wrong. She knew many
men and women who, although wonderful, proficient medical professionals, insisted on keeping a professional distance from their patients. Courtesy was always there, but
kindness? That was more rare...

She claimed the first ambulance that returned for her
man with the broken femur, taking in the clamminess of
his skin—worried that he might be going into shock.

The ambulance attendants lifted him onto a stretcher and
into the back of the vehicle, Kate following, worrying—

'The doctors at the hospital are excellent—they'll take
good care of him.'

She spun around to see Fareed right behind her.

'I was going to claim that ambulance for one of mine
but I think you were right to get that man out of here fast.
The complications of a break in the femur can be life-
threatening.'

Another ambulance returned, then the third and the
fourth, and they were able to load the rest of the casualties
into these, some sitting by the stretcher in the side seats
in each one.

Red taillights flickered in the darkness then disappeared,
and Kate was left with Fareed in the eerie moonlight on
the mountain whose jagged peaks looked like dark dino-
saur teeth against the star-spangled purple velvet of the
night sky.

It was a place of peace and beauty, and suddenly she
longed to see it in daylight, to see all of it—the desert,
the mountains, the sea. And the pain she'd felt when she'd
accepted Ibrahim's bargain lessened, was replaced by the
first stirrings of excitement.

'Some wedding night!' Fareed said, and Kate laughed
not only at his words but because they'd broken into her

thoughts at that precise moment. Not that he or wedding nights were any part of those stirrings.

Were they?

To distract herself, she waved her hands towards the view beneath them, the sands of the desert stretching to a distant sea, visible only as a deeper darkness than the sky.

'Where's the city?' she asked, puzzled that the lights of the towering buildings she had glimpsed there would not be visible.

'It is to the right, but hidden by the lower reaches of the mountains and the trees in the fertile plains that lie at the foot of them. The winds from that direction bring rain and even snow, which falls in the mountains and drains down to that area.'

'An oasis?'

He paused before he replied, and when he said, 'Of such great beauty you could not imagine it,' his voice was full of pride and wonder and something else, that, to Kate's sensitive ears, could well have been love.

And could a man who loved his country be all bad?

Not that she thought him bad—just judgmental.

And if she wasn't feeling very tired and just a little disoriented, she probably would have ignored it, for didn't most people love their country?

Fareed studied her in the light of the moon, a small woman, gazing out over the desert, drinking in the beauty of it, her lips slightly parted, the sprinkle of freckles on her pert nose barely visible.

'I am grateful for your help tonight,' he said, and wondered if she'd heard him for it took a moment or two for her to turn and face him.

'I am here to be a doctor for a year. If you could just think of me that way, it would make things easier for both of us. So we're married at the moment, but really that means nothing. Let's just get on with being colleagues.'

It made sense, yet the knowledge that she'd been bribed to come here—bribed to marry him—bit deeply into his pride and aroused such suspicion, of her as well as his uncle, he knew he couldn't let down his guard. This woman might act all innocent, but her deal was with his uncle and though he loved his uncle, he knew the man could have taught Machiavelli a few lessons in deviousness.

'Shouldn't we be getting back to the hospital? Won't the staff on duty need more help with that influx of patients?'

She was making sense again—of course they had to get down to the hospital. He could hardly dislike her for being sensible, although he could regret that she was being sensible right now, when he'd have liked to have lingered on the mountain and watch a slim, pale woman with white skin and red-gold hair take in the beauty of his country.

'Are you always sensible?' he demanded, as he drove them back down the precipitous road.

'Nearly always,' she said, in such a way he had to wonder when she hadn't been. She'd shown no sign of regret about coming here—why would she if she was being offered vast sums of money?—so it must have been something in her past.

A man?

What kind of man would appeal to her?

And why the *hell* did it matter to him?

Would it be so hard to act as she was acting, and not only treat her as a fellow professional but accept her as such?

But they'd reached the plains and he heard her gasp and turned to see her face light up with excitement and her lips part as she breathed the word, 'Camels!'

His groin stirred—again!

Perhaps it *was* because it was his wedding night—not that he'd been looking forward to going to bed with any strange woman, let alone deflowering a virgin, as his bride had suggested—but maybe the words *wedding night* had subconsciously stirred up his libido, which would explain why it was playing up right now.

She had twisted around in her seat to catch a last glimpse of the camel train they'd passed—a string of at least twenty stately beasts travelling in the cool of the night—so he was able to study her and keep some of his attention on the road.

He wondered if his uncle had chosen her because she was the antithesis of the women he usually dated—either blondes or brunettes, always tall and beautifully groomed. Women who knew the world and how relationship games were played—women he'd liked enough to enjoy their time together but had never had regrets about when they or he moved on.

He'd put it down to the disaster that had been his parents' marriage, this inability he had to enter into even a semi-permanent relationship with a woman, always finding an excuse to back away before things became too serious—before one of them was hurt...

Something about this woman told him she wouldn't have a clue.

Which was why he had to stop—right now—thinking of her as a woman at all and concentrate on her as nothing more than a colleague, in spite of the fact that she was, of course, his wife.

CHAPTER SIX

'IS THAT THE HOSPITAL? I can't believe it. I've never seen anything so fantastic in my life.'

The building resembled a long, low-slung tent, dark in colour, although it was a tent with the sides rolled up so light showed from within, through windows up to three stories high.

But it was the forecourt that stole Kate's breath away. It gave the impression of a giant Persian carpet, although it had to be made up of tiny tiles, not material. And set squarely in the middle of the carpet was a piece of artwork, something she couldn't name because it wasn't a statue but a representation of a campfire, warm and welcoming, flames flickering, although she knew they must be an optical illusion of some kind.

'It's done with lasers,' Fareed explained, as he drew into a parking area off the magic carpet. 'The carpet and the fire are symbols of welcome for the Bedouin people, from whom most of us are descended. The desert is too dangerous to turn away a stranger, so the carpet and the fire—and you'll see a coffee pot by it if you go closer—they say welcome.'

'And the shape of the hospital—it's a Bedouin tent?'

Fareed smiled in reply, and although Kate knew it was tiredness playing havoc with her emotions, she found herself smiling back.

As he held the door and helped her down from the high vehicle, Fareed tried to forget about the smile. He studied his colleague dispassionately. There was a smear of dirt on her cheek that he was tempted to wipe away—sliding his thumb across her skin. Her clothes were grubby from their hours on the mountain, and tiredness had smudged dark shadows under her eyes and drawn lines down her cheeks.

Yet she stepped briskly away from him and walked towards the building, still looking around, taking it all in, turning back to him to ask if the cluster of palms were date palms.

For some obscure reason her interest—no, her *obvious* interest and even more obvious delight—pleased him, even made her seem attractive to him.

Or maybe that was exhaustion, both emotional and physical...

'I need to wash and grab some scrubs before I see any patients,' she said, bringing him back to the reality that the night had not yet ended.

'I'll introduce you to someone who can fix you up,' he said, and hoped he sounded as matter-of-fact as she had.

But as he handed her over to one of the nurses on duty he felt a strange sensation that couldn't possibly have been loss.

Time to pull himself together—there was work to do and no way could he start feeling anything at all for this woman. She'd been right when she'd said all they had to do was work as colleagues—she was just another doctor.

But when she appeared with the too-big set of scrubs swamping her figure, the legs and arms rolled up so she could actually move around without falling over, he couldn't help but notice that the green of the garment made her eyes look greener, and the shower had brought some colour to her cheeks.

She held out her arms for his inspection then grinned at him.

'Like being an intern again, isn't it, working double shifts and getting that wonderful second wind halfway through the night.'

'Maybe I'd better have a shower and hope I get it, too,' he grouched, more disturbed by his reaction to the woman than his tiredness.

How could he possibly find her attractive? She just wasn't his type. And then there was the hair, which, while nothing like his mother's lustrous tresses, was definitely a reminder of childhood pain he had no wish to remember.

Kate watched him go and felt a little lost, but that was only because she was among strangers in a facility she didn't know. She wandered through the large admissions area. There were a few men seated as if waiting for treatment, or perhaps waiting for a loved one who was being treated, and some of the less injured patients from the bus were also sitting around.

Finding the desk where the paperwork would be done—and what hospital didn't have one?—she introduced herself and was steered towards treatment room six, where a pregnant woman lay on an examination couch, a female nurse taking her blood pressure through the cloth that covered her arm.

Cloth covered all her body, in fact, from the top of her head to the tip of her toes—a long robe, slippers, a hijab over her head and hair, and a mask of some kind that allowed only her eyes to shine through.

Anxious eyes.

Hiding her surprise that the bus-crash victims weren't getting priority, Kate stared at the woman, wondering where to begin. She needed to listen to the woman's chest and heartbeats and didn't want to do it through what looked like layers of material.

'How much do you know?' she asked the nurse.

The young nurse gestured to a computer screen—a very modern hospital—where a note explained the patient was twenty-eight weeks pregnant and had been experiencing some bleeding. Her blood pressure was slightly low but there was no other indication of trouble.

'Is there an obstetrician on call to see patients like this?' Kate asked, and the nurse nodded.

'I have called him, he is on his way.'

So what am I supposed to do? Kate wondered.

Examine the woman, presumably.

She began with the obvious, asking her patient if she spoke English.

'No, she doesn't, but her husband does. We could ask him to come in but Dr Fareed prefers the women to handle their own consultations. I can translate.'

Kate glanced at the earnest young nurse and didn't doubt that she could, but would this woman speak even to her?

'Could you tell her I'm going to listen to her heart and then to the baby's heartbeat. I'll be sliding the stethoscope inside her clothes to put it on her skin.'

The woman struggled into a sitting position.

'Better and better,' Kate said. 'I can check her lungs, as well.'

But as she approached the woman began to scream and within a minute there was a large, robed man in the room with them.

The nurse spoke harshly to him—words Kate couldn't understand—but she put her hand on the nurse's arm and steered her away, facing the man herself.

'Do you speak English?' she asked.

'A little,' he said. His guttural tones did nothing to ease Kate's concern but husbands accompanied their wives on prenatal visits in most places, so why not here?

'I'd be happy to have your help,' she said to the man, and held out her hand. 'I'm Dr Kate.'

The man ignored her hand and moved to stand protectively beside his wife.

It took time, but finally Kate was able to establish, by using her stethoscope on the square inches of flesh the man revealed through partings in his wife's clothes, that the woman was healthy and the baby's heartbeat was strong. She entered the information into the computer and was wondering how to tackle the next hurdle—the blood loss—when the obstetrician arrived.

Introducing himself as Akbar, he wasted little time in ordering the husband to take a seat over by the wall— still in the examination room but out of the way.

He then won Kate over completely by washing his hands, donning gloves then lifting the woman's skirts and drawing them up over her abdomen. The nurse, obviously used to his ways, draped a small sheet modestly over the woman's belly.

'You have to be firm with them,' he said to Kate. 'We understand he's anxious about his wife, as he should be—it's a first baby -but you can't let the men bully you. We need women doctors but they must be strong women doctors.'

He finished his examination and was stripping off his gloves.

'You strong?' he asked Kate.

'I think so,' she said.

The man nodded at her and favoured her with a charming smile.

'Good,' he said. 'I'll see you around. In the meantime, I want this woman admitted to the maternity ward at the hospital. That way I can keep her in bed for a week and see if the bleeding settles down. Send her home and she'll be back shopping and cooking and cleaning and probably grooming her husband's camels, and what she needs is rest.'

Kate returned his smile.

'Are you going to tell him or am I?'

Akbar put his hand on her shoulder.

'This one time I'll do it, but the referrals usually come from this place so it will be up to you in future.'

The hand on her shoulder was such a casual gesture Kate thought nothing of it until Fareed entered the already crowded room.

He spoke to Akbar and Kate wondered if the harshness in his voice was because of the language or something else.

Not that she had to wonder for long. Leaving the nurse to make the transfer arrangements, she went to the desk, seeking more work.

'That man is a lech, steer clear of him.'

Fareed was right behind her, and although she understood exactly what he meant, she decided to ignore him. They were both tired and telling Fareed she was quite capable of looking after herself—*and* recognising a lech when she met one—would be pointless right now and probably provoke an argument.

Though why he should care did bother her a little. Surely it wasn't a possession thing—*you're my wife, therefore...*

She shook the thought away and found the next patient to whom she'd been assigned. This *was* one of the bus victims, but he needed nothing more than a few stitches in a gash in his arm, a dressing on it and a general health check to make sure they hadn't missed anything major.

Two patients later, as Kate's second wind had faded completely and she was wondering if there was such a thing as a third wind, Fareed appeared.

'The staff on the new shift are arriving—they'll double up for a while to clear the backlog of patients so we can go home.'

Home! The word caught unexpectedly at Kate's heart and she had to blink suddenly.

'Home where?' she demanded, probably sounding more aggressive than she'd intended because of her sudden fatigue.

'We'll go back to the palace.' Fareed was watching her closely. Had he seen the weakness? 'There are three bedrooms in that suite, there's no reason why we shouldn't use them, especially as our clothes are there.'

'His, hers and theirs?' Kate asked, trying desperately to make light of the situation, although returning to that ornate bedroom in the palace filled her with misgiving.

But Fareed was not amused.

'Exactly,' he said. 'There's no need for us to hide away in hospital accommodation when we can be more comfortable there. And you'll have the pool to swim in and the courtyard should you wish to be outside.'

He had taken her arm and was walking her towards the exit as he spoke. She wanted to pull away. He was too close—deliberately close—as if he wanted that closeness so his body could talk to hers.

Or was it nothing more than politeness on his part and the only body doing any talking was hers? Talking to *her*, telling her it was enjoying the closeness.

Surely not!

They reached the vehicle and something in the way he regarded her seemed to suggest it *hadn't* only been her body.

Desperate to get all thoughts of the man and the way her body was reacting to him out of her head, she went for lightness.

'And will we have to ruffle up the big marriage bed every morning to make it look as if we've slept in it?'

The look he was giving her intensified, and a small smile played around his lips.

'I didn't say *I* wouldn't use the bed,' he murmured, and a shiver of pure excitement ran down Kate's spine.

More likely it was fear, her head muttered as she hauled herself up into the passenger seat in an attempt to escape both the man and the feelings he was generating in her body.

And she *was* tired—emotions were always more raw when one was tired.

But was attraction stronger? Particularly unwanted attraction?

Why would it be?

Of course, it had to be the tiredness—why else would she be feeling it?

Fareed drove home with a feeling of satisfaction, knowing he'd rattled his new wife's composure.

He'd discovered it was fun to tease her just a little—to watch her react then hide her reaction with smart talk.

Though the word *home* had hit her hard. Just what could Ibrahim possibly have promised her to make her come so far from a place she obviously loved?

And, to his surprise, Fareed found himself wondering how he could make things easier for her—only as far as her being homesick was concerned. She was still a conniving, money-hungry woman who, instead of selling her soul to the devil, had sold it to Ibrahim. But he didn't like the people around him being unhappy.

That was probably why it had taken him so long to realise his mother didn't love him. He had been a fool to think that love had been the reason she'd sent for him as soon as she'd arrived on one of her rare visits to the palace. He had thought spending time with him had made her happy, never dreaming that she'd endured his presence so they could have a photo taken together in order to wring more money out of his father.

As he turned onto the road leading to the palace, he realised the sun had yet to rise. Given all that had happened, the previous sunrise might have been a week ago, but, no, he could see the colour in the eastern sky and knew the great red orb would soon be rising over the desert sands—a sight he loved so passionately he *had* to see it now.

And for some reason he felt an insistent desire to show it to Kate.

She was resting her head against the window and had her eyes closed as he turned off the palace road and onto a rough track that would lead to the top of the closest dune. The vehicle jolted as it left the tarmac, and Kate straightened in her seat.

'Oh, we're in the desert. It's hard to realise it's right there, so close to the city, although I suppose the city was built on it.'

She turned to look at him.

'Where are we going?'

'To see the sunrise,' he said, and enjoyed the look of surprise on her face.

'Just a little farther and we turn towards the east. See?'

He spun the car and then looked out towards the painted sky, rich with pink and purple, orange streaked, the desert sand beneath the horizon reflecting back the vivid colours.

'Can I get out? Walk in the sand to watch it?'

'It's what I always do,' he told her, surprised by the pleasure he felt at her request, and as he watched her peel off her sneakers he felt a sense of pride in this woman who was his wife.

'I wanted to feel the sand between my toes,' she explained when he joined her on the very top of the dune, so they could see the city below them to the right, and in front of them the first red glow of the sun rising majestically above the horizon.

'Oh, Fareed, that is so beautiful!'

The whispered words, full of genuine wonder, shifted something in his chest, and although he knew touching her was fraught with danger, he slid an arm around her shoulders and held her close until the sun completed its won-drous act and the colours faded to gentler tones, reflecting *their* colour on his companion's fair skin.

Kissing her had definitely not been on the agenda—any agenda, not ever—but the stirring inside him must have provoked a momentary madness, for he bent and touched his lips to hers—a breath of a touch, no more. But the moment skin met skin, a fiery longing seized him and he wanted nothing more than to devour those pale lips and slide his tongue along the pearly teeth, and take her, right here and now, as his bride.

He'd touched his lips to hers, and suddenly she was all aquiver. Kate edged away from him because that touch, though she knew it was a kind of 'the end' to the bit of magic they'd shared with the sunrise, had set her nerves jangling through her body and had stirred up all the fight-or-flight reactions that came from the area of her brain that warned of danger.

Danger with a capital D.

She hoped Fareed hadn't noticed her response, hadn't felt it in her body or tasted in on her lips.

Maybe he had, for he was studying her, the mask that hid all his thoughts back in place.

Had she upset him?

She hadn't meant to, so she rushed into speech, hoping to cover the awkward moment.

'That was the most beautiful experience,' she told him, as she edged back towards the open passenger-side door then realised she'd timed it badly. 'The sunrise, I mean,' she added, desperate to recover lost ground. 'Thank you so much for sharing it with me.'

She scrambled into the car then discovered, once he was in, that they were far too close to each other.

'I'm obviously not used to doing all-night duty,' she

muttered. 'Please tell me we're not on again until tomorrow—or *I'm* not on again until tomorrow?'

He glanced her way then turned his attention back to the road.

'You don't *have* to work, you know.'

'I came here to work,' she told him. 'For me, that was the main reason. The marriage thing was just Ibrahim's bargain. But surely he told the truth when he said you need doctors and that I'd be usefully employed?'

Another glance, this one a little grim but that was probably because she'd used the M word.

'We do need doctors with ER experience, I won't deny that. Ibrahim and I have different views on the sex of the doctors. He would like a lot more women working here so women could always see a woman doctor.'

'And you don't agree?'

He sighed.

'It's complicated. It's not the women doctors. I have nothing but respect for them and, in fact, find many of them far more suited to ER work than men, who don't see it as a career path but—' He stopped abruptly, adding more quietly, 'We'll talk about it some other time. Let's get back to the palace. Shall I order you some breakfast so you can eat before you sleep?'

Hmm, Kate thought. *So you don't really want to talk about this disagreement. I must remember to bring it up again, if only because it just might give me some insight into how you think.*

But, 'Breakfast would be lovely,' was all she said for now. 'Can we eat out in the courtyard again?'

Foot in mouth again with that 'we' but she wasn't going to try to take it back. Surely eating breakfast together wasn't going to compromise either of them.

CHAPTER SEVEN

SHE ATE ALONE, a delicious meal of fruit and pastries and yoghurt topped with honey. Ate too much but her tired body needed fuel.

Back inside the wedding room, she found the sumptuous bed turned down, ready for an occupant.

Or two?

No, hadn't Fareed said he'd sleep in it?

In which case she'd have to find another way in and out of the courtyard, because it was beginning to feel like a special sanctuary to her.

Fareed appeared as she was mulling over this.

'You might as well use the bed,' he said. 'The wife's bedroom in this suite is through the dressing room and has no direct access to the courtyard.'

Only to the husband's bedroom? Kate wondered. And was it access for her or for him?

Bur Fareed had made his suggestion and departed and she didn't really want to know the answers to her questions anyway. It was only tiredness playing with her mind.

She pulled off her clothes, had a quick shower. Tomorrow she'd try some of the lotions and potions. She pulled on a her favourite pyjamas—a present from Billy and soft from many washings, the pattern of tiny frogs almost completely washed away—and climbed into the enormous bed.

It was like lying on a cloud, so softly did it wrap around her. She snuggled deeper and—

Woke to darkness, and a small night-light burning somewhere over by the window, so she could take stock of where she was. Still half-asleep, she brought to mind the events of the past twenty-four—or maybe thirty-six—hours.

Slowly she let the images roll through her head—the wedding gaiety, her as a parcel, Fareed's disgust, but even as he'd felt it, him being kind in his own way. The accident and getting back to work—always a good thing—then the sunrise—

She shut down the film show, not wanting to go further, but, thinking of the sunrise, she realised she must have slept through a whole day for it to be dark again.

Reaching for the bedside light, she must have touched a sensor on the base for it sprang to life, casting a soft glow across her side of the bed.

Her side of the bed?

Did Fareed have a side he preferred?

Silly thought when she'd never have the opportunity to find out, and wasn't even thinking about it a waste of time?

She eased herself out of the cloud and headed for the dressing room. Obviously his side of the bed would be the other side because his dressing room was that side!

She shook her head, hoping to regain the sanity she'd need to get through the day—or night, as it happened to be.

But once in the dressing room, the dilemma of actually dressing seized her. What was she supposed to be doing next? Where was she supposed to be now she was awake?

Who was she supposed to be?

The soft knock on a side door of the room was so welcome she called, 'Come in,' before considering who it might be.

Or realising the room beyond that door would be Fareed's dressing room.

He was wearing dark slacks and a lighter polo top that must have been silk the way it clung so lovingly to his chest and shoulders, and her heart scrunched a little in her chest in the realisation that all of this was just pretend.

'I saw the light and thought you might be feeling a little lost,' he said, the words kind enough, though his attention seemed to be centred on her night attire.

'Wedding-night finery?' he added, the slight smile she'd seen before just a suggestion on his lips.

'Comfort after a long day,' Kate said, and hated sounding so defensive. 'But what comes next? Do we hide away in here, venturing out only to go to work, or is there stuff we should be doing, people we should see?'

She flung out her arms. 'I haven't a clue what I'm doing in this place!'

'Earning whatever Ibrahim is paying you, I imagine,' Fareed replied, then immediately regretted the bitter remark. But he'd walked in and seen her in her ridiculous pyjamas, her hair escaping from the plait so bits of it stood up everywhere. She'd looked like a sleepy child but, unfortunately, not enough like a child for his body not to react to her presence.

His reaction and the fact that he'd hit out at her, if only verbally, annoyed him to the extent he'd have liked to turn on his heel and walk away, but that first image of the child—a lost child—held him back.

'If you press a blue button either by your bed, in your bathroom off the dressing room or on a desk in the little day room beyond the bedroom, someone will come. You can order food, clothes, a car—whatever you might want.'

Now he could turn and walk away, although when he'd first come in it had been to—

'What if you get dressed and I'll take you to dinner?' he heard himself say, and cursed inwardly.

It *was* what he had intended saying earlier, as a way of thanking her for her help, but then the mention of his uncle and the unanswered questions about this relationship had reminded him he didn't want to get close to this woman, not even vaguely close.

So why had he asked her to dinner?

And, given how he'd just insulted her, would she come?

She was peering intently at him, frowning slightly as if not entirely sure who he was. And why wouldn't she be puzzled? He'd come in as a friend then had sniped almost immediately. But there was something more in her regard.

'No glasses?' he said. 'Can you see well enough to find them?'

The words broke whatever spell had enveloped her.

'They'll be by the bed, they always are,' she said, 'but I was wondering why you're asking me to dinner. You don't have to, you know. I'm happy just to work out my year at the hospital. I don't expect a social life.'

There was a trace of something just behind the words—regret? hurt?—but he didn't know her well enough to guess.

Would probably never know her well enough...

'One dinner is hardly a social life,' he muttered, some-how disturbed by the fact he *wouldn't* ever know her well enough.

This situation was ridiculous. She was just a woman, nice enough looking but not in the class of women he usually dated; what's more, she'd been bribed into marrying him by his uncle.

Which made her a conniving woman!

But as she seemed willing to work at the hospital and, thrown into the bus accident, had been more than competent, perhaps they could forget the marriage thing and get on with their lives.

Individual lives...

'Well, we *do* have to eat!' he added, determined now to

get her to agree. Since when had a woman turned down one of *his* invitations?

She smiled suddenly, the expression lighting up her whole face so the pale skin seemed to glow from within.

'Okay!' she said. 'Give me ten minutes to pull on some clothes and— Oh!'

'Oh?'

'That's where I was when you came in. I've got clothes I brought from home, jeans and T-shirts and a couple of skirts and tops, then the women who swamped me with kindness before the wedding kept producing these long floaty trouser things with long tunics to go over them. Given you're a public figure and I'm supposed to be your wife, if we're going outside these rooms, should I wear one of those outfits?'

Could she really be as unworldly as she seemed? And have so little interest in clothes? The women he'd known in his life—all of them, from aunts and cousins to lovers and friends—were absorbed by clothes to the extent that asking his fashion advice would be as likely as them hesitating over a dinner invitation.

And, from the way she spoke, she'd only said yes because she thought maybe others would expect it of her.

Others like Ibrahim?

Though why should he, Fareed, care why she'd said yes? He'd only asked her out of kindness—pity really. After all, she *was* a stranger in a strange place.

'Wear trousers and a tunic,' he said. 'I'll meet you in the big bedroom in half an hour.'

'Okay,' she agreed. 'Only don't expect the fine clothes to suddenly turn me into a ravishing beauty, like in the stories where the secretary takes off her glasses and shakes out her hair and she's beautiful. With me, if I shake out my hair it's all tangles and if I take off my glasses I'm practically blind, so what you see is what you get, I'm afraid.'

She turned away before he'd made sense of the words—off to get her glasses, no doubt.

Had she been apologising for her looks?

He didn't think so—just telling it like it was. He remembered her on the mountain the night before. She hadn't hesitated about going with him, and once there she'd got straight to work and had worked through what had been left of the night without a murmur of complaint.

Remembered her, too, at sunrise, her face lit by her delight in the magical time that was so special to him, taking off her shoes to feel the sand between her toes...

Without doubt she was the strangest—no, that wasn't the word—perhaps the most beguiling woman he'd ever met!

And while she might not be a ravishing beauty, the sight of her ten minutes later in local dress, a pair of deep blue trousers with a sea-green and blue tunic, splashed somehow with gold thread, did something peculiar to his heartbeat. She had gold sandals dangling from her hand, and had somehow bunched her hair on the top of her head so she looked taller—womanly! And although he was fairly sure there was a light coating of make-up on her pale skin, the little gold freckles still shone through.

Kate knew she'd brushed up well—no ravishing beauty but passable by most standards—not that Fareed had anything to say about her looks, simply nodding to acknowledge her and leading her out of the door she'd first entered as a parcel late the previous afternoon. Or was it two afternoons ago? She'd lost count, but right now all she had to do was follow Fareed through the corridors of the palace.

And keep up if she didn't want to get lost!

She lengthened her stride in an effort to catch up to him then wondered if there was a protocol she didn't know.

'Am I *supposed* to walk two paces behind you?' she asked.

He looked so startled she had to smile.

'Of course not,' he muttered at her. 'Why ever should you?'

'I just wondered. You were going so fast it was hard to keep up then I thought maybe that's how it should be.'

He stopped, turned to stare at her and shook his head.

'It has *never* been like that, understand! Not from a servility point of view. In times past when no one knew what danger lay ahead, a man would walk in front of his womenfolk to protect them, but now—'

He stopped, shook his head again, and added, 'Let's talk about it over dinner.'

Upon which he strode off once again, leaving Kate to hurry behind, puzzling over what she'd done to annoy him this time.

The question of why Ibrahim had chosen this particular suite of rooms for the newly married couple continued to eat away at Fareed. He recalled all those times when he had rushed here on hearing his mother was in residence, hoping for the smallest show of affection, even permission to swim in the pool she never used. But, no, the cold, unhappy woman would allow him to kiss her cheek then she'd wrap an arm around him for the photographer and he'd be sent on his way—never a hug, or a word of love, nothing but the emptiness in his chest when he left the suite yet again.

He recalled the horror of finding his father, too… But he didn't want to think of that now—too many raw emotions…

A redhead and this suite… Was Ibrahim playing some deep game? Could it be that he didn't really feel the affection for his nephew that Fareed had always felt he had? Was Ibrahim perhaps regretting that Fareed was heir to the throne? Would his uncle have wanted it to go to one of his own children?

No, he couldn't believe that, although the thought left a hollow in his chest.

He'd been fooled by his mother, fooled into thinking—again and again—that she might actually love him. Surely he couldn't have been fooled by his uncle—not all this time—surely not…

He must have been striding again for he heard the shuffle of hurrying feet behind him. This time when he stopped he took her arm, and once he'd touched her, all thoughts of Ibrahim vanished like a wisp of cloud, his mind filled with the woman by his side, the feel of her arm beneath her tunic, the faint scent of rosewater—reminiscent of weeks he'd spent camping in the deepest desert with Bedouin relations.

Most of the women in the court—and women he had courted from without it—smelled of designer perfume, not the fragrance that was as much part of his life as his skin and bones and tissues.

'So, tomorrow do we go to work? I must say I'm excited to see more of the hospital you've built—to see what facilities it has and to learn the procedures you use regarding referrals to specialists, and hospitalisation.'

'Really?' he asked, glancing down at her, finding it hard to believe that a woman here purely for the money Ibrahim would pay her should be bothered about such things.

'Of course,' she said, glaring at him. 'I've told you I was here to work. How else am I going to fill in a year?'

He wanted to tell her most of the women he knew filled their time quite easily. Visits to the big malls where European and American designers displayed their wares, trips to the big international hotels for tea and cakes. Then they had appointments for their hair, their nails, their waxing and polishing, massages and yoga and perhaps a little not-too-strenuous gym work.

But he had a feeling if he told her this she would stare blankly at him, or possibly disbelieve him completely.

And to give her her due, she'd insisted on going to the accident site and had then worked in the hospital while she'd been needed.

'You haven't answered me.'

He looked at her, her eyes still on his face, and for the life of him he couldn't remember what she'd asked, the sudden stirring of attraction towards her blotting out all thoughts.

Totally confused, he dropped a kiss on her lips—soft and pink and slightly open so he could see the pearl-like teeth.

'We'll talk about it later,' he said, and hoped he'd be able to go back through his thoughts to rescue the conversation.

She studied him a moment longer.

'That kiss was nothing but a diversionary tactic and don't think I don't know it,' she said. 'But if we're going to eat tonight, we should get going.'

Which they should, but his feet were stuck to the ground, and his body was demanding another kiss, a proper kiss, not a diversionary one, as she'd correctly said.

'Now?' she suggested.

He pulled himself together, took her arm again, and led her onwards, along the corridor that would eventually open near the old stables where the cars were kept.

But once outside it was she who slowed, for not all the stables were used for cars.

'Oh, look at that magnificent fellow,' she said, pointing to where Fareed's stallion, Muhib, peered from his stall.

'Not tonight,' Fareed said firmly. 'Tomorrow I'll show you the horses.'

Though he had no idea why he'd made *that* offer!

A driver pulled up beside them in a low-slung, sporty coupe.

'I'll drive tonight, Ahmed,' Fareed told him, as he opened the passenger door and helped Kate inside. He pulled the seatbelt free and passed it to her, his hand accidentally brushing against her breast, and again, for all this was an arranged marriage that held nothing but questions for him, he felt the tightening of attraction.

Think of his disdainful face, Kate told herself. *The way he surveyed our property, and us, really, as if we were beneath him. And his jibes about Ibrahim's money. Just because he's taking you to dinner, and dropping careless kisses here and there, it doesn't mean a thing. Don't think of that sunrise; don't think of that kiss...*

But the casual kiss then the brush of his hand across her breast had set her heart racing. Apparently you didn't have to like someone to be attracted to him.

The thought was so bizarre, she pondered it as they drove to wherever he was taking her. She supposed attraction could work like that. After all, it was put into people to ensure they propagated and the human race lived on. Dogs didn't have to be in love to have sex, or horses, or—

'Do you enjoy seafood?'

She'd been about to add fish to her list of species, so his question made her smile.

'Very much so.'

'Good,' he said, as he approached a roundabout. Turning off it to the right, he drove a short distance onto an esplanade that ran along a sandy beach, the dark waters of the sea lit by silvery foam and, here and there, by the lights along the road.

He pulled up into a parking lot opposite a dilapidated-looking shack, stopped the car, got out and came around to help her alight. She was already halfway out by the time he reached her, hurrying so there'd be no need for him to touch her again.

'It doesn't look all that great, but the seafood it sells will have been caught only hours earlier and you will get no finer food in Amberach.'

'Yet it looks quiet, almost deserted,' she said, as they

crossed the road and walked up a rickety jetty to where the shack perched above the water.

'Most locals and the expatriates prefer the fancy restaurants in the big hotels. This place doesn't have the ambiance they like.'

'But it's beautiful,' Kate whispered, as a young man bowed low to Fareed and led them to an outer veranda, where they sat above the sea and looked out at the moonlight playing on the water.

Was she genuine or was she simply doing what she felt she'd been paid to do?

Fareed wished he knew, although for now he was happy to give her the benefit of the doubt, because this was a special place and the faint flush on her face and the shine in her unpainted eyes suggested her words were genuine.

'May I order for you or would you prefer to choose dishes for yourself?' he asked, to get his mind back on the meal.

'Go ahead and order for me,' she said. 'There's no seafood I don't like.'

He ordered a lobster thermidor for her main course and for an appetiser a platter of tiny prawns, baby octopus, fish pieces, oysters and mussels, something they could share, picking at it as they talked.

If they talked!

He need not have worried. As they waited for the first part of the meal to arrive, she sipped at her water then asked, 'So, is tomorrow a workday?'

Fareed felt a twinge of disappointment. Here they were in one of the most romantic places in his land and she wanted to talk about work.

Of course she wanted to talk about work. What else would she want to talk about—the sham of a marriage she'd got herself into?

So he told her, yes, if she wished, she could work the next day.

'I'll get the staffing officer to draw up a roster for you,' he said, adding to himself, *leaving me off it as much as possible.*

'I think Ibrahim has already allocated you a driver. If you let him know the roster he will always be waiting for you.'

To his surprise, Kate smiled—and once again his body yelled attraction.

'Then I should probably ask for some extra bread to take back with me so I can leave a trail of breadcrumbs from the stables back to the suite. How else will I find my way there in the morning?'

He found himself smiling back. And ignoring his own warning to never work the same roster as her.

'I will take you there in the morning, show you around and introduce you properly. We will leave at eight, if that suits you.'

'That would be great, but please don't feel you have to look after me all the time. Once I've found my way around enough to get to the car and back to where I'm sleeping, I'll be fine.'

'You don't want to mix with the other women? You must have met some of them since you've been here. Your life shouldn't be all work.'

She studied him for a moment then sighed before explaining, 'I have met many of them and they have been wonderfully kind and supportive, but they are women with curiosity and I would be uncomfortable with them because of the pretence. I would rather work and sleep, swim in the pool, maybe do a little sightseeing, but I don't want to be answering questions about you, or my life with you. I don't want to deceive them. It was bad enough deceiving you on the drive from the airport but I had promised Ibrahim I'd say nothing.'

Fareed shook his head. In his experience women revelled

in a little deception and intrigue and would have thought nothing of making up stories about their marriage, their husband and even his prowess—or otherwise—in the bedroom. Hadn't whispers of such things come back to him from women he had once thought loved him?

She was definitely different, this woman.

The food arrived and they began to eat, using their fingers to pick up the delicate morsels, using flat bread to savour the juices. Fingers brushed from time to time, but the conversation focused on the food, with Kate letting out little moans of delight with each new mouthful.

'This is so delicious,' she said. 'I've eaten this kind of food before but the spices and the way it's been cooked make it more delicious than anything I've ever had. The only trouble is, if I keep eating I won't be able to eat my lobster.'

'We can take our time,' Fareed said quietly, and Kate glanced up at him, trying to read behind the mask that was his face.

He was an enigma, this man. Definitely kind, caring even, yet he hid every emotion from view. Even when he'd kissed her in the corridor, shocking her into silence for a while, nothing had shown on his face.

Though he *had* smiled earlier, she reminded herself, then had to wonder if it had actually been a smile or a simple movement of his lips that had looked like a smile, but without any emotion behind it.

CHAPTER EIGHT

SHE DID FINISH her lobster, although by the end of the meal she knew she'd overdone it.

'I think I should walk back to the palace after that,' she told him, as she pushed away from the table.

Again what might have been a smile.

'That would be a bit drastic, but we could take a stroll along the beach.'

By the sea?

In the moonlight?

With this man to whom she already felt a fine, fragile thread of attraction?

I don't think so.

'That sounds lovely.'

She knew the words were hers, knew she'd said them, because even if she hadn't recognised her own voice she could feel the tension they had caused in her body.

They left their sandals and shoes on the path along the foreshore, and walked down onto the sand, smooth and cool underfoot, sliding between Kate's toes.

'Is it the same sand as in the desert?' she asked, and he bent to lift a handful, letting it trickle into her out-held hand.

'The very same but the beach sand becomes bleached by the water while the desert sand retains the redness of the mountains from which it is born.'

She closed her fingers on it, feeling the warmth of it in her palm. Amberach sand—the world was a truly wonderful place and somehow she'd found herself in a particularly magical corner of it. Surely it was all right to enjoy it...

They had walked a little, paused, and walked again, but now Fareed asked what she was thinking and she tried to explain.

'I know I have been the means of putting you in a very awkward position, but I cannot regret coming here. It is so different, so special somehow, I wouldn't have missed it for anything.'

'Yet you have seen so little of it.'

'I'll see more, but look ahead—at the ridge of rock tumbling down into the sea, and the moon shining on the desert closer to where we are—these are beauties I had never imagined, and although it probably sounds daft to you, it touches my soul.'

'Not so daft,' he said quietly, then he bent his head and kissed her lips, very slowly and barely touching at first, although soon his mouth firmed on hers, his arms enclosed her, and she found herself responding, her lips parting at his insistence, and from her own desire.

A month at least, it lasted, that kiss.

It stole her breath, and teased her into thinking things she shouldn't think—things like marriage and marriage beds and—

Now his hands were moving on her skin—well, not skin but on the fine-woven silk of her tunic. He was learning her by feel, all the time keeping her pressed against him so she could feel his reaction to the kiss was as strong, and probably as startling, as her own.

'It is unseemly for a prince to be behaving like this in public.'

The husky whisper sent a shot of pure lust downwards through her body and she clung a little tighter.

Slowly he eased her off, took her hand, and began to walk back to where they'd left the car—*and* their footwear.

No words spoken—no laughing off the kiss—it was as if they were held in a bubble that existed beyond this world. A bubble of both time and place that could burst any minute with one false step or one unconsidered word...

He had to think! Had to stop kissing this stranger—who was his wife—and try to work out exactly what was going on in Ibrahim's mind. Heaven forbid he take her to bed—which he desperately wanted to do—and she became pregnant...

Was that Ibrahim's plan?

No! There was no way on this earth or the next Ibrahim could possibly have realised that some peculiar chemistry would attract the two of them to each other. Ibrahim knew the type of women he dated—the kind of women to whom he was attracted.

And surely Ibrahim knew him well enough to know a red-haired woman was more likely to repel him than attract him.

He glanced towards the woman at the centre of this puzzle—big mistake, as she was looking out the window but smiling at the same time—a soft, beguiling kind of smile that made him want to stop the car and kiss her all over again.

Then rip her clothes off and—

Some echo of the groan he'd thought he'd concealed deep inside his body must have escaped for she turned to look at him, concern on her face.

'Are you okay?' she asked, spreading soft fingers on his arm.

'As can be!' he answered roughly, then regretted it, but it was better to be back at odds with her than the attraction thing.

Could it be genetic, this attraction to a red-haired woman? His father had been besotted, and then destroyed...

Was Ibrahim testing him, marrying him to Kate? Testing his strength of character—his ability to be heir to the Sultanate?

Growing up in the palace, he'd heard enough gossip about his parents to know his mother had expected to become a queen immediately she'd married, not realising the old sultan, Fareed's grandfather, had still been alive.

And so she'd left—left her little son and her husband— returning only when she'd wanted money, tormenting her husband until—

He pulled into the castle grounds, and drove more slowly towards the converted stables, reluctant now to leave this woman, yet...

She'd lost him.

Somewhere between the kiss and the car, she thought. Not that she'd wanted more—

Liar!

Attraction was a peculiar thing. Here she'd been, thinking a marriage of convenience would be safe from attraction—from the longings, and stirrings, and demanding needs of desire.

Especially after Mark, who, for all his declarations of undying love, had dropped her like a hot potato when she'd said she had to go home. No sympathy, no hint of understanding, just, 'Well, if you go don't expect me to wait.'

So much for love!

Not that this was love—it was far too urgent, too primal to be covered by that gentle word...

Now her husband, the man she didn't know yet had kissed with passion, led her back to the suite, suggested she continue to use the big bed, and departed, leaving behind an emptiness Kate couldn't understand.

* * *

Waking in the morning, determined not to brood on Fa-reed's peculiar behaviour the previous evening, Kate dressed, ate her breakfast, then asked the maid to take her to where she'd meet her driver.

Fareed wasn't anywhere in sight when she reached the hospital, but a nurse she'd met the day of the acci-dent showed her around. They'd barely covered the im-portant things when three young women, covered in the all-concealing black cloaks called *abayas*, their hair hid-den by scarves, appeared in the waiting room and greeted Kate with cries of delight.

'Oh, thank goodness you are here. We did hope we'd get a woman doctor but getting you is even better. You have an oath thing, don't you, doctors? You can't talk about what we tell you?'

Mai, Suley and Farida crowded around her and while as-suring them all of confidentiality she ushered them into an examination cubicle and drew the curtains to close it off.

'I didn't recognise you at first in your cloaks. So, what is wrong?'

The young women—girls, really—looked puzzled, then Farida caught on.

'You mean the *abayas*? We always wear them when we go somewhere public like the mall but this time we wore them so we could come here without anyone recognising us as part of the royal family and fussing over us.'

'I see,' Kate said, as they settled themselves, Mai and Suley on the examination couch and Farida on the only chair.

Kate propped herself on the equipment cabinet and stud-ied them. There was something wrong—not health-wise, she suspected—but...

She didn't have a clue. It wasn't drugs or alcohol, they were all too healthy looking.

'So?' she asked, and waited, until, slowly and with obvious reluctance, Mai pulled back one sleeve of her black, all-enveloping gown.

Kate's heart missed a beat at the sight of the bandaged wrist, although there didn't appear to be blood staining the bandage so maybe the damage had been minimal.

'Want to tell me about it?' she said, as she gently unwrapped the bandage.

As usual it was Farida who took over the explanations.

'We were—we thought—we...'

But the usually confident Farida faltered and now Suley, her arm around Mai, hung her head and whispered the words Kate needed to hear.

'We had this silly idea, back when we were children. We decided that we didn't want to be married off to just anyone. We wanted to be free to choose our own husbands. We took a vow and pricked our fingers and mixed our blood, that we would all stand together and...'

Suley stopped, obviously unable to go on, but Kate could guess at what the young women had decided.

She had laid bare the cuts on Mai's arm, not deep but reddened at the edges. She could use a couple of stitches in one of them but guessed that was the last thing Mai would want.

A nurse appeared at the end of the curtained room but Kate stepped in front of her young friend and sent the nurse away.

Finding antiseptic and butterfly sutures, she bathed the wounds and put the strips of tape across the cuts to hold them together. She was nearly done when Suley spoke again.

'This was my fault. My father told me last night that he'd chosen my husband, and I phoned the others to meet me at the mall. We went into one of the restrooms and I had a razor blade but I was too scared to cut myself, so Mai said she'd show me how, then she saw the blood and fainted and we didn't know what to do, then Farida remembered you might be working here and could help us.'

'My father will kill me if he finds out I did this,' Mai whispered, 'and poor Suley, what can we do to help her?'

Kate was fitting a clear adhesive dressing over the wound but her mind was churning with the scraps of information she'd been given.

'There,' she said, as she finished. 'Now, tell me the plan you had back when you swore the oath and mingled your blood.'

Farida must have recovered her confidence for it was she who spoke.

'We were all going to kill ourselves,' she announced, and Kate had to hide a smile at the melodrama of youth, although by now they should have had more sense.

'I imagine you were about ten years old and the drama of it was so exciting you didn't think past the actual act. Killing yourself is so very final, you know. You end up dead before you've had time to think of all the wonderful things in life you're going to miss out on—university, careers, love, children and just having fun. There's no coming back from dead—or very rarely.'

'But it was to be a protest to our families,' Mai told her. 'How else could we make them realise that arranged marriages are so out of date—that we should be allowed to choose our own partners.'

Kate took a deep breath.

'I really do not know enough about your customs to talk about such things, but surely—'

The curtain opened again and this time it was Fareed who stalked through.

'I will see these girls, Dr Andrews,' he said crisply.

'I don't think so,' Kate replied, feeling Mai hurriedly

hiding her wrist behind her. 'They actually wanted to see a woman doctor.'

'That's as may be,' Fareed muttered, 'but they are related to me, I know their parents and I just heard you say something about not understanding our customs.'

'That doesn't lessen my effectiveness as a doctor,' Kate snapped, 'so now I'd like you to leave so I can continue my consultation.'

He stood there, glaring at her, and for a moment she thought she might have won the argument, then he drew in a deep breath and began again.

'The women in this country, the young ones in particular, want gender equality. It is my opinion that if they are so eager for it, they should accept it in all aspects of their lives. They should be just as willing to see a male doctor as a female one.'

Kate straightened her spine and fought back.

'For some things, yes, and I'm sure they would be. But there are some things, I, as a woman, would prefer to discuss with a woman doctor, just as you would probably prefer to discuss something like—oh, impotence—with a male doctor.'

She heard the collective gasp from the young women behind her, and saw colour leach from Fareed's face as anger fired his eyes and stiffened his body.

'I will talk to you later,' he said, each word delivered like a death threat.

And with a final slit-eyed glare he left the cubicle.

'Is he really impotent?' Suley whispered, and with a groan Kate dropped her head into her hands, shook her head, and wondered what on earth she had done.

Of all the things to have said, and in front of witnesses, but he'd made her so angry, so furious, the words had just come tumbling out.

'No, he's not, it was nothing more than an example of what a man might not wish to discuss with a woman doctor.'

She looked sternly at the three, adding, 'And if any one of you mention this outside this cubicle I will tell everyone about your silliness. Now, let's get back to it.'

They nodded in unison, but were still watching her, wide-eyed with awe.

'Firstly, tell me this, do you all love your parents?'

Three more nods.

'Can you talk to them both, or to one or other of them, about most things?'

'I can talk to my mother about absolutely anything,' Suley said, 'and Farida's parents are fantastic, they are more like an older sister and brother than parents—we all talk to them about sex and boys and stuff.'

'And you, Mai?' Kate asked gently.

'Usually I can,' she said, 'to both my parents, although they are quite strict. All our parents are strict as far as our behaviour goes, like we're not allowed to go out with boys alone, or go to nightclubs.'

'Could you tell them what has happened?'

Suley shook her head.

'My father would be very angry. He would say I was stupid and how could a stupid girl like me go away to college?'

'Farida, could you explain this to your parents?'

Farida was quiet for a while then asked, 'But why would I need to?'

'I'm just worried one or other of your sets of parents will hear about this visit to the hospital from Fareed and you will be asked to explain. Although there is confidentiality between you and me, I must fill out some kind of information about your visit and he, as head of the hospital, can easily access it. If the three of you would be happy to explain it all to someone like Farida's parents, they could settle the other parents down before it blows up into something far bigger than it was.'

The three spoke among themselves, quickly in their own language, finally facing Kate again.

'Would you come with us to Farida's house? Would you explain?'

Kate looked at three pairs of beseeching brown eyes.

'I could,' she said, 'but not until my shift ends. Could you go back to the mall until four and I'll meet you there then?'

Apparently this presented no problem. Kate asked when Mai had last had a tetanus injection, checked the dressing on her wrist, suggested she buy some bangles at the mall to cover it, and sent them on their way.

Fareed must have been watching from somewhere because she'd no sooner left the cubicle than he appeared beside her.

'What happened with those girls?' he demanded.

'I sorted it,' Kate said, trying hard to ignore the signals his body was sending hers, as well as the anger that was simmering behind his eyes.

'But they are family, I must speak to their parents.'

'I'm doing that later,' Kate said, as airily as her tension would allow. 'They knew me, you know. They were part of the entourage that helped me prepare for the wedding and were with me at the henna party. I'm sure that's why they asked for me, rather than for you.'

She knew he wasn't appeased and she was probably adding fuel to the fire, but she couldn't resist adding, 'And there is such a thing as patient confidentiality, you know!'

He greeted this with a derisive snort and stormed away, leaving Kate shaken by the encounter and upset that she'd torn apart whatever tentative bonds they'd forged the previous night.

A little sadness seeped into her soul because, for all her bold talk of it being nothing more than sexual attraction, she was beginning to see that other emotions were mixed up in her feelings for Fareed.

She was without doubt *the* most infuriating woman he had ever met! Firstly, defying him when he'd demanded to take over her patients, then accusing him of impotence—him!

And in front to those silly young women!

It would be all over Amberach, and believed, given his own bride had said it.

He'd kill her!

Somewhere in the ancient laws of his tribal ancestors there had to be one that covered insolence towards the crown prince, and he was certain it would be punishable by death.

Unfortunately, death was so very permanent and every time he looked at the wretched woman he had a jolt of lust rush through his body—lust, he knew, that wouldn't be satisfied by just any woman right now.

Maybe he could imprison her in the suite—in the bedroom—tied to the bed…

His groin stirred painfully and he cursed again, unable to believe where his thoughts had strayed.

Fortunately he was called to another patient, a woman, while he was pleased to see a robed man objecting when he was led towards Kate and introduced to her as his doctor.

She glanced across the wide room and raised her eyebrows and he could almost hear her asking if gender equality shouldn't work both ways.

The man, he realised, was refusing to be seen by Kate, who treated him with respect and suggested he sit down and wait until a male doctor was available.

The man was voluble in his protests but just then an ambulance attendant brought in a young labourer with an obviously horrific wound to his arm and shoulder.

Kate hurried the pair into the cubicle, calling for a nurse and a pathology runner to take blood to the lab.

Every instinct told him he should go to this case, but the woman he'd been walking to a cubicle was groaning now, and he realised she was definitely in labour.

All part of a day's work in the ER.

Kate sat the young man on the bed so recently vacated by her friends, and listened as the ambulance attendant gave his report. Her patient had already been given morphine for the pain and had fluid running into his good arm.

The man had fallen on a building site, probably about twenty feet, but he'd brought down a pile of bricks with him, and they had landed on his arm and shoulder.

Kate cleaned the wound as best she could, picking out bits of brick and grit.

'We'll take him through to X-Ray,' she told the nurse who'd appeared to help her.

The nurse called for an orderly, who wheeled the man through to the back of the main room, where every kind of machine was set up to provide the very best of patient information.

An X-ray was all Kate needed now, but she was pleased to see an echocardiogram and what looked like a nuclear scanner.

The X-ray clearly showed a compound fracture of the humerus, close to the shoulder, a situation that would require orthopaedic surgery and any number of pins and plates to stabilise.

She asked the nurse to call an orthopaedic specialist, then back in the cubicle worked out what she could fix herself to save the young man extra time under anaesthetic.

She could stitch the gash below his elbow, so, while the nurse flushed the wound with saline to clean out any remaining debris, Kate repeated the checks that the ambulance attendants had already done. Pulse, blood pressure, oxygenation and temperature were all taken then recorded on the man's file. Now she began a more careful examination of him, checking every area of his skin, palpating his stomach, listening to his chest, gently checking for damage to his rib cage.

He seemed all right, although he didn't understand the questions she kept asking, and when the nurse repeated them in the local language, she drew a blank, as well.

'He must be a migrant worker,' the nurse explained. 'There are many hundreds of them in the city.'

'Do we have translators?' Kate asked.

The nurse shook her head.

'They do at the big hospital where he will go for his operation, so he will be all right.'

He would, Kate knew, but she'd have liked to talk to him, even through an intermediary, because only the patient could tell you exactly how he was feeling, and where he had pain.

Could she talk to Fareed about this? Ask if would be possible to have translators here, or would there be too many nationalities concerned?

Perhaps—

'I am Dr Livingstone.'

The man who appeared through the curtain made the announcement as if he was, indeed, the famous African explorer.

Kate had to laugh.

'Kate Andrews,' she said, holding out her hand to the big, bluff, middle-aged man looming over her patient.

'Mike!' Dr Livingstone told her as he shook her hand. 'You've got yourself something you can't handle.'

Kate pointed to the X-rays still in the light boxes on the wall.

'Hmm, nasty one indeed. What's he had?'

Kate listed what she knew.

'I was about to sew up that gash below his elbow,' she explained.

'Not to worry,' Mike told her. 'I'll have one of my lackeys do it while he's under. Okay if we take him now?'

Slightly bewildered by the speed at which things were happening in this very different ER, Kate nodded.

'See you again, then,' Mike said, as he followed the trolley with his patient on it out of the cubicle. 'We have monthly socials at the big hospital and often a group of us will get together for dinner in between. I'll get someone to put your name on the list, and get your contact details from HR so we might see you soon.'

Just what she hadn't wanted to happen—getting dragged into a hospital social scene that, once her relationship to Fareed was known, would lead to never-ending questions and speculation.

Never mind, when an invitation came she could say no.

Would have to say no!

Wouldn't she?

The day continued to be busy, and it was only when she remembered she had to leave to meet her young friends at the mall that Kate realised she'd missed lunch.

She explained to the woman who'd shown her around that she had to go, and asked how she could let her driver know.

'Oh, he'll be waiting for you outside. Once he sees you come out the staff entrance, he'll collect you immediately.'

Kate frowned at the woman.

'You mean he's been sitting there all day, just waiting for me to reappear.'

The woman shrugged.

'It's what drivers do.'

Kate shook her head, unable to believe such things could happen.

'Where are you headed?' her informant asked.

'I'm meeting some friends at the mall,' Kate explained.

'Not with that hair,' her new friend told her. 'Wait, I'll get you a scarf and an *abaya*—there are always spare ones hanging around in the staffroom in case one of the women on the staff decides not to go straight home.'

'Do all women wear them all the time in public?'

The young woman smiled and led her into the staffroom.

'Most of the expats don't, but you're different, aren't you? You're married to our prince and everyone knows you've got red hair so if you want any peace while you're out and about, you'll have to cover up. In here it's okay, our patients will be delighted to think they're being treated by a princess. Stand still, I'll show you how to tie the scarf. You need pins to keep it tight under your chin, then the rest just flows around your shoulders and down your back. Should have put the *abaya* on first, but we'll manage.'

Once clothed from head to toe in black, Kate looked at herself in the mirror.

'The pale skin and glasses are a bit of a giveaway,' she said, but her friend—now introduced as Roberta—shook her head.

'When you're dressed like that you're anonymous. No one will look twice at you.'

Kate thanked her and found her way to the staff entrance where, as if by osmosis, her driver was pulling in.

And probably not by osmosis, Fareed was looming.

'You do not need to wear that outer clothing to ride back to the palace,' he said, his voice still tight with anger.

'I'm calling in at the mall on the way back,' Kate told him, 'so Roberta suggested I cover up. Is that right?'

It took every ounce of courage she possessed to look directly into his face while she spoke—directly into that anger.

Was she hoping to see it soften?

She didn't know, but a small pain in her chest told her she was sorry this had happened—that she'd lost what little rapport she'd had with him already.

'Why the mall? Is there something you need? You have only to ask one of the servants at the palace and she will fetch it for you.'

'Are you saying I can't go to the mall? That my life will be limited to the hospital and the palace, with perhaps a little sightseeing as a special treat?'

Her own anger was building now, although she remembered claiming it was all she needed.

'I am not saying that at all,' he growled. 'I am just not happy about you going alone to such a place. You should have a maid with you, and a manservant. Anything could happen!'

'At a mall? Anyway, I'm going to meet the girls—the young women—and have a coffee with them. Is that a crime?'

He gave a huff of frustration.

'Of course it's not a crime. Somehow you turn my words against me, but you're a stranger here and my responsibility, I only want that you be safe.'

Seeing him at a loss, her anger vanished and she saw he'd left himself wide-open for a tease.

'That wasn't all you wanted last night with that kiss,' she reminded him, and skipped over to where the ever-patient driver was holding the car door open.

Had Thalia the soothsayer led Ibrahim to this woman knowing she was some kind of witch? Had his uncle chosen her knowing she'd cast some kind of spell over his nephew and drive him to distraction with her behaviour? Thalia had certainly been a presence in the palace prior to the trip to Australia.

He shook his head in disgust at his thoughts. Thalia wouldn't have known of a witch way out there in Australia.

Not a witch with milk-white skin and glinting green
eyes...

Yet in one day at work and she'd defied him, made him
look a fool in front of his young cousins and now taunted
him and departed before he could hit back.

And there was something going on with those girls, he
knew it, and as a man in the family, surely it was his duty
to find out what it was.

Kate found the three friends sitting in a coffee shop, behind
a screen that provided a private place for women on their
own to sit and enjoy each other's company.

Beyond the screen men and women sat together, families with small children, and men with men, some robed in
traditional costume, others in western clothes.

Good-looking men, all of them, and the women, even
with only their faces visible, were beautiful.

But she wasn't here to talk about the beauty of the local
people—

'Have you thought about what you're going to tell your
parents?' she asked.

'Why?' Farida asked, and Kate thought about her answer.

'Although it was only a minor incident, and Mai wasn't
badly hurt, any attempt at suicide must be reported—well,
in my country it must, at least.'

'But we didn't mean it!' they cried in unison.

'Except you thought you did,' Kate reminded them. 'You
know now it was silly, and juvenile, and something you
just did without thinking, but I do believe you should talk
to your parents, all of you. Tell them about the oath you
swore when you were too young to understand what death
meant, but more than that talk to them about arranged marriage and how you feel about it. I am sure your parents all
love you very much, and would not do anything to cause

you distress, so talk about these things, and listen to them, as well—listen when they explain why they wish the best for you.'

'They *do* always want the best for us,' Mai said gloomily. 'And they allow us a lot more freedom than some of our friends at college get.'

'So will I come with you now to talk to Farida's parents, then maybe they could arrange for the other parents to join us and we can get it over and done with?'

'But you haven't had a coffee,' Farida objected, and Kate smiled.

'I'd rather go now—putting things off never helps,' she said.

Suley led the way to where her driver was waiting for them. She spoke quietly to him, obviously telling him to take them all to Farida's house.

'Will both your parents be there?' Kate asked, and Farida assured her they would be.

'It is Thursday and my father is always home from the office early.'

The car swept along the esplanade then turned into a high-walled enclave, the ornately carved metal gate swinging open at some electronic command.

Farida's mother greeted Kate warmly, showering praise on how beautiful her guest had looked at her wedding.

Of course these people would have been there, Kate realised, not that she remembered any of the hundreds she had met.

Farida explained Kate had come to talk to both her parents, and one servant was dispatched to bring coffee and cakes, while another was sent to get Farida's father.

'Is this bad?' Farida's mother asked Kate quietly as the friends led the way into a small lounge room.

'Not bad but a little complicated,' Kate told her. 'Silly

schoolgirl stuff, really, but something I couldn't not talk to someone about.'

Farida's father arrived and bowed low to Kate, making her feel very uncomfortable, but once they were all settled, it was Farida who took over, kneeling at her father's knee, holding his hand and telling the story from the beginning, blinking back tears at times but going on determinedly.

'Oh, my darling girls,' Farida's mother said, taking Mai in her arms and hugging her, then gathering Suley on her other side, while Farida's father lifted his daughter from the floor and held her on his knee as if she were two years old again.

'Thank you,' he said to Kate. 'You were right to come. I will call the other parents and tell them what has happened, and although all three will be scolded, no harm has been done as long as all three of you swear that you will never do anything so foolish again.'

'And that you will talk to us, or to Dr Kate, if you are troubled by anything,' Farida's mother added. 'There is nothing so bad in all the world that you cannot tell us, is there, Dr Kate?'

Kate shook her head, blinking back her own tears, probably brought on by seeing this close family when her own was so far away.

So far away and living in ignorance of her deceit! The pain of *that* stabbed again and she stood up rather hurriedly.

'I'll leave you with it and be going,' she said, then remembered she'd been driven here with the girls.

'Oh, I left my driver at the mall,' she said, feeling embarrassed by her casual behaviour.

'He will have followed us here,' Mai told her. 'Come on, we'll walk you to the door to make sure he's waiting.'

He was, which didn't make Kate feel any better about not telling him where she'd been going. But when she tried to apologise he waved her words away.

'I will always be waiting for you,' he said, and after her earlier moment of weakness she felt strangely comforted.

'That girl had attempted suicide!'

The accusation hit Kate as she walked into the suite, surprised to find Fareed there and too weary for an argument.

'And good evening to you, too,' she muttered, slumping tiredly into one of the chairs by the window.

'You should have told me. I must speak to the parents.'

'All done, all fixed,' Kate said, 'and, anyway, it wasn't a serious attempt—she was demonstrating to the others how easy it was to do, then fainted when she realised she'd drawn blood.'

She looked across at Fareed, who was pacing the space beyond the bed.

'And I refrained from telling them that if they were serious about wrist slitting as a means of suicide they should cut long ways along the vein, not across where the tendons protected it.'

He halted on the spot and stared at her, so much disbelief on his face that Kate had to laugh.

'Joke, Fareed, joke!'

'It is not funny, such things are very serious. Suicide is a crime in my country.'

'Mine, too, I think,' Kate told him, then, not wanting to get into another argument with him, she shook off her lethargy and stood up. 'I think I'll have a swim.'

She opened her mouth to ask him to join her then closed it again, imagining just how much trouble she'd be in with this man almost naked in the water beside her, the sensual slither of water on skin magnifying the silly attraction she had towards him.

'I'll join you,' he said, startling her so much by this about-face from angry man to companion that she almost decided against the idea. He'd disappeared into his dressing room, and she made her way more slowly into hers, thinking about the cool, revivifying water—and droplets of it on tanned skin...

He had to do something about his impulse control, Fareed decided as he shut the door on the woman who seemed determined to torment him.

He'd always prided himself on control, but just lately it appeared to have taken a holiday.

Or he'd taken leave of his senses!

He should get out of this place—go for a drive or, better still, a ride.

A memory of a woman on a horse flashed through his mind.

He burst back into the bedroom of the suite, crossing to the door into Kate's dressing room, knocking, then opening it slightly to call through the gap.

'Will a swim suffice this evening or would you like to go for a ride? There's a full moon rising early so even if we go too far, we'll have moonlight on our return.'

Riding by moonlight? In that magical desert?

Kate tossed her swimsuit back into the cupboard.

'Give me five minutes,' she said, as she pulled old jeans and a checked shirt out of the cupboard, then searched through what seemed like dozens of pairs of sandals for her boots.

'Thank you, Fareed,' she said, as she met him in the bedroom. 'This will be much better than a swim.'

Partly because our near-naked bodies won't be frolicking closely in the sensual water, but also because there's nothing as good as a ride for blowing the cobwebs from the brain, and allowing it to think more clearly.

And her brain certainly needed to do that.

He'd been waiting for her, dressed much as she was, but projecting such arrogant masculinity she had to restrain her body from flinging itself at him.

'Beach or desert?' he asked, as he led her along a now more familiar corridor towards the rear of the palace.

'Beach or desert?' she echoed.

Her bewilderment must have been evident in her voice for he turned and smiled.

The smile had even more effect on her body than the sight of him had earlier—the man was sex personified.

'To ride—the beach or the desert?'

'Oh!' Kate managed, swallowing hard and hoping her errant thoughts had been swallowed at the same time. 'Desert for sure. Maybe the beach some other time, but I've never ridden in a desert. How do the horses manage in the soft sand?' *Good work, Kate, you sound almost normal.* 'I know camels have specially developed hooves but horses?'

He turned away again and she hurried to catch up.

'The sand is good for their hooves and very good for strengthening their legs.'

Duh!

'Of course, I did know that,' Kate said, remembering the countless times her parents had taken horses to the beach—taken her along, as well, as a rider on the string. It was just that Fareed's presence was causing brain melt.

Or she hoped that's all it was!

A stablehand was holding the bridle on the stallion whose head she'd glimpsed over a stall, while a smaller boy held a saddled gelding, a dark grey-black, and possibly the most beautiful horse Kate had ever seen.

'Oh, you beauty,' she whispered, as she walked quietly towards it, holding out her hand so the horse could check on the stranger.

'He's very well behaved,' Fareed said, and Kate wondered if he'd added 'unlike some women' under his breath.

Moving automatically, Kate checked the gear, sliding her fingers beneath the girth to make sure it hadn't loosened. Satisfied, she put a foot in the stirrup and vaulted into the

saddle, happiness flooding through her at the familiarity
of a horse beneath her.

'Oh, Fareed,' she said, 'this is so much better than a
swim.'

'You haven't gone anywhere yet,' he reminded her, but
she thought she detected that little smile she'd seen before—a smile he didn't really want to smile...

He swung easily into the stallion's saddle and led the
way sedately out of the yard, across a big training paddock
behind the stables, through a wide iron gate held open by a
wizened old man, and straight from grassy field to desert,
the sand painted red by the setting sun.

The stallion was prancing, held on a tight rein but obviously ready to take off.

'He needs a run. I'll go ahead and come back when he's
shaken out his fidgets,' Fareed told her, and Kate nodded,
her breath stolen by the sight of the man she'd married
astride the powerful, cavorting animal with the red glow
of the sunset behind them.

He swung the horse around and took off, the stallion
streaking across the soft sand. Kate's horse pranced now,
wanting to join the action, but, not knowing the animal,
she started slowly, getting the feel of him as he trotted
then cantered and finally stretched his legs in a full gallop,
following some path only he could see towards the other
horse and rider.

Fareed rode back to meet her, and they moved at a more
sedate pace towards a high outcrop of rock. As they drew
closer, Kate made out the shape of a building at the top.

'Is that the old fort?' she asked. 'It looks different from
this side.'

'Would you like to see it? We can ride there.'

Kate turned towards the man who rode beside her, wondering just how much of this togetherness she could take.
But her interest in the old building overcame the warnings

her head was offering—warnings about spending too much time with Fareed—too much 'friendly' time…

'I'd love to see it,' she said, and although she meant the words, she still felt a shiver down her spine—as if by committing to the destination she was moving into the unknown.

'Race you to that palm tree,' she challenged, in an attempt to clear her mind of fancies she didn't understand. It was also a good idea because his horse was so much faster she'd be spared his proximity for a little while.

Maybe that would help her sort out what was going on her body.

And her mind!

He'd beaten her easily, but Fareed turned so he could watch her, see the effortless way she rode, at one with the animal, strands of red hair flying loose from its restraining plait.

He imagined that hair splayed across a pillow—a pillow next to his—and his body quickened. Would a physical relationship be possible?

He knew he wanted it, but Kate—Katya as he now thought of her… Of her feelings, he had no idea, although she *had* responded to his kisses—responded with a fire as vibrant as her hair.

But she *had* married him for money, which made everything she did and said suspect. A woman who'd accept a bribe like that would do anything for money—or so he imagined.

She pulled up, flushed and laughing.

'That was wonderful,' she said, breathing deeply to slow her heart rate. 'Just wonderful!'

And all aglow like that, she was almost…

Beautiful?

She put herself down over her looks, but—

'Well,' she said, while he was still trying to work out

why the sight of her flushed and panting had affected him so deeply, 'are we going on to the fort?'

The sky was streaked with the last colours of the fading day, but the track to the fort was wide and well marked and by the time they came down the moon would be out.

'If that is what you'd like,' he said, uncertain now that spending even more time with her was a good idea.

She studied him for a moment, then smiled and said, 'It definitely is!'

Now she was smiling as well as looking almost beautiful. He led the way around the hill to where the track began, but his mind was on the woman following him—the woman who had been paid to be his wife—and why he was suddenly feeling very confused about her.

Kate's horse picked its way delicately up the track, allowing her time to sit and admire the broad shoulders, slim hips and straight back of the rider in front of her.

Was this little adventure a good idea or a bad one? By the time they returned and ate dinner it would be late and she could plead tiredness and retire to bed, although maybe he wouldn't be around, wouldn't eat dinner with her, so there'd be no danger of them taking those kisses they'd shared any further.

And surely that wasn't disappointment squelching away inside her?

Did she actually *want* to get sexually involved with this man?

Wouldn't that just complicate matters too much?

And how could she separate out sexual feelings and emotional feelings? Could she have sex with someone she didn't love?

Wouldn't there have to be an element of love somewhere in there for the sex to be enjoyable?

And surely enjoyable sex and love weren't all that far apart...

CHAPTER NINE

'TAKE CARE ON this corner,' Fareed said, and Kate turned her mind from sex and love to concentrating on her horse.

Although once around the corner, she paused and looked around, amazed at how close the shoreline was, edging the red desert sands that flowed from the mountain.

'It's fantastic,' she said. 'I really have to get a map and drive around so I can orient myself. From here, you'd never know there was a city out there. It's so peaceful and serene, so untouched somehow.'

'The desert, like the ocean, is forever renewing itself. It is little wonder my forbears, seeing how this happened, believed life could do that too—believed in an afterlife in which you were rewarded for the good you did on earth.'

Kate nodded, looking into Fareed's dark eyes, aware how easy it would be to drown in them—liking him far more than she'd admit even to herself in case liking led to love and this was a bargain with a time limitation, not a real marriage.

He'd moved his horse towards the rocky edge of the track and she drew up beside him so they could look out together.

'The desert is my past,' he said quietly, 'the past that is in my blood. But although it's hidden from us now, the city does exist.'

He turned towards her, the reins loose in his hands, which rested on the stallion's neck.

'That city, Kate, is the future, although my people are ill prepared for it.'

He sighed, and Kate stayed silent, willing him to keep speaking, wanting to learn more of this man she didn't know.

'Ibrahim is doing his best, but his roots are more deeply buried in the desert, so seeing to the transition, getting it right, will be my job.'

'You make is sound like an enormous burden,' Kate said quietly, and he smiled at her.

'Only when I'm looking at the desert and thinking of the freedom it offers, or when I'm on this beauty and feeling the freedom of his stride.'

He patted the stallion's neck.

'Could no one else do the job?' Kate asked, hearing the pain in his voice as he spoke. 'You already run the hospital and work there many hours past your roster. Does Ibrahim not have sons who could take over?'

Fareed shook his head.

'My father was the eldest brother, so it is my duty,' he said, 'and one I will one day take it on with pride, but it worries me how best to help my people move forward. The hospital was a trial run, you might say. There I've been putting some of my ideas to work, employing as many women as possible in an effort to bring in some gender equality—but, on the other hand, I want the people, our patients, to accept this equality. You were right to point out there are times when it is appropriate to see a doctor of one's own sex, but for a cut toe or a headache? Surely whatever doctor is available should do?'

'But the people don't see it that way?'

He turned from the desert to look directly at her.

'I think it must be something in our blood—the blood of our men—that we are so protective of our women. Here I am, a modern man, yet when I saw you in that *abaya* I

wanted to forbid you to go to the mall, or at the least send
a phalanx of guards along with you.'

Kate laughed and touched his arm.

'All change takes time, you must know that,' she said
gently, but he didn't reply, simply turning his horse back
onto the track and riding on.

Kate's horse followed closely, while she considered this
side of Fareed she'd never seen. She couldn't help but feel
empathy for this man who longed for freedom yet was
bound by duty to his people, chained by the need to do his
best for them at what was obviously a very difficult time.

They rounded another bend and there was the fort. An
earth-coloured building, looking as if it had grown out of
the rock, it had the same air of permanence as the rock itself. An outer courtyard was lit by lamps hung along the
walls, and carpets were spread across it.

'People live here, then?' she asked, remembering something Fareed had said about it but not the details.

'A caretaker and his family are permanent residents,
and sometimes artists and artisans stay here while they
are doing restoration work. The only vehicle here now is
the caretaker's so maybe it's just his family at the moment.'

He waved his hand towards a decrepit old four-wheel
drive parked in one corner of the courtyard, then dismounted and turned to hold Kate's horse while she swung
off.

She straightened up, moving her feet and shaking off a
little stiffness while Fareed led the horses to a corner and
hitched their bridles on a rail above a trough of water.

'Come,' he called to Kate, and she crossed a faded, sandy
carpet towards a door that opened into the largest of the
round towers she'd seen from the car that first morning. It
was set at one end of a long, low building.

'This was the main lookout tower but it was also the

quarters for the headman of the village and his family when the village was raided from the sea.'

Inside, lamplight threw strange shadows on the spiral stairs that curved up out of sight. To the right of the staircase, an open arch led into a round room, made smaller on one side by the staircase. On the other side, a long, thin window let in the last of the daylight.

Fareed flicked a switch and lamps around the walls lit the room with an amber glow.

'When I was a child, we still used oil lamps when we came here—my uncle and cousins and friends. It was a great adventure then, to play games by lamplight and snuggle under rugs to sleep by the light of the one lamp that stayed lit.'

He sounded more sad than nostalgic and Kate fought an urge to put her arm around him and give him a quick hug. He'd walked to the window and was looking out, and she lost the fight.

She followed him, standing beside him and slipping her arm around his shoulders as she asked, 'Your uncle and cousins? Did your parents never come?'

She felt him stiffen and withdrew her arm, embarrassed by her action, moving away, back to the opening, changing the subject as quickly as she could.

'Does the staircase go to the top?'

He was still at the window, staring out, lost, she imagined, in the past.

But was he in the happy past of camping out in the tower with friends, or some unhappy past her question had revived?

Oh, bother him! she decided, and began to climb the stairs. A landing and another arched door, another room inside the arch, then up again, this time to the top, a terrace surrounded by battlements, but no longer a place of war because half of it was shaded by a frame that held up filmy draperies, making an elaborate gazebo, open on one side, to reveal carpets and piles of cushions—a party place or just a place of peace and beauty where people could relax.

But the battlements drew her first, and she crossed to one of the slits in the high stone walls and peered out, pleased to see the sea, dark now, with just the silver wash of foam on the little waves that broke upon the beach.

She felt him before she heard him—felt his presence right behind her—then his hand slid around her shoulders as hers had earlier held his.

'I'm sorry. My family—close family—was dysfunctional, to say the least. Ibrahim and his wife brought me up with their children so all my good memories are of times I shared with them.'

Kate moved so she rested against his body.

'I'm the one who's sorry, hurting you with an unthinking question. My family has been my life, and after seeing Farida with her family today I imagined family was just as important here as it is at home.'

'It is,' he said, holding her closer. 'But nothing's ever perfect, is it?'

He turned her slightly, looked down into her face for a moment, then his head bent and his lips touched hers, igniting all the nerves he'd awoken in her the previous night.

It's just a kiss, she told herself, but herself took no notice, responding as if it was an invitation to whatever wild and wonderful sex he might propose.

The kiss deepened, stole her breath, had her melting against him, then cool air brushed her lips and he was gone, striding to another part of the roof, peering out into the darkening night.

Fareed closed his eyes to the beauty and tried to make sense of his actions.

They'd been talking about his family yet still he'd kissed

this paid-for wife of his—the woman who was no better than his mother.

Kissed her until she'd responded...

He could hardly say she was seducing him when it was he initiating the kisses.

And wanting more!

He ached for her, something that was very new and strange in his contained and controlled lifestyle.

Was this how his father had felt?

It *had* to be some genetic code written into them that made them fools over women with red hair...

And Ibrahim—did he know this? Had he chosen Kate for that reason?

And now he, Fareed, had spoiled their time together— spoiled the small adventure that she had begun with such delight, as if he'd handed her a very special gift.

He walked back to where she stood, still looking out to sea, and took her hand, turning her so she faced him.

'Are you hungry? Do you want to go back for dinner, or could we sit and talk a little?'

The moon was rising but its light was not strong enough for him to read her face.

She was silent for a moment, then nodded.

'Yes, perhaps talking would be good.'

He led her to the cushioned retreat beneath the silken curtains and held her hand to support her as she settled amongst them.

Held her hand when they were both seated, close but not touching, apart from her hand in his.

'My mother was a foreigner,' he began. 'My father was besotted with her, but she hated Amberach and used any excuse to get away from it. The only time I saw her was on her rare visits to the palace.'

'She didn't take you with her when she left?'

Kate had moved so she could see his face when he answered, but the little tent was shadowed so reading it was impossible—or maybe that should be more impossible than usual!

Fareed sighed and his grip on her fingers tightened.

'That could have been my father's fault—he might have insisted I stay here.'

'You don't sound as if you believe that.'

Another sigh, deeper than the last.

'I don't, not for one minute!'

The words were blunt, but Kate heard hurt behind them—hurt and anger.

Pain caused by a red-haired foreigner, Kate realised, remembering the women's chat at the henna party!

'Oh, Fareed,' she whispered, and she slipped her free hand around his neck and held him close.

The kiss, she realised later, had been inevitable, as had been all that had followed it. The touches, the exploration, the building excitement that had turned to hot, ferocious need and the furious, winner-take-all coupling that had left them lying exhausted, entwined and breathless, but holding hard to each other as if they needed anchorage to the earth.

'I'll never find my clothes,' Kate grumbled, not moving from within Fareed's arms.

'Are you in such a hurry to move away from me that you need your clothes?'

There was a hint of laughter in Fareed's voice and Kate responded by snuggling closer.

'I suppose it's being naked or near naked in a strange place,' she said, murmuring the words against the satiny skin on his shoulder, licking at it when she'd done talking.

'Keep doing that and you won't need clothes for a while longer,' he growled, but Kate knew they had to move. Down in the courtyard the horses were waiting, and her stomach was telling her it needed dinner.

But what did this mean?

Would this Fareed, who'd shared more of himself than his body, ride home with her, eat dinner with her, sleep in the same bed as her, or were they back to being polite strangers—colleagues?

She moved and found her clothes, pulling them back on, wondering why she'd thought a ride with her husband would be less likely to end in sex than the two of them swimming together.

The ride home was magical, the moon now throwing its silvery light across the desert so Kate felt as if they rode across the sea; the dunes were waves so the sea was solid, but so serene and beautiful, she wondered how anyone could not fall in love with this fantastic country.

They were handing their horses over to stable hands when Fareed's mobile rang.

He answered it, turning from her and walking away slightly, talking English, but she couldn't hear the words.

Finishing the call, he turned back towards her and raised his hands in a helpless gesture.

'I have to go back to the hospital. One of the duty doctors has gone home ill.'

'Do you need me? I could come,' Kate said, but the Fareed she barely knew and definitely couldn't read was back and he thanked her politely, led her back to their suite, then said goodbye.

He wouldn't have wished his colleague ill, but the phone call had been a lifesaver, Fareed decided as he made his way to the hospital. He'd had no idea how to proceed as far as his marriage was concerned.

He knew it for a sham, despised the fact that Kate—she was only Katya in his other thoughts—had married him for money, and he was still determined not to become emotionally involved with her.

That had been his father's problem—fancying himself

totally in love with a woman who had only had eyes for the money she could suck out of him—a beautiful flame-haired leech.

Yet every instinct told him Kate—Katya, anyway—was different, although that might be part of the ensnarement.

Al'ama! What was he to do?

Put aside the problem of the woman and concentrate on your work, the sensible, and obviously nonsensual side of his brain told him, but could he?

He'd work it out tomorrow!

Kate pressed one of the buttons that summoned a servant and asked if she could have dinner served in half an hour.

After the hospitable companionship of eating with the other women before her wedding, this seemed weird to say the least, and she hoped they wouldn't think she was avoiding them.

But she had no idea what she should be doing—whether she should be seeking them out.

Except that might make them think Fareed was neglecting her.

Oh, hell and damnation, was nothing easy?

She showered, and emerged to find her dinner waiting, a tray full of delicious-looking dishes, ice cream in a wide cooler and a bowl of fruit.

Had they sent enough for both her and Fareed? It certainly looked that way.

And when she'd barely eaten half of it, what would the servants think? What gossip would ensue?

Bother this! She'd eat her dinner, send some emails—including a long one to Billy about the horses and the fort and the desert—then go to bed and tomorrow she'd have a long talk to Fareed about just what was expected of her in her role as his wife.

Would she be isolated like this for ever?

Or would she be shunted into the women's part of the palace—she already knew it reasonably well—and only see her husband when he...?

Tomorrow!

She'd sort it out tomorrow!

She slept in the big bed, woke early and alone, and decided to have a swim before breakfast. The ritual of pushing buttons to summon servants was still strange and uncomfortable for her, but she pushed a button anyway, ordered breakfast in an hour, then asked the young woman to tell her driver she'd be leaving for the hospital a half-hour after that.

Would this kind of thing ever become 'normal'? Kate doubted it, at least not in a year, which was all she'd promised Ibrahim she'd stay.

And why did thinking about that promise cause anxiety in her stomach, a kind of cold dismay?

It was the limit of a year—she knew that. Less than a year now that she'd share with Fareed? Barely time to get to know him—yet time enough to fall in love?

Last night, at the top of the tower at the old fort, it had felt like love, lying with him, listening to talk of his childhood, his mother, hearing his pain...

He was at the hospital when she arrived, already doing a handover to one of the other doctors coming on duty.

The smile he greeted her with was tired, but even a tired smile set her heart thumping in her chest.

'I will see you later—I'll go home and sleep and be back this afternoon,' he said, walking with her to the staff room where she could drop her bag.

'You're all right? Not too busy a night?' Kate asked, while inside she was cursing herself for the pathetic conversation. This man was her *husband*, for heaven's sake!

Okay, so over here she couldn't hug or kiss him in public, but shouldn't their conversation be easier?

Less forced?

'A pretty good night. The only busy time was when some young men, joy-riding, as they do, wiped out their car on a roundabout. One's in hospital up the road, head and spinal injuries, but the others were lucky and escaped with only assorted broken limbs and bumps and bruises.'

'Which would have kept you busy for quite some time,' Kate guessed, and was rewarded with another smile, a better effort this time, but they were talking work, so he probably felt smiling at her was safe.

'It did,' he said, holding the door open for her.

Kate slipped inside and was surprised when he followed, dropped a kiss on her cheek, squeezed her shoulders, then said, 'I'll see you later.'

Boy, oh, boy! A kiss on the cheek and I've gone weak-kneed!

She stood in the staff room, holding the palm of her hand to the cheek he'd kissed, and felt like an idiot. It was obviously too late to decide not to fall in love with him.

The morning was quiet apart from one man refusing to be treated by a woman for a nasty wound on his hand, and one woman whose husband insisted she only be seen by a woman.

Another pregnant patient! This one had had a fall, and both of them were beside themselves in case the fall had done some damage to the baby.

Kate helped the woman onto an examination table and sat the man on a chair.

'The baby's really well protected in there,' she assured them. 'He or she is floating around in a sac of fluid that's a bit like airbags in a car, designed to protect the occupant. But I will check your wife, and the baby's heartbeat, and then, if you wish, do a scan to check on the baby. You've had a scan before?'

The man shook his head.

'No photographs.'

Not rudely said, but definite.

'That's okay. We did it all before the machines were invented, there's no reason why we can't do our checking without them now.'

Questions about where and how the woman had fallen provided little information.

'She just fell,' the man said bluntly, and a shiver down Kate's spine suggested domestic abuse.

But the man seemed genuinely concerned for his wife and the wife very dependent on him, shaking her head rather than speaking, so Kate set it aside.

'Do you know how pregnant your wife is?' she asked the man.

'Twenty-two weeks,' he said with no hesitation, giving Kate a base from which to work in her examination.

'Has she had any bleeding?'

The man shook his head, looking so embarrassed, Kate found herself believing him.

Pulse, blood pressure...

Uncertain about the protocol of baring a woman's arm, she wrapped the blood-pressure cuff around the fine material of the woman's tunic.

The machine puffed and clicked, the eventual reading one hundred and eight over seventy. Given that blood pressure dropped in early pregnancy, and picked up towards the middle, this was almost clinically perfect. Pulse and respirations were also good and when she worked out the mean arterial pressure, it also came out perfect.

Now she asked the woman, who'd been sitting on the table, to lie down on her back. Kate put her arm around her to help ease her down, but the husband took over and as he settled his wife on the table the gentleness in his hands and the anxiety in his eyes told Kate he genuinely loved this woman.

The nurse, who'd been standing quietly at the end of the cubicle, stepped forward with a small sheet to cover the woman, and Kate spread it across her belly and legs.

Kate reached beneath it for the bottom of the woman's tunic, ready to lift it then ease down the trousers, so she could listen to the baby's heart, but she'd no sooner touched the cloth than the man rose from his seat again.

'Do not touch her clothes. You must do what you do through clothes.'

So why did you want a woman doctor? she thought, but she obediently felt around her patient's body, seeking any sore spots from the fall. The woman gasped when Kate touched the right hip.

'She fell on her hip?' she asked the man, accepting he was the voice of the patient.

'On the step outside. It must have been wet and she slipped.'

'I imagine there's quite a bruise. I can give you something to rub on it to ease it. Now I'll listen to the baby's heart.'

But not through a sheet and her tunic and her trousers.

The nurse handed Kate a Pinard's stethoscope, something she hadn't seen for many years, but right now, in these circumstances when she couldn't press a foetoscope to the woman's distended belly, it would be ideal.

She pressed the wide end to the clothing, carefully put her ear to it, then removed her hands so her own heartbeats wouldn't interfere with what she heard.

Definite heartbeats, faint and rapid. The faintness she put down to listening through layers of clothing and the rapidity was normal. She moved it around, heard nothing to worry about and lifted her head.

'It all sounds good,' she told the woman. 'Are you feeling movement?'

The woman spoke for the first time, not to Kate but to her husband.

'She said the baby kicked when you put that instrument on her belly. She said the baby didn't like it but she is pleased because the baby hadn't been moving and now it is.'

He was beaming at Kate, as if somehow she'd performed a miracle.

'Take her home, but make sure she rests for a few days,' Kate told him, 'and if you are worried about anything, come back.'

'You will always see her?' the man asked.

'Perhaps not, but there will always be a woman doctor on duty, and you must have a regular doctor—are you seeing an obstetrician?'

The man nodded.

'But she is busy-busy, only one woman doing this in Amberach, so very hard to get in to see her without an appointment.'

He had helped his wife to her feet and was now guiding her out of the cubicle, his arm around her shoulders.

Kate asked the nurse to find a jar of arnica for the bruising, and with repeated thanks, the pair departed.

Later, Kate decided, she'd have to have a long talk to Fareed about customs and protocols for dealing with the locals. In fact, shouldn't she have had a proper orientation tour and talk, rather than a nurse showing her around?

Her life seemed to be straying farther and farther from any known path and while she wasn't willing to believe it was completely off track, she had no idea what track it might be taking.

CHAPTER TEN

FAREED WOKE IN his apartment at the hospital, answered a dozen messages waiting on his phone, then decided it was time to think about his situation—his marriage.

What was going on that he was so drawn to this woman—physically drawn?

Would a psychologist put it down to his longing for some mother love? Was it as simple as that?

But he wouldn't have wanted to be racing his mother off to bed, so surely that wasn't right!

This morning, as he'd walked Katya to the staff room and followed her inside, he'd had an almost overwhelming urge to kiss her properly, although he'd known full well where kissing her would inevitably have led.

He'd even had the notion that the door had a lock on it flash through his head.

He *could* put it down to tiredness, this morning's episode, but last night at the fort?

Part of his brain told him not to let it worry him, the woman was his wife, it was natural he should enjoy sex with her, but enjoy hardly covered it, and was it natural to *crave* sex with her?

He clasped his hands to his head and squeezed hard—hoping to squeeze out memories of delight?

To squeeze out answers?

The demanding beeping of his phone saved him from further soul-searching and frustration.

Suley's mother, asking if he and Kate would have dinner with them that evening.

'Farida and Mai will be here, and their parents, of course. We would like to thank your wife for the sensible way she handled the girls and have a talk to them with both of you present if that is all right.'

Fareed agreed, while at the same time wondering just what Kate had handled.

All fixed, she'd said to him and nothing more, changing the topic of conversation by talking of a swim, which had turned into a ride, which had —

No, he was over the soul-searching, for a while at least. Best he get back and find Kate—or Katya?—to tell her about this evening.

She was talking to Roberta, the English nurse who had been here since the hospital opened.

'Kate's just had a pregnant patient whose husband refused to let Kate remove clothes to listen to the foetal heartbeat.' Roberta was smiling. 'I told her your stories of the old days when doctors were supposed to diagnose what was wrong with women by looking at a hand, or even one finger, the only part of the woman's body the husband would allow the doctor to see.'

Fareed smiled back.

'Times are changing but we cannot hurry change. It was a win for us that the man brought his wife here.' He turned to Kate. 'Do you think if you'd asked him to put the stethoscope on his wife's belly while you turned your head but listened—would that have worked?'

The two women seemed to be considering it.

'It might have worked,' Kate said, 'but I would have had to be standing very close to him—possibly our bodies touching—and he might not have liked that.'

She was good, this wife of his, Fareed conceded mentally. She seemed genuinely concerned not just for the patient's physical health but for his or her cultural sensibilities.

'I haven't done a lot of midwifery,' she was saying now, 'but do you have those monitors used on women having an induction or in labour—the ones with two discs, one measuring the contractions and the other the foetal heartbeat? They just trace a line on a screen, not a picture—would that work?'

Kate looked directly at Fareed for the first time since he'd joined them—looked and thought she saw a softening in his usually stern face.

Or perhaps that was nothing more than wishful thinking...

'We do not do inductions here but we have at least one of those for emergency admissions when a woman is in labour,' he was saying, and, no, she hadn't been wrong, he was actually smiling at her. 'I'll get someone to show you where—in fact, maybe tomorrow I can ask someone to cover for me and give you a proper orientation.'

It was basic medical talk and exactly what she knew she needed, so why did the words sound suggestive to her—make her insides squirm just slightly?

'In the meantime,' he continued, oblivious of her reaction to his words, 'we need to be getting home. Suley's parents have invited us for dinner, with the other girls and their parents.'

Kate knew she was probably frowning as she looked at him this time.

'I do hope I haven't got you into any trouble,' she said, ignoring Roberta's almost palpable interest.

Another smile from Fareed!

'On the contrary, apparently the dinner is in your honour, to thank you for sorting out something with the girls.'

Relief swept through Kate, although it was not quite

enough to cover her trepidation over going to a private dinner with Fareed.

'You are bothered?' he asked as they walked towards the staff room so she could collect her handbag.

'Only because I've got no idea how I'm supposed to behave at a private dinner.' She stopped and looked at him. 'In fact, I've no idea how I'm supposed to behave anywhere, or any time.'

She would have asked more, except the smile was gone and a frown had taken its place. It didn't bother her as she was far more used to his frowns than his smiles, and his frowns didn't make her twitchy inside.

'Did Ibrahim not appoint someone to teach you some of our ways—at least instruct you in the marriage rituals?'

Kate shook her head.

'Everyone was very kind and they told me things about the clothes to wear and talked about the food as we ate together, but I suppose...'

'Suppose what?' Fareed demanded.

Kate's courage wavered but in the end held firm.

'I suppose they thought that you would tell me anything I needed to know.'

She knew she was blushing, probably from her chest up to her scalp, but he *had* asked.

'Of course!' he said shortly, then he put his hand on her elbow and steered her out of the building. Her driver drew up but Fareed waved him away, leading Kate into a large car park hidden behind shrubs and bushes.

He steered her towards his big black SUV and opened the door for her, again taking her arm to help her into it.

'Ibrahim has used you shamefully,' he muttered as he drove out of the hospital. 'I thought he'd done badly by me, but you! He hands you a pile of money to marry me then leaves you to fend for yourself without any instruction or information or even help.'

'He didn't hand me a pile of money!'

The words were out before Kate could stop them, but that hadn't been the point so she continued with what she'd been going to say. 'And, anyway, he's always busy. He worked on the plane, worrying all the time about things he had to do, and on top of that I don't think he's very well. I think your anaphylactic shock shocked him more than it shocked you. I think it made him realise how vulnerable we all are and that it was time to get his affairs in order.'

Fareed had pulled over to the side of the road as she'd been talking, and was now studying her intently.

'He *didn't* give you a pile of money?'

Kate waved the question aside. 'We had a bargain, something else,' she said, 'but it's Ibrahim you should be thinking about, not me. I haven't seen him since before the wedding but even on the plane coming over, I felt he was unwell. And the day I did see him, not long before we were married, I thought he was a bad colour, a little sallow, like a hepatitis patient. Are you his doctor?'

Fareed was frowning at her—again—but this time it was more a puzzled frown than an angry one.

'What kind of bargain?' he asked, and Kate wanted to scream with frustration.

'Will you just get off that subject and talk to me about Ibrahim? Don't you care that he might be ill? Do you know who looks after him if you don't? When did you last see him?'

Fareed could have answered easily. He hadn't seen his uncle to talk to properly for weeks. Ibrahim had been busy—busy avoiding his nephew, Fareed now realised—since the wedding, and he'd been angry, and now it wasn't money—

No, he had to stop thinking about that, and consider what Kate was telling him.

Could Ibrahim be ill?

Had he rushed Fareed into marriage thinking the sultan needed a wife and that Fareed would be Sultan sooner than he realised?

'I'll go and see him now,' he announced as he put the car into gear and drew back onto the road. 'There'll be time before we go to dinner.'

The drove home in silence, each lost in their own world of thought.

Once back at the palace, Fareed escorted Kate to the door of their suite and paused to say, 'Convention says we should spend forty days and nights in the suite, but you need not worry about it. You are free to go wherever you wish.'

'Except if I join the women for evening meals, say, they will wonder what is happening in our marriage.'

He nodded.

'Later,' he promised, 'we will talk about it later, but please believe I would rather put up with gossip than have you feeling imprisoned and alienated in my land.'

And to Kate's surprise he kissed her cheek, just as he had when he'd left her in the staff room earlier in the day. Only this time she refused to put her hand across the bit of kissed skin—bad enough to be silly over something even once in a day!

She crossed to the window and looked out at the little courtyard. She could hardly be in a more luxurious prison, and did she really want to be mixing with the other women?

She was still standing there when Fareed returned.

'Ibrahim isn't in but I spoke to his private servant, who assures me he is well. I'll see Ibrahim himself in the morning.'

'That's good,' Kate said, then felt she had to explain. 'I don't feel imprisoned, but not knowing the customs I wondered if the women would think I was being rude not joining them. Now I know, I'm only too happy to go to and from the hospital and to have my meals on my own here.

It's such a beautiful and peaceful place—who would not be happy, staying here?'

'My mother!' Fareed said shortly, then he crossed the room, opened the door to his dressing room and disappeared.

The door opened again a few seconds later.

'We'll leave in an hour,' he added, and once again closed the door behind him.

His mother must certainly be one of the ghosts Ibrahim had spoken of, but wasn't having another redhead hanging around the same rooms more likely to bring the ghosts back than banish them?

Kate decided she had no idea, so she headed for her dressing room, determined to find an outfit Suley had given her before the wedding.

It was pink, a colour most redheads avoided, but Kate had loved it from the moment she'd seen it. Rusty red embroidery—the colour of her hair—wove intricate patterns around the neck and hem of the tunic and along the bottom of the trousers, while the fine material caressed the skin, making her feel sensually alive.

Possibly not a good when she was going out with Fareed...

Especially Fareed in local dress—the first time she'd seen him dressed this way since he'd escorted her off her stage on their wedding day, and back then, without her glasses, he'd been nothing more than a tall, fuzzy figure clad in white and gold.

He wore a long white—dazzlingly white—robe and over it a kind of full-length vest, the edges trimmed with two inches of delicate gold embroidery that matched the gold cords he wore to keep his headdress in place.

'Oh, my!' Kate said, unable to stop staring at the vision in front of her.

Not that he noticed her wide-eyed amazement, because he, in turn, was staring at her.

'You look stunning,' he finally said, his voice gravelly with emotion.

'Same to you,' Kate whispered, still too overawed to move—to go towards him and the door. 'So different, so regal—you look magnificent.'

He smiled, which all but finished Kate. Her knees went weak, and nerves danced through her body, her brain sending heat to her nipples and lower to between her thighs.

'Shall we go?'

Obviously Fareed was more in control than she was, but she forced herself to move, one step at a time, towards the picture-book prince who awaited her.

A drive took them along the esplanade that ran below the fort and through an open gate into a complex almost as big as the palace. Only this one was made up of many houses—huge houses.

'As each son marries, he builds himself a house, usually larger than his brother's,' Fareed explained.

'So they live as families in their own homes?'

'They do—it's the modern way—but the houses still have some rooms that are for women and some for men—we haven't been entirely westernised as yet.'

Kate heard a smile in the words and wondered whether, if this had been a normal marriage, Fareed would have built a house for her.

'Would you like a house of your own--one you could run as you wish?' he asked, as if her thoughts had flashed through the air into his head.

'I doubt I'd run it properly,' she told him. 'Telling servants what to do is way beyond my comfort zone and probably beyond my capabilities.'

'But you manage it at the palace.'

The car had stopped outside one of the huge houses so

Kate felt she didn't have to answer, but although the driver was now holding the door open for them to alight, Fareed remained seated at her side.

'Well?' he prompted.

She tried to find the words she needed, not wanting to sound rude or to offend him.

'There, it's different,' she said. 'I really have no choice, do I? I mean, if I want to eat I have to press the bell and ask a servant to bring me food, but I look at it like room service at a hotel.'

'Something temporary?'

The question held a hint of steel and Kate was flummoxed.

'Not really,' she told him, 'but it's kind of what I was saying earlier—I feel I'm in a situation where I don't know the rules.'

To her surprise he kissed her lightly on the cheek—three in one day?—then climbed out of the car, reaching back to take her hand and help her out.

'For someone who doesn't know the rules you're doing very well,' he told her, just as Suley, Mai and Farida came running down the stairs to welcome them, kissing Fareed on both cheeks then hugging Kate and kissing her, as well.

'Come in and meet my parents,' Suley said, taking her by the hand and leading her up the stairs, pausing while they slipped off their sandals, then directing her into the house, which seemed even larger than it had looked from the outside.

'Last brother to marry?' she whispered to Fareed as he caught up with them and took her free hand.

He nodded, and smiled, and Kate's heart leapt in her chest, ignoring all her warnings that she shouldn't fall in love with this man. After all, she was only here for a year and to leave him if she loved him…

They were led into a huge reception room, to where the

three sets of parents waited in a grouping of comfortable
armchairs and lounges about halfway down the room.

Introductions done, they were offered cool drinks and
appetisers, tiny nibbles of food so delicious Kate would
have been happy to make it dinner.

Suley's father sat beside her and took her hand as he
thanked her formally for taking care of the three silly young
women.

'We had no idea such adolescent fantasies still lingered
in their heads,' Suley's mother said. 'They should all have
known that even if we suggest someone we think would
make a suitable husband for them, these days they will have
the opportunity to meet him and decide for themselves. We
are not so strict about such things as some people.'

'Of course, they would be chaperoned at these meetings,'
Mai's father put in. 'That protects their reputation, but none
of us would want our daughters to be unhappy so we would
never force them to marry someone they did not like.'

'I think they all knew that,' Kate said, 'but you must
remember that they are still at an age when there is a lot
of hormonal change going on, particularly in their bodies.
So the highs of excitement are higher and their low moods
lower—everything is more dramatic, exaggerated!'

Farida's mother nodded.

'You can say that again. Farida's been a drama queen for
the last few years—we're just hoping we're nearly through
it.'

Farida pulled a face at her mother, who answered with
a loving smile, and the conversation turned more general,
Kate's hostess asking about her family and how she was
handling being so far away from them.

'I've worked away from home before,' Kate explained,
'and while my mother's busy at home and my brother is
happy, I am content just to be in touch by phone and email.
And these days it is so easy to get to anywhere in the world.

Should something happen, I could be home within a couple of days.'

She felt Fareed stiffen beside her but didn't turn to look at him, still overwhelmed by seeing him in his local dress.

'Kate's mother bred and is training one of Ibrahim's horses,' Fareed told the company, and something in his voice told Kate he was wondering about her bargain.

Had he guessed?

Did it matter?

They moved in to dinner, and the conversation turned to local and international affairs, the three young women drawing Kate into talk of shops and shopping, and making plans to take her to the mall again—

'Only this time to shop,' Suley said.

Fareed held his wife's arm as she slipped on her sandals, then continued to hold it as they went down to the car. They had said their farewells in the front vestibule, so now were alone—or as alone as they could be with a driver.

His mind played back the bits of conversation they'd had earlier. Kate's denial that Ibrahim had given her money, the talk of a bargain, then the light-bulb moment.

Or was he wrong?

Only one way to find out.

'Was your bargain with Ibrahim that your mother would train the horse?'

He was sitting close to her and felt the tension build in her body.

'Yes!'

One defiant word.

'You talk of a loving family. What did your mother think of *that*? Selling yourself so she could train a horse? How could she have allowed such a thing?'

Silence, then, 'She doesn't know.' No defiance now,

more quiet resignation. 'I've worked abroad so much, when I told her I was coming here for a year she wasn't surprised.'

'And the marriage?'

More silence.

'She doesn't know about that either.'

The whispered words did something to Fareed's heart—caught at it and twisted it somehow, yet words she'd said earlier needed explanation.

He hardened the twisted heart.

'And the one year? Is that all Ibrahim asked of you? Did you intend to serve out your sentence of marriage to me then walk away?'

The questions, so coldly put, numbed Kate for a moment, but she knew she had to answer. Fareed deserved that, at least.

'I never saw it as a sentence.' She spoke quietly, trying to get through the armour Fareed had rebuilt about himself. 'I told you on our wedding night that I was happy just to work here, that as far as I was concerned we didn't need to live as man and wife, or even see each other very much, but, yes, Ibrahim had said if, after a year, we found we didn't suit, then I could leave.'

'And if I ask you to leave now?'

'I have no idea,' Kate admitted. 'I suppose I leave.'

And Ibrahim takes the horse to another trainer and breaks Billy's heart.

Her own heart ached at the thought, but at least she'd tried...

They had pulled up at the rear of the palace building and the driver once again had the door open for them.

'Unfortunately, you can't leave for forty days,' Fareed said, icicles hanging off the words.

'The forty days from our wedding?' She could understand that. To leave earlier would be to embarrass him in front of his people.

'No, forty days from today before we can divorce,' and with that he was out of the car and stalking, not into the corridor that led back to their suite but off into the night, towards the stables.

Heartsick, Kate climbed out of the car and made her own way to the suite.

Once inside she showered but the water didn't wash away the feeling of grubbiness that talking about her bargain with Ibrahim had left behind on her skin.

She pulled on her old pyjamas and climbed into bed, feeling the emptiness of it echoing the emptiness in her heart.

CHAPTER ELEVEN

HE MUST HAVE told the staff to let him know, for as soon as Kate arrived at the hospital next morning, Fareed appeared.

'I will show you around,' he said, so formally she wanted to weep.

'Did you see Ibrahim?' she asked as he led her to the back of the reception room where the radiology and pathology suites were.

'I did, and you're right, he doesn't look well, but I also spoke to his physician, who told me Ibrahim is just getting over a hepatitis attack and will be well again within weeks. He assured me that I won't need to give up my day job in the near future.'

'Oh, I'm so glad!' Kate said, feeling genuine relief that the man she liked was on the mend.

'Glad for me or him?' Fareed asked.

The question jolted Kate and this morning she really wasn't in any state to be coping with jolts.

'For him, of course. I like him.'

'And you don't like me?'

Kate stopped outside the pathology lab and shook her head as she stared at her husband.

'Now you're being downright adolescent,' she told him. 'You knew from the start this was an arrangement, now somehow my agreeing because of my family is worse than my taking money.'

He glared at her and stalked away.

'Someone else will come to show you the back section.'

Fareed knew he was behaving badly but he couldn't seem to stop.

He'd somehow come to terms with being attracted to a money-hungry female, so why was the knowledge she'd done this for her family—not for money—annoying him so much?

Because 'family' was a foreign concept to him?

Nonsense, he'd had enough family growing up—a huge family.

It might have been lacking in the loving mother and father department, but Ibrahim and his wife had never shown anything but love to him—the same love they gave their own children.

Fortunately, with Kate being shown around, the ER was busy, so he let work push all other thoughts from his head until she returned to help him with a badly dehydrated man, found lying by the side of a road in the desert.

Kate was dripping water into his mouth through a wide-bore syringe while a nurse sponged the emaciated body and he searched for a vein so he could set a catheter in place and get a saline solution flowing into him.

'Will you have to do a cut down for a wide-bore catheter?' Kate asked, thinking Fareed might have to open up the subclavian vein or internal jugular near the patient's neck to get a catheter seated and fluid flowing as swiftly as possible into the almost comatose patient.

'I'm thinking subclavian,' he responded. 'Want to do it?'

It was a challenge and she rose to it, having done a number of them in the past, usually on burn victims.

A nurse swabbed the area while Kate checked equipment and pulled on a gown and mask, then fresh gloves. Still not sure of protocol, she went with what she was used to doing and that was being sterile for even simple operations.

Fareed made no comment, busy administering a local anaesthetic around the site.

Kate moved in, feeling along the man's clavicle, finding the spot she needed along the inferior surface of it. With Fareed so close, the tension between them still twanging in the air, she worried she'd get it wrong, but the needle she'd attached to a syringe slid in beneath the skin, along the clavicle and finally into the vein.

She drew out some blood to make sure it was seated properly, then carefully detached the syringe, capping the needle she'd left in place to prevent air entering the vein.

Now for the guide wire! Carefully she inserted it into the hollow needle, advancing it into the vein then retracting it just a little. Holding the wire firmly, she withdrew the needle, then used a scalpel to stab a small hole beside the wire to enlarge the catheter site.

Now it was just a matter of threading the different pieces of equipment over the wire—first a dilator to enlarge the hole, twisting it gently as it went into the vein, then another tiny piece of plastic slid down the wire and into the dilator, taking its place so she could remove the dilator.

'You're doing well,' she heard Fareed murmur, but even the unexpected praise didn't distract her, because through every move she had to keep the wire in place while fiddling with something else. Now the catheter, down over the wire and safely into the vein. Kate checked the monitor that was showing every detail of what was going on inside the patient and sighed with relief.

Now she could withdraw the wire and cap the end of the catheter until they flushed the line, took more blood for testing then attached the IV tube and began restoring the patient's fluid balance.

Next step was to stitch the catheter into place.

'I'll take over,' Fareed told her, and she gladly handed over, realising that the tension of performing even this minor surgery with him so close had left her feeling weak-limbed and exhausted.

A nurse was labelling the blood samples and Fareed had plenty of help, so Kate headed for the bathroom, where she stripped off her gown, mask and gloves and had a good wash.

When Fareed finished, he would order an X-ray of the man's chest to make absolutely certain the catheter was in a vein and not in a nearby artery.

'All good,' he said when he caught up with her later, and as his tone sounded almost friendly, Kate began to hope his anger over her bargain might have dissipated.

But his non-appearance when she was leaving the hospital—so no lift home with him—and his absence from the suite when she did get home suggested she'd been fooling herself.

Could she really live like this?

Forty more days with a man who obviously despised her? The word came to her out of her childhood, some old book with tales of sultans and harems and women kept in isolation—purdah!

Except she didn't have to accept it.

She was reluctant to cause gossip in the palace or do anything to embarrass him with the servants, but what the hell.

She found her phone and called Mai.

'Fareed's not in this evening, so do the three of you want to come over for a swim and then some dinner?'

'In the wedding suite?' Mai asked, in almost reverent tones.

'Of course,' Kate told her.

'We'll be there as soon as we can.' Mai's excitement made Kate smile.

Kate called a servant and explained the young women

were coming over, there'd be four for dinner and could it be served in the pergola in the garden at eight?

The servant didn't seem taken aback, so maybe it was okay for a woman in purdah to have friends.

Showering quickly, she put on a black bikini, thankful the garden was private as she hadn't thought to bring a full swimsuit. Over it she pulled a black-and-white patterned caftan, also brought from home because it had been a present from Billy on her last Christmas at home.

Right now she needed to feel close to her family despite her betrayal of them...

The three friends oohed and aahed over the hidden garden, then used the bathroom to change. Out in the pool they splashed like dolphins, playing in the water with such excitement Kate finally had to ask.

'Do you not have pools at home?'

Three shakes of the head.

'Our parents are very modern in some things,' Suley explained, 'but for us to be cavorting like this—no way! When we go to a pool in a hotel or even if we go to the beach, we may wear a swimsuit but we must wear our *abayas* over it, and our scarves, so we bob around in the water like big black blobs because air gets caught under our *abayas* and they blow up like balloons.'

The picture of any number of blobby women swimming in scarves and *abayas* made Kate smile.

'Well, here it's completely private so you can enjoy it all you want.'

It was the noise—the shouts of laughter and high-pitched squeals—that drew Fareed to the window.

He'd stayed back at work, telling himself it wasn't to avoid his wife but not really believing it.

Arriving home, he'd decided to find her in the suite,

compliment her again on the work she'd done today then perhaps try to close the gap that had pushed them apart.

Gap?

More like a chasm.

And knowing it was his fault only made it harder. Cerebrally he knew he was at fault. The fact she'd agreed to marry him for the sake of her family should have made the so-called bargain more acceptable.

So why didn't it?

He had no idea.

Except he *had* come home hoping to make things right— or perhaps less wrong.

Which he could no longer do as she was obviously entertaining.

Pushing his feet reluctantly towards the window, he looked out into the secret garden.

His wife was sitting on one end of the pool, her tantalising body clothed in nothing but two strips of black material—making it more, not less, tantalising.

She was watching three young women frolicking in the pool, smiling at their antics and encouraging their silly behaviour. Her three young friends…

Had they come to call on her?

During her wedding month?

Unlikely—they would know the rules…

So she'd asked them over…

Not that he could blame her. She was enduring isolation she'd never have known before.

Which was his fault for not being here for her.

Al'ama—he *had* to get his head straight.

He moved away from the window, not wanting to embarrass her guests, but the sounds of laughter wormed their way inside him and he wondered how long it had been since he had laughed in such a carefree way.

He pulled a servant, and learned that the friends were staying for dinner.

Caution suggested he go for a ride and eat later in his dressing room, but instead he asked the servant to take a message to his wife, advising her he was home for dinner and suggesting he join her and her friends in the pergola.

Would she refuse?

He doubted it. She was still so uncertain about their customs she would probably take the suggestion as an order.

Was it wrong for him to take advantage of her this way?

For sure, but what the hell. Why *shouldn't* he eat with his wife and her friends? Laugh with his wife and her friends?

Silently acknowledging that he'd somehow got himself into an impossible situation, he headed for his bathroom, showered, then put on traditional clothes—'at home' traditional in the form of a simple white robe.

Because she admired you in traditional garb yesterday? an imp whispered in his head.

He refused to answer it, merely waiting in his study off his private bedroom until the dinner was carried out into the pergola.

The friends greeted him with kisses and apparent glee, his wife more calmly, although he thought he detected a gleam of surprise in her eyes when she saw how he was dressed.

She poured him juice then looked at the pretty women lounging under the pergola, dressed now in jeans and tops—the uniform of youth.

'Now tell me this,' she said, addressing her visitors but waving one hand towards him as she spoke. 'You have to cover up—wear *abayas* and scarves—when you go to the mall, and even when you swim at the beach, but here, now Fareed has joined us, you don't have to cover up?'

They laughed and all tried to explain at once.

Fareed held up his hand.

'They are family. They can appear uncovered in front of the men in their family, their fathers, brothers and in my case even cousins because I grew up with them—well, not exactly but I've known them all their lives.'

He knew by the little frown between her eyebrows that Kate wasn't satisfied.

'But when marriages are arranged, aren't they often within the family—to cousins or second cousins? I'm sure Suley's mother mentioned that,' she said.

'It's different with cousins our own age,' Farida explained. 'We might have played with them when we were little but now, if they're around, we cover up. Fareed's more like an uncle so he doesn't matter.'

'Well, thank you very much!' Fareed said, but he was pleased to see Kate smiling at the remark.

Maybe things weren't broken beyond repair.

Why had he joined them?

Kate ate and talked—well, listened—all the time so aware of Fareed she could feel her skin tingling. Fooling around with the friends, teasing them, asking questions about their studies, offering advice in a casual way, she saw a side of him she hadn't seen before.

Fareed, the family man?

Not really, just Fareed the man.

Up until now he'd been a stranger, then her husband but still a stranger, then a colleague and a lover…

She shivered at the memories of the lover, and her body grew warm beneath her all-encompassing caftan.

But Fareed the lover was gone and in thirty-nine days Fareed the husband would also be gone.

Thirty-nine days alone in that big bed…

Couldn't they at least enjoy the unexpected attraction that had flared between them like a forest fire?

Look on it as a holiday romance?

Oh, yeah, and just how are you going to put it to him?

I know you hate me for making the arrangement with Ibrahim but could we at least sleep together until I go?

Like that would happen!

Coldness now where the warmth had been, and Fareed bringing her out of her thoughts—back to the present.

'Our guests are leaving,' he said—oh, so smooth, so suave when they'd been *her* guests, not *theirs*.

She walked behind the other four towards their suite then accompanied her visitors to the front door, where their driver was waiting.

Fareed stopped at the door, kissed and hugged the three-some, then disappeared back into the palace while Kate saw them into the car.

'So much for suggesting we enjoy a holiday romance,' she muttered to herself as she made her way back to the suite.

Angry and unhappy, she slipped back out into the garden, heading for the pergola where she could sit and think.

Except it was already occupied

'You enjoy their company?'

The voice of her husband—an unnecessary question, surely, so what was he really asking?

'They are fun,' Kate replied, moving past the pergola to stand by the side of the pool.

'And I'm not?'

The anger Kate really didn't understand fired up again.

'How would I know?' she demanded. 'I barely know you, any more than you know me! Oh, you're quite happy to judge me, but actually getting to know me—perhaps that isn't part of marriage over here.'

'Getting to know someone takes time.'

He sounded so calm she wanted to throw something at him.

'Time together, not time apart,' she said. 'Anyway, it

doesn't matter—there's no point in us getting to know each other now. Only thirty-nine more days and I'll be out of your hair and you can get on with enjoying whatever life you were leading before I came into it.'

Silence that stretched and stretched, eventually for so long Kate took a step back towards the pergola, peering into the shadows so she could make out his form, check he was still there.

She was one step closer when he finally spoke.

'There wasn't much enjoyment in it, my old life,' he said quietly, and Kate took the steps she needed to join him in the shadows, sitting down beside him, taking his hand, holding it in both of hers.

'Tell me,' she said, and as he had the evening at the fort, slowly and carefully he did.

Telling her the things he'd thought were fun—buying the fastest of cars and racing them along empty desert roads, vying with his cousins for affairs with glamorous women, university studies overseas where he'd tried alcohol and drugs, partying wildly...

'In the hope of having fun,' he finished quietly.

'But at the time it must have been good,' Kate protested, and heard a smile in his voice as he answered.

'Oh, yes, at the time I thought it very good, but it was empty fun, Kate—bought fun. If you have money you can buy anything.'

'Even a wife,' she whispered, and he stood up and walked away, pacing at the end of the pool.

'That's different,' he said harshly. 'It's our custom—there is always a bride gift—brides *are* bought.'

She'd felt so close to him but now?

She could let it go and maybe he'd sit again, they could recover what they'd lost...

But she had to know.

'So why was my arrangement with Ibrahim so upsetting for you?'

'Because it was family business and Ibrahim knew how I felt about family, and to put us in that suite, redecorated or not... I found my father's body in that suite—his body and a note that destroyed any illusion I might have had about my loving family!'

She moved swiftly to his side, putting her hand on his arm.

'Why? How? What did the note say that made you feel that way?'

He spun towards her, his eyes glittering in the moonlight.

'You really want to know?'

She nodded, and though he turned away from her again she heard the words ring clearly through the night air.

'It wasn't addressed to anyone,' he began, 'but I was the first to read it. It said, "She doesn't love me, never did, and cares for Fareed even less. My death will end both my pain and my beloved son's so it is best I do this."'

Kate shook her head as she tried to process the words. She wanted nothing more than to hold him but he was already striding away, away from her and their marriage and towards the place that held such horrific memories for him.

'Well, you *had* to know!' she muttered to herself, then she returned to the pergola, sank down on the cushions and considered whether a good cry would help.

Not in the slightest—all it would do was make her eyes all red and puffy!

So she thought instead, thought about Fareed and the ghosts Ibrahim had told her of, wondered just where he'd found his father.

Surely not in the big marriage bed.

His mother must have used it—the big bed. She had seen

it as her right so his father had probably used the bedroom off Fareed's dressing room—rooms she'd never seen.

Of course, he might not have gone to bed, but if he had, could she let him sleep alone in there with the memories she'd evoked so unthinkingly fresh in his mind?

He'd been a child.

A lost child, for all the family love around him.

She sighed, got off the cushions, left the garden, took a shower, pulled on a robe, then went in search of her husband.

The room she found was dark, but once her eyes adjusted to the gloom she could make out the form of a body—a live body, she was sure—beneath the covers.

Coming closer, she slipped off the robe and slid between the sheets, reaching out a tentative hand, finding an arm and resting her hand on it, stroking lightly.

A movement told her he wasn't asleep so she slid closer, put her arms around his body, pressing herself against his back.

'We don't have to make love, Fareed, but I guessed this was the bed, and I didn't want you sleeping in it alone when I've hurt you by bringing back those memories.'

She said no more, just lay there, spooned against an unyielding body.

At least he hadn't kicked her out, and this felt so good, just being close to him.

CHAPTER TWELVE

HE WAS GONE when she woke in the morning, disoriented and confused. At some time during the night he'd turned to her, touched her, arousing her desire so she'd responded fully and completely, so a frantic coupling had been followed by a slow, seductive, teasing act of what to Kate had been love.

Freed from all inhibitions by the knowledge that soon she'd lose this man, she'd let her hands explore him fully, let her lips brush against his smooth skin, let her teeth nibble at his ear, his shoulder and let her tongue wander at will, finally arousing him again, so that time, in her mind, they'd made love.

But this morning he was gone, and soon she'd be going, and in the meantime she should get to work.

Or not?

The thought occurred to her as she stood under the shower, rinsing conditioner from her hair.

At least at work she'd see him, if only across the room, and hear his voice, if only from another cubicle. To not see him, to not hear him, to not take whatever she could of him for these last few weeks would be unbearable.

Don't be pathetic, woman!

Get a grip!

You'll go to work because at the moment it's still your job and other people are relying on you.

*And you will not get all weak-kneed over seeing him or
hearing his bloody voice.*

Kate sighed and did pull herself together, though reluctantly. She plaited her still-wet hair, slapped moisturiser
on her face, dressed in her usual work uniform of jeans
and a shirt, and sat down at the table where her breakfast
had been set.

Without being ordered?

She checked it out—fruit, yoghurt, cereal, coffee—exactly what she usually ordered, so perhaps the servants
simply brought it now.

Except there was a red rosebud in a tiny silver vase, right
in the middle of the tray.

Fareed?

She shook her head and told her heart to not get over-
excited, but somewhere inside, a tiny bud of hope, much
smaller than the rosebud, began to unfurl a tentative leaf.

Which withered and died when she arrived at work to
find her husband wasn't on duty.

'The boss does his prince-of-the-realm thing on the first
Tuesday of the month,' Roberta told her. 'Didn't he tell
you? He sits with the sultan and people come and tell them
their troubles and they sort it out. It's a tradition, going
back for ever.'

Of course he hadn't told her, not that or anything about
his 'prince' life.

It was realising just how little she knew of him that
killed the bud.

Fareed tried to listen to the supplicants as they told their
stories to Ibrahim, but his mind kept wandering—to the
previous night, to the need to talk to Ibrahim, to working
out exactly where his marriage was…

Or wasn't!

He'd offered her a divorce—actually, demanded more

than offered—told her that in forty days—thirty-eight now—she could go back to the family that meant so much to her.

It would be for the best. He'd marry again, someone from his own culture. Ibrahim of all people should have known how disastrous mixed marriages could be.

Yet Ibrahim had planned this...

He must have sighed, for the supplicant in front of them turned to him, assuring him it wasn't such a big problem and that all would be well.

'Would that it could be,' Fareed told him, then realised he'd spoken in English and changed his translation to a blessing for the man.

He came in late in the afternoon, striding into the ER with an injured child in his arms, issuing orders as he carried the child into a cubicle, sending nurses scurrying to help.

Kate followed him into the cubicle, where he was placing the little boy carefully down on the examination couch, his hands gentle as he spread the small limbs.

'What happened?' Kate asked.

He didn't glance her way, intent on examining the boy.

'One of those idiots on a motorbike—the young men with too much money and not enough to do with their time who sit outside the malls on women's shopping days, revving their bikes to make the teenage girls notice them. He was swerving through the crowd near the market and hit the child a glancing blow, sending him flying into a market stall. Didn't even stop!'

Kate heard the anger in his voice and understood it. How could anyone be, first, so careless and then so uncaring?

'Did no one come forward to claim him?'

Fareed shook his head.

'There are people searching for his parents, asking through the markets, but I think he may have been a beggar, possibly the child of a migrant worker who either didn't want him or who died. It happens, although there are services out there that usually pick up children like this and take them into care, find caring foster-families for them.'

He finished his examination, found a vein in the child's arm and took some blood, all the time talking quietly to the boy, although he was unconscious.

'Let's take him through to Radiology, see what an X-ray tells us.'

Not having anything else to do, Kate followed, realising how much she enjoyed watching Fareed in action as a doctor.

A caring doctor!

Just one more thing about him she'd have to forget.

The X-rays revealed a hairline crack in the base of his skull, which explained his concussion.

Further tests showed no bleeding or swelling in his brain, yet he remained comatose.

'I'll keep him here and stay with him. I'm sure he was conscious when I picked him up—I was right behind the motorbike when it happened—so at least I might be a familiar face to him.'

Kate started to remind him that with concussion most patients remembered little of what had happened during and straight after an accident—or even just prior to it—but she stopped herself, realising Fareed would stay there whatever she said.

So no night of love, not that night or the next. No rosebuds on her breakfast tray, and no communication outside of work.

She caught him in the staff room three days later, where he was cursing the coffee machine.

'How's the little boy?' she asked, as she took over from him, bumping the machine on the left side, a trick she'd learned that would make it work.

'How did you do that?' he demanded, and she showed him, trying desperately to remain as cool and in control as he was, although her body wanted nothing more than to melt against him.

She handed him a coffee, got one for herself, and took it to a lounge chair, needing a break after a busy morning.

'The little boy?' she asked, when she realised Fareed was still hovering in the room.

'I've had him admitted to the hospital. He's still unconscious, although scans of his brain tell us there's nothing wrong there, and his blood tests have come back normal.'

'How old would you say he is?'

'The paediatrician says five or six, although he's small for his age.'

Kate thought about a child that age left to roam the streets.

'Do you think subconsciously he doesn't want to come out of his coma? Do you think he could just have closed down? If you think how bad his life must have been, maybe this is a nice way of avoiding it.'

Fareed stared at her.

'Do you think humans have the power to do that?'

Kate shrugged.

'I don't know but we all try to block out bad things that happen in our lives, yet we still remember them, probably more than the good memories. And who knows what he might need to block out?'

Fareed didn't answer, simply finishing his coffee and leaving the room.

Two more nights in purdah, although by now Kate had convinced herself she didn't care.

So why, when he did appear in the suite after dinner on the third night, grave-faced and stern, did her heart leap in her chest and her blood rush hotly through her veins.

He hasn't come for fun, she told her errant body, and she

crossed to the window, looking out at the garden that had become her refuge, knowing, somehow, that this might be her last view of it.

'Ibrahim has heard from his man in Australia,' Fareed said, then must have seen her shock for he immediately added, 'No, your family is all right, it is the horse. Apparently some hooligans were out with guns—rifles, probably—shooting in the bush. They shot the horse.'

'Shot Tippy?'

Kate sank down into a chair and stared blindly at the bearer of bad news.

Fareed nodded.

'What about Billy? Is Billy all right?' She stood up again, panicky now. 'He would have been with Tippy, surely?'

'As far as I know, your brother wasn't injured.'

Kate nodded while her brain kept throwing up any number of consequences Tippy's death might have had on Billy.

'I'll phone home,' she said to Fareed. 'I might have to go, to help Mum with Billy, with the stables probably. Ibrahim won't leave his men there now.'

'And, of course, your "bargain" with him is null and void?'

Kate stared at her husband, unable to believe he'd spoken so coldly. They might not be friends but they had shared some passion.

'I wasn't thinking of that, but of helping my family,' she said, her own voice as cold as she could make it. 'Something you wouldn't understand because although you had all the love Ibrahim and *his* family could give you, you kept yourself apart, nursing the hurt your own parents did to you, peeling the scabs off the scars so you could continue to feel sorry for yourself. Don't you realise you've got to put it all behind you? Yes, you were hurt, but pain is part of being alive, you get over it and move on—how else can you become the best you possibly can be when you're letting the past cripple you?'

'You don't know me,' he said, his anger so tight it seemed to suck the air out of the room.

'I know enough to know you're a fine man, a caring man, and a wonderful doctor, but you could be so much more if you would just let go of all the anger seething inside you.'

She moved closer, stood in front of him, looked into the dark, dark eyes.

'You talk about freedom, Fareed. Free yourself from the past, from the ghosts that take up far too much space in your head.'

For a moment she thought she might have got through to him but, no, he turned his back on her and stalked out of the room, pausing at the door.

'You know nothing of me. Go home to your family!'

His words pierced her heart, leaving her shaken by his coldness. Not that she hadn't asked for it, bringing up all the things he'd told her in confidence, telling him he had to get a life!

But even so, before she'd spoken, could he not have offered just a little comfort? Asked her if she needed help to make arrangements? Suggested she return?

Well, that last was never going to happen. He was probably glad of a reason to get rid of her before the forty days were up.

A knock at the door—a servant summoning her to Ibrahim.

Kate followed the young woman through the endless passages of the palace, coming at last to a small study where Ibrahim sat in a leather lounge chair. He rose as she entered, taking her hand to lead her to a chair beside his.

'I have spoken to your mother. She had trouble getting hold of you at the hospital so she phoned the palace. You will want to talk to her yourself and can phone her when you get back to your suite. But I can tell you your brother is all right—unhappy, but your mother thinks he will handle it, although when I suggested you would probably want to be with them, she was very relieved.'

'Thank you, Ibrahim. I do need to be with them.'

'My plane is being prepared as we speak,' he said, 'and will take off in three hours. Your driver will take you to the airport, unless your husband wishes to drive you.'

Kate looked into the kindly eyes of the older man.

'I somehow doubt that,' she said.

'He is a fool!' Ibrahim muttered. 'A fool not to see how happy the two of you could be together. He has told me he intends divorce, but it cannot happen for forty days, my dear, so if you wish to return…'

'To a man who doesn't care for me?' Kate tried to smile but her lips wobbled and she breathed deeply instead, not wanting to cry in front of Ibrahim.

'You must do what you think best,' Ibrahim told her, patting her hand.

So once again she was up in the air, in the luxurious jet, heading home at a million miles an hour, heartsore at leaving, angry at herself for being stupid enough to fall in love.

Because that was what she'd done. She'd fallen in love with a man who'd been tricked into marrying her and to whom she was everything he most disliked in a woman—foreign, red-haired, out for what she could get…

She tried to think of Billy, of how he must be feeling, coping. Told herself her pain was nothing but self-pity, and she had to think of others, not herself.

But the 'other' who crept into her head wasn't her mother, or Billy, but Fareed. Fareed on his beautiful stallion, king of the desert over which he rode. Fareed at work, so calm and competent, caring enough for the little boy to stay with him overnight...

Fareed who didn't love her, and why should he? They barely knew each other...

She slept and woke in airspace over Australia—home.

He got through one day, but the night was too much. They may not have slept together the previous few nights as he'd been at the hospital but he still felt her presence in the suite.

He was tortured by her presence in the suite!

Yet he'd let her go without a mention of that torture, without telling her he'd miss her or asking her if she'd come back—without offering to go with her, to support her as a husband should.

At midnight he phoned the airport, arranged for a plane to be made ready, a pilot organised, a flight plan registered. He'd leave at dawn.

Kate arrived home in one of the big black limousines that had brought Ibrahim and Fareed to the stud the first time, people from the embassy having met her at the airport.

'You didn't have to come,' her mother said, although the hug she gave Kate told her otherwise.

'Billy?' Kate asked, and her mother shook her head.

'I don't know what to do with him,' she admitted. 'He sits on the deck and looks out at Tippy's paddock, not speaking, barely eating. The mares are due to start foaling so I'm busy with them as well as the horses in work and can't give him the attention he probably needs, but I don't know how to help him.'

Kate gave her mother another hug and went to find her brother. She'd been seven when Billy had been born, a baby she'd looked forward to with all her heart. A real, live doll had been how she'd thought of him. Except he'd come too early, and the doll had been a wizened little thing in an incubator. So many premmie babies did well, they'd all hoped for the best, and when he hadn't reached his milestones, not talking or attempting to walk, her parents had put it down to her doing everything for him, interpreting his wishes before he'd had a chance to talk, carrying him around with her.

But it had been more than that. Investigations had shown a rare syndrome, a debilitating condition that meant he was slow to develop, and vulnerable to illness. It hadn't been until he'd been six that he'd discovered an affinity with the horses, spending all his time following his parents around the stables and yards, starting to speak so he could talk to his 'friends'.

Then Tippy! Tippy had been special...

'It hurts, doesn't it Billy, to lose something you love?'

She pulled a chair over close to him, refused to think of being here with Ibrahim, and took her brother's hand.

'First Dad, and now Tippy. I know you're sad but Mum probably needs you in the stables. The mares are due to start foaling—you usually help her.'

Billy shook his head.

'Isaac will help her.'

It took Kate a minute to realise Isaac was the man Ibrahim had organised to work at the stables—and had been paying for!

'Is he still here?' Kate asked, and Billy nodded.

'Him and Tony. Tony is my friend.'

Perhaps Ibrahim was going to ease them out of their employment here, Kate thought, but aloud she said, 'Then couldn't you be helping him?'

'Don't want to!'

Billy in a stubborn mood, Kate knew it well.

'Okay,' she said, 'although I wouldn't mind going down to have a look around. Come with me?'

The shake of his head told Kate it was the end of the

conversation, but she *did* need to go down to the stables, to talk to her mother and find out why Ibrahim's men were still here.

That conversation didn't happen, as Isaac and the young lad called Tony were both down at the mares' paddock with her mother, and she could hardly talk about it in front of them.

'We're checking on them because there's a big race meeting in Sydney this weekend and we've got Tippy's brother and two other horses entered in races,' Sally explained. 'I feel bad leaving you when you've just arrived but I'm so glad you're here because I really want to see these three race and I couldn't have left Billy otherwise.'

'Of course you should go, Mum,' Kate said. 'It will be good for me to have some together time with Billy anyway.'

Her mother still looked worried.

'Mum! It's not as if the mares don't usually manage on their own and I know the vet's number off by heart if anything untoward happens. Just go and enjoy yourself. Once the foals arrive and the mares are being mated again, you won't have a spare moment.'

Kate hoped she sounded firm enough, although being left with—she counted quickly—eleven pregnant mares was slightly daunting.

Her mother turned and hugged her.

'Thank you,' she said, then she slipped through the fence and walked around the animals, talking softly to them, probably, Kate realised, telling them who'd be in charge over the weekend. Billy wasn't the only one who talked to the horses!

The horses going to the races left early the next morning, so when Kate toured the stables at what she considered the early hour of seven o'clock, they were quiet.

Old Josh, who'd been with them for as long as she could remember, greeted her with a horsy-smelling hug.

'Your mum's doing real well,' he told her. 'We've got owners from all over asking her to take their horses for training. I'm taking this fellow to the locals tomorrow, and the mare in the stall next to him will go to the midweeks in town.'

He walked her through the old building, introducing her to the new horses, but Kate was more interested in trying to work out what was different about the place, other than the new horses.

It still smelled of horse, and liniment and tack polish, but...

Was it tidier in some way?

Her mother had always tried to keep things tidy, insisting on everything being in its rightful place, but somehow there'd always been a saddle stuck on a rail somewhere, and a bridle hanging from a nail on the wall of a stall.

And clean—the place was almost spotless—another condition her mother had aimed at but rarely achieved.

'Everything looks good,' Kate said to Josh, who smiled and nodded.

'That Isaac, he's a quiet man, but he sees the jobs get done. Just what you mother needed, someone with a firm hand.'

And for the first time Kate wondered just how her mother had managed, taking care of the horses, the business paperwork and the family, while Dad, wonderful as he'd been, had been off chasing his dreams.

Thinking about this, she wandered down to the mares' paddock, slipped through the fence, then walked around them, talking quietly, checking for signs of imminent delivery—wax on their teats or milk leaking from them, restlessness, walking round in circles, shaking their legs, lying down and standing up again.

These were the signs her mother had told her to watch for, although now she stood in the paddock with the mares it all came back to her from the times she'd done the same thing with her mother.

'Not that they all show any of the signs,' Kate remembered her mother saying as she climbed back through the fence. She'd check them again this evening and in the meantime she'd have another talk to Billy.

Billy still wasn't talking so Kate occupied herself making a huge pot of chicken soup that could be frozen in portions ready to be heated when needed. With mares usually foaling in the early hours of the morning, the humans checking them would often need hot food at odd hours of the night.

Once that was on she made her way down to a smaller shed behind the stables where two birthing stalls had been set up. The large stalls were spotless and had bales of hay ready to be spread. Although her mother preferred to leave the mares in the paddock to foal, if there was an emergency and they needed the vet, it was easier to bring them here where there was good light.

Satisfied everything was in order but desperate for work to keep her mind off the life—and husband—she'd left behind, she found the paint she'd been using on the fences and took it out to continue the never-ending job.

Within an hour Billy had joined her, arriving with his own paintbrush, working with her on the other side of the fence, still silent but at least he was there.

Fareed sat on the plane, his mind running over the tumultuous month since he'd first met Katya.

The woman on the horse, later calling him a big lunk because he'd been struggling against her, her lips on his, breathing life into his lungs.

Then the parcel that was his bride.

His fury at Ibrahim for doing this to him.

Except it hadn't all been fury. Right from the moment he'd seen her there'd been something—a connection—

No, he had to be imagining that!

Although he'd certainly been attracted to the termagant he'd unwrapped, his body stirring at the sight of the pale skin, golden underwear barely covering anything...

He shook his head as he remembered his anger at the deception—anger at her and at Ibrahim. Kate—sensible Kate—had been right about him holding on to his unhappy childhood memories, using them as a shield against love.

Was it too late to woo and win her now?

He knew he wanted to—more than wanted, needed to.

The realisation that Ibrahim—and the old crone, Thalia—had been right in choosing her for him still didn't sit comfortably with him, yet in his heart of hearts he knew they were right.

Katya definitely was the woman for him; now all he had to do was convince her of that.

Billy and Kate had chicken soup for dinner, phoned their mother to check she'd arrived safely at the city stables and the horses had settled in, then went out, torches in hand, to check the mares again.

Kate knew her mother walked among the mares several times a day, so they were used to someone being there. Tonight she pulled on her mother's coat, knowing she wouldn't fool the mares but hoping the scent of it would be reassuring to them.

'The problem is,' she said to Billy as they walked down the track, 'that a mare can stop her labour if she's disturbed—sometimes stop it for several days—and that's not good for her or the foal.'

To her surprise, Billy actually responded.

'I know that,' he said, and Kate could have hugged him, although she refrained, guessing he, too, needed his own space right now.

They walked among the mares, talking quietly.

'Sarina's restless,' Billy said, pointing to Tippy's mother, moving a little apart from the others.

'We won't go near her,' Kate said, 'but I'll come down again later to check on her.'

'Me, too. Don't go without me,' Billy said, and this time Kate *did* put an arm around his narrow shoulders and give him a hug.

Back home she suggested they go to bed. She set the alarm to wake in three hours and prayed she'd made the right decision.

Fareed had arrived in Sydney midafternoon but getting out of the city then finding his way to the stud, even with the latest GPS, took him until close to midnight.

Fortunately he could see lights on in the house as he drove down the long, fenced track towards it because only now had it occurred to him that people might not appreciate a visitor arriving in the middle of the night.

But the house was empty—unlocked and obviously with people in residence, for a smell of toast still lingered in the kitchen and butter, jam, and dirty toast plates were on the table.

Two plates?

Kate and her mother having a midnight chat?

About the marriage perhaps?

Confession time?

Shaking the thoughts from his head, he walked out onto the deck and saw the property spread before him in the moonlight. And down towards the stream two flickering lights.

Torches?

What he should do was drive back to the town where he'd been hospitalised and spend the rest of the night in a motel, but torches in a paddock this late at night suggested there might be trouble.

Forgetting what he should do, he headed towards the lights, following a track down towards the river.

Hadn't it been down here somewhere he'd met the bee—or the bee had met him? They'd been going to the mares' paddock. He tried to think whether he knew how pregnant the mares had been, but couldn't remember a thing except Katya's face bent over him, telling him to calm down, holding him, breathing into his mouth, her lips on his for the first time…

He lengthened his stride, chasing away the silly fantasies, and as he drew closer called out a quiet hello.

'Is that you, Josh?' Kate answered—definitely sensible Kate, not his seductive Katya.

'It's Fareed,' he said, close enough now to see two shadowy forms walking a horse round and round in a corner of the paddock.

He heard Kate's sharp intake of breath then she used it to breathe his name.

'Fareed?'

He'd reached the fence and now he stood, leaning over the top rail, aware that if the mare was foaling, another intruder might startle her.

'Keep walking her, Billy,' she said quietly, before coming towards him in the darkness, lowering her torch so she could pick her way to the fence.

'Why are you here?' she asked, but seeing her face in the moonlight, her eyes wide behind her glasses, his chest grew tight and his throat thickened and all the things he'd rehearsed saying on the plane flew off into the night air.

He reached out and touched her cheek, ran his hand over her hair and finally found his voice.

'I forgot to ask you if you'd come back—if you'd please come back?'

Even in the moonlight he could see her frown, and his nerves tightened.

It was too late!

He'd lost her!

Then, her eyes on his, she murmured, 'Back to Amberach or back to you?'

He had to say it—needed to say it, needed her to hear it. Drew in a deep breath, 'Back to—'

'Kate! Come now.'

She slipped away, walking swiftly towards the mare and her attendant.

'It's okay, Billy, let her lie down. That was her waters breaking, so the foal will come soon.'

The mare lay on the grass in the corner of the paddock, but even from the fence Fareed saw the red bubble protruding from her vulva. The placenta was being delivered first and without it the foal would have no oxygen.

He clambered through the fence, saying urgently, 'Bill, go up to the stables as quickly as you can and bring back the first-aid box. You know where it is?'

'Of course,' the young man answered, vaulting the fence and sprinting towards the stables.

"What's happening?' Kate asked, looking up anxiously from where she knelt beside the mare.

Fareed explained, slipping one arm around her as he spoke, giving her a quick hug.

'I've seen it before, helped the mare deliver, back at home,' he assured her, as Billy returned with the first-aid kit.

'Watch this, Bill, in case you ever have to do it yourself. We just cut through this sac—a lot of blood will come out—but after we make the opening, the mare will be able to deliver normally. You just have to do it really quickly but be careful you don't go deep enough to cut the foal's leading leg.'

By the time he'd finished explaining to Billy, he'd pulled on gloves, unwrapped a scalpel and was preparing to cut. Setting aside his awareness of Katya right behind him, he sliced the placenta and eased it to one side, then breathed a sigh of relief as he felt the little hoof already coming through the birth canal. The second foreleg was right where it should be, tucked neatly behind it.

'Here's the head,' Billy said, and within five minutes the foal was on the ground, waving spindly legs as it tried to right itself, finally getting up and staggering around in a circle before finding its mother—his mother—and nuzzling at her teat.

Sarina was on her feet, turning to lick at her baby.

'I'd let them be,' Fareed said, as he wrapped the soiled scalpel in several layers of elastic tape to protect from accidental injury then putting it and his soiled gloves into a plastic bag.

'Do you have some place to dispose of sharps?' he said to Billy, but Kate answered for her brother.

'I'll do it,' she said, and Fareed knew she was escaping—from him or from what his arrival might mean to her.

In the time he'd known her he'd given her no indication of how he felt about her, now here he was asking her to return to him.

Not that he'd known how he felt about her until she'd gone...

Billy was talking to him, asking questions about horses, how he, Fareed, knew things like that, what horses did he have, and, finally, would he take Kate away again?

'Would you mind?' Fareed asked him.

'I would miss her,' Billy said, 'but I'm really good on social networks now so we can talk and send each other pictures so she's not really gone and maybe one day I could visit her over there.'

'I'm sure she'd like that,' Fareed told him. 'But you'll probably have to wait until this little foal is older. He's going to need you to show him all the things you showed Tippy.'

'Tippy died.'

The sadness in his voice caught Fareed unawares, but he knew he had to say something.

'People and animals do die, Bill,' he said gently, 'and it's right to be sad about that. But there are always more things coming along, like this new foal, so we have to keep going to give the very best we can to the people and animals that are here.'

He hadn't done the very best he could for Katya—had been so resentful, he hadn't been able to think straight. And here she was.

'The vet's on his way. I phoned him in case there was some placenta retained inside Sarina. He said you did exactly the right thing but the placenta coming away like that is usually a sign of an infection. He wants to check her and the foal out.'

She sat down on the grass a little away from the two men, her knees up and her arms looped around her legs.

'Kate's sad,' Billy said, and Fareed turned to look at his wife. 'She's been sad since she came home.'

Kate wished she could strangle her brother, but as he seemed to be speaking freely for the first time since she'd got back, she couldn't stop him now.

She could say she was sad over Tippy, but couldn't bring herself to tell a lie—or even a half lie—because she *was* upset that the horse had been killed.

Instead, she rested her head on her knees and hoped they'd think she was having a sleep while they waited for the vet.

But Billy had other ideas.

'When I'm sad, Mum gives me a hug. You could give her a hug, couldn't you, Fareed?'

Murder wouldn't be enough, Kate thought, but she sensed movement then a body lowered to sit beside her and a strong arm came around her shoulders.

'Were you sad?' Fareed whispered to her, and she lifted her head enough to nod.

'Because of leaving Amberach or leaving me?' he asked, and now she lifted her head right up and looked at his face, so clear and dear in the moonlight.

'I think I asked that question first,' she said, and although he looked puzzled for a moment, she saw his face clear and something spark in his eyes.

'Back to me is my answer,' he said, the words so definite, she had to believe him.

'Now your turn,' he prompted.

'Both,' Kate said, smiling because she knew it wasn't the answer he wanted to hear. She touched his face, which had grown stern again. 'Even in such a short time I'd grown to love both the place and the people.' She sighed then turned so she could kiss him gently on the lips. 'And to love you, awkward sod that you are.'

With Sarina and her foal safely medicated, they finally made their way back to the house as dawn was breaking.

'You'll have to sleep in the spare room,' Kate told Fareed as they reached the house. 'Billy seems to be okay but I wouldn't want to shock him by us sleeping together.'

Fareed held her tightly and groaned.

'I imagine I can wait one more night to get you alone,' he whispered against her neck, his warm breath sending spirals of delight right through her body.

Waking at midday, Kate went down to check on the new arrival, finding Josh, Fareed and Billy there before her. Billy was already in love with the foal he'd helped deliver.

'If everything's okay I'm going up to the house to make lunch, then we can watch the races on television. You guys coming?'

'I'll stay here and watch with Josh on the stable's TV. There'll be some food in the fridge there,' Billy said, then to Kate's utter amazement he added, 'And call me Bill now, please, Kate. I am a grown-up, you know, and Billy is a name for a kid.'

'Probably my fault,' Fareed said, slipping an arm around Kate's waist as they walked up to the house. 'I called him Bill last night and he's right, really, he's ready to be a Bill.'

Kate turned and kissed him.

'You are a wise man,' she said.

He kissed her back, not a thankyou kiss like she'd bestowed on him but a loving, tender, exploration of her mouth, her lips, her tongue, his strong arms holding her hard against his body, while his lips told her everything she'd ever wanted to know. 'Not wise enough,' he told her when he'd finally released her, 'to realise just what a gift Ibrahim had given me in my wife. You were right, I was so tied up in the past I couldn't see the present. And although I was attracted to you from the beginning, I wouldn't let myself fall in love with you—'

'Because you saw your mother in me. I understood that, Fareed, yet somehow Ibrahim knew that we were meant to be. The man's a genius.'

Fareed pushed some strands of the brilliant red hair off Katya's face.

'He did have help,' he said, smiling at her. 'You might not believe this—in fact, I didn't when he told me just before I came out here this time—but he'd been worried about me, about the things that had happened in the past and how they had affected my life, so he'd called in a *kahin*—a fortune-teller—to ask what to do, and she threw sticks on the sand or poured oil on a dish of water and somehow came up with the idea that if he took me on a journey with him to a foreign country he would find a wife for me and never have to worry about me again.'

'A fortune-teller told him that?'

Kate looked at him in complete disbelief.

'But how did he know I was the one? You must have met other women while you were in Australia.'

'Dozens,' Fareed told her with a smile, 'but Thalia—the old *kahin*—kept talking about things green and Ibrahim says as soon as he saw you on the horse in the green paddocks he knew you were the one. After that it was just a matter of getting you to agree.'

'Which, once he saw how rundown the place was, wasn't really a challenge.'

Fareed drew her close, and felt her body fit to his as if they'd been designed to be together. He looked around at the green of the place, and decided green wasn't nearly as bad as he'd thought it.

'Food,' Kate said, pushing away from him. 'If we don't go now we'll miss the first race.'

In the kitchen, with a television perched on top of the refrigerator, Kate made sandwiches while he watched the beginning of the TV coverage of the afternoon's races. He'd rather be taking her to bed after their lunch but the races were important to her and her family and, now he was part of that family, important to him.

So they sat and ate the simple meal, cheered the first of the stable's horses to a win, groaned as the second one lost, then moved into the living room where there was a mammoth TV, to watch the big race of the day.

To Fareed's surprise, he was on his feet, jumping up and down as much as Katya, as the horse swept to the outside and flew to the finish line a head in front of the second horse.

Flushed and excited, his wife flung herself into his arms,

hugging and kissing him, stopping only when the phone rang, her mother phoning home.

'Sarina foaled last night, a little colt, and Fareed's here,' Kate said, unable to keep this most exciting arrival a secret from her mother.

'Ah,' her mother said. 'I gathered from constant mentions in your emails that he might be something more than your boss. But just how long were you going to wait before you told me more about him?'

'Mu-u-u-m,' Kate said. 'I've barely seen you.'

'We'll talk about it later, but I'm so glad for you, darling,' her mother said.

'I will have a lot of explaining to do,' she muttered to herself, looking so worried Fareed took her in his arms again.

'We'll do it together,' he promised. 'How about a whirlwind romance then, because of my position, we married? We can offer to do it again here.'

He looked into her eyes.

'In fact, I'd like to do it again, do it properly, your way, holding your hand and promising to love, honour and obey you for ever.'

Kate kissed his lips.

'I think we'll both leave out the obey bit,' she teased, then as tears of happiness threatened to spill from her eyes she nestled close to him, aware that this was where she wanted to be.

Forever...

* * * * *

COMING SOON!

We really hope you enjoyed reading this book. If you're looking for more romance, be sure to head to the shops when new books are available on

Thursday 2nd May

To see which titles are coming soon, please visit

millsandboon.co.uk/nextmonth

Want even more
ROMANCE?

Join our bookclub today!

LET'S TALK
Romance

For exclusive extracts, competitions
and special offers, find us online:

 facebook.com/millsandboon

@MillsandBoon

@MillsandBoonUK

Get in touch on 01413 063232

For all the latest titles coming soon, visit
millsandboon.co.uk/nextmonth